About [illegible]

Kim Lawrence was en[illegible] husband to write when the unsocial hours of nursing didn't look attractive! He told her she could do anything she set her mind to, so Kim tried her hand at writing. Always a keen Mills & Boon reader, it seemed natural for her to write a romance novel – now she can't imagine doing anything else. She is a keen gardener and cook and enjoys running on the beach with her Jack Russell. Kim lives in Wales.

Three-time Golden Heart Award finalist **Tina Beckett** learned to pack her suitcases almost before she learned to read. Born to a military family, she has lived in the United States, Puerto Rico, Portugal and Brazil. In addition to travelling, Tina loves to cuddle with her pug, Alex; spend time with her family; and hit the trails on her horse. Learn more about Tina from her website or friend her on Facebook.

Jessica Lemmon is a former job-hopper who resides in Ohio with her husband and rescue dogs. She holds a degree in graphic design currently gathering dust in an impressive frame. When she's not writing emotionally charged stories, she spends her time drawing, drinking coffee, and laughing with friends. Her motto is 'read for fun', and she believes we should all do more of what makes us happy. Learn more about her books at jessicalemmon.com

Second Chance

June 2025
His Unexpected Heir

July 2025
Their Renewed Vows

August 2025
A Cowboy's Return

September 2025
The Prince's Desire

December 2025
A Love Rekindled

January 2025
Their Enemy Sparks

Second Chance:
Their Renewed Vows

KIM LAWRENCE

TINA BECKETT

JESSICA LEMMON

MILLS & BOON

First Published in Great Britain 2025
by Mills & Boon, an imprint of HarperCollins*Publishers* Ltd
1 London Bridge Street, London, SE1 9GF

www.harpercollins.co.uk

HarperCollins*Publishers*
Macken House, 39/40 Mayor Street Upper,
Dublin 1, D01 C9W8, Ireland

ISBN: 978-0-263-41746-3

MIX
Paper | Supporting responsible forestry
FSC™ C007454
www.fsc.org

This book contains FSC™ certified paper and other controlled sources to ensure responsible forest management.

For more information visit: www.harpercollins.co.uk/green

Printed and Bound in the UK using 100% Renewable Electricity
at CPI Group (UK) Ltd, Croydon, CR0 4YY

WAKING UP IN HIS ROYAL BED

KIM LAWRENCE

To Jane and the 'Artists Unlocked'.

CHAPTER ONE

BEATRICE RESISTED THE instinct to fight her way through the layers of sleep, instead easing her body closer to the warmth of the hard male contours she was lying… *Male*... The shocked acknowledgement hit at the same moment a distant clatter was joined by the melodic voice of her sister, who had clearly recovered from her migraine of the previous night and was singing something catchy and irritating downstairs.

One of the major differences between them, beyond the fact her sibling was not blonde, did not have blue eyes and was frequently referred to as petite and delicate, was that Maya was a morning person who woke with a smile on her face and a spring in her step. She could also hold a tune, and finally Maya would never have woken up beside a man who had walked into a bar alone and walked out minutes later *not* alone!

A protective hand went to Beatrice's face before she conquered her sense of dread and opened her eyes, widening her fingers fanlike to peer through them.

Maybe it was all a bad dream—with some very good parts.

It wasn't a dream!

Connecting with the pair of dark polished ebony eyes framed by lashes too thick and curling for any man, containing a sardonic gleam that stared right back at her, she loosed a low moan, scrunched her own eyes tight and twisted away.

The reaction of the owner of the eyes and the body, which even fully clothed had had every woman in the bar regarding her with envy as she had left with him, prevented her rolling into a foetal bundle of denial.

In her head she had stiffened in reaction to the heavy arm thrown casually across her ribcage; in reality her body softened and the determination to put some distance between them was overwhelmed by a fresh surge of toe-tingling heat, as a voice as deep and sinfully seductive as the warm breath against her earlobe sent sharp tingles outwards from the core of liquid warmth low in her belly.

'What's the hurry?'

Eyes closed, she loosed a quivering sigh and then moaned as he brought his hard body suggestively up against the curve of hers, providing enough reasons not to go anywhere as her resistance to the heavy throb of desire that robbed her limbs of strength dissolved utterly.

For several long languid moments she allowed herself to enjoy the feel of strong, sensitive hands and clever fingers moving up her ribcage, tracing a line down her belly, causing her to suck in a shocked, excited breath, before lifting to cup the weight of one breast, his thumb rubbing across the tight, aroused peak.

'Stop it?'

Now where did that question mark come from? she wondered, feeling a stab of frustration when he did just that, pulling his hand away. An action that caused her to squirm backwards a little and catch the thumb of the hand that came to rest on the curve of her jaw between her teeth.

'Play nice, Bea.'

Before she could react to the husky remonstrance, she found herself flat on her back. It wasn't his superior strength that kept her breathless there—she could have easily slid from underneath him. There was air between their bodies as, hands braced flat on the pillow either side of her face, knees either side of her hips, his body curved above her.

She was pinned there as much by the hungry ache inside her as his predatory bold dark stare fastened onto her face, lingering on her lips that still felt swollen from the kisses that had continued last night, even as they had torn each other's clothes off as they had stumbled across the room to the bed.

Her eyes darkened at the memories of the passionate coupling. The stress of discovering him beside her was pushed to the fringes of her mind as she stared back. His face was really a total miracle. Perfect was too mild a word to describe the sculpted arrangement of his perfect bone structure, the deep golden tone of his skin, dusted on his hollow cheeks and square lower jaw by a shadow of dark sexy stubble, the sensuality of his mouth, the firm upper lip counteracted by the full sensual lower.

She blinked and cleared her throat. 'I don't want to play.' She husked the words out past the ache in her throat. It was true there was nothing light or playful about the ache. It was on a par with the need, the *craving* for oxygen as she opened her eyes and managed to disconnect from his stare, but only escaped as far as his mouth, which did an equal amount of damage to her nervous system.

The sharply etched angle of his carved cheekbones, the hawkish dominance of his nose blurred as his head lowered. The first kiss was a warm, tormenting whisper across her parted lips, drawing a fractured moan from her throat. The second, still soft on the side of her mouth, drew her body up into an arch as she tried to deepen the pressure. The ones that followed increased the torment until, unable to bear it any longer, she reached up, her fingers sinking deep into the thick dark hair, her hands locking on the back of his head as she dragged his face downwards, glimpsing the glitter in his dark eyes, before she pressed her mouth to his and closed her eyes.

Restraint gone, they kissed with a wild hunger, and they fell back. Warm bodies sinuously twisting to deepen the contact, driven by a passion that drove every other thought from Beatrice's head.

'Bea, are you coming down or shall I bring your coffee up?'

Beatrice stiffened as she was jarringly jolted back to reality. Eyes scrunched, a moan of self-recrimination locked in her throat, as without a word she rolled away from the warm body she was pressed against.

'Weak…stupid…weak…stupid!' she mumbled, beating herself up verbally as she swung her long legs over the side of the bed and, with a sinuous, graceful swoop, grabbed a sheet that had at some point fallen on the floor. She didn't stop until she reached the far corner of the room, where she stood, shoulder blades pressed to the wall, holding the sheet against her body. It was an inadequate shield but better than nothing.

She glanced nervously at the door; a nightmare scenario played in her head of the door opening and Maya appearing.

'I'll be down just now!' she yelled. 'You need to go!' she whispered, transferring her agonised glance to the man lying in her bed.

He looked in no hurry to go anywhere any time soon as he rolled onto his back, tucking one hand behind his head, causing the light sheet that lay across his narrow hips to slide another inch lower. He was totally at ease with his naked state but she was not. He was a living, breathing sculpture of perfectly formed muscles and warm olive-toned skin—just looking at him made things shift deep inside her.

The mockery in his expression was not quite in tune with the dark frustration in his heavy-lidded eyes as his glance came to rest on the swell of her full breasts above the sheet she held clutched against herself.

As he watched her struggles to control the white swathe, he visualised the slim curves beneath the tented fabric. The smooth, warm scented skin, the silk touch of her long legs as they wrapped around him. The thousand razor cuts of desire that came with the memory darkened his eyes to midnight.

'That is not what I need, *cara*.'

Before she was fatally distracted by the bold challenge of the seductive gleam in his heavy-lidded eyes, the timely interruption of her sister's voice drifting up the stairs again saved her from getting sucked back into the dangerous sexual vortex.

She clenched her even white teeth so hard she could hear the grind of enamel. She didn't feel saved at all, or maybe she didn't want to be saved?

'Oh, my God!'

He grinned a slow devilish smile of invitation.

'Oh, my God!' she whispered again with even more feeling as she realised how close she had come to ac-

cepting the invitation in his sinful eyes. She took a deep breath and thought, *Do not go there*. Her eyes flickered towards the figure in the bed—*again*!

Once was enough—actually it was too much!

She cleared her throat. 'I'll be right down!' she belted out, then directed an accusing glare at the figure occupying the bed, even though she knew the guilt was as much hers. When it came to Dante, why was she such a weak idiot? 'Do not make this any more difficult. You need to get out of here.'

His brows, dark, straight and thick, lifted above polished ebony mocking eyes. 'Why?'

'You can ask that?'

He casually levered himself into a sitting position with a distracting display of contracting muscle in his washboard belly. 'I really don't see what your problem is.'

Eyes indignantly wide, she managed to drag her gaze upwards, not that the breadth of his muscled shoulders and chest offered much respite for her wildly surging hormones.

'What?' he responded with an innocent look and a seemingly mystified shrug that intensified her murderous glare. 'Unless you have forgotten, we *are* married.'

CHAPTER TWO

HUFFING OUT A defiant gust of breath through clenched teeth, Beatrice refused to drop her gaze from the challenge she saw in the dark eyes of Dante Aristide Severin Velazquez, Crown Prince of San Macizo.

Her husband.

'If only I *could* forget.' Her mumble came with a resentful glare, at odds with the mood of their civilised divorce.

She never had really understood what a civilised divorce entailed, but she was pretty sure it did not entail having a night of passionate sex with your soon-to-be ex. But on the plus side, her peevish attitude did provide some sort of cover for her deep inner despair.

Everyone made bad choices, and she was no exception, but it sometimes felt that from the moment Dante had walked into her life the only sort of choices she'd made were of the bad variety—actually, *disastrous*!

She had always operated on the principle that your actions had consequences, and you lived with them. Or, in her case, you neatly plotted a course around them, or at least the more dangerous ones.

Then Dante happened and she forgot her philosophy; her navigation skills took a vacation. She didn't so much forget as didn't give a damn about the consequences.

The primitive instincts that he had awoken in her were totally in charge. Instincts that had drowned out the warning bells that she had remained determinedly tone deaf to. Actually, last night there had been no bells, just a fierce *need.*

She had lifted her head and seen the reason why the crowded bar had fallen silent, and had felt a bone-deep desperation, much like any addict who found their drug of choice was close enough to smell. Dante was her addiction, the virus in her blood she had no antibody to.

Which made it seem as though she'd had no choice, but she had. She hadn't sleepwalked into the situation. She had known what she was doing every step of the way. Admittedly she had not typed his name into a search engine when she'd accepted the offer of dinner, knowing that he wasn't actually talking about a dinner. But you didn't need a bio to see at one glance that he represented the sort of danger she had spent her adult life avoiding.

The idea of experiencing an attraction strong enough to make her share intimacy with a man she didn't know had been a concept she had considered with a disbelieving smile, tinged, if she was honest, with smugness. But she'd had total confidence in her belief that any relationship she had would come from friendship and respect.

She'd slept with Dante that first night. She had been so determined to have that first night end the way she had imagined from the moment she had set eyes on him that she hadn't told him that this…that *he*…was her first, in case it made him back away.

Her instincts there had been bang on because Dante had not been pleased by the discovery she was inexperienced, sternly telling her that virgins were *not his thing* and demanding an explanation.

It could have ended there—it should have—but it hadn't, because she hadn't wanted it to.

When she had retorted that she wasn't a virgin any more so that was one obstacle gone she'd made him laugh, and he'd laughed again when she had explained that it hadn't been a conscious choice. She hadn't been waiting for the right man or anything, she simply wasn't a particularly *physical* person.

They had spent the next three days and nights in bed disproving this theory. Nothing and no one had disturbed them in the penthouse with million-dollar views that she'd never even looked at, and Beatrice had savoured every hot, skin-peelingly perfect moment of the intimacy because she'd known this heaven wasn't going to last. Dante had made that painfully clear.

He had left no room for misinterpretation when he'd explained that he was not into long-term relationships, or actually any sort of relationship at this point in his life.

Facts she'd already known, having finally typed his name into her phone's search engine—even if a tenth of the women he was alleged to have slept with were actually real, it would be amazing that he found time to be so hands-on with the charitable foundation that he had founded.

It made a person wonder if he ever actually slept, except she knew he did. She had watched him and been utterly fascinated by the way the strong lines on his face relaxed in sleep, made him look younger and *almost* vulnerable in a way that made her conscious of an empty ache inside her.

There had been more than one occasion over that weekend when he had felt the need to drag her feet back to earth by reminding her.

'This is just sex—you know that, right?'

The fantasy bubble she had spent the weekend in had ended when she'd opened her eyes and found him standing there, suited, booted and looking every inch the exclusive playboy prince who was always good for a headline.

She remembered fighting the self-respect-killing urge to run after him when he had stopped of his own volition, his long brown finger curled around the doorknob. She had managed a response as cool and offhand as his suggestion that they meet up in three weeks when commitments would be bringing him back to London.

By the time three weeks had come around things had changed, and the consequences of her actions had been impossible to ignore. Even without the multiple tests she'd *known* why she felt different; she'd known even without the blue line that she was pregnant.

She'd also known exactly how this next step was going to go, with a few gaps she'd left for his shocked, angry reaction. She had played the scene out in her head and, allowing for a few variations, she'd known exactly what she was going to say.

When she'd been buzzed into the building she'd *still* known *what she* was going to say, as she'd been escorted in the glass-fronted lift by a silent suited man.

She'd walked in, and she'd known not just what she was going to say but when she was going to say it. She'd allow herself their *last* night and then she would tell him.

In the event, the door had barely closed before she had blurted it out.

'I'm pregnant and, yes, I know we…*you* were careful.'

She had a vague recollection of dodging his eyes,

allowing her hair to act as a screen to hide her guilty blushes. The memory even now had the power to make her insides squirm.

'I've done three tests and…no, that's a lie, I did six. I am not…do *not* suggest *that*… Just know that I want nothing from you. I'm going home tomorrow to tell my mum and sister and we'll be totally fine. I'm not alone.'

He had stood there totally motionless during her machine-gun delivery of the facts. Strangely, saying it out loud had made the secret she had nursed to herself seem slightly less surreal.

She'd thought she'd been prepared for his every reaction, most had involved noise, but him turning on his heel and walking out of the door before she could even draw breath was not one she had been prepared for.

It might have been minutes or an hour, she didn't have a clue, but when the door had opened again she hadn't moved from the spot where she'd been before his abrupt departure. He had re-entered, still pale but not with shock now; determination as steely as his stare had been etched into the lines of his face.

'Well, obviously we need to get married. I don't need to involve my family in this—it's one of the advantages of being the spare. Carl is getting married and they probably won't even notice. How about you?'

Carl? What did his older brother have to do with this? *'Family...?'* Her thought processes had been lagging a confusing few steps behind his words.

'A big wedding, given the circumstances, is not an option, but if you want your immediate family to be there I can accommodate that. I have business in the area, so how does Vegas next week sound to you?'

He had paused, presumably for breath. She had definitely needed to breathe!

'You're not joking…? Dante, people don't get married because of a baby… Let's forget you ever said that. You're in shock.'

He didn't appear to appreciate her consideration. 'I may only be the spare but I am still second in line to the throne…*my* child will not carry the stigma of being a bastard. Believe you me, I've seen it and it's not pretty.'

'You're insane.'

Every argument she'd made against his plan he'd had a counterargument to. The most compelling one having been it was the right thing to do for the baby's sake, the new life that they had made.

She had ended up agreeing, of course. Saying yes to Dante was a habit she had to break if her life was going to get back on track.

As for last night! How could she have been that stupid *yet again*? And she had nobody to blame for it but herself! Dante didn't have to do anything to make her act like a lemming with her sights on a cliff edge, he just had to *exist*.

And nobody had ever *existed* as much as Dante—she had never met anyone who was *so* alive. He had a presence that was electrifying, and there was an earthy, raw quality to the megawatt vitality he exuded that made the idea of forgetting anything connected with him laughable.

But she had to. She had to put last night behind her and start again—it would get easier. It had to! First, she couldn't run and hide or pretend that last night didn't happen. She just had to accept she had messed up and move on.

Again…!

'What are you doing here, Dante?' Falling in love was not at all as she had imagined it—in fact it really should come with a health warning, or at least a misery warning!

'You invited me. It seemed rude—'

'How did you know where I was? How did you know we had gone away?' For the first few weeks after she had left Dante she had moved in with her mother, then she had taken residence on Maya's couch until a flat they could afford together had come up.

He arched a sardonic brow and she sighed.

'All right, stupid question.' She had considered fighting the insistence that she needed any sort of security, even the ultradiscreet team of men who in pairs watched her around the clock, but she had learnt that it was better to fight the battles you had a chance of winning. 'You know, there was a time when my life was my own.'

'It will be again.' Unlike Dante's. The moment his brother had stepped away from the line of succession had been the moment that Dante had known his life had changed forever. He was no longer the playboy prince and unexpected father-to-be. He was the future of the monarchy.

His flat delivery brought a furrow to her smooth wide brow, but his expression told her nothing. 'A friend of Mum's owns the place. We used to come here when we were kids.'

His glance lifted from his grim contemplation of his clenched hands and his future, as she glanced around the wood-lined walls of the modest ski lodge.

'Ruth, that's Mum's friend, had a last-minute cancellation and offered it to us for the fortnight for a song. Maya is working on ideas for a sports line and we thought the snow might inspire her.'

'So the business is going ahead? The fashion industry is notoriously tough.'

'Slowly,' she said, bringing her lashes down in a glossy protective sweep as he adjusted his position, causing a rippling of the taut muscles of his lean torso. He didn't carry an ounce of surplus flesh; his broad-shouldered frame would have made many a professional athlete sigh with envy.

She would have retreated if there had been any place to retreat to. Instead she ignored the pelvic quivering, and pretended her skin wasn't prickling, and tossed her hair as she adjusted her sheet once more.

'It would go a lot quicker and easier if you made the bank that is playing hardball aware of the settlement that will be yours. Do they even know you're going to be a very wealthy woman soon?'

Wealthy and single. She refused to acknowledge the sinking feeling in her stomach.

'And I'm more than happy to make the funds you need available to you now.'

Her lips tightened. If people called her a gold-digger that was fine, so long as she knew she wasn't. 'I don't want your money. I don't want anything—'

I want to go back to the person I was, she thought forlornly, aware that it was not going to happen. She might only have been married for ten months, and been separated for six more, but she could never be the person she was before, she knew that.

'Well, then, *cara*, you chose the right lawyer. Yours seemed more interested in golf than your interests.'

'Could you pretend, even for one minute, that you don't know every detail of what's going on in my life? I repeat, why are you here?'

Good question, Dante thought as he dragged a hand through his hair, leaving it standing in sexy tufts across his head.

He'd told himself when Beatrice left that it would be easier if he could focus on his new role, without the distraction of worrying how she was coping, of knowing that behind her smile she was unhappy, resentful or usually both. That no matter how tough his day had been, hers had probably been worse.

Dante had never been responsible for another person in his life. He'd lived for himself, and now he had an entire country relying on him and Beatrice—that really was irony, of the blackest variety.

Except now she wasn't relying on him. The reports that landed on his desk all said as much. She was doing well…he had just wanted to see for himself. It was an option that would soon not be open to him. The list of potential successors to fill the space in his life Beatrice had left, candidates who would know how to deal with life inside the palace walls without his guidance, was already awaiting his attention. His stomach tightened in distaste at the thought of the breeding stock with good bloodlines.

'There are a few papers for you to sign,' he said, inviting her scorn with his lame response and receiving it as he skated around the truth in his head.

'And now you're a delivery service?'

He sighed out his frustration as his dark, intense gaze scanned her face hungrily. She was still the most beautiful thing he had ever seen in his life and for a while their lives had meshed. But things had changed. He had another life, responsibilities, duty. At some level had he thought coming here would offer him some sort of closure?

'We never actually said…goodbye.'

She blinked, refusing to surrender to the surge of resentment that made her heart beat louder. 'Didn't we?

You probably had a meeting, or maybe you left me a memo?' She bit her lip hard enough to raise crimson pinpricks of blood. Could she sound any *less* like someone who had moved on?

'You felt neglected?'

'I felt…' She fought to reel in her feelings. 'It doesn't really matter. This was a conversation we never had, let's leave it at that. Let's call last night closure.'

He shook his head, the antagonism leaving his face as he registered the glisten of unshed tears in her eyes. His shoulders dropped. 'No, it wasn't planned. I just… I'm sick of receiving any news about you through third parties.'

'I miss…' She stopped, biting back the words she couldn't allow herself to admit to herself, let alone him. 'I think it's safer that way,' she said quietly.

'Who wants safe?'

The reckless gleam in his eyes reminded her of the man she had fallen in love with. There was an irony that she had to remind him he wasn't that man any more. 'Your future subjects and, frankly, Dante, I have all the excitement we can handle without…'

She closed her eyes and pushed back into the wall until the pressure hurt her shoulder blades. It was true—after she had walked away from the royal role she had never been equipped to fulfil, she had thrown herself into her life, and there were new, exciting and sometimes scary challenges to fill her days. She had recovered some of her natural enthusiasm, though these days it was mingled with caution. A caution that had been sadly missing last night. Dante walked into a room and all those instincts and hungers he woke in her roared into sense-killing life.

Sense*less*, she thought, underlining the second syllable in red in her head. Last night had had nothing to do with sense. Her insides tightened as the warm memories flooded her head. It'd had everything to do with passion, craving and hunger!

So she had a passion for chocolate, but if she gave into that indulgence Beatrice knew she'd need a new wardrobe. Exercise and a bit of self-control meant she could still fit into last year's clothes.

The trouble was Dante was a perfect fit, in every sense of the word, and he always had been.

When in one of her more philosophical moments she had told herself that she would take away the good bits from her marriage, she had not intended it this literally. Though even when everything else was not working in their marriage the sex had still been incredible. The bedroom was one place they always managed to be on the same page. Unfortunately, you needed more than sexual chemistry and compatibility for a marriage to work, especially when it had hit the sort of life-changing roadblocks theirs had.

With a self-conscious start she realised that during her mental meanderings her glance had begun to drift across the strong sculpted breadth of his chest, and lower, to the ridged muscular definition of his belly, before she realised what she was doing, and brought her lashes down in a protective sweep. Not that they provided much protection from the raw sexual pulse he exuded, or his unnerving ability to read her mind.

'Do you regret it?'

Her response to the question should have been immediate, a reflex, and of course she did regret what had happened, on one level. But on another, shameful level she would not have changed a thing, because Dante bypassed her common sense. She only had to breathe in the scent of his skin to send her instincts of self-preservation into hibernation.

I really *have to break this cycle!*

Easy to say, easy to think, but less *easy* when every time he touched her something inside her said it was *right*.

Then don't let him touch you!

Cutting off her increasingly desperate internal dialogue, Beatrice cleared her throat to give herself time to think of a next move that would manage to convey that last night didn't mean she wasn't totally over him. An action that wouldn't draw attention to the skin-prickling awareness and the warm pelvic heaviness.

A next move that established that she could walk away just as easily as he could after satisfying a primal itch. That he wasn't the only one who could compartmentalise his life.

'Last night was—'

His deep voice, the edges iced with impatience, cut across her before she could establish anything. 'Considering you are standing there huddled in a sheet, acting like some outraged virgin, I'm taking that you regret last night as a given.'

The accusing note in his voice brought a tinge of angry colour to her cheeks.

'That's really astute of you,' she drawled sarcastically. Where Dante was concerned her virginal outrage had always been zero, even when she'd had a right to the title. She had had no qualms about giving him her virginity, though he had been a lot less *relaxed* about receiving the unexpected gift.

'Do you regret marrying me?' Asking the second time did not make it any clearer to him why her answer mattered to him…except to lessen his guilt, maybe?

The irony was not lost on him. There could be few people who had spent a life where guilt featured less heavily… His upper lip curled in a bleak smile.

If he'd been a man who believed in karma he might think that his present situation was Fate's way of making him pay for an empty life of utter hedonism. Where the only way was the easy way. Having once rejected the concept of duty, now he was ruled by it.

He'd imagined that he was doing the *right thing* when he had proposed, never for one moment asking himself what the right thing was for Beatrice. He'd been the one making the ultimate sacrifice. Unwilling to own his thoughts, jaw clenched, he pushed out a breath through flared nostrils.

She blinked, her long lashes brushing the smooth curve of her cheeks like butterfly wings. 'There's no point regretting, is there?'

'Which means you do.' Did she ever ask herself if things might have ended differently if their baby had clung to life and not simply been a heartbeat that had vanished from the screen?

His guts tightened like an icy fist as the memory surfaced of the doctor relaying the news alongside the information that the baby had just faded away.

He had been consumed by a devastation that had felt as if he were being swallowed up. It had made no sense. He'd never wanted children—hadn't wanted a child.

'I'm looking forwards.'

His glance lifted as his thoughts shifted back to the present moment.

The intensity of his stare made Bea lose her thread, but after a momentary pause she managed to regain control and her defiance.

'The past is done and gone. I'm not interested in

revisiting—' She felt the sheet slip and yanked it up. As she did the colour seeping under her skin deepened the golden-toned glow as the irony of what she was about to claim hit her. Sometimes honesty, wise or not, was the best, or only, policy.

Her shoulders lowered as the defensive antagonism drained away, exposing the vulnerability that lay beneath. Dante looked away but not before he felt something twist hard in his chest.

'I have a lot of lovely memories that I will always treasure. I'm just not as realistic as you are sometimes.' She bit down on her quivering lower lip before the emotion took her over.

A spasm played across the surface of his symmetrical features that had more than once been called *too* perfect. 'Maybe I have lower expectations… You should try it, Beatrice. Less disappointment in life,' he suggested harshly.

'You want me to be as cynical as you are? That's a *big* ask, Dante.'

Heavy eyelids at half mast, his eyes gleaming, he quirked his mobile lips into a mocking smile that invited her to share his joke as their eyes connected. 'You call it cynicism. I call it realism, and it's all about baby steps, *cara*.'

It wasn't just her expression that froze, time did too. He could almost hear the seconds count down before her lashes came down in a protective sweep, but not before he had seen the hurt shimmer in her eyes.

Jaw clenched, he silently cursed himself. Of course he knew the self-recrimination might have been of more use if it had come sooner. Like when the loss of their baby had become not a personal tragedy, but one debated by palace mandarins and *sources* close to the throne.

It had come as no surprise to him—he'd known the moment his brother stepped away from the throne what lay ahead for him. But to Beatrice it must have felt like an alternative universe.

She waited for the toddler in her head with Dante's eyes to take his first faltering steps before she let the image go and looked up, ignoring the ache inside her. Dante didn't meet her eyes—maybe he was thinking about the *practical princess* he would replace her with…the one that could give him babies.

The babies she had tried so hard to give him; ten months of married life within the palace walls and ten months of waiting and hoping, then the awful inevitable sense of failure.

He swung his legs over the side of the bed, causing the rumpled sheet across his middle to slide a few treacherous inches lower.

Fighting the dormant protective instincts that Beatrice woke in him, Dante shrugged, but the truth was the thing she actually needed protecting from was him.

'I'm sorry.'

Cheeks hot, eyes wary, she dragged her wandering gaze up from his muscled thighs, but his expression was frustratingly hard to read.

'For what?' If he said he was sorry for last night she would hit him, she vowed grimly. 'Marrying me? I knew what I was doing,' she retorted, not happy at being cast in the role of victim.

'And now you're getting on with your life.' *Without him.*

'That might be easier if you weren't sitting in my bed.'

'I need to be in Paris tomorrow. The meeting was delayed and—'

'You wanted to mess my life up some more?' There was more weariness than reproach in her voice.

'I didn't invite myself into your bed, Beatrice.'

Colour scored her cheeks. Did he really think she needed that spelt out? 'Sorry. I'm not blaming you. You've been very good about making it easy for me to leave.

'So are there any papers?'

'There are papers, but…'

'But?'

'The tabloids love to—'

She tensed, suddenly seeing where this was going, and why he wasn't quite meeting her eyes. Pale but composed, she cut him off. 'Congratulations.'

His brows knitted into a perplexed frown. 'For what?'

'You're *engaged…*?' Her racing thoughts quickly joined the dots, swiftly turning the theory in her head to fact in seconds. It would be something official. He wouldn't have come all this way to tell her in person that he had a lover. She had kind of taken that for granted. A sensual man like Dante was not built for celibacy.

His steady stare told her nothing, but she knew and she was totally fine with it, or she would be if she didn't throw up.

'Aren't you?'

Finally, a low hissing sound of amazement escaped his clenched teeth. 'Engaged would be a little premature. I'm not divorced yet.'

Her eyelashes flickered like butterflies against her cheeks. 'Oh, I just…'

'Made one of your leaps based on the well-known

scientific theory that if something is totally crazy it is true.'

'It was a perfectly reasonable assumption,' she retorted huffily, hating that she felt almost sick with relief, but adding for her own benefit as much as his, 'You will get remarried one day—you'll have to.'

His gut twisted in recognition of the accuracy of her words *have to.* She said *have to*—the people around him, his family, the courtiers, called it duty. Every word he spoke, his every action would be observed and judged. *He* would be judged.

The bottom line was his life was no longer his own. Even as he opened his mouth to respond Dante recognised the hypocrisy of his occupation of the moral high ground. 'So, you think that I'd be engaged and sleep with you?'

'Yes,' she said without hesitation, the damning shame curdling inside her reserved for herself, not him, because she knew that nothing would have stopped her sleeping with Dante last night. 'You'd only be keeping up the family tradition,' she sniped.

One corner of his mobile lips quirked upwards as he remembered how shocked she'd been when she'd realised that his parents both had lovers who upon occasion slept over. His normality was her shocking.

'Will you sit down? I'm not about to leap on you.'

'No.' She backed a little further into the corner. It wasn't *him* she was worried about; they were both naked, and sitting was just one touch away from lying down. Her eyes widened as another equally and actually more probable explanation for his presence occurred to her. 'Is this about the divorce?' Her voice rose a shrill octave as she gulped and tacked on, 'Is there a problem?'

'No, it is not about the divorce. It is about Grandfather.'

'Reynard?' She stopped nervously pleating the fabric she held tight across her breasts and smiled. The old King, who had stepped back from the throne in favour of his son, Dante's father, after he suffered a stroke. Reynard had been one of the very few people she had been able to relax around in the palace.

Known for his acerbic tongue and a wit that took no prisoners, he'd made Beatrice laugh, though she had not realised until after the fact that being taught chess by him was considered a rare privilege.

They still played chess online. 'One of these days I'm going to beat him.'

One corner of Dante's mouth lifted in a half-smile. 'If you ever do it'll be for real. He won't let you win.'

'I hope not… So how is he?' She read enough in his face to make her panic; it wasn't so much his expression that made her heart lurch, more the careful lack of it. 'Oh, my God, he's not…not…?'

'No…no…he's all right,' Dante soothed.

She had barely released a sigh of relief when he added, 'He has had another stroke.'

'Oh, God, no!'

'Don't panic, the doctors gave him the clot-busting stuff in time, so they say there's no permanent damage, no further damage at least.'

She huffed out a sigh of relief but still felt shaky and sad because one day her worst-case scenario would be true, and a world without that irascible character would be a lesser place.

'We've kept everything in-house but it's inevitable that the news is bound to leak soon, and you know how they play up the drama disaster angle. I wanted you to know the facts, not the exaggerated fiction.'

'Why didn't you just say this was why you came?' His eyes captured her own and Beatrice felt the blush run over her skin. 'All right,' she cut in quickly before he could point out that last night had not involved much talking. 'You could have messaged me…rung…?'

'Yes, I could.' He released her eyes suddenly.

'It wasn't kind coming here. This hasn't been easy for me…'

His jaw clenched. 'You think it has for me?' he pushed out in a driven tone.

'Right, so let's just call last night goodbye.' It had to be because she couldn't do this more than once. 'Give my love to Reynard. I really wish I could see him. He *really* is all right?'

'He really is. You *could* see him.'

Beatrice gave a bitter laugh. 'Come back to San Macizo? I presume you're joking.'

'Were you so unhappy there?'

She kept her expression flat. 'I was irrelevant there.' The only function that would have made her acceptable was producing babies and she hadn't done that. The month after month of raised expectations and then… Dante must have been relieved when she had announced that she'd had enough. The recognition made her throat tighten; she ignored it.

She was ignoring so hard she nearly tripped over the draped sheet. Enough was enough!

Head high, not glancing in his direction, she stalked across to the wardrobe and, presenting him with her back, pulled the turquoise silk robe from its hanger on the door.

There was a sheer ridiculousness to her display of

false modesty around Dante, who knew every inch of her body—intimately. She let the sheet fall.

'I tried for ten months,' she said, throwing the words lightly over her shoulder, glad that he couldn't see her face. 'I tried to do the *right* thing, say the right thing. I tried to fit in. I tried…' She didn't finish the sentence, but the unspoken words hung between them like a veil. They both knew what she had tried and failed to do, the only thing that would have made her acceptable to his family: provide an heir.

CHAPTER THREE

BACK TURNED TO HIM, Beatrice tightened the sash before she turned, doing her best to not notice the molten gleam in his eyes as he watched her cinch the belt a little tighter.

She tilted her chin to a defiant angle and tossed her hair back from her face before tucking it behind her ears as she stomped over the sheet, her pearly painted toenails looking bright against the pale painted boards scattered with rustic rugs.

Despite the snow that had begun to fall again outside, the temperature was if anything too warm, thanks no doubt to the massive cast-iron radiator that didn't seem to respond to the thermostat.

Pretty much the way her internal thermostat ignored instructions when Dante was in the vicinity.

'You were the one who was hung up on that.'

The claim made her want to throw something at him.

'You were never irrelevant. A pain in the…but never irrelevant,' he drawled, unable to stop his eyes drifting over the long sensual flow of her body outlined under the silk. 'Have I seen that before? It brings out the colour of your eyes.' Which were so blue he'd initially assumed that she wore contact lenses.

She sketched a tight smile. 'It's been six months. I've

added a few things to my wardrobe. You probably have a list somewhere.'

'Six months since *you* left, Beatrice. I didn't ask you to go.'

She'd left. It was not an option for him; he could never walk. He was trapped, playing a part. He would be for the rest of his life. Typecast for perpetuity as a person he would never be.

Beatrice felt her anger spark, the old resentments stir. He made it sound so simple, and leaving had been the hardest thing she had ever done. How much simpler it would have been if she had stopped loving him, how much simpler it was for him because he never had loved her, not really.

It was a truth she had always known, a truth she had buried deep.

'You didn't try and stop me.'

'Did you want me to?'

'Even if I had got pregnant, a baby shouldn't be used to paper over the cracks in a relationship, which is why this can't happen again.'

'This...?'

'This, as in you turning up and...' She caught her eyes drifting to his mouth and despaired as she felt the flush of desire whoosh through her body. This *need* inside her frightened her; she didn't want to feel this way. 'I think in the future any communications should be through our solicitors,' she concluded, struggling to keep her voice clear of her inner desperation, making it as cold as she could.

Dante felt something tighten in his chest that he refused to recognise as loneliness, as he pushed back fragments of memories that flashed in quick succession through his head. The tears in his brother's eyes as he said sorry, the coldness in his parents' eyes as they informed him that the future of the royal family rested on his shoulders.

'So, you don't think that exes can be friends.'

Her hard little laugh sounded unlike the full, throatier, uninhibited laugh he remembered. A few weeks into their marriage and she hadn't laughed at all.

'This isn't friendship, Dante. Friends *share*.'

Share, she said. He almost laughed. The last thing he had wanted to do was share when he was with Beatrice. He had wanted to forget. He didn't want to prove himself to his wife; he was proving himself to everyone else.

For the first time in his life Dante had been experiencing fear of failure, something so alien to him that it had taken him some time to identify it. Worse than the weakness was the idea of Beatrice seeing those fears, looking at him differently… He knew the look. He had seen it every day and he couldn't have borne it.

He had seen that look in the eyes of the team who had been put in place to coordinate his own repackaging, even while they *told* him they had total confidence in him, before asking him to embrace values that he had long ago rejected. They appealed to his sense of duty.

The real shock, at least to him, was that he possessed one. He'd spent his life trying to forget the early lessons on duty and service, but it seemed that they had made a lasting impression.

He didn't share this insight, unwilling to give anyone the leverage this weakness would have afforded them. Instead he listened and then worked towards cutting the team down to three people he could work with.

He would have liked to get rid of the lot, but he was

a realist. It had taken his brother a lifetime to recognise what he had grasped in weeks wearing the mantle of Crown Prince. You really couldn't have it all, you had to make sacrifices.

His glance narrowed in on Beatrice's lovely face. *What* you were prepared to sacrifice was the question.

'I can't be half in, half out, Dante, it's not…fair. It's cruel…' she quivered out.

His glance flickered across the lovely, anguished features of the woman he had married. Finally *seeing sense* was how his father had reacted when he had broken the news that they were splitting up.

'She has come to her senses. Beatrice is leaving me.'

Dante had pushed the fact home that this was her choice, though not adding that fighting the decision was about the only noble thing he had done in his life. Lucky for him *nobility* was not a prerequisite for the job of King-in-waiting, unlike hypocrisy.

He knew that he ought not to be feeling this rage, this sense of betrayal. Their marriage had been about a child, then there was no child. Beatrice's decision had been the logical one. He could not see why it had shocked him so much.

Most successful marriages owed their longevity to mutual convenience and laziness, or, as in his parents' case, they were business arrangements, two people living parallel lives that occasionally touched. This was not something that Beatrice could ever understand.

In the end, the official line had been trial separation, while behind-the-scenes lists of replacements were drawn up for when the *trial* was officially made permanent.

He wasn't much interested in the lists, or the names

of those that were added, or deleted after a skeleton emerged from their blue-blooded closet.

One *suitable* bride was much the same as another to him, though he wondered if the woman who had been chosen to share the throne with his brother, and had unwittingly been his brother's tipping point, had been included. He could not remember her face or name, just that she belonged to one of the few minor European royal families he and Carl were not related to.

Carl had choked before it was made official, choosing to step away from the lie and his life…because though San Macizo was considered progressive, the idea of an openly gay ruler unable to provide an heir was not something that could be negotiated.

His option had been walk away, or live a lie.

Dante had wondered whether, if the situations had been reversed, he would have shown as much strength as his brother.

One of the things that had struck him, after his initial shock at the revelations, was that he *was* shocked that he really hadn't seen it coming. When his brother had revealed his sexual orientation and his deep unhappiness, Dante hadn't had a clue. But then he never had been much interested in anyone's life but his own, he acknowledged with a spasm of self-disgust.

There was an equal likelihood that he hadn't recognised his brother's struggles because it really wouldn't have suited him to see them.

His glance zeroed in on Beatrice's face, the soft angles, the purity of profile, the glow that was there despite the unhappiness in her eyes. Just as he had tried not to see Beatrice was unhappy.

'And you're out.' His shoulders lifted in a seemingly negligent shrug. 'Fair enough.'

She blinked, hard thrown by his response, a small irrational part of her irked that he wasn't fighting. 'You agree?'

'I already did. We are getting divorced, so relax, things are in hand,' he drawled.

'Are they?' Yesterday she'd have agreed but yesterday she hadn't been breathing the same air as Dante. Since then she had been tested and had come face to face with her total vulnerability, her genetic weakness where he was concerned.

'It's in everyone's best interests for this to happen. We're all on the same page here.'

'Pity the same couldn't be said for our marriage.'

It shouldn't have hurt that he didn't deny it, but it did.

Her decision to leave had been greeted with thinly disguised universal relief, which gave a lie to the myth that divorce didn't happen in the Velazquez family. It made her wonder if there had been others before her who had been airbrushed from royal history.

'I don't think anyone expected it to last, not even you...?'

Dante shrugged and deflected smoothly. 'I never expected to get married. I think it has a very different meaning for us both.'

In his family marriage was discussed in the same breath as airport expansion, or hushing the scandal of a minister who had pushed family values being caught in a compromising position, and the latest opinion poll on the current popularity of the royal family—it was business.

His heart had always been shielded by cynicism, which he embraced, but maybe it was the same cynicism that had left him with no defence against the emotional gut punch that Beatrice and her pregnancy had been.

'You're right.' He unfolded his long lean length and stood there oblivious to his naked state before casually bending to retrieve items of clothing, throwing them on the bed before he began to dress.

She couldn't not look; his body was so perfect, his most mundane action coordinated grace. She just wished her appreciation could be purely aesthetic; just looking made her feel hungry and ashamed in equal measure.

'I am?' she said, the practical, sane portion of her mind recognising this was a good thing, the irrational, emotional section wanting him to argue.

He turned as he pulled up his trousers over his narrow hips, his eyes on her face as his long fingers slid his belt home.

'Our lives touched but now—' Touched but nearly not connected—maybe it had been the sheer *depth* of his reaction that had made him show restraint, and it had required every ounce of self-control he possessed not to seek the glorious woman with endless legs and golden skin he had seen across the crowded theatre foyer, or at least find out her name…but he had walked away.

When, days later, he had found himself in the front row of the catwalk show of the hottest designer of the season with…he really couldn't remember who he had arrived with, but he could remember every detail of the tall blonde under the spotlight drifting past, hands on her hips, oozing sex in a way that had sent a collective shiver of appreciation around the audience. She had been wearing an outfit that was intended to be androgynous but on her it really hadn't been—it had felt like Fate.

He had allowed his companion to drag him to the sort of back-slapping, self-congratulatory, booze-fuelled backstage party that he would normally have avoided, where he got to know her name, Beatrice, and the fact she had already left.

His companion, already disgruntled by the lack of attention, had stayed as he'd run out of the place…in the grip of an urgency that he hadn't paused to analyse.

An image of her face as he'd seen it that day supplanted itself across her features. She'd stood too far away then for him to see the sprinkling of freckles across her nose. But they'd been visible later, when he had literally almost knocked her down on the steps of the gallery where the fashion show had been held. She'd looked younger minus the sleeked hair and the crazy, exaggerated eye make-up and he had decided in that second that there was such a thing as Fate—he had stopped fighting it. Never before had he felt so utterly transfixed by a woman.

She didn't fit into any stereotype he had known. She was fresh and funny and even the fact she'd turned out to be virgin territory, which ought to have made him run for the hills, hadn't.

A clattering noise from downstairs cut into his reminisces and made Beatrice jump guiltily.

'How is Maya?' he asked.

'People are finally recognising her artistic talent.'

Her sister might think that talent spoke for itself but Beatrice knew that wasn't the case. That was where she came in. She had done night classes in marketing during her time modelling, while everything she'd earned during that period had gone into their start-up nest egg for their own eco-fashion range.

Dante grunted, in the act of fighting his way into his shirt. Beatrice willed her expression calm as his probing gaze moved across her face.

'Will you be all right?'

'I'll be fine.' She would be; she wasn't going to let her Dante addiction of a few months define her or the rest of her life. She had accepted that it would be painful for a while, but she was a resilient person by nature, strong. Everyone said so.

So it must be true.

When her dad had died people had said how strong she was, what a rock she was. Then when Mum had married Edward she had been there for Maya, who had been the target of their stepfather's abuse. For a time, she had been the only one who had seen what the man was doing, because there had been nothing physical involved as he had begun to systematically destroy her sister's self-esteem and confidence.

For a while their mother had chosen the man she had married over her daughters, believing his lies, letting him manipulate her, controlling every aspect of her life. It had been a bad time and for a long time Beatrice, more judgemental than her sister, had struggled to forgive her mother her weakness.

The irony was that marriage to Dante had shown her that the same weakness was in her, the same flaw. Dante hadn't lied, which perhaps made her self-deception worse. She had wanted to believe he was something he wasn't, that they had something that didn't exist.

She pushed away the memories, focusing on the fact that she and Maya had forgiven their mother; their bond had survived and so had they. Now all they both wanted was their happily divorced mum to stop feeling so guilty.

'And how are your parents?' She felt obliged to enquire but could not inject any warmth into the cool of her voice.

'Pretty much the same.'

She lifted her brows in an acknowledgement as the memory of that first-night dinner in the palace with his parents flashed into her head. The shoulder-blade-aching tension in the room had taken her appetite away, and, if it hadn't, the unspoken criticisms behind the comments directed her way by the King and Queen would have guaranteed she was going to bed hungry.

And alone.

It had been two in the morning before she'd sat up at the sound of Dante's tread. She remembered that waiting, checking the time every few minutes. In the strange room, strange bed, in a strange country it had felt longer.

She had switched on the bedside light.

'Sorry, I didn't mean to wake you.'

She remembered so clearly the empathy that had surged through her body when she saw the grey hue of exhaustion on his normally vibrantly toned skin. Her throat tightened now as she remembered just wanting to hold him. If that day had been tough for her, she had told herself, it must have been a hundred times worse for Dante.

'I wasn't asleep,' she'd said as he'd come to sit on the side of the bed.

'You were waiting up.'

She'd shaken her head at the accusation. 'You look so tired.' She'd run a hand over the stubble on his square jaw—he even made haggard look sexy as hell.

'Not too tired.' She remembered the cool of his fingers as he'd caught the hand she had raised to his cheek and pulled her into him, his whisky-tinged breath warm and on his mouth as he'd husked against her lips, 'I just want to…bury myself in you.'

She pushed away the memories that were too painful now. They reminded her of her own wilful stupidity—for her that night it had gone beyond physical release. Dante had always taken her to a sensual heaven, but this connection had gone deeper, she had told herself as she'd lain later, her damp, cooling body entwined in his, tears of emotion too intense to name leaking from the corners of her eyes. She had felt so…complete.

But it had been a lie, her lie, and the cracks had started to appear almost immediately—before their heated, damp bodies had finished cooling in the velvet darkness.

CHAPTER FOUR

BEA WAITED UNTIL he had finished dressing before voicing the question that had inserted itself in her head and wouldn't go away. If she didn't ask she knew from experience the anxiety would start to eat away at her.

'I was wondering…' She paused, wishing she possessed Dante's enviable ability to distance himself from negative emotions. The world could be falling apart, panic endemic, but Dante, all calm, reasoned logic, would stand apart.

'Wondering?'

'Will last night affect the divorce?' What was the legal take on sleeping with your *almost* ex-husband?

'That's what you're worried about?'

'Well, aren't you?'

He gave a twisted smile. 'Are you going to tell anyone about it?'

The colour flew to her cheeks. 'Of course not, though of course Maya will—'

'Will be waiting for our walk of shame.'

'Maya doesn't judge.' Or blab, which was just as well when you considered the things she had told her sister.

'Of course she doesn't.'

She ignored the sarcasm and pushed him for an answer. 'Well, will it?'

‘I see no reason it should.’

‘Right, so we can forget last night happened and get on with our lives.’

‘You seem to be already doing that…’

Underneath the smooth delivery she picked up *something* in his voice, an unspoken *suggestion* that she shouldn’t be. It brought a flare of anger and she embraced it, embraced anything that wasn’t the emotions of this slow, never-ending, nerve-wracking goodbye.

‘Well, I *thought* about sitting in a room and fading away, but then I thought there might be life after Dante and you know what—’ she widened her eyes in bright blue mockery ‘—there is.’

Jaw clenched, Dante viciously shoved a section of shirt in the waistband of his trousers and dragged a hand across his hair. ‘So, who is he?’

‘Who…what…?’ She expelled a little sigh of comprehension as enlightenment dawned. This time she didn’t need to jab her anger into life. ‘Oh!’

For a split second she was tempted to invent an active love life—after all, she seriously doubted a man with Dante’s appetites would have been celibate. His morals were certainly flexible enough for him to not allow something like a *nearly* ex-wife to keep him faithful.

Would he be jealous?

It was a sign that she had a long way to go in her journey to not caring to know that she wanted him to be.

‘Does there always have to be a man?’ she countered, viewing him with arch-browed disdain. ‘I don’t need a man to complete me! *Any* man! I am not my m—’ She stopped before she voiced the comparison that was in her head.

It took a moment for his muscles to unclench and banish the image in his head of a faceless male exploring the delights of Beatrice's body. He'd get used to the idea, but it was too soon yet, which sounded like a rationalisation and was, which was new territory for a man who had never understood the concept of jealousy in relationships.

But now the idea of another man appreciating Beatrice's long lush curves, beautiful face, the shape and intensity of colour of her wide-spaced sapphire eyes, the wide, generous curve of her lips and the smooth pallor of her flawless creamy skin filled him with an impotent rage.

The idea of the laughter in her eyes and her deep, full-throttle, throaty laugh being aimed at someone who was not him made his grip on his self-control grow slippery.

'We should have had a wild passionate affair.' Wild passionate affairs had a beautiful simplicity. They burned bright, they hit a peak and they faded. Controlled madness that was temporary, that left no regrets, no sense of unfinished business.

His words made her flinch. 'Instead I got pregnant… The irony is, of course, that if we'd just waited there wouldn't have been a baby to get married for.'

His expression darkened. 'That wasn't what I meant, and you know it. I know you blame me for the miscarriage but—'

'I blame you?'

His lips twisted in a cynical half-smile that left his dark eyes bleak as he challenged, 'So you have *never* thought that if you hadn't been forced to transplant yourself to another country, an alien environment, being isolated from everything you knew, your entire support system, you might not have lost the baby?'

'I thought none of those things.' But it was clear

from his expression that he did. Why had she never suspected that Dante felt guilt for the loss of the baby? 'The doctors told us that a high portion of pregnancies end early on—a lot of women don't even know there ever was a baby.'

'Stress plays a part in these things. And an affair would inevitably have burnt itself out and we could have parted friends.'

'I think we have already established that isn't going to happen. You do realise that that was spoken like a true commitment-phobe.'

Dante shrugged. He had no problems with the description, though it implied that he had been running or avoiding something, which he hadn't.

Dante had never felt anything that inclined him to believe that he was marriage material. He would, he had always suspected, make a terrible husband. Well, on that at least he had been proved right—he had been, and he was.

'You need to leave.' She caught her lower lip between her teeth, her eyes swivelling from him towards the door, recognising the danger, the anger between them often found release in a *physical* way.

'Yes, I do.'

It had all gone quiet downstairs but the main thing was making Dante vanish and failing that…there was no way she could smuggle Dante out without Maya seeing him. She paused mid thought, almost wanting to laugh that she had been considering the smuggling option!

About time you took responsibility for your own actions, she told herself sternly, knowing full well it wasn't Maya's judgement she was trying to dodge but her own. She tightened the belt on her robe, causing the neckline to gape and drawing his eyes like magnets to the smooth swell of her cleavage.

Beatrice swallowed. His eyelids had dropped to half mast; the gleam below made her throat dry.

'That's the exact same colour as the top you were wearing when we first met. You had something in your eye.'

'Did I? I don't remember,' she lied.

'You were making it worse, stabbing your eyes with that tissue. And swearing like a sailor. You bumped into me.'

'You bumped into me,' she contradicted, her breath coming fast as she remembered him taking the tissue from her fingers, ignoring her protests. *'Let me,'* he'd said and she had—soon she had let him do a lot more.

She'd *begged* him to do a lot more!

'You looked so—' Young, fresh and a million miles away from the sleek creature on the catwalk, but even more sexy without the dramatic make-up, her pale hair no longer sleeked back but loose. It had spilled like silk down her back. He should have realised then that she was an innocent but he hadn't, and when he had, it had been too late.

You think it would have made a difference? his inner voice mocked as he dragged himself back to the moment and watched as Beatrice shook her head.

The effort to escape the memories in her head hurt but it was worth it. She had moved on and, more importantly, *she would never become her mother.*

'So, we have an understanding. From now on any communication will be through our legal teams,' she said, making her voice cold.

'You don't have a team. You have a solicitor who

spends more time watering his roses than looking after his clients' interests.'

Left to that guy Beatrice would be walking away from their marriage just as poor financially as she'd walked into it, if he had not issued some instructions that made his own legal team look slightly sick. There were some lawyers who recognised a moral scruple when they saw one, but none of them worked for the Velazquez family.

'Bea, shall I bring the coffee up?'

Dante watched as Beatrice responded to the voice that drifted up the stairs with an 'over my dead body' expression on her face, which she backed up with a dagger look.

Not analysing his motivation, he walked past her and pulled the door open.

'We'll be right down, Maya!' He let the door close with a snap.

Feet apart, hands on her hips, she fixed him with a glare of seething dislike. 'Well, thank you for that.'

'Call it a parting gift.'

'I'd call it a cheap shot.'

He sighed out his irritation. 'Would it be preferable for me to just appear? At least she's had some forewarning. Unless you were going to smuggle me out?'

Beatrice felt the guilty wash of colour stain her cheeks. 'Let's just get this over with. Don't say *anything*,' she hissed.

'Is there anything left to say?'

'I suppose not.'

Her expression was as blank as her voice. Once, he had been able to read everything she felt because she had worn her emotions so close to the surface. Was this what palace life had done to her?

What you did to her.

He'd set her free, which ought to make him feel good. It didn't, but then he'd always thought doing the right thing was overhyped.

Her sister, dressed in dark ski pants and a chunky cable sweater she wore with the sleeves rolled up, didn't turn as she continued to stir the scrambled eggs on the stove.

There was an unmistakable chill in the air.

'Good morning, Dante.'

'Dante was just—'

'Let's not go there, shall we?' Maya stopped stirring and turned, spoon in hand. She blanked Dante, which was something not many people could manage, and slanted a wry look across at her sister.

Beatrice bit her tongue, though not sure of the words she was biting back. Would the jumble in her head have emerged as a defence or apology?

Maya turned back to her stirring. 'Want some breakfast, Dante?' she asked, still not looking at him.

'No, he doesn't,' Beatrice said before Dante could respond. 'He was just going.' To emphasise the point she went to the door and opened it. The waft of cold, fresh, snowy air made her gasp but she stood her ground, appeal mingled with the determination in the glance she sent to Dante.

'Nice to see you, Maya.' The petite figure continued to stir, presenting her back to him, but he could feel the disapproval radiating off her in waves.

The door closed; the tension left Beatrice's body. She grabbed the back of one of the dining chairs and lowered herself into the modern plastic bucket seat. 'How's your head? The migraine gone?'

'Fine. All I needed was an early night, but it seems

that things got interesting after I left.' Maya took her pan off the stove and poured a coffee from the full pot. She placed it on the table in front of Beatrice, a worried frown puckering her brow as she scanned her sister's face.

Beatrice cleared her throat. 'You must be wondering.' Now there was an understatement.

Maya shook her head. 'Just tell me you're not getting back together, you're not going back to San Macizo…'

'I'm never seeing him again,' Beatrice said and burst into tears.

As for San Macizo, the last time she had left she had left behind part of herself. If she went back she knew she'd lose what she had left.

'Thank God!' Maya hefted out a deep sigh of relief.

Beatrice sniffed and dashed the moisture from her face with the back of her hand.

'Oh, I know it's not my…and I'm *trying* to be objective, but honestly, when you came back last time looking like a…a…'

Shocked by the expression on her sister's face, Beatrice covered her small hand with her own. 'I'm not going back,' she cut in, holding her sister's teary, scared gaze.

'So what was he…?'

'Reynard has had a stroke.'

Dismay spread across Maya's heart-shaped face, melting away the last wisps of disapproval. 'Oh, I'm so sorry. Reynard was such a lovely man, with such a wicked sense of humour. When is the funeral? I'd like to come if I may?'

'It wasn't fatal,' Beatrice said quickly. She got up, picked up a piece of toast and started to butter it, not because she could have eaten a bite, just for something to do. 'So those buyers lined up to view the samples…'

'Changing the subject, Bea?'

'I know you don't like Dante.'

'I think Dante is perfectly charming,' Maya inserted, her lips curving into a wry smile, before adding, 'But I don't, I can't, *like* anyone who makes you unhappy.'

'I'm not unhappy.'

It was an obvious struggle for Maya not to challenge this statement, but lip-biting won out.

'And Dante is gone. He's never coming back.'

This time the crying went on a long time.

CHAPTER FIVE

'*DATES!*'

Beatrice blinked, caught between confusion and panic. She dragged her wandering blue gaze back to the young GP's face and allowed the professional encouraging smile to drag her back from the brink of panic. Though kick-starting her brain remained a non-starter—she felt utterly incapable of forming coherent thoughts.

'Dates...?' she echoed, as though she were thinking about it, which she wasn't. Thinking was simply not an option.

The reality was she could barely remember her name, let alone the information the locum GP, a young woman her own age, was asking for. Her regular doctor was, ironically, given the circumstances, on paternity leave.

'I know... I think...' She clenched her hands as she struggled to push past the loud static buzz in her head, which she explained by telling herself she needed a sugar hit. She hadn't managed to keep her breakfast down or, for that matter, last night's supper...*again*!

'Take your time,' the woman said, even though Beatrice was sure she had overrun her allowed time slot by a long way. An image of the foot-tapping disapproval as fellow patients glanced at the clock on the waiting-room wall flashed into her head—she'd been there, done that herself.

This doctor, with the relaxed attitude to time, seemed nice and sympathetic, which might not be a good thing. She had reached the point where it would only take a kind word to release the tears she could feel pressing against her eyelids.

So Beatrice avoided the sympathy and focused on the hole in the woman's tights as she wrapped her arms around herself in a self-protective hug to combat the cold inside her that was making her teeth chatter and sending intermittent tremors through her body.

'So, I'm assuming that this wasn't planned?' the medic, who had scooted her chair around to Beatrice's side of the desk, suggested.

Beatrice shook her head and wished the medic's calm were contagious, but then the professional had seen this a hundred times before and this wasn't professional for Beatrice.

'Statistically pregnancies rarely are planned.'

Tell me about it, she thought, swallowing the ironic laugh locked in her aching throat. 'Really?' If that was meant to make her feel better, it didn't.

'Did someone come with you?'

Beatrice reeled in her wandering thoughts, back from the unknown and scary future they had drifted towards, and tried very hard to focus on the here and now and not fainting—she *never* fainted.

'Someone...?' She moved her head, a tiny jerky, shaking motion, before clearing her throat, relieved when she responded with a close approximation of someone who had not totally lost it. 'Yes…yes, my sister.'

Who had refused to take no for an answer and had tagged along to the appointment that Beatrice had made after the stomach bug had not cleared up. Had Maya sussed the truth…had she?

Of course she had, but she'd buried the knowledge so deep…constructed so many perfectly reasonable, safe alternatives that it had not lessened the mind-deadening shock when confronted with the inevitable reality.

Despite the shock, her body continued to perform all its automated responses: she was breathing and moving, putting one foot… Actually she wasn't—she was sitting down and her knees were shaking. She was thinking, *Well, maybe not.* Her thoughts continued to refuse to move beyond the big mental brick wall. *I am pregnant.*

In her head she tacked several large exclamation marks on the acknowledgement, which did not make it feel any more real.

'I'm six weeks,' she said suddenly, her tone making it clear there were no ifs and buts or maybes about this. A warmth heated her pale cheeks as her thoughts drifted back to the night she'd spent under the duvet in the ski lodge with Dante. Sometimes on top of the duvet and sometimes… She felt a shameful flash of heat and closed down the thought of the night they had made a baby. 'It's our eighteen-month anniversary today…'

'Congratulations. Your husband isn't here today?'

Beatrice watched the doctor tap some keys on the computer and grimace as she noticed the hole in her tights.

'He's out of the country,' she said carefully.

'Would you like me to…? Shall I ask your sister to come in?'

Beatrice gave a pale smile of gratitude. 'Yes, please.'

A short while later she and Maya were out of the surgery and back in the fresh air. Beatrice expelled a long shuddering sigh and squeezed her eyes closed, opening them as she felt Maya's arm link with her own.

'Fancy walking back through the park?'

'Didn't we drive here?' If she had imagined that she was in even worse shape than she thought, Beatrice decided.

'Yes, but the fresh air might do us good… I'll pick up the car later.' She glanced at the little vintage car they had jointly bought when they first set up home together. It had seen better days.

Beatrice shrugged. 'Why not?'

The watery spring sun had come out from behind the clouds as they trudged beneath the skeletal branches of a row of poplars and past the snowdrops that were pushing up through the cold ground.

It was Maya who broke the silence.

'I love the smell of spring, all that promise of new life…' She pulled her wandering gaze, which had drifted to her sister's flat stomach, upwards. 'Sorry, I didn't mean to be profound or anything.'

Beatrice turned her head, then, as her eyes connected with the concern clouding Maya's eyes that her sister was unable to hide, she quickly looked away. 'You knew?' she asked, digging her hands into the deep pockets of her coat.

'It seemed…a…possibility…'

'You must think I'm a total idiot!' So must the doctor, not that she could remember the things she had said or any details of her own responses.

'I will think you're an idiot if you carry on saying daft things like that.'

Beatrice produced a pale, lacklustre smile in response. 'I suppose I must have known,' she admitted, thinking of all the signs that had been there. 'But I didn't think it would happen again…after…' Her voice trailed away, a faint ironic smile tugging at the corners of her lips as her thoughts drifted to the words of unbidden advice Dante's grandfather, still autocratically regal despite the fact he had passed on his official title to his son after a stroke, had offered. *'Relax, woman.'*

His words had stuck in her mind, mainly because at the time everyone else had been telling her to panic, if not in so many words—it had not been hard to read between the lines or the glances and conversations that halted abruptly when she appeared.

Well, it turned out that old Reynard was right all along. All she had needed to do was relax…

Oh, God, no one had ever accused her of having good timing.

Beatrice turned her head. The worried expression on her sister's face pushed her into speech. 'It's just everyone was waiting, every month…and letting myself hope, and then having to tell Dante when it didn't happen.' He had acted as though it didn't matter, but she knew it did; she knew that as far as the palace was concerned her fertility had stopped being a private matter the moment Dante became Crown Prince.

She looked down at her flat belly and tried to separate the confusing mess of conflicting emotions fighting for supremacy in her head. 'A year ago, this would have made him so happy.' Frowning, she worried her full lower lip and wondered about his reaction now. Who was she kidding? She knew *exactly* what his reaction would be when he discovered that she was carrying the heir to the throne.

This was the end of her new life; there was no way he would allow her to bring up his child outside San Macizo.

'Is that why you left…?'

'Left?' Beatrice gave a vague shake of her head.

Maya studied her sister's face and glanced around for a convenient park bench, hoping they would make it there before Beatrice folded.

'You never said *why*, just that it was over, when you got home.'

Beatrice gave a sad smile. 'I'm pretty sure that it was why Dante made it easy for me to go.'

Maya caught her hand as Beatrice's voice became suspended by tears.

'You never asked me before,' Beatrice said.

'I thought you'd tell me when you were ready.'

'It's hard to explain my life. I felt like I'd stepped into a trickling stream and ended up trying to keep my head above raging white water. Things happened so fast—one minute I was me and the next I was pregnant and married.'

'Then you were a princess.'

Beatrice forced a laugh. 'A very bad one…then I lost the baby and there was no time to grieve.' She compressed her quivering lips. 'I was expected to do my duty and provide an heir. People acted as though our first baby had never existed. I hate now that I kept apologising, when I wanted—' She had wanted to hear Dante say that she didn't have anything to apologise for, that a baby shouldn't be about duty, it should be about *love*.

But he hadn't.

But then love had not been a word her husband had ever used. *Did he even believe it existed?*

He had been happy to tell her how much he *wanted* her, his throaty voice making her insides dissolve. But even then, sometimes she'd got the impression that he'd given in to the desire she awoke in him reluctantly.

She had told herself that discussing feelings was hard for some men, but beneath the rationalising she had known it was more than that.

She couldn't acknowledge her secret fear that the issue wasn't his inability to acknowledge his deep feelings; no, she worried that he just didn't have them. After the baby was gone, there was nothing deep connecting them, just passion... And now there was another life.

She gave a bleak little laugh and turned to Maya. 'I wonder if there are any statistics about the rate of divorce for Vegas marriages?'

'You sure there is going to be a divorce now?'

Beatrice decided not to acknowledge the doubt she could see in her sister's eyes. It was a doubt she shared, a doubt she was trying very hard not to confront.

'I think you need to sit down,' Maya added, stepping off the pathway and approaching a bench.

It took Beatrice a few moments before she roused herself enough to react to the prompt of her sister patting the seat beside her.

Hunched forward, Beatrice planted her hands on juddering knees.

Maya put one small hand onto one of hers. 'Tell me to shut up, it's none of my business, but what happened, Bea?'

'I found it pencilled into my diary.'

'What?'

'An appointment with an IVF specialist,' she said. Maya was the only one who would know the full significance of that.

Her sister did. 'Oh, my God, what did you do?'

'Other than not be like Mum, you mean? Oh, you

know me, very subtle and royal to my fingertips. I charged into Dante's meeting with a room full of the island's captains of industry and told him that enough was enough. That I didn't want staff, I didn't want a diary and that my childbearing hips were not a subject for staff meetings!'

She remembered the white line of fury outlining his sensual lips as he had escorted her from the room.

Beatrice shrugged, her eyes following the antics of a squirrel that was running through the branches of a nearby tree.

'He called me naive and said I was overreacting.' The lingering bitterness hardened her voice. 'I probably was, and, oh…it's hard to describe what it's like in the palace.' She lifted her hands, her long fingers sliding through her silky blonde hair, lifting the tangled strands off her neck before she let it fall in silky waves down her back.

'I wanted to wait. I didn't want a baby then. I was still grieving for the one I'd lost… Oh, I know they were only a bundle of cells, but—'

'Of course you needed time. Didn't Dante understand how you felt?'

'I never told him. We didn't discuss it…or actually anything much. With Carl gone, he was under a lot of pressure. Maybe I'm more like Mum than I thought,' she mused, remembering her words of moments ago—it would have made *him* happy.

When did she stop asking herself what would make her happy?

Like her own mother, she had seen what she wanted to; she had put her own needs to one side to please a man.

'Oh, Bea, you know that's not true!'

Beatrice's glance fluttered from her sister's face

across the flash of cheery yellow where winter jasmine was in bloom.

'I'm going to have a baby.' She said it like a practice run, imaging herself throwing the line into the conversation, but no, her imagination fell short. It still didn't feel real. 'I really do have great timing, don't I?'

'I wouldn't say the timing is just down to you,' her sister responded drily.

'I will have to tell Dante.'

Maya's expression softened into sympathy as she saw the realisation hit home for Beatrice, who began to scrabble for her phone in the bag that was looped across her shoulder.

'Give yourself time first, to get your own head around it,' Maya advised, trying to hide the worry she felt behind an encouraging smile.

Beatrice, her teeth worrying at her full lower lip, shook her head. The way she felt right now, that moment might never come and the longer she left it—well, it was never going to get any easier.

'Do I have to tell him?' she said with a surge of wild hope that vanished into guilt as she connected with the sympathy in her sister's eyes. 'I didn't mean that. It's just that everything will change. This baby is second in line to the throne.' It seemed like a terrible responsibility to give a child before they were even born. 'Dante had a bad childhood, you know, and now this baby will be brought up in that world…'

'Dante had a bad childhood because his parents are vile self-centred narcissists. This baby will have you.'

'If I go back.' In her heart she knew there was no *if* about it. The baby made it a forgone conclusion. 'It won't be like the last time. I won't be brought out like some sort of—'

'Don't tell me, Bea,' Maya cut in. 'Tell him. Did he know about Mum and the IVF thing?'

Beatrice shook her head. 'It seems like yesterday sometimes.'

The sisters' eyes met, their glances holding as they both remembered the period in their teens when, in an attempt to satisfy her husband's demands for a child of their own, their mother had turned to IVF to give him the *real* child he had wanted, which he had said would make them a *real* family.

Witnessing the physical and mental toll that cycle after cycle of treatment had wrought on their mother's health had been bad, but what had been worse was the blame game that had come after each failure from the man who held his wife responsible for not providing him with his *own* child.

'Do you have any idea what this is doing to me?'

The familiar petulant response had soon set the tone of their stepfather's reaction to having *his* plans disappointed. It had always been *her* fault: if she had *rested* more, if she had been more motivated, healthier, thinner, fatter…*if*…*if*… The list of accusations had been endless.

When one specialist had refused to treat them any more because of the impact on their mother's health, they had moved on to the next clinic.

'I used to think that I'd never go down that road…' Maya said suddenly. 'But, do you remember Prue?'

'The Prue who married the cricket player, but is much more famous for doing your maths homework?'

'She and Jake had twins through IVF. I've never seen two people happier.'

'That's not the same. Prue and her cricketer wanted a baby because they loved…' Beatrice felt her eyes fill.

'It wasn't duty. I left of my own volition, but it was only a matter of time before Dante would have been forced to put me aside for someone with a more reliable reproductive system.'

'He is a total bastard,' Maya said conversationally.

'He's the father of my child.'

Maya grimaced. 'I'm sorry…'

'I'm not.' Beatrice pressed her hands to her still-flat stomach. The panic was still there but it was pushed into the background by a certainty. 'You probably think I'm mad, but I *want* this baby.'

Maya smiled. 'I don't think you're mad, I think you're… I think you'll make a marvellous mum and I intend to be a pretty great auntie too.' Her eyes widened with awed realisation. 'God, with you as a mum and Dante as a dad, this baby really has hit the gene jackpot.'

CHAPTER SIX

'I'm afraid His Highness is—'

'Unavailable at the moment?' Beatrice inserted, her words dripping with saccharine-coated sarcastic venom, not caring by this point that she was killing the messenger.

This messenger at least.

It had taken all her courage to make that first call and she had felt physically sick as she had punched in Dante's personal number, only to have her call diverted to someone who had identified herself as 'His *Royal* Highness the Crown Prince's office'—not actually an office but a snooty-sounding female, whom Beatrice took an instant dislike to.

Over the last few hours her instincts had proved to be bang on. She also knew that her husband was ghosting her—every single number or email address she had for him came up as unrecognised or no longer available.

The only number that was taking her calls was this one.

'His *Royal* Highness is not taking calls but I can pass on a message.'

'Yes, you mentioned that,' Beatrice cut her off before she went deep into auto message mode.

This was the fifth time now that she had tried to

contact Dante and the fifth time she had been given the same runaround by this faceless underling with the nice line in patronising.

'But if you would prefer to address your questions to His Highness's legal representatives... Do you have the number of the law firm? I can—'

Eyes squeezed tight, Beatrice told her exactly what she could do, and heard the shocked, offended gasp on the other end. She wasn't proud of it, but there were limits, and she had reached hers and then some.

In the periphery of her vision she was aware of Maya's frantic hand signals as she mimed zipping motions across her lips.

She ignored them and smiled. She wasn't enjoying herself, but it was a relief to stick her head over the parapet and stick it to Dante's messenger.

'I don't actually have any *questions*, I just want to deliver some information.'

'I will pass on any important information.'

'It is personal information. Sensitive information.'

'I am a *personal* assistant.'

'In that case...why not?' Beatrice came back smoothly. 'Do you have a pen? Fine, yes, well, take this down, will you? Tell my *husband...*' She ground the title home as she jabbed the pencil she had picked up into the stack of unopened post on the table. 'Tell him that I thought he might like to know that he is going to be a father. Got that?' she asked pleasantly, and decided to take the choked sound at the other end of the line as an affirmative. 'Well, thank you so much for your help. I'll be sure to mention your name when I speak to my husband!' Her breath gusting fast and frantic, she ended the call, her glance moving from the phone, still grasped in her white-knuckled hand, to her sister.

She pressed her hand to her mouth and gave a nervous giggle, her eyes flying to Maya, who rolled her own.

'You didn't stick to your script.'

'No, I didn't.' Beatrice looked at the stack of bullet points printed on cards that had been meant to aid her calm delivery of the facts, even factoring in a potential mind blank when it came to telling Dante.

She had not factored in a red-mist moment.

'I imagine you might get a response now,' Maya murmured as Beatrice continued to look at the phone in her hand as if it were an unexploded bomb.

'I lost my temper. What have I done now?'

It had been three in the morning before Beatrice had finally managed to drop off, so it took her a few moments to orientate herself and realise that the noise was not part of her dream, but real.

Someone—it didn't take too many guesses who—had their hand pressed to the doorbell, filling the flat with a continual tiny rendition of the 'William Tell Overture', their landlord's tasteful choice.

Maya appeared as Bea was dragging on a robe over her nightshirt.

'How did he get here this quickly?'

Beatrice shrugged.

'Shall I get it, tell him to come back later?'

'Like that's going to work…' She dragged a hand through her tousled hair and tried to dredge up some calm. 'No…no, I'll be fine.' She took another deep breath, and tightened the sash on her full-length robe as she lifted her chin to a defiant angle.

Maya looked doubtful. 'If you say so. I'll be in my bedroom if you need me.'

'Thanks.' Beatrice smiled but barely noticed her sister go; her thoughts had already moved on to the person outside the door.

She was vaguely conscious of her sister's bedroom door clicking closed as she blew out a slow calming breath, which didn't slow the speed of her pounding heart even a little, and reached for the handle.

Leaving the safety catch in place, she opened it. The action would normally have revealed the communal hallway, with a worn rug that covered the scratched parquet floor, and a noticeboard. But today all she could see through the door was Dante, who effectively blocked everything else from view.

He pushed himself off the wall and far enough away for her to see more of the dark suit he was wearing. Not his normal immaculate self—the fabric was crumpled and his white shirt was open at the neck, revealing a section of warm brown skin—but she barely noticed these details. All she saw, or rather felt, were the powerful, raw emotions that were emanating from him.

'You moved.' Dante had been keeping his emotions in check, but the sight of her standing there and he could feel them slipping through his fingers like a wet rope, taking his control with it. 'No one told me.'

The journey here—he'd been mid-Atlantic when he had received the message, a sentence that was going to literally change his life in ways he was still too shocked to imagine—had already pushed his control to the limits.

The sight of her big blue eyes looking warily at him through the gap, rimmed with red from where she had been crying, didn't make him any less furious. It just added another layer to the emotions fighting for supremacy in his chest.

'Last week—it's bigger.' Just as she would be soon. An idea that still seemed deeply strange and not quite *real*.

Dante was very real though, and *very* angry.

'The people who live there now seem… I left my security team persuading them I am not dangerous.' While he had spent several frustrating minutes finding the correct address to give his driver.

'What are you doing here?' The accusing words floated through the gap and drew a low feral disbelieving growl from his throat.

'Are you *serious*?'

'It really wasn't necessary for you to come in person. A simple acknowledgement you'd got the news would have done fine.'

'Well, I am here.'

'I'm sure everyone in the building knows that. Come back tomorrow.'

Was he meant to care what people thought?

'That isn't going to happen and we both know it. Are you going to let me in or would you like to have this discussion here?' He bestowed a scathing glance at his surroundings before fixing her with a steely bitter stare. 'Sorry, I forgot my megaphone, but I have several paparazzi on speed dial…if that is your preference? Sure, let's share the news! Oh, I forgot, you already have.' It would be interesting to know just how many people she had told before she had told him…but then he was only the father.

Her lips tightened at the sarcasm. 'Lower your voice and don't be so unreasonable.'

'I suppose I should consider myself lucky you didn't send the news by text!'

Although on second thoughts, he decided as he experienced a stomach-clenching chilled aftershock of what he had felt as he had listened to his stand-in PA tell him he was going to be a father, a text might have been preferable!

She slipped the safety chain and hastily backed away, standing there, arms folded across her chest, as he entered a hallway that had been described in the rental details as a spacious dining hall.

A slight exaggeration, but it had never felt this claustrophobically cramped before.

'I tried to contact you.'

'You didn't try very hard.'

Her lips compressed. 'I suppose it depends on your definition of hard. The number I have for you no longer exists. Though why I'm telling you this I don't know, because I assume that you're the one who arranged for my calls to be diverted to your robotic PA.'

'She's a very good PA.' And he might have sacked her, he realised, a furrow forming between his dark brows as he replayed the in-flight exchange.

The details of the incident were a little sketchy, but in his shocked state of mind he presumed he must have asked her to repeat what she had just said, because she had repeated, word for word, the message that had left him literally rigid with shock.

The second time of telling had involved the same words, but no longer a statement, more a question conveying a snide implication that he had taken exception to.

'She says *she is pregnant? Are you calling my wife a liar?'*

'She is very efficient,' he said now.

'Oh, I have no doubt that she was only saying what she was told to. I assume that it was you who told her that any further communication would be through our legal teams.'

'That,' he reminded her grimly, 'was your idea.'

'I should have known it would be my fault.' Without warning the fight drained out of her, leaving her feeling weak-kneed, shaky and fighting back tears.

'Are you all right?'

She scraped together enough defiance to throw back a querulous, 'I'm pregnant, not ill.'

His chest lifted in a silent sigh. 'So, it's true?'

'Obviously not. I just made it up.'

'Sorry, that was a stupid thing to say.'

She squeezed her eyes closed and felt his hand on her elbow. 'Yes, it was.' She opened her eyes and shook her head, unable to keep a quiver of emotion out of her voice as she tilted her head back to look him in the face.

'You should sit down.'

'I should be in bed. I *was* in bed.' Conscious of her shaky knees and the fact she was grateful for the support of his hand, she nodded to the door just behind him. 'The sitting room is through there,' she said, afraid that he might take the next door, to her bedroom. Bedrooms were where all this had started. 'Be careful. There are boxes we haven't got around to unpacking yet.'

Skirting the packing cases, he continued to hover protectively until she had sat down on one of the sofas.

'So, have you seen a doctor?' he asked, dropping into a squat beside her. He scanned her pale features and felt a gut punch of guilt. She looked as if she had been crying for a week. Maybe she had. She looked so fragile that he was afraid to hold her. She looked as if she might break.

She nodded.

‘So, there’s no mistake.’ Under the fresh wave of guilt he was conscious of something new. A possessiveness, a protectiveness.

She shook her head, feeling tears threaten again as she wondered if that was what he had been hoping. That this was all some mistake that they would laugh about. She couldn’t really blame him.

‘And a scan?’

‘Not yet…what are you doing?’

He lifted the phone away from his ear. ‘Making arrangements.’

‘Dante, it’s half three in the morning.’

He shook his head as though the relevance passed him by.

‘I know in your world you can demand anything you want at any time of day and people will jump, but in my world we make appointments in daylight hours and get put on waiting lists.’

‘*Waiting* lists?’

‘If you want to do something, make me a cup of tea. Ginger. It helps the nausea. The kitchen’s through that way.’ She tipped her head in the direction of an arch at the end of the room that fed into the galley kitchen. ‘Teas are in the bottom cupboard, first right.’

She closed her eyes, pretty much too exhausted to see if he reacted and definitely too exhausted to argue. She didn’t open them until she felt a hand on her arm.

‘Drink,’ he said, watching her.

She did, blowing on the surface of the liquid first to cool it as he took a seat on the opposite sofa. He appeared lost in his own thoughts.

Feeling like someone sitting in the eye of a storm, knowing that any second all hell would break loose again, she drank and felt a little less wretched.

She set her mug down on a side table and waited, tensing when Dante unfolded his long, lean length and got to his feet.

'I didn't think about the time,' he admitted. 'I was—'

'In shock—I know.'

'I realise that you must feel… I know this isn't what you wanted, but it is happening, and we have to deal with it.'

'We don't need to deal with anything.' She still felt as if she had been run over by a truck, but the tea was making her slightly more coherent. 'I am already *dealing*,' she added, anxious to correct any impression to the contrary she might have given. 'I'm booked in for my first scan, just to confirm dates, I think, in a few weeks.'

'Right, I'll cancel and have them schedule one for when we get back,' he murmured half to himself.

'Back?' she said, pretending a bewilderment she wasn't feeling as a cold fist tightened in her stomach.

'I'm not going anywhere. I'm here and I'm staying here.' She drew her knees up to her chest and wrapped her arms around them. 'Relax, once the divorce comes through we can sort out the details, how things will work.'

'What the hell are you talking about?' he ground out, realising that his life had changed the moment he had met Beatrice. Nothing had been the same since that day.

'There isn't going to be a divorce now you are carrying my child.'

She looked into his eyes and saw the same steely conviction that his voice carried. She half rose and subsided, shaking as panic spilled through her body.

She looked up at him, eyes looking even bigger. The dark rings around them making him think of a trapped animal.

'You are carrying our child, the heir to the throne. That changes everything.'

'He…she won't want that,' she said, pressing a hand to her stomach, the gesture unconscious.

'Shouldn't that be their call? Are you going to try and rob that child of their heritage, their birthright?'

'It didn't make you or Carl very happy,' she slung back.

'We don't have to repeat the mistakes of my parents.'

She lifted a shaking hand to her head. 'There has to be another way. I can't go back to *that*…' She shook her head. 'I won't be manipulated and managed.'

He was looking at her with the strangest expression. 'Is that how you felt?'

His shock seemed genuine.

'It is the way it was.'

'It won't be like that when you go back. There will be changes.'

She didn't have the strength to hide her extreme scepticism even if she had wanted to. 'What changes?'

'To hell with opinion polls, I'm putting my family first. This is not about having an heir. It is about being a father.' Until this moment he had never appreciated the massive difference between the two. 'We'll make it work.'

'For the baby.'

He said nothing, the steely determination she saw shining in his eyes said it all as he took her chin between his fingers.

'You can't bring this child up alone…'

She fought the urge to turn her cheek into his palm. 'People do every day, some out of choice, some because there is no alternative.'

'But you *have* an alternative,' he cut in smoothly. 'We've had a trial separation, why not a trial marriage?'

'Another word for a sham? Been there, done that,' she said tiredly. The emotional and physical stress of the past days, and maybe the pregnancy hormones, were making their strength-sapping presence felt and her fight was being replaced by a dangerous fatalism.

Perhaps sensing her defences were failing, he leaned in towards her, bringing their faces level; she met his eyes and felt guilty for doubting his sincerity. There was nothing sham about the emotions rolling off him.

When she thought about it later, she decided it was the emotion in his face, the concern and self-recrimination that made her stop fighting the inevitable.

She lifted her chin. 'Things will *have* to change…if I come back,' she tacked on quickly.

'I promise there will be no *managing*.'

'I want to be more than a decorative accessory; I want to be treated as an equal, not patronised. Oh…' Her head dropped a little as she looked at him through the veil of her dark lashes. 'I don't want you to tell anyone, not until I'm three months along and things are…*safer*.'

'My parents?'

She gave a tiny laugh that left her blue eyes sombre. '*Especially* your parents.' She did not think she could stand any of their insincerity. They wanted a royal baby and for a while she'd be flavour of the month, but she knew that before long they'd be planning behind the scenes how to detach her from the baby.

Did the conviction make her paranoid? Well, better that than naive.

'They don't like me, they never liked me…which is fine, because I don't like them either.'

After a moment, he nodded. 'This waiting, secrecy… did the doctor indicate that anything was amiss? That there is a potential problem with this pregnancy, with you?' The tautness in him rose visibly as his sharpened glance moved across her face.

'No, it's just early, and if anything did happen like before…' She felt the tears form in her eyes and looked away, the muscles in her pale slender throat working as she fought to contain her fears. 'I don't want anyone else to know. I don't care what you tell them, just—'

Dante dropped the hand that lay curved around her cheek and, rising to his feet, stepped back. The ferocious surge of protectiveness he was experiencing as he watched her was less easy to step away from.

'Nothing will happen.'

'You can't say that,' she choked back, looking at him through glistening blue eyes. 'Because it does, for some people, over and over and—' Her voice cracked as she swallowed and felt a big fat tear trickle down her face as she felt his hand slide to the back of her head. 'I really don't think I could bear that,' she whispered, her voice muffled against his chest.

Helplessness and a fierce wave of protectiveness arched through him as he pressed a kiss to the top of her silky head and stroked her hair as she wept out her fear.

The sobs that shook her subsided but she allowed herself a few moments of lying there, taking comfort from the solidity of his chest, the strength of his arms, finally heaving a deep sigh as she pulled free.

'Thank you,' she said with a loud sniff.

Dante felt something nameless twist hard inside him as he rose from the kneeling position he had fallen to beside the sofa. 'You are welcome.'

'I must look terrible.'

'Horrific. That's better,' he approved as she gave a watery smile. 'And soon you will get fat and you won't be able to see your feet.'

Will you still love me?

The words stayed in her head because he didn't love her now.

CHAPTER SEVEN

THEY EMERGED FROM the low-lying fog that had blanketed the area around the private airport into the spirit-lifting blue above. Beatrice's spirits didn't lift; the nervous tension making her shoulders ache didn't dissipate as she undid her seat belt and leaned back in the seat that bore an imprint of the Velazquez crown on the leather headrest. It had more of a welcoming embrace than any she had received from the Velazquez family, but then they were not really a *tactile* family.

She was under no illusions that any welcome she had in the future would be because of the baby. She didn't care about that, but the equally inescapable fact was that Dante only wanted her here because of the baby. She avoided the temptation to read anything else into his determination to rekindle their marriage.

The pilot's disembodied voice spoke, adding to his words of welcome the less welcome fact that there was the possibility of some turbulence ahead. *Tell me about it*, Beatrice thought, looking around and seeing that someone had already whisked away the fur-lined parka coat she had worn for the journey to the airport. She wouldn't need it, or the layers she had on underneath, at the other end. San Macizo enjoyed an all-year-round temperate climate.

She continued to exchange her boots for the flats she had pushed into her bag as Dante translated the pilot's Italian words.

She smiled and nodded absently, even though she hadn't needed him to translate. She had continued the lessons she had begun without much optimism during her brief sojourn in San Macizo where Italian, introduced to the country by the royal family centuries before, was the official language. Though she had never encountered a native who didn't speak English and French fluently, like Dante, who was also fluent in Arabic and Spanish.

Free of her layers, she adjusted the cuffs on her white shirt and watched as Dante unfastened his own seat belt and the buttons on his dark grey suit jacket and waited, wondering if it was worth getting the paperback out of her bag. She doubted she'd be able to concentrate—her nerves were too wound up.

No massive surprise there. What she had committed to was about as sane as deliberately opening a half-healed wound, and, as it turned out, just as painful. Up to the point of being welcomed onto the private jet she had not allowed herself to think about what lay ahead. Now she couldn't *stop* thinking about it.

After a few moments, a small frown appeared between her brows. Dante hadn't got up to seek a quiet, private office space to work in; he hadn't even reached for the laptop that lay on the seat next to him, let alone buried himself in it.

She found this break in familiar routine slightly unnerving. She searched her memory and could not remember a time, at least not since he had stepped into the role his brother had walked away from, that Dante hadn't immersed himself into work at every opportunity.

She had teased him at first about his ability to totally shut out distractions until she had realised that she was one of those distractions, then it had seemed less amusing.

Dante still showed no sign of moving away, and doing so herself would seem a bit obvious, so she exhaled a resigned sigh and reached for her book. Even if she could not lose herself in the world of fiction she would have somewhere to look that wasn't directly at her husband. *Husband...* She could remember saying that word out loud and smiling—it seemed a long time ago.

These days she felt impatient with her younger self for being so naive; while she had been walking on air she doubted that, despite what was written on a piece of paper, Dante had ever felt he was her husband, not really. But he *was* the father of her child.

She desperately wanted this baby. It was that utter certainty that was getting her through; the life growing inside her was light at the end of the tunnel.

She couldn't assume that Dante would feel the same way. She had to see things the way they were and not the way she wanted them to be.

Attracted to the wrong man and refusing to see the things that she didn't want to. *Now, where have I seen that before?* An image of her mother's face floated into her mind.

Beatrice found the idea of history repeating itself through the generations deeply depressing and she intended to break that cycle. It was just a pity she hadn't displayed the insight earlier, instead of spending her short marriage living in a fantasy world of her own making.

Just thinking about it, she could taste the self-disgust

in her mouth. The irony was, of course, that when she had finally opened her eyes to the reality of her marriage it had been impossible not to be struck by the fact she had been guilty of the same weakness that she had struggled to forgive in her own mother.

But though she couldn't avoid the glaring comparison with her own mother, she had never extended it to include Dante, who was nothing like her ex-stepfather, who had been a manipulative, cruel bully with a sadistic streak.

Dante was not the man she had *wanted* him to be. She had created a fiction; that did not make him a bad person. He was absolutely straightforward, strong, complex, impatient, arrogant and had zero tolerance for incompetence, but his only real sin had only ever been not to be in love with her.

But that didn't mean she had the right to rob their child of a father's love, nor rob their child of his heritage. But she was equally determined not to allow that heritage to emotionally damage the baby.

'Are you all right?'

She jumped as the sound of Dante's voice broke into her thoughts.

'What? Yes. Why…?'

One sardonic brow hitched, he nodded towards the book on her lap. 'It's upside down.'

She felt the guilty flush climb up her neck as she turned it around and then closed it. 'I never liked flying much.'

'There are no barriers, medically speaking, for you to fly at this stage.' He caught her surprised look. 'I have been reading up a little.'

'This is staying between us for now…*right*?'

'I have made some enquiries concerning obstetricians. *Discreet* enquiries. I understand that early monitoring is important.'

She thought about that and nodded. 'So, what have you told your parents?'

'I have told them we are back together.'

'That must have gone down well!'

'They need not concern you. If it makes you feel any more relaxed about it, I stopped trying to please them a long time ago, about when I realised it was never going to happen.'

He remembered the exact moment. He had been watching the flames of an open fire lick the Christmas card he had made them. The Christmas card they hadn't even bothered to open.

By the time it had collapsed into a pile of ashes he had decided that if they considered him the wild one, the unreliable one, the one who always caused them a headache, he might as well enjoy himself and do what people expected him to.

'Ah, I almost forgot. My grandfather sends his best wishes and says he hopes you can give him a decent game.'

Still wondering about his previous comments, she allowed herself a smile. 'At least I have one friend in the palace.'

Something flicked across his face that she struggled to interpret. 'You have a husband…'

Her glance fell. 'I haven't forgotten,' she said, thinking that it was a pity he couldn't say the same about her. The moment the palace doors had closed behind them she had been delegated out, the only use he'd had for her recreational.

'That was a big sigh… It is a steep learning curve, for me too.'

Surprised by the unexpected admission, she stared at him.

'Sadly, there are no intensive courses on being a Crown Prince. I had some valuable advice. My parents advised I delegate, which, as you might have noticed, is their management style. Grandfather, whose advice was actually quite helpful, said that I should trust no one and don't believe a word you're told.'

As he had hoped, his comment drew a laugh from Beatrice. The sound made him smile too, then his smile faded as he realised how much he had missed that sound.

'And now you have found your own style?'

'I like to think I have steered a personal course somewhere in between idle disregard for anything but my own comfort and paranoia, but the jury is out.'

As their smiling glances met and clung, she was aware of the perceptible shift in the atmosphere.

She pulled in a tense breath and looked away.

'Is something wrong? You can tell me.'

The unexpected addition brought her glance sweeping upwards. 'You just seem…?'

She paused, pulling in a long steadying breath, and wondered if the day would come when she could look at him and feel only aesthetic appreciation rather than an ache of need. You'd have thought that after a while boredom would have kicked in, but she could have happily stared at him forever.

'Seem?'

'Maybe it's just that you're—'

'I'm what?' he prompted with slightly less patience.

'It's that you're still…' Her hands moved in a descriptive sweep that made the collection of silver bracelets she wore on her left wrist jangle. 'You're here.'

His dark brows knitted; he looked genuinely mystified. 'Where else would I be?'

A small laugh burst from her lips. Had Dante *really* never realised that from the moment the news had been delivered that his brother had decided to renounce his claim to the throne, Dante had tuned her out, more than distance, much more than an understandable preoccupation with the role that had been thrust upon him?

She had felt at best surplus to requirements, at worst, an embarrassment.

'Busy with more important things?' she flung out and bit her lip as her unthinking retort was laden with an inch-thick layer of bitterness.

She lifted a hank of slippery, shiny hair that was crawling down the collar of her crisp white shirt, then catching the direction of his gaze made her glance towards the folded cashmere sweater she had discarded as she gritted her teeth and fought the ludicrous impulse to fasten another button, or pull her sweater back on. Instead she smoothed the non-existent creases in the tailored pale cream trousers and fussed with the buckle on the narrow red leather belt that held them up, just to give her hands something to do.

Her lips twisted as she noticed that Dante seemed to be having a similar problem. His long fingers flexed and clenched as if he was fighting an instinct to reach for his laptop after her comment.

She vented an internal sigh. Ah, well, this looked like it was going to be a nice relaxing journey—always supposing you were the sort of person who found nail-biting tension and sitting on the edge of your seat while looking for an escape route relaxing!

She adopted a carefully neutral expression as she lifted her chin and crossed her feet neatly at the ankle. The soft leather flats she had changed into proved you could look fashionable and be comfortable. Well, at least from the ankle down—being comfortable elsewhere was hard when she remained so acutely conscious of the restrained power Dante exuded. Always a challenge to cope with, but overpowering in any enclosed space, and right now her feelings were too raw and close to the surface to make her feel confident about disguising her vulnerability.

'I'm fine, feel free to…' She made an all-encompassing motion with her hand before she gave an elaborate yawn. 'I didn't get much sleep last night.'

She and Maya had talked into the small hours, and after her sister had gone to bed she had lain fully dressed on her bed staring at the ceiling, dreading the morning. She had finally fallen asleep half an hour before her phone alarm sounded, and had felt like death warmed up.

'Nor the night before,' she continued unthinkingly, then tacked on, 'That wasn't a dig.'

'I'm sorry I disturbed your sleep.'

'It wouldn't be the first time.'

The quiver of her stomach could have been connected with the lurch as they hit a pocket of turbulence, but she knew it wasn't.

'All right?'

'Fine. I always liked roller coasters.' She breathed through a wave of nausea and missed what he said next. 'Sorry…?' she pushed out, her hand pressed to her throat.

'I said…' He paused, his heavy-lidded glance lingering on the dark smudges beneath her glorious eyes.

Dante didn't know where he stood on the nature, nurture debate, whether he'd inherited the trait from his parents or simply learnt by example didn't seem the point, but whatever the truth he had always possessed the ability to step back and observe events and people from an objective perspective.

Except with Beatrice.

'You do look tired.'

'Thanks,' she murmured drily, translating the comment that he'd framed more like an accusation as, *You do look awful.*

'Maya and I were trying to decide what to do now that I'm, well…not there.'

'Setting up a business is challenging.' And he suspected that most of the work fell on Beatrice's shoulders. He had nothing against Maya, but she didn't seem that *dynamic*, and as far as he could tell she had a habit of not finishing things. From what Beatrice had let slip he had decided Maya was one of those people who were wildly enthusiastic, then lost enthusiasm when the project needed hard work.

Not the sort of person you'd choose to enter a partnership with.

'Is your sister intending to go it alone now?'

Beatrice felt a resurgence of her guilt. She was letting Maya down once more and her sister was being so damned nice about it, but they both agreed that she couldn't put her plans on hold again. 'She says she'd be happier to go for a less ambitious format.'

'You think she's lying.'

'Of course she is.'

He looked thoughtful. 'I was actually going to suggest that… I have some contacts—would she be open, do you think, to the idea of experts coming in to offer advice? And I know someone who might be interested in investing.'

'Someone, as in…you?'

'Someone anonymous,' he said smoothly.

'That is very generous of you.'

'It is in my best interests that you not spend your pregnancy worrying.'

'Well, I'll speak to her, but she can be a bit touchy. She has come up against a lot of prejudice, a lot of people who can't see past a young pretty face.'

'I wouldn't bet against either of you once you put your mind to something.'

Bea reacted with a glowing smile to the unexpected compliment; she couldn't help it, even though she knew his good opinion shouldn't matter. 'We like a challenge.'

He watched her smile fade.

'What is it?'

'I *want* to be a good mother.' Her eyes flickered wide in dismay. Standing in front of a TV camera and confessing she was afraid she wasn't up to it would have been only *slightly* less embarrassing than revealing her insecurities this way.

'Then you will be.'

'You really think so?'

Before Dante could respond to her equally mortifying appeal for reassurance—her tongue seemed to have developed a will of its own—an attendant appeared.

Dante watched as the male attendant predictably went red and started stuttering when he spoke to Beatrice. He looked as if he was going to faint when she smiled encouragement.

Dante spoke sharply and the guy made an obvious effort to pull himself together, though his glance did keep straying to Beatrice.

While the young man waited, he turned to Beatrice. 'I ordered coffee and sandwiches, do you want some?'

Beatrice's smile held a hint of teasing triumph that he didn't understand until she turned to the young man and asked for tea and biscuits in halting but pretty good Italian.

Dante waited until the young man had vanished. 'So, when did that happen?'

She shrugged, and tried not to look complacent. 'I had a grounding. Even a not very good student can pick up quite a bit in ten months, so I carried on after I left. There are a lot of really great online courses available and some night classes at our local college. A second language is a useful skill.'

'That's a change of tune.'

'I'm doing the lessons now out of choice, not—'

His long fingers curled around his coffee cup as he raised it. 'You make it sound as though you were forced,' he said, looking at her over the rim.

'Forced? Maybe not,' she conceded. 'But I was definitely *not* consulted. Nobody asked if I wanted to have lessons.' It was only after she'd left and she'd found herself in an Italian restaurant that she had realised how much of what she had learnt had stuck. It was actually a shock to realise that she had learnt anything at all!

'And Maya has joined me, so we practise our conversational skills on each other…though Maya is much better than me. She's so much quicker than I am at picking up languages.'

He made a non-committal grunt that had her hackles rising. 'So now *you* don't believe *me*?' she challenged.

'Your sister has a gift for languages, fine, if you say so.' He put down his coffee and leaned back, planting his interlaced fingers on the tabletop.

'I *do* say so.' She fixed him with a dangerous, narrow-eyed stare. 'Just what is your problem with my sister?'

'I don't have a problem…' he began and then stopped. 'All right, do you realise how much you sing her praises? It's constant. Maya is brilliant, Maya is beautiful, Maya says, Maya thinks,' he bit out. 'From what I understand Maya had all the same advantages as you but left school with virtually no qualifications, squeezed onto a degree course and then dropped out, worked for a charity, was it…? And yes…walked away…' He could feel his antagonism building. It was always *Maya's* birthday that deserved the special celebration, her crossing a road seemed to rate a hashtag, but it was Beatrice who was the powerhouse, the real talent!

'That was because…' Beatrice flared, then bit her lip. Maya was a private person and she respected that, even though she wanted to throw his assumptions in his face.

'Maya quits—*you* are the one with the exams, the degree, the successful career. Why do you defer to *her*?'

She reeled back, her hands gripping the armrests, shocked by the sheer vehemence of his attack. 'I don't…' She stopped, her fluttering lashes framing the realisation that dawned in her deep blue eyes as she saw how her relationship with her sister might appear to him. 'You wouldn't understand.'

'Try me.'

Her desire to defend her sister outweighed her reluctance to confide details. 'I say those things…' She cleared the constriction in her throat. Her fists clenched, but so was everything inside too. 'I say those things, because for a long time nobody else did.'

His dark brows flattened into a line of confusion above his deep-set eyes as he shook his head. 'You're talking as if your sister is some sort of victim.' The petite brunette he knew had a core of steel under the delicate exterior. She was quiet, yes, but no shrinking violet. He judged it would take a very brave man to cross her or for that matter pierce the shell under the deceptively placid exterior.

'Not a victim, a *survivor*,' she bit back fiercely. Self-pity was not one of her sister's traits. 'You know our father died?' Beatrice had known then that their lives had changed, that nothing would be the same as it had been without his big warm presence, but she hadn't known how much it would change.

He nodded, wondering where this was going.

'And Mum made a second marriage.'

He nodded again. Rachel Monk had been divorced for some time when he had met her; it had been hard to tell what she would have been like under normal circumstances because the day they had met had not been *normal*. How did a mother respond when her daughter announced she had married a man the week before in Las Vegas and—cue drum roll—here he is?

He hadn't anticipated being welcomed into the bosom of the family, and he'd been prepared for worse than he'd got, but his own parents had more than made up for it. Luckily he'd been about ten when he'd last cared about their disapproval…or maybe that was when he'd started enjoying it.

After the initial shock, his new mother-in-law had been polite but not warm and on the handful of subsequent occasions they had met she had never relaxed in his company, continuing to view him as a threat to her daughter's happiness. She'd been proved right.

He remembered Beatrice mentioning the second marriage in passing, but she had not dwelt on the circumstances and he hadn't thought it warranted much curiosity in a world where very few marriages lasted long term, and those that did last, much as his parents', did not because they were happy, but because ending it would be too costly.

'They divorced years ago?'

'Yes, thank God!' There was nothing at all *in passing* about this emotional declaration.

'You didn't like him?'

'He was vile.' Beatrice aimed for statement of fact but it came out more hissing vehemence, which made it pointless to claim that time had done anything to lessen her feelings when it came to her stepfather.

Dante froze… His eyes went black; a chill slid down his spine. Suddenly it was hard to breathe. 'He *hurt* you?'

'Not me, no.'

The bunched aggression in his pumped muscles lowered fractionally, but the nerve beside his mouth continued to beat an erratic rhythm.

'He wasn't violent, he never raised a hand.' People always assumed that abuse was physical, but torture came in many forms. 'He didn't need to,' she said with quiet emphasis. 'And he never really bothered much about me. I was not his target. It turned out there are some inbuilt advantages in being too tall and gawky, which I was at that age.'

Dante's eyes swept across her face, taking in at once the soft, moulded contours of her smooth cheeks, the sensual curve of her full lips and her expressive cobalt blue eyes beneath the sweep of dark brows. It was hard to fit that face, those glorious supple curves, into an ugly duckling analogy. Impossible to imagine her anything other than jaw-droppingly beautiful.

But it might explain why she put so little store by her own beauty. Beatrice was the least vain woman he had ever met, with the most cause to be vain.

'He always liked to be the centre of attention, certainly Mum's attention, and he didn't like competition for it. He didn't consider me pretty or clever—people didn't smile when I walked into a room, unless I fell over my own feet.

'But he took against Maya from the start. She was so pretty, "like a doll" people would say—she actually hated that, she was a bit of a tomboy. And she was gifted—a precocious talent, they called it—and, you know, I think he sensed her bond with Mum… It was special.'

She paused, her blue eyes clouding with memories before she made a visible effort to compose herself.

'Mum and Dad always told her she was special because they didn't want her to feel second best when I came along. They wanted her to know that she was as much their real daughter as I was.'

'I had forgotten she was adopted.'

The description of the family dynamics brought his protective instincts to the surface. It seemed to him that it was inevitable the well-meaning parents had favoured their adopted daughter.

'What about you?'

She looked at him, startled, and shook her head.

'While Maya was being told she was special and enjoying her bond…?'

She gave a laugh and shook her head. 'No, I'm not explaining this very well.' Frustrated by her inability to describe the dynamics when they were growing up, she paused a moment before trying to explain. 'Mum and Dad wanted us to know we were *both* special, and the Maya and Mum thing…you can be loved by both parents but closer to one. I was a daddy's girl,' she admitted with sadness in her eyes. 'I was always closer to Dad than Mum.' He watched a shadow cross her face before she turned her head in a sharp negative gesture as though she was dislodging memories. 'We were just a happy family, even after Dad died. We had each other and then—'

He watched as she swallowed. She seemed unaware of her actions as she pressed a hand to the base of her throat.

'Everything changed almost overnight, but we clung together, and it was getting better. At first it was lovely to see Mum happier and getting dressed up. Maya and I would help her with her make-up before a date, and Edward was a charming man.

'Until they were married—he changed then. It was insidious, the way he cut Mum off from everything, everyone, including us. You didn't see it at the time and we were just kids. And he was careful to appear caring in front of Mum, but when she wasn't there, one of his weapons of choice against Maya was finding fault.' It sounded innocuous when she said it, but the cumulative effect had been devastating. 'He just chipped away at her on a daily basis. Nothing she did was good enough. He ridiculed her, laughed at anything she did and told her she was hopeless.'

In the end her sister had believed it.

Bea's eyes lifted from her determined contemplation of her clenched fingers in response to the harsh curses that Dante spat. They were not Italian words she was familiar with but she got the gist without a dictionary.

'He had a sadistic streak. He *wanted* to see her cry.'

Dante swore again, feeling the rage that a strong man felt for a bully. They called it coercive control; he called it being a pathetic coward. Lost in her memories, Beatrice didn't register it.

'And she tried so hard not to.' Beatrice brushed away the tears that had spilled from her eyes with an angry hand, recognising that there was an odd sense of relief that she was sharing things she had held close for years.

'She always had artistic talent. Early on, her teachers noticed it, encouraged it, and she is a brilliant artist. But Edward destroyed her confidence. He'd hold up her drawings and mock…' Her voice cracked at the painful memories that flooded her head. 'He made her feel useless. From a bright, bubbly girl she became withdrawn, but worse than all that was that Mum, when I told her, didn't believe me—not for a long time.' She sighed and looked at him, sadness behind her forced smile. 'So, you see, I do say Maya is brilliant a lot, because she is.'

'Yes, I see that.' It seemed to Dante that Maya was not the only *brilliant* Monk female.

Beatrice had been her sister's champion; there was no trace of envy in her and when he compared it with the resentment he had felt as a child, when he was pushed to the background with all the attention focused on his brother, the heir, he felt ashamed.

He felt a fresh kick of shame when he recalled how irritated he had felt about Beatrice's closeness to Maya, and his attitude when she became unreasonable, as he had seen it, at any hint of criticism of her sister.

Clearly the events of their childhood had created an unbreakable bond. If he had known, he wouldn't have wanted to break it, but he hadn't known, maybe because he had never asked. In fact, he had switched off when she'd spoken of her sister and not bothered to hide his lack of interest.

'I think the hardest part was feeling so helpless, but then I suppose I was meant to—it's all about power for creeps like Edward.'

As she stared out of the window it was almost as if she had forgotten he was there. She was saying things he wondered if she had ever said before. It was clear to Dante that Beatrice had not escaped as unscathed as she liked to think.

'Seeing what he did to Maya and then Mum, with the blasted IVF—he made her feel a failure too. Mum couldn't give him the family he wanted, his own family, and even though it was affecting her health he kept pushing her to try again and again. Telling her if she was a real wife, a proper wife, she wouldn't be sabotaging the attempts.'

His deep voice cursing jolted her free of the dark memories.

'Your mother had IVF?'

She nodded, and he swore. 'That is why you reacted to the consultation so…extremely. If I had known—'

'I don't think my reaction was extreme,' she rebutted, turning in her seat to face him. 'And, irrespective of my family history, I don't think something that personal, that intimate, should be delegated. It is something that is *discussed*.'

'I thought your reaction meant that you didn't really want children. That after the miscarriage, I assumed…'

Her hand went to her stomach, the gesture unconscious. 'I *knew* you didn't want children. You wanted an heir.'

He felt a flash of shame as he found himself thinking about the events in her life that had moulded Beatrice into the woman she was today.

He found this new experience unsettling, as he considered this woman who didn't carry resentment. Her recount had focused on how her mother's ill-fated marriage had affected her sister, but the childhood trauma had to have impacted her too.

Men who hurt those in no position to hit back were one of the things in life that made Dante see red. He'd met them; they came in all guises, and he did everything within his power to make sure they did not flourish.

What he saw, and Beatrice did not, was that she had been a victim too, watching her sister and mother suffer and feeling helpless, going to a person who was meant to protect her and being disbelieved.

'Why didn't you tell me any of this?'

'It's not really my story, it's Maya's and…' She paused, her clear blue eyes meeting his with a directness that made him think she could read his shame. 'We never reached that point, did we? We were married, but really we were still two people dating.'

He looked about to say something, but he closed his mouth when she added quietly, 'And in the end, we skipped the bit of getting to know one another and went straight to divorce. We were on fast forward, all intense and…' She shook her head, suddenly overcome by emotion. He was there, a few feet away; all she had to do was reach out. The sheer craving inside her to seek the physical comfort of his strength was, for a split second, so overwhelming that she began to move towards him.

Then at the critical moment, the pilot's voice made her snap back.

'He's inviting me to…' Dante paused. 'You already know?'

'Go join him,' she said with encouraging brightness.

He half rose and subsided. 'No, it's fine.'

'I can cope for a few minutes without you.'

'I know you can—you have been for the last six months—but now you don't have to.'

CHAPTER EIGHT

BEATRICE TOOK SOME time freshening up. She reapplied some lipstick, smudged some more soft grey shadow on her eyelids and that was it—the recent exposure to the winter Alpine sun had given her skin a deep glow that made her look deceptively healthy, even though she felt tired and washed out.

Her freshly washed hair resisted her efforts to pull it back from her forehead and into a sleek ponytail on the nape of her neck, but she persevered and got a result that made her nod faint approval at her reflection.

A quick spritz of perfume before she shrugged on a long-line oversized blazer in a swirly print. She thought she might pass muster. Her lips curved into a small, reflective smile as she remembered the first time she'd stepped off one of the royal fleet of jets onto home tarmac. Except it hadn't felt like home as she knew it.

When Dante had said *private* she had assumed that this covered both the flight and the arrival—she'd been wrong! Stepping into the sun, she had found herself faced with a military guard of honour, several dignitaries and half the royal family, complete with hats and heels. She'd stepped out wearing jeans and a tee shirt emblazoned with a cartoon of a smiling monkey, and trainers that had seen better days. Her hair, waist-length, loose and wild.

Given the way she made her living, she was used to being the focus of attention, but that was playing a part. That day she hadn't had any fake sexy persona to hide behind—she had worn less in public but she had never felt more exposed.

She had been furious with Dante for not warning her, and he had added insult to injury by suggesting that she was overreacting.

She hadn't asked about today, but she was pretty sure that, given the circumstances, this would be low-key and not a hat-and-heels-and-handshakes occasion. But even if it had been, she no longer had anything to prove.

It was quite liberating to have already flunked the exams, and actually the intervening months had made her grow in confidence. Something that hadn't really hit home until now.

With a toss of her head that set her ponytail bobbing, she pushed up the sleeves on the oversized tailored blazer and went to join Dante. She tilted a smile up at him.

'So, let's do this.'

Dante had been scrolling through his phone as he'd waited. At the sound of her voice he slid it back into his pocket and turned his head. She sounded like a sports coach giving a confidence-boosting pep talk, but she looked like a goddess. He felt the heat flash down his front and settle painfully in his groin. Beatrice could make a sack look sexy; along with a perfect supple body, she had an innate sense of style.

He remembered the first time she'd arrived; the image would stay with him forever—Beatrice dressed in jeans that showed off her incredible bottom and endless legs, carrying off the military escort reception with a queenly confidence that had filled him with pride. She'd been mad as hell, he recalled, a reminiscent smile turning the corners of his mobile mouth upwards.

Beatrice felt the heat inside her rise as his dark gaze settled on her. She stood her ground and fought not to react.

'You look good.'

She tipped her head in acknowledgement; it hid the rush of blood that warmed her cheeks.

Their arrival was indeed low-key and, like the Italian lessons, it seemed she had learnt more than she'd thought. She nodded through the handshakes and smiles in a way she would once have thought unimaginable... Maybe it was because she had not had to impress anyone.

There was something quietly liberating about it. Was this the way Dante, who never tried to impress people, felt? She slid a glance at him as she stepped through the open door of the limousine. He was conversing with someone who had a serious expression and wore a holstered gun. She gave a little shiver. That was something she could never feel nostalgia for, along with bulletproof glass.

She had settled in her seat when the door opened, and Dante joined her. 'Sorry about that, just a message from Carl.'

She nodded but didn't ask. She was aware in the periphery of her vision that Dante was watching her.

'How is he?' she forced herself to ask.

She understood being close to a sibling, but she had never understood why Dante had never, ever displayed *any* resentment towards his older brother.

She had always been careful not to show how she

felt but his next words suggested she hadn't been entirely successful.

'Our marriage problems were not down to Carl.'

'I don't think that,' she tossed back with a small unconvincing laugh. 'I never did.'

Strong marriages survived the storms, some were even made stronger, but theirs had sunk without trace at the first squall.

Why do you think it will be any different now?

She pushed away the doubts. 'What is the hold-up?' she gritted, bouncing out of her seat as she virtually pressed her nose to the window.

His eyes went from her foot tapping on the floor to the visible tension in her slim neck.

'This is going to work, you know.'

'Are you basing that on blind faith, or have you been reading the tea leaves again?' She stopped and grimaced, instantly ashamed of her outburst. 'Sorry. I… I'm a bit nervous about this.'

He reached out and curled his hand around hers, drawing it onto his lap. His action was so unexpected that for a moment all she could do was stare at his strong fingers, dark against her pale skin.

Her emotional reaction to his action was way over the top, she knew that, but she had no control over the tears that began to spill down her cheeks.

She pulled her hand free, mumbling, 'Hormones,' as she sniffed and dashed the moisture away with the back of her hand.

He could feel the tension rolling off her in waves; he felt a stab of guilt that his first reaction was to pretend he couldn't.

'Try and relax.'

She shot him a look; did he think this was easy?

Perhaps he did, and why wouldn't he? In the past this was the point she would have nodded and hidden her nerves under a smile.

'This is me *trying*—I promise you.'

'You know what to expect this time.'

'That's the problem…' Panic closed her throat.

A wave of emotion moved through him as he watched her struggle, and he had no defence against the uncomfortable mixture of tenderness and guilt that stirred inside him as he looked into her beautiful unhappy eyes.

How many times had he made her unhappy?

Bea turned her head away, her thoughts drifting back to Dante's comments about his brother. 'I like Carl.' Although Dante was right, there was a tiny part of her that did blame Carl.

Carl doesn't want to be King.

The sentence that had changed her life, but at the time it had elicited a muted but sympathetic response from her. She remembered thinking that she could not imagine what it was like to have your life mapped out from birth.

'I am supporting his decision.'

'His decision?'

'He is renouncing his title and his claim to the throne.'

Still she hadn't got what he was telling her. 'Is that even possible? What will he do?'

'Be happy.'

She had got a horrible feeling in her stomach at that moment that his happiness might come at a cost, and she'd been proved right.

She sighed, feeling petty and mean-spirited. She did not normally struggle with empathy, but when it came to the erstwhile Crown Prince he would be linked in her head forever with losing Dante on the heels of losing their baby. But then you couldn't lose what you'd never had.

'If it helps, I will be able to be there more than—'

Her glance swivelled his way, and she arched an enquiring brow.

'More than I was. There were a lot of people waiting for me to fail.' The admission seemed drawn from him almost against his will.

Beatrice stared. He had never said anything like that to her before. He sounded almost...*vulnerable*?

'We made this baby together, and we will make decisions about this baby together. I want to make this work.'

She swallowed. 'So do I.'

He nodded and sat back in his seat just as the convoy of armoured limousines, the metallic paint catching the sun, finally drove along a wide chestnut tree–lined boulevard that dissected the capital city of San Macizo. The strict development laws meant there were no skyscrapers to compete with the old historic buildings.

There were modern buildings, the glass fronts reflecting back images, but they blended in seamlessly with the old. Traces of the historic waves of invasion and occupation were everywhere. The eclectic mix extended to culture and food—the capital featured highly on international foodies' wish lists.

As they drove past the government building, Beatrice watched Dante's face as his eyes lifted to the national flag fluttering in the breeze. She wondered what he was thinking.

As they reached the high point on the road, the panoramic vista widened and Beatrice caught a glimpse of the sea through the dense pine forest that bordered the white sand on the eastern side of the island. The western coast was where the famed colonies of seabirds nested in the protected area around the high cliffs, drawing naturalists from around the world every breeding season, and giving inspiration for countless nature documentaries.

Beatrice had read all the guidebooks about the place that Dante called home before she'd arrived, but she had quickly realised that until you experienced the place you didn't really *get* just how dramatic the contrasts they spoke about were. It wasn't just the geography of the place. San Macizo had been conquered several times over the centuries, and each successive wave of invaders had brought their own culture and genes to the mix. There was no such thing as a *typical* San Macizan, but as you walked the streets of the capital it soon became obvious there was an above average quantity of good-to-look-at people.

Great climate, pretty faces, an exceptional standard of living—small wonder the island kingdom frequently topped the list of happiest places in the world to live, and small wonder that few spoke out against the status quo of the monarchy.

Beside her, Dante was now on the phone as they left the city limits and went onto the flat plain that, though interspersed by villages and hamlets, was mostly agricultural, consisting of vineyards that produced the unique grape species that made the wine produced here famous the world over.

She didn't know if the tension she could feel in him was connected to the conversation he was having, or his recent declaration of intent. Given her tendency to hear what she wanted, she tried to retain a sense of proportion.

There was nothing proportionate about the palace that loomed into view. It was visible for miles around because of its position on a hill that rose in the middle of a flat plain. She felt *heavier* as she looked at it—not physically, more emotionally. This might be some people's happiest place to live, but it had not been hers!

A perfect defensive position, the history books she had pored over had explained, before they spoke of the family who had taken control of the island five hundred years earlier, and the generations' contributions to the towering edifice to their wealth and power.

The palace was not a home, or even a fortress, which it originally had been; it was a statement of power and in reality a small city covering many acres of ground. The main body was devoted to state apartments, but many wings and towers were private apartments housing family. Other areas, like the world-famous art gallery, were a draw for international tourists and open to the public at certain times of the year.

The closer they got, the more daunting it became.

'That's a big sigh.'

Her head turned from the window. If the expression in the blue depths was an accurate reflection of the thoughts she had been so deeply lost in, they were not happy ones. In the time it took him to push away the inconvenient slug of guilt, the shadow vanished. Beatrice really had got good at hiding her feelings…which was a good thing, he acknowledged, but also…*sad.*

His lips tightened at the intrusion of emotion, and he wondered if there was such a thing as sympathy pregnancy hormones. He'd heard of sympathy about labour pains.

'You were wishing you were somewhere else?'

The question was as much to silence the mocking

voice as anything else, but it opened the door to a question he had exerted a lot of effort to avoid. *With someone else?*

He had not forgotten her explosive reaction when he had casually dropped the subject into the conversation. His *innocent* comment had produced such an explosive response that you had to wonder if her overreaction was not about guilt.

Why guilt? asked the voice in his head. *Just because you have chosen to be celibate doesn't mean she has to follow suit...*

The golden skin stretched over the slashing angle of his cheekbones tightened, emphasising his dramatically perfect facial contours as he fought a brief internal battle to delete the images that came with the acknowledgement.

Celibacy was not a natural state, at least it wasn't for him. Sex, just plain, uncomplicated, emotion-free sex of the variety he used to enjoy, was a great stress-buster.

So, problem solved, mocked the voice in his head, *except you don't want sex, you want sex with Beatrice.*

'Wishing…?' she echoed, breaking into his thoughts.

Wishing was not going to be much practical help at this moment. Her time was better spent mentally preparing herself for what lay ahead.

As their eyes connected Beatrice pushed out a laugh that held no amusement, while Dante told himself that she would not have future relationships; he would be enough for her.

He would enjoy being enough for her.

'Wishing is for little girls who want to marry a prince. I was never one of those little girls.' One of life's little, or in this case massive, ironies. 'Actually,

I was still thinking about Carl. I wanted you to know that I think he is very brave.'

She had liked Carl on the occasions they had met. He had been about the only member of the Velazquez family other than Reynard who had made her feel welcome.

'So do I.'

'We wouldn't be here today if it wasn't for Carl's choices. I wonder sometimes where we would be, don't you?'

Dante leaned back, his head against the corner of the sumptuously upholstered limo interior as he turned his body towards her, his languid pose at odds with the tension in his jaw and the watchful stillness in his face.

Embarrassed now and wishing she'd never started this rather one-sided conversation, she dodged his stare.

'Say whatever it is you need to say. If you're going to explode there is no one here to hear.'

There was a hint of defiance in her face as she responded. 'Doesn't it ever occur to you that when we got married we never planned, we never spoke about where we would live or anything?'

He dismissed her comment with a flick of his long brown fingers, irritation at her persistence sliding into his eyes. 'I have homes.'

'Across the world, I know—the penthouse in New York, the LA beachfront villa, the Paris apartment. Yes, you own endless properties, but not *homes*.'

'I am sure you are going to tell me why my real-estate portfolio seems to bother you so much.'

'Did you plan for your life to change at all? Was I ever meant to be more than a pretty accessory?'

'Well, my life has changed now.'

'Because of Carl, and the baby,' she conceded, dashing a hand across her face. 'But not out of choice, not because you got married. People who commit plan a future. We never did. That's all I was trying to say.'

'You were never pretty. You were, you are, beautiful.'

His voice, low and driven, sent a siren shudder down her spine, and as her eyes connected with the heat in his whatever she had been about to say vanished from her head, leaving nothing but a whisper of smoke.

She squeezed her eyes closed, pushed both hands into her hair as she shook her head to shake free the sensual fog and gave vent to a low groan of frustration, before fixing him with a baleful glare that gradually faded to one suggestive of tired defeat.

'Please do not change the subject.'

'I was—'

'You haven't got a clue what I'm talking about, have you?' she said wearily.

'We—'

'No, there was never a *we*.' She forced a smile, struggling to inject some lightness into this conversation, which she wished she had never started. 'I was always a bad fit, not just here. I never would have fitted into your playboy lifestyle. I was always pretending to be something I'm not.'

'In my bed?'

She coloured. 'No, not there,' she admitted, her eyes sliding from the suggestive heat in his.

'Why do I get the feeling that all this is leading up to a declaration of hostilities?'

'Not hostilities, just a declaration of intent.'

'You are warning me.' He sounded astonished at the concept.

'I'm telling you that I'm not fitting in any more. I'm being me. I owe myself, and this baby, that much. I never want him to look at me and feel ashamed that—'

She stopped, realising a heartbeat after him where she had been going.

'You're still very angry with your mother, aren't you?'

'No…no…' she stammered out, disturbed by his perception. 'Not angry, I just… I don't want to be her.'

'You are not her and, for the record, I have no problem with you being yourself.'

She stopped and followed the direction of Dante's gaze through the tinted window. His eyes flickered to the edifice that dominated the landscape.

'Home, for me these days be it ever so humble.' He glanced her way. 'For us?'

She didn't react to the question, just nodded. 'It is beautiful. I always thought that it looked like something from a dream.'

Up close it looked real and solid, but it was not the carved stone that made her stomach tighten with nerves, it was the life inside it. A life she had never fitted into.

She had not married Dante because of his royal connections, but *despite* them. An inner voice of caution had told her she was playing out of her league, but she'd been too intoxicated by loving this incredible man and the baby they had created together to listen, and anyway he had never traded on his royalty. Dante didn't need to.

It was not his title, his blue blood or his wealth that made people listen when he spoke. She could hardly deny there was a sexual element to it; his sheer physical presence made an impact, but it was more he had an aura, a natural charisma—he was the sort of man who dominated any space he occupied.

She had turned away from him again but was no less conscious of his presence as she trained her eyes on the massive gates across the arched entrance that slid open as they approached. In profile, the purity of her golden features was quite breath-catching.

'Dream or nightmare?' he murmured sardonically.

She smiled faintly, but didn't turn her head, so he allowed himself the indulgence of allowing his gaze to drift in a slow lingering sweep over her smooth, glowing skin. The resulting tightening in his guts was as painful as it was inevitable.

She turned her head and caught a look on his face that was almost pain. 'Don't worry. I will try to make this work.'

'I never doubted it.'

CHAPTER NINE

'So, what is the cover story?'

'Cover story?'

'I mean, what is the press office going to release, or are you keeping me undercover for the time being?'

'I have a cupboard you would fit right in.'

His wilful imagination conjured a scenario where she was not alone in that space, their bodies pressed against—

He sucked in sense-sustaining air through flared nostrils and tried to halt the heat building inside him before it reached the critical point of no return.

His flippancy caused her frown to deepen. 'You know what I mean. I am assuming you want me to keep a low profile.'

'The press office will not be briefing.'

She stared. 'But that's—'

'The way it is. If asked directly the response will be the family is happy to have you back.'

'Irony, that's a change.'

'*I* am happy to have you back.'

'Oh!' She faintly willed herself not to read too much into his words, or the expression in his eyes.

'Is anyone going to believe that?'

It was clear to him that she didn't, and Dante realised

that her belief was all that mattered to him. He wanted to be the father of their child; he wanted to be half the man she deserved.

'I thought you weren't a fan of the spin doctors. Would you prefer to be in their hands or mine?'

She stared at the long brown tapering fingers extended for her scrutiny and felt her stomach muscles dissolve as she remembered how they felt on her skin, stroking…touching…

'Spin…you mean I don't like being patronised, manipulated and talked over? Yes, I am a bit odd that way.'

'Welcome to my world.'

The world she had been glad to leave. 'Nobody would dare patronise you—and as for talk over you!' She gave a hoot of laughter.

'Present company excepted?'

She fought off a smile in response to the gleam in his eyes, a gleam that held enough warmth to make her oversensitive stomach flip dangerously.

'I hate them, but they were right, weren't they?'

Despite her misgivings the supercilious suits had been right: nothing had leaked about the divorce proceedings. Certainly not to the journalists and opportunistic paparazzi who had dogged her steps for the first few weeks, along with the security detail that she had decided not to confront Dante about. They were discreet, which was a plus—there were days that she'd forgotten they were there.

The press pack had gradually lost interest when she hadn't been seen doing anything even vaguely newsworthy; she never reacted to questions and had no social media presence. A nun had a more interesting life, someone had written, and there were only so many times they could report on the length of her legs.

Beatrice had concluded being boring had its plus points.

'Did they fly back with us?'

He shook his head. 'They?'

'Seb, Roberto, Luis and the one with the really nicely trimmed beard. The security detail—my minders.' Did he really think she wouldn't notice just because she hadn't kicked up a fuss?

'You knew their names.' He swore under his breath—so much for covert surveillance. 'They stayed behind. Your sister could be a press target. You are safe with me.'

Strangely, considering how objectionable she had initially found their presence, she felt oddly comforted by this information, and felt quite guilty about the fact.

'Safe?' She slung him an ironic look and, rubbing the bridge of her nose, pushed back in her seat, digging her head into the soft leather upholstery to ease the muscles of her aching neck before she turned her head in his direction.

'You *really* think it will be that easy? I just reappear and it's all happy families? Your family must be planning your next marriage. Won't me being here throw a spanner in the works?'

'Oh, I think they were doing that before you left.'

She had been joking but, looking at his face, she wasn't sure he was. Of course it made sense. He was going to be King one day and he needed a queen and why wait? It was all about continuity.

Ignoring the sharp stab of something that could be jealousy, or loss, or hurt, she managed a flippant comeback to prove to herself as much as him that her heart was not broken.

'So, any prospective candidates standing out yet?'

'Perhaps you're better placed than most to decide what would make my perfect bride.'

'Are you flirting with me?'

Before she could react to his wicked grin, she realised that while they had been speaking they had entered the palace proper. The cars in front of them and behind had peeled away at some point, and they were now drawing up between the two elaborate stone fountains that stood outside the porticoed entrance to the private apartments she had left eight months ago.

She sat there, fighting a deep reluctance to get out of the car. Once she did it would all seem real, which up to that point it hadn't. She felt as if stepping onto the gravel would be akin to ripping a scab off a healing wound, releasing the pleasure and pain of past memories.

She took a deep breath and reminded herself this was the new, improved Beatrice. Sane Beatrice who did not lose her mind, or become malleable mush when breathing the same air as Dante.

'I am a bit tired after the journey,' she said, setting the scene for when she excused herself. A bit of aloneness was looking very tempting right now.

'Ah...'

She looked at him, bristling with suspicion. 'Do you mind translating that *"Ah"* into something I won't like?'

'There is a reception tonight for the French ambassador and his wife. It was arranged some time ago and it was deemed to be diplomatically unwise to cancel. We have already postponed once. Mother had a headache—actually she was hung-over.'

'Fine, don't worry, I can amuse myself.'

'Ah…'

She regarded him with narrowed eyes.

'The point is that should the ambassador become

aware that you are here your non-attendance could be construed as an insult.'

'You even sound like a diplomat.'

'A bit harsh, Bea.'

She fought off a grin. 'Couldn't you say I had a headache or something?' She wasn't at all sure she didn't, she decided, rubbing her temples with her fingertips before she gave a resigned sigh. 'All right, tell me the worst.'

His expression tensed. 'There is no question of you attending if you feel unwell. I will have the physician visit. In fact, this might be a good idea. You've had a long day and you shouldn't overexert yourself. Stress isn't good for the baby.'

'I'm fine,' she promised, adopting a businesslike tone. 'So, who will be at this dinner?'

As he listed the guests she gave several eye-rolls, interspersed with theatrical sighs.

'So basically, the snootiest, stuffiest—'

'I'm sure you'll cope admirably,' he cut back with an utter lack of sympathy that made her eyes narrow. 'Just be yourself.'

She opened her mouth and closed it, realising that this was almost like talking to the man she had fallen in love with, the one who didn't give a damn about protocol. They had always shared the same sense of humour, and appreciation of irony.

'Oh, I'll be fine after a bottle of champagne,' she said airily and watched the look of utter horror cross his face before adding with a sigh, '*Joke...?* You remember those?' Nine months of sobriety was not going to be a big ask for her—her normal alcohol consumption mostly involved nursing a glass for the sake of being sociable.

Not that she was making a statement. She had just never really liked the taste.

'I remember *everything*, Beatrice.'

The silence stretched as *something* in the atmosphere of the enclosed space changed. Impossible to put a name to, mainly because she didn't dare to, but it made her pulse race and her throat dry as he leaned in.

When he broke the silence all she was thinking about was his mouth and the way he tasted, the way he always tasted.

'Let's skip the dinner and go to bed!'

The feelings fizzing up inside her were making her breathless. 'You're not serious.'

He arched a brow and gave a wicked grin. 'I don't know, am I…?'

His laughter followed her out of the car as she hurried to put some safe distance between them.

She marched towards the door and past the men who stood either side, staring straight ahead. They wore bright gold-trimmed ceremonial uniforms, but the guns slung over their shoulders were not ceremonial but unfortunately very real.

It wasn't until she entered the echoing hallway with its row of glittering chandeliers suspended from a high vaulted carved ceiling that Beatrice took a deep breath, fighting against the tangle of jumbled memories that crowded her head.

For a split second panic almost took control. She had no idea if she was standing, sitting or lying, then, as she exhaled and the panicked thud in her ears of her own heartbeat receded, she was able to reel herself back to something approaching control.

The breath left her parted lips in a slow, measured,

calming hiss before she turned, masking her emotions under a slightly shaky smile.

Dante was standing a couple of feet away, his hands shoved in the pockets of his well-cut trousers. He had been watching her almost lose it. The enormity of what he was asking her to do hit him between the eyes like the proverbial blunt object.

She was distracted from this uncomfortable possibility by the fact that he was standing right in front of a larger-than-life portrait of a previous King of San Macizo, though this painting captured him when he had been Crown Prince.

She had noticed the striking similarity between the two men the first time she'd walked in, though she'd not then noted the far more modest portraits of his several wives hidden on a wall in a rarely used part of the building.

Legend had it that the first, rather plain-looking wife, who had died in childbirth, had been his one true love, but then legends rarely had substance. Still, it was a pleasingly romantic tale and she had liked to think it true.

The illusion that the figure staring down with hauteur etched on his carved features had actually stepped out of the frame lasted several blinks.

The man standing watching her had all the hauteur along with the perfect symmetry of features his ancestor had possessed. Had his ancestor possessed the same earthy sensual quality that Dante had? If he had, the artist hadn't captured it, though with those lips you had to wonder.

She pulled her shoulders back, feeling some sympathy for the long-ago wives, wondering if they too had stopped trying to figure out why their responses to their prince bypassed logic or common sense. Like her, had they just come to accept and guard against it as much as possible?

Dante watched as she made a visible effort to gather herself, but the expression on her face reminded him of a fighter who had taken too many punches, and maybe she had in the emotional sense.

He was prepared for the guilt and he accepted it. He had anticipated it. What he had not anticipated was that seeing her here, in this setting, would actually make him *more* aware of the ache that he had lived with since her departure. An ache he had refused to acknowledge, an ache that indicated weakness he couldn't own up to.

His upbringing had developed a strong streak of self-sufficiency in Dante. He had been sent to boarding school at six, where the policy was to discourage contact between siblings, the theory being part of the institute's ethos that was intended to develop a strength of character and independence.

Which in Dante's experience in practical terms translated as an ability to look after number one ahead of all others, and he had learnt the lesson. Well, the option had been enduring the misery of those who didn't, and there had been more than a few who'd never understood that showing weakness exposed you to the bullies.

Dante never had shown weakness; he had gone into the school system privileged and come out privileged and selfish as hell. The strategies developed at a tender age were coping mechanisms that had stood him in good stead. One kicked in now, stopping him acknowledging the emptiness.

'I can make your excuses?'

Her chin went up. 'I can make my own,' she began hotly and stopped, an expression of guilt spreading across her face as she saw through his offhand manner. 'There is no need to be worried about the baby. I would never do anything that put him at risk.'

'Him?'

'Or her.'

'Do you want to know?'

'I'm not sure…' Sadness settled across her features. Their first pregnancy had not lasted long enough for it to be a question she had been asked. 'Will the sex matter?' she asked, pushing the sadness away. She knew it would never go away, and she knew it was all right to feel it, but she didn't want it to overshadow the miracle that was happening to her body now.

'Matter?'

'I mean, can a female succeed to the throne?'

Her eyes widened with shock as she saw his hand move towards her; she gave a little gasp as he placed his hand on her flat belly. 'By the time it matters to this one's future, she will.'

His hand fell away, and she wanted to put it back. A dangerous shiver ran through her body as warning bells clanged in her ears.

'You intend to change things.'

'Baby steps.'

This time the words did not injure; they made her smile.

The lines around his eyes crinkled, totally disarming her fragile defences, which were jolted back into life when he angled his head towards the curving staircase with the elaborate wrought-iron balustrade that led to their private apartments that stretched along the first floor of this wing.

'I actually think tonight is a good idea. I'm going to see your parents at some point. It might as well be now.'

Meeting them in company would hopefully limit their ability to make snide digs. After all, appearances were everything in this household. 'What time…?'

'An hour?'

Dante stopped with his back to the glass-fronted lift and nodded towards the staircase. He knew that Beatrice was not keen on enclosed spaces and would walk up a heart-stopping number of steps to avoid a lift. 'After you, you know the way.'

'Which room?' she began and stopped, her eyes flying wide as his meaning hit home. 'I'm in our…*your* room?' she blurted. It was only seconds before a flush began to work its way up her neck.

Their room, but he would have long vacated it.

He was probably trying one of those suitable candidates for size in another room?

The images that accompanied the possibilities made her feel nauseous and then mad because she had been suffering and celibate and it only seemed fair that he should have been too. But then life here had never been fair or balanced; it worried her that she needed to remind herself.

'I never got around to moving my things out.'

The warning made her freeze. 'You mean you're still…!' She would have laughed outright at the suggestion that he would have been personally involved in any moving if his comment hadn't raised a number of issues. Mainly, was he assuming that they would be sharing the room? She could see how spending the night with him in the ski chalet might have led to this assumption.

'Your things are still there.'

The casual throwaway information added another layer of confusion. It could've been a housekeeping error, except such a thing did not exist inside the palace walls.

There was literally an army of people that would have made it possible for her to wake up in the morning and not have to do a single thing for herself right up to the end of the day.

There was always someone hovering, ready to relieve you of the burden of tying your own shoelace should you find that a bore, or too tiresome. It had been one of the *royal* things that she'd never got the hang of. She simply couldn't ask someone to perform a task that she was more than capable of completing herself, and she couldn't for the life of her see how it was demeaning to be seen making her own sandwich or washing out her own tights, but both had been activities that had been frowned on.

She had expected Dante to laugh with her at the sheer absurdity of people having so much time on their hands that they thought sandwich-making was a sin worth passing up the chain of command when she told him about her sugar-coated reprimand—the sugar had made it so much *less*, not *more*, acceptable—but he had just looked at her with a frown indenting his forehead.

'Can't you just go with the flow for once? Is it really worth the argument?'

It was the moment she had realised that they had stopped laughing at the same things. Actually Dante had stopped laughing altogether—that Dante had gone forever. Sometimes she wondered if he had ever really existed.

There was sadness and regret in the shaded look she angled up at his lean face.

'It's your room. I'll take one of the others.'

'It was our room,' he said without emphasis. 'You

might as well take it. I think you'll find most of your things where you left them.' Nobody had questioned his instructions to touch nothing, not even him, though now he might have to face the question that he had avoided because Beatrice was going to.

He'd kept telling himself that he'd get around to it, that he didn't like the idea of someone else touching Beatrice's things, but somehow it was a task he'd kept putting off.

He didn't sleep there any more; he slept, the little he did, on a couch in his office. Not because he was avoiding anything. It was a matter of convenience.

There was always a spare set of clothes in his office, and his running gear. He could shower there, he could shrug on a fresh shirt. It worked because he didn't keep office hours.

He wasn't avoiding anything. It wasn't in any way symbolic; it wasn't as if he were in denial. Bea had gone and it was better for her and better for him.

She was looking at him with a puzzled expression.

'But I wasn't coming back.' She had assumed her belongings would have been boxed as soon as she had gone. She had wondered more than once about asking for them to be sent on.

He shrugged, appearing exasperated by her persistence as he dragged a hand through his dark hair and sighed, managing by the flicker of an eyebrow to make her feel she was making a big deal out of nothing at all.

Maybe because you *want* it to be a big deal for him? Maybe you want it to hurt for him too? Before the horror of acknowledgement hit home, she pushed away the preposterous idea, conscious that she was guilty of overanalysing.

'But you are back.'

She couldn't argue with that, but it meant sleeping in the same bed they had shared…as if this weren't hard enough anyway. She'd stepped out of this life—stepping back in was going to present challenges regardless of where she slept.

This time, when his hand curved around her cheek, she did let her cheek fall into it.

'Look, I know this is hard for you but—' He broke off, cursing as the opening of a door to their left made Beatrice jump away from him.

Giggles entered the hallway a moment before two uniformed figures. One saw Dante and stopped so quickly that the smaller figure bumped into her.

'*Scusi*, Highness…' Eyes round with shock, her face pink with embarrassment, she dropped a curtsy and the woman behind her followed suit.

Dante addressed them, speaking Italian, and they responded in the same language. Considering she had been boastful about her language ability earlier, Beatrice didn't have a clue what was being said. Her brain wasn't functioning through the jam of conflicting emotions in her head.

She stood there with a fixed smile throughout the exchange and one thing was clear: if her arrival had not been officially announced, it had now.

He gave a sardonic smile as the women vanished through the door they had entered and closed it behind them.

'They think I don't know they use this suite as a shortcut when we're away,' he said, sounding amused. 'Don't worry, word will get around we are back.'

'My ears are already burning.'

'They'd be burning some more if we slept at opposite ends of the building,' he predicted drily.

'Was that ever an option?' she asked, with a catch in her voice.

He held her eyes and her insides tightened as he didn't say a word. The look, even without the shake of his head, was enough.

'But relax,' he added as she swung away from him. 'There's still the bed in my dressing room if that is what you want.'

Walking behind her, he watched as she almost missed the next step but after a pause carried on walking.

He caught up with her, pulling level as he added in a low voice that dragged like rough velvet across her nerve endings, *'Remember?'*

Her hand tightened on the banister as she stopped and flung him an anguished look. 'Why are you doing this, Dante?'

Remember? Of course she remembered…

She'd made her complaint after Dante had not slipped into their bed before three in the morning and had then been up before six for two weeks straight. It had been intended to ignite a discussion about his unhealthy work-life balance.

That had always been optimistic. Dante took the entire caveman-of-few-words thing to extremes, missing the point entirely and, working under the assumption she was concerned about her own disturbed beauty sleep, he'd had a bed put up in the adjoining dressing room so that he would not disturb her.

The one occasion he had used it she had lasted five minutes before she had left the massive bed they'd shared and joined him, sliding in beside him in the narrow bed. Images floated into her head, warm bodies entwined, his need to lose himself in her, her need to give. The cumulative effect had always generated heat.

She felt heat now ripple through her body and, resisting the temptation to feed it, lowered her eyes, her glance snagging on his strong brown fingers that were curled lightly around the cool metal of the banister a bare inch away from her own.

Conscious of the tingling and the tug, she pulled her own hand away and pressed it against her stomach.

'I really don't think our sleeping arrangements are anyone else's business,' she said, even though she knew this view would not be shared. The palace was filled with spies loyal to differing factions, the King's spies, the Queen's spies… Everyone took sides, at least that was how it had felt to her, or maybe she had been infected by the paranoia of the claustrophobic life inside the palace walls?

Her eyes went to Dante's face. Presumably he now had his own army of spies reporting to him. 'And now you're *making* the rules.'

She hitched her bag onto her shoulder, not anticipating that her remark would evoke much reaction, certainly not the ripple of complex emotions she saw flicker across his face.

Had she inadvertently hit a nerve?

'Well, don't you?'

'So is that how you think of me? A dictator?' He vented a wry laugh as they began to climb the sweep of stairs together. 'I sometimes think it would make life easier.'

He felt he was not just combating his own perceived inexperience but a father who, while he was reluctant to relinquish any power, was equally reluctant to leave the golf course for a long boring meeting, and senior courtiers who, accustomed to winding their King round their collective fingers, thought modernity a dirty word and equated stability with immobility.

She realised they were standing outside the open door to Dante's study. Opposite was a small salon, where her Italian tutor used to try and be polite about her progress. They were a few doors down from the bedroom suite they had shared, but he went directly to the first door and opened it.

'This is me. I've had the doors to both the adjoining suites opened up, so if you hear any noise you'll know…'

Beatrice immediately felt foolish for making such an unnecessary issue out of the room situation. 'Not very likely, the walls are about ten feet thick.'

'And there are locks on all the interconnecting doors, should you be concerned I might ravish you.'

'Maybe I'm worried that I might ravish you. It wouldn't be the first time,' she flung back recklessly.

He stood there, his eyes burning into her… Very slowly he raised his hand and, with one finger, tilted her face up to him.

'What are *you* trying to do, Beatrice?' he said, turning her own words back on her.

His hand dropped and she gave a shuddering sigh of shame, tears standing out in her eyes as she passed a shaky hand across her mouth.

'I'm sorry,' she whispered, before turning and running down the corridor to her own bedroom door. She felt his eyes burning into her back but she didn't turn around, she didn't breathe, until she was safe behind the closed door.

CHAPTER TEN

SHE STOOD THERE, back against the door, her eyes squeezed tight shut until she heard the faint sound of a door closing.

Up to this point the necessity of maintaining rigid defences had kept the exhaustion of the day, as much emotional as physical, at bay. Now as her shoulders slumped a wave of deep weariness swept over her.

Struggling against the memories being in this room evoked, images that were buzzing in her head like a swarm of wasps, she headed for the bed and sank down.

She felt her eyes fill but she was too tired for tears. How had she allowed herself to get into this position?

By saying yes to Dante—so no change there!

She was here and this was not the time for a post-mortem as to how she had put herself in this position. She just had to deal and get on with it.

This was about the baby. A soft smile curved her lips as she rested her hand on the non-existent swell of her belly.

'Your daddy loves you,' she whispered, hoping that it were true.

Dashing the hint of moisture that had seeped from the corners of her eyes, she gave a loud sniff. Puffy eyes were not a good look for a formal dinner. She pulled herself up off the bed and stood there, ignoring the heaviness in her legs and the ache in her chest. She didn't examine her immediate surroundings; instead she opened the wide interconnecting doors into the adjoining room. Outside the bedroom she was able to breathe a little easier.

Wandering through the rooms where she had lived, it was all the same, but not really.

It took her a few moments to realise that though the antique furniture was still the same, some of the heavier items that she had requested to be stowed away, like the priceless, but to her mind ugly, set of cabriole-legged chairs, had been returned. The walls were covered in the paintings that had been in situ when she had arrived; the ones that were more to her taste had presumably been put back in some vault labelled not cultured enough.

As she wandered from room to room it dawned on her that actually *all* the personal touches she had introduced had vanished from these rooms.

She had been wiped from the rooms and probably Velazquez family history.

In the west-facing sitting room where she liked to spend her morning, the light was so beautiful, she glanced wistfully at the carved stone mantle where the natural sculpted driftwood she had collected during walks on the beach was no longer evident. In its place there were pieces of delicate porcelain, which were beautiful but had none of the tactile quality she had loved.

Likewise, the church candles she had lit in the evening when it was too warm for a fire no longer filled the elaborate grate and the vases she had filled with bare branches now held rigid formal floral displays.

Without the bright splashes of colour from the cushions and throws she had scattered throughout, the rooms looked very different from how they had in her mind. Even the bookshelves had become colour-coordinated and stripped of her piles of paperbacks. There was not a single thing that could have been termed eclectic in any part of the apartment.

Leaving the places where her presence had been clinically expunged, she reopened the door to the bedroom and, with a deep sustaining breath, walked inside.

It was just a room.

No, she realised, it was the *same* room.

The same room she had walked out of eight months earlier. After the complete removal of anything that was remotely her in the other rooms, the contrast was dramatic. The room was like some sort of time capsule where her presence had been preserved.

It really was almost as though she had just walked out of the room. Stunned, she stood poised in the doorway, her wide blue eyes transmitting shock before she stepped inside.

She ran her fingers across the paperback on the bedside table, the spine still stretched open at the page she had been reading, before walking over to the dressing table where the messy pile of earrings, bracelets and make-up she had left behind still seemed to be in exactly the same place she had left them.

Every item she touched carried distracting memories, which she struggled to push away. Instead, aiming for a practical focus, she pressed the hidden button and the massive walk-in wardrobe slid silently open while the overhead recessed lights burst into life, along with those over the mirrored wall ahead, reflecting her image back at her.

She blinked, and saw her sister's face appear, her

dark eyes laughing as she walked inside the wardrobe she declared to be bigger than the entire flat they had once shared. She was laughing as she spun gracefully around, her arms spread wide as she took in the space.

The image was so real that Beatrice found the corners of her mouth lifting as she remembered Maya's reaction, then wobbling as the memory of her sister's assessment swam to the surface of the recollections.

'Oh, my God. Perfect for people who love looking at themselves.' Her husky laughter had rung out as she'd stepped inside and begun to open myriad doors to reveal racks and shelves; her laughter had turned to silent awe.

'When you said you'd stopped off in Paris to shop…' She'd rubbed her fingers across a silk catsuit that they had both last seen and admired in a high-end magazine spread. 'When will you ever wear all this?'

Beatrice had shrugged. 'I know. It's crazy.' How was she to have known that the personal shopper thought her trying something on and saying she liked it equated to *I'll take it—in several colours*?

Dante had laughed at her horror and overruled her when she'd announced her intention to send back the stacks of clothes that had come draped over hangers inside cellophane wrappers and in layers of tissue paper in ribbon-tied boxes.

'You want me to charter a plane for your clothes? Imagine the carbon footprint,' he had taunted.

Beatrice pushed away the lingering memory and replaced his voice in her head with an amused Maya saying that she might work her way through this lot in ten years or so, if she changed outfit three times a day and four on a weekend.

She never had because she hadn't stayed for ten years; she had barely stuck it out for ten months, and now she was back and all the suppressed emotions had surfaced, combining with her baby hormones to make her feel raw and vulnerable.

She dashed a hand across her eyes; she was just too tired of soul-searching. Today had gone as well as she could have expected.

Dante seemed to be making a genuine effort for the baby's sake, and that was the problem. It was for the baby. She wanted him to want her, to need her as much as she needed him.

Giving her head a tiny brisk shake, she pushed away the thoughts and turned to a section that was devoted to evening wear.

After pulling out a few dresses she finally settled on a full-length white silk gown, the style a modern take on classic Grecian. The heavy fabric swirled on the hanger as she held it up. It left one shoulder bare, the hand-embroidered sections on the skirt alleviating the stark purity of the design.

It took her half an hour from choosing suitable shoes to complement her choice—the plain court style was secondary to the fact they were made of a silver jewelled glittering fabric and the spiky heels elongated her long legs even more—to putting the finishing touches to her hair. The fact the ends were still damp made it easier to pin it into a simple topknot and at the last minute she pulled out some loose shiny strands and let the shiny wisps fall, creating a softening effect against her cheeks and long neck.

She added a light spritz of her favourite perfume, ignoring the voice in her head that said it had only become her favourite since Dante had said it was his, when there was a tap on the door that connected the adjoining suite.

She had time to suck in a hurried restorative breath,

take in the flush on her cheeks and the sparkle that was part excitement, part fear in her wide-spaced eyes, before the door opened and Dante stepped into the room, his dark head slightly bent as he adjusted the cufflinks at his right wrist.

It gave Beatrice time to close her mouth and paste in place an expression that fell disastrously short of neutral, but at least she wasn't licking her lips or drooling too obviously.

A lot of men looked good in formal evening wear, the tailoring could hide a multitude of sins, but Dante had nothing to hide and the perfect tailoring emphasised the breadth of his shoulders, the length of his legs and...well, his perfect *everything.* One day she might be able to view his earthly male beauty with objectivity, but that day was a long way off.

She felt the heat unfurl low in her belly and ignored it as she opened her mouth to offer to straighten his tie and changed her mind. Less wisdom and more self-preservation as she remembered more than one occasion when a tie-straightening offer had made them late for an official engagement.

Dante took his time over the cuff adjustment to give the heat in his blood time to cool and recover from the razor-sharp spasm of mind-numbing desire that had spiked through him in that brief moment before he'd lowered his gaze, the electricity thrumming in a steady stream through his body.

She always had been the chink in his armour, the beautiful downfall for a man who, over the years, had become smugly confident in his ability to control his carnal appetites, not have them control him.

And once again she was carrying his child. He had never expected that they would be here again, but the knowledge she was carrying his child only increased the carnal attraction.

He performed another necessary adjustment and lifted his head. He had regained some level of control, but there were limits. He didn't even attempt to prevent his eyes drifting up from her feet to the top of her shining head, knowing the effort would be useless. He recognised it was a dangerous indulgence, but things could be contained so long as he didn't touch her. Experience had taught him that the explosion would be madness.

Everywhere his eyes touched shivers zigzagged over the surface of her skin, awakening nerve pathways, making her ache. The smoky heat in his stare and the clenched tension in his jaw were some sop to her frustration. At least she wasn't the only one suffering.

'I'm ready,' she said, her voice brighter than the occasion justified. She could hear the tinge of desperation, she just hoped he couldn't.

The intensity of his hungry stare did not diminish and the longer it lasted, the harder it was for her to resist the impulse to fling herself at him. Then when he did break the silence his voice sounded so cool that she was relieved she had not reacted to it when it was quite possible that the heat she had felt pounding the air between them had been a product of her febrile imagination.

'So I see, punctual as always and, I imagine, just as impatient about being kept waiting, so you see… I didn't.' He extended a crooked arm and after a moment she moved forward to rest her hand lightly on it, aware as she did of the muscled strength of his forearm.

'You look perfect,' he said, without looking at her.

'Thank you.'

As they approached the shallow steps that led from the private apartment into the corridor that linked to what she thought of as the palace proper, Beatrice raised her gown slightly with her free hand, exposing her sparkling shoes.

The glitter caught Dante's attention; he arched a brow. 'What all the princesses are wearing these days?' he teased, not looking at her ankles any longer. His gaze had progressed to the long, lovely lines of her thighs outlined against the heavy silk fabric of her dress.

Though her heart was trying to climb its way out of her chest, she tried to replicate the blank look on the impassive faces of the two uniformed figures they were walking past.

'Do I look different?' She flashed him a worried look. She *felt* different. 'Do you think anyone will guess?'

He paused and, capturing her wrists, pulled her towards him. 'Would it matter if they did?'

'I know you think I'm being stupid about this.'

'It's your call.'

'Well, if anyone did guess,' she added on a philosophical note, 'it couldn't be any more excruciatingly awful than the last time the subject of babies came up at the dinner table.'

His blank expression made it obvious that he didn't have a clue what she was talking about.

Beatrice envied his amnesia. She would never, *could* never, forget the silence around the table that night, when she had responded to a thinly veiled hint when she had refused a glass of wine.

Suddenly everyone had been exchanging knowing glances and saying how very well she looked…positively glowing.

There had been any number of similar moments after the early loss of that first pregnancy where it had been made clear that should she prove to have good child-bearing hips all her other shortcomings might be overlooked.

Dante didn't seem to realise how agonisingly embarrassing she'd found the entire situation. Previous to that night she had risen above the comments, had damped down her hurt over their insensitivity, but on that occasion something inside her had snapped. She had tried to do it Dante's way, it had been time for hers, and she had always found that the best way to deal with most situations was by being upfront, despite the fact that she'd agreed with Dante up to a point. It hadn't been anybody's business, but then no one had been staring at *his* belly waiting to see a royal bump!

Of course, there had never been any official acknowledgement of her miscarriage, but she'd known that her personal loss was the subject of palace gossip and speculation.

She had tried not to care, to rise above it, but as she'd looked around the table she'd known full well that there wasn't a single person present who didn't know the details, a single person who hadn't discussed her fertility.

Despite her outward composure her voice had shaken a little with the effort to control the surge of emotion inside as, looking at the woman seated opposite her, she'd deliberately pitched her words to reach the entire table as she'd remarked how much she loved children and hoped to have several.

The approving smiles that had followed this group-share announcement had faded when she'd gone on to explain that she would be following her own parents' example, that she wanted to adopt as well as give birth, but that she didn't plan on doing either just yet.

By the time she'd finished speaking the entire table

had been sitting in shocked silence, broken finally by the King himself, who had announced quite simply that adoption for a member of the royal family was not an option, before proceeding to make a lot of pronouncements about bloodlines and breeding that had made her blood boil before he'd risen and left the table, indicating that the discussion was over.

So Dante hadn't leapt to her defence. She'd been prepared to cut him some slack as there hadn't been much opportunity once his father had gone into regal-pronouncement mode.

She hadn't expected to have Dante intervene on her behalf, she could defend herself, and the first lesson on royal protocol that she had learnt was that you didn't contradict the King, although she had seen Dante calmly face down his father, with an emphasis on the calm, when it had come to something he'd thought important. Dante had always emerged the victor without raising his voice, no matter how loud his father had got—but this had never happened when there were people present outside the immediate family, as there had been that night.

But she had been quite glad of his silently supportive arm around her shoulders as they'd returned to their apartments. It wasn't until the door had closed that she'd realised that the arm hadn't been supportive, more restraining, and Dante had been quite royally *unhappy* with her.

In fact he'd blamed her for reacting the way she had and making a situation where none had existed.

And now there *was* a situation.

'Are you all right?' he asked her now, scanning her face.

'A bit light-headed, that's all.'

'This is not a good idea,' he said, dragging out one of the ornately carved chairs that were set at intervals along the wall.

'No,' Beatrice said, resisting his efforts to push her into it. 'I didn't get all dressed up for nothing. I really am fine. Please stop looking at me as though I'm an unexploded time bomb. The baby is fine. I am fine.'

'You are not fine—you escaped and now you're back. The doors have closed and locked and you're wondering what the hell you were thinking of.' He smiled at her shocked expression. 'You think I have never felt that way?'

'You?'

He tipped his dark head and gave a faint twisted smile. 'I sometimes feel as if the walls are closing in on me.' His dark eyes lifted to the ornately carved ceiling high above.

'What do you do?' she asked, fascinated by the new insight. Did Dante ever think about escaping?

'I used to escape in your arms, inside you, *cara*.'

'Dante?' Her stomach clenched with helpless desire as their eyes met.

He stroked her cheek with one finger. 'Lately I remind myself that I am here to change things, that I can knock down walls, change mindsets. So long as no one guesses I don't have a clue what I'm doing I might become a man my son is not too ashamed of.'

She was moved beyond words and for several moments could not speak. 'You do know what you're doing,' she protested indignantly.

'Do I?' he said, self-mockery gleaming in his eyes. 'Frankly,' he continued in the manner of someone making a clean breast of it, 'it doesn't matter so long as people think you know what you're doing.'

She took an impetuous step towards him and almost stumbled. He caught her elbow to steady her, his own heart thudding hard in reaction to the burst of adrenalin in his bloodstream.

'Be careful!' The surge of protective concern edged his voice with gravel.

It was possibly good advice.

'Those heels are a little high, considering…'

Her smile of gratitude half formed froze in place as the warmth in his eyes hardened. 'Considering *what*?'

'Isn't that obvious?' he said, seemingly oblivious to the danger in her voice.

'Please do not try and wrap me up in cotton wool, Dante. I am a woman, not an incubator, and I'm pregnant, not ill.' Having made her point, she hoped—it was hard to tell from his expression—she didn't dwell on the subject. She took a deep breath and moved the conversation on. 'So, who is there tonight, again?'

Him going over the guest list gave her the opportunity to gather a little of her composure.

'Wow, it sounds like a fun evening.' Her mocking smile faded as she looked up at him, conscious of the gaping gap that had grown between them as they'd walked. Was there ever a time when she could have bridged it without a baby?

If so, it had gone, because without the baby she would not be here.

She damped the beads of moisture along her upper lip as she struggled to banish the questions and doubts swirling in her head.

'What am I even doing here?'

'Is that a rhetorical question?'

She shook her head. 'Sorry, just a mild panic attack, but don't worry, I'll be on my best behaviour.'

'No, don't.'

Her blue eyes fluttered wide. 'What?'

'All I want is for you to be yourself.' Infuriating, foot-in-mouth but always honest self. 'I get tired…of people…'

'Polishing your ego?'

He gave a cynical grin. 'I'm sometimes tempted to announce the world is flat just to watch them admire my amazing intellect.'

She laughed. 'I'd pay good money to see that.'

'It isn't too late to change your mind.'

'Yes, it is,' she countered as they passed into the palace proper, as she called it in her head.

The carpet underfoot now was inches deep and scarlet with a border of gold; the crystal chandeliers glittering overhead lit the long corridor that seemed to stretch into infinity, guarded by rows of portraits of more of Dante's ancestors, ancestors' wives, children and dogs and, in one case, a leopard with a jewelled collar looking almost as supercilious as its mistress.

If the intention was to impress or intimidate, it did both.

They were the last to join the guests and family in the drawing room, where the mingling involved a lot of diamond tiaras, medals on lapels and stiffly formal conversation.

'Did all conversations stop just now, or did I forget to put my clothes on?' Beatrice asked, her cheeks already starting to ache from the effort of maintaining her meaningless smile.

Her comment invited Dante to see her naked, every sleek, smooth, glorious inch of her, and his imagination obliged, which meant his smile was forced around the edges and he felt the need to loosen his tie, an action which, across the room, earned a horrified glare from his mother.

'Forget the gossips, we owe them no explanations.'

She slung an 'easy for you to say' look up at the tall, imposing figure of her husband as she gritted out through a clenched smile, 'I feel like I've stumbled into one of my nightmares. Do you think there are odds on how long I'll stay this time?' She took a deep breath and allowed her veiled blue gaze to take in all the details. 'Wow, this really is vintage Velazquez. Reminds me of everything I don't miss.'

'On the plus side, so is the champagne,' Dante said, appropriating two flutes from a passing waiter, then, realising what he'd done, slammed them back down on the tray and selected the alternative sparkling water just before the Queen, wearing a staggering amount of diamonds, bore down on them.

'How delightful you look. Good flight?' The Queen greeted her with gracious frigidity and raised a pencilled eyebrow when Beatrice drained the glass of sparkling water in her hand.

The King appeared and ignored Beatrice, so she returned the favour.

'Dante, you are escorting the countess into dinner. You can't escort your wife.'

Dante smiled at his father. 'Actually, I can.' He held out his arm to Beatrice, who, after a pause, took it, and they went to join the other guests who were pairing off to process into the state banquet hall.

'If looks could kill.' She had enjoyed the expression on her father-in-law's face, but she enjoyed even more the feeling that she and Dante were on the same team.

'They don't.'

'Don't?'

'Kill. I have conducted pretty extensive research into the subject. There have been occasional reports of minor injuries but absolutely no fatalities.'

Beatrice's gurgle of laughter drew several glances and several comments on what an attractive couple the future King and Queen made.

'Thanks for having my back.'

He looked down into her beautiful face and felt shame break loose inside him. She shouldn't be thanking him; it should have been something that she took for granted…but why would she? He had never had her back when it had counted.

He watched as she took a deep breath and straightened her shoulders, and felt the shame mingled now with pride. When had he ever acknowledged the courage she had shown?

She had wanted to blend in but she never would, he realised with a rush of pride, because she was better than them. Better than him, he decided, not immediately identifying the tightening in his chest as protective tenderness.

He didn't want her to blend in!

'I'm here if you need me.'

Under dark brows drawn into a straight line above his hawkish nose, she struggled to read his expression but made the obvious assumption he was worried she was going to fall apart. 'Don't worry. I'm not going to fall apart.'

It seemed to Beatrice that the present King had decided to deal with her presence by directing every comment he made to a point six inches above her head. For some reason Beatrice found it very funny.

Absence had not made the King any less angry than she remembered. Her glance drifted from father to son, where Dante sat with his head bent attentively to catch what the person on his left was saying.

Despite her experience of a toxic stepfather, she had known what a *proper* father should be like. How could Dante know when all he had was his own father, who was a distant, cold figure, to go by?

What sort of father would Dante make?

It was a question she had asked herself the first time around, and it had bothered her because she simply couldn't see him that way. But now? Her eyes flickered wide as she realised how surprisingly easy it was to see him in that role. Had he changed, or was it the way she saw him, thought of him, that had altered?

What did they say? Expect the worst and hope for the best? Actually, against all expectations, this evening was not so bad, as her experience of official engagements went.

A fact in large part due to the conversation she'd struck up with one of the guests of honour, who protocol decreed had been seated to her right.

The ambassador's wife, an elegant young thirty-something Frenchwoman, who Beatrice soon discovered was a new parent and self-confessedly besotted.

'Sorry, I must be boring you. We have very little conversation between night feeds, teething and the general brilliance of our son,' she admitted, glancing fondly to where her husband was holding a stilted conversation with the Queen.

'I'm not bored.' Beatrice grinned and lowered her voice. 'But if you get onto the best vintage this decade to lay down for an investment… I might doze off,' she admitted with a twinkle as she glanced to the retired general seated on her left, who was giving all his attention to his glass of red.

It was refreshing to be around someone who was so obviously happy. Maybe it would rub off, she thought wistfully. 'Did you have Alain here?' she asked. The opening of the new maternity wing of the hospital had been one of her last official duties, frustrating as usual because her expressed wish to speak to some staff and patients without the photographers had been vetoed. 'Or did you go back home?'

'Oh, I didn't give birth. I can't actually have children. We adopted.'

At the opposite end of the table Dante was conscious that several people had begun to eavesdrop on the young women's conversation, though they themselves seemed unaware of the fact. It was as if people were shocked that nobody had told the women that this event was business, not pleasure.

'Really? My parents adopted too.'

As Beatrice's voice floated across the table, he was aware of his mother looking tenser by the moment.

The ambassador leaned across; he was smiling. 'Thank you.'

Dante lifted his brows.

'These formal events are a trial for Lara—she finds them something of an ordeal… The Princess has drawn her out.'

Dante was aware of something like proprietorial pride breaking loose inside him as he nodded, and found himself wondering how differently things might have worked out if his family had decided to consider Beatrice's natural warmth and genuine interest in people a positive rather than a handicap.

And you threw that warmth away. So, what does that make you?

Maybe it was true that you didn't value what you had until it was no longer there, but now she was there, and he was determined that she would stay. She was the mother of his child; her place was with him. It was an explanation that he could live with. It meant he didn't have to delve too deeply into his tightly boxed emotions.

'Listen to them.' The ambassador's voice cut into Dante's bitter reflections.

Dante was, as were several other people who had tuned into the animated conversation between the two attractive women.

'So you're adopted?'

'No, my sister was adopted. My mum and dad had given up on getting pregnant by that point. They adopted Maya as a newborn, then a couple of months later Mum discovered that I was not a grumbling appendix.'

Lara Faure laughed and clapped her hands.

'So, you are almost twins.'

'That's what we say, except definitely not identical. Maya is dark and petite and I'm…' her brows hit her blonde hairline '…*not*! The irony is that Mum is dark and petite. I take after our dad, who was tall and blond, before he went bald, so I hope I haven't inherited that from him.' Her hand went to her head, where her frequently disobedient hair appeared to be in place, before dropping. Her fingers curled around the stem of her water glass as she swirled the contents, giving the impression she was breathing in the scent of wine as she lifted it to her lips.

'Your hair is natural!' the Frenchwoman exclaimed, her envious glance on Beatrice's glossy head.

'I had some blue streaks when I was at school.' The

admission freed a grin. 'And was a redhead for about five minutes. That's about the limit of my rebellion, but these days, yes, this is *au naturelle*.'

'How lucky. Mine costs me a fortune and far too many hours to maintain. I've forgotten what colour I actually was.' The woman patted her elegant head and gave a self-deprecating shrug. 'Your sister is the brunette, you said?'

Beatrice nodded.

'I always wanted a sister. I was an only child. We hope one day we will be able to give Alain a brother or sister…'

'Maya and I are best friends and sisters,' Beatrice said, her voice warm with affection as she thought of her sister. 'We squabble, but I know…' She paused, becoming belatedly aware that the table had grown silent and that everyone was listening to every word she said. Well, too late to stop now, even though she knew she'd strayed onto a dangerous subject area. 'I know that she is always there for me.' She put down her glass and kept her eyes steadily on the woman beside her and imagined the thought bubbles of disapproval above the collective regal heads.

'And I'm sure you have always been there for her. You know, I have a few friends coming for brunch next week, you might know some? We have started up a book club, and on the side we have some pet projects at the moment. You might know that I am…was a violinist before the arthritis…?'

She briefly extended a hand displaying swollen knuckles while in a sentence she dismissed an unfair roll of the dice that had robbed her of a short but glittering career, and the world of someone considered one of the greats in the music industry.

Her bravery was humbling, and Beatrice knew this was someone she would like to know.

'They have a great system in place here for music in schools—an innovation of your husband, according to my sources?'

Beatrice said nothing, aware that the other woman's sources were a lot better than her own.

'But the younger appreciation of music starts, the better, so we are hoping to raise some money for instruments to introduce music lessons into the nurseries in a fun way.'

'That sounds great,' Beatrice began, her smile deepening as she realised that she'd made a friend.

'Though I should warn you, you might be bored. Two others of our group are new parents too and another is pregnant, so you might get a bit tired of all the baby talk.'

Beatrice could not control the guilty colour she felt rising up her neck, even though she knew logically that nobody was about to suspect the truth. As far as anyone else was concerned they had been estranged for the last eight months and, while there might be a lot of speculation as to why she was back, a baby was not going to be on their list of possibilities.

As she continued to struggle to frame a response, aware that Lara was beginning to look puzzled by her silence, it was Dante who came to her rescue.

'Hands up.'

He held up his hands, the long tapering fingers splayed in an attitude of mea culpa that caused conversation to halt and every eye to turn his way. 'My fault.'

Beatrice's initial relief was immediately tempered with wariness. What was he going to say?

Lara Faure raised a delicate brow, her teasing eyes

flashing between the handsome Prince and his wife. 'It is in my experience that it is always the husband's fault.'

Beatrice held her breath as she waited for Dante to speak. The gleam in his dark eyes as they brushed her reminded her of the Dante she had fallen in love with, the Dante who made the outrageous sound normal, and had delighted in making her blush in public.

'I have been complaining,' he drawled, leaning back in his seat while his long, sensitive brown fingers now played an invisible tune on the white linen as they lightly drummed, 'that she spreads herself too thin—she has just so much *enthusiasm*.' His shoulders lifted in an expressive, fluid shrug. 'It makes her take on too many things. I have to book an appointment to see her.' He threw the words out, along with a heavy-lidded caressing look that sent Beatrice's core temperature up by several degrees.

Ignoring her burning blood, she focused on his ability to lie through his beautiful teeth and continued to conceal her true thoughts behind an impassive mask.

'Books and music. Two of her favourite things.' And both offering no physical danger that might harm mother or child. 'Though I have to warn you, she can't hold a tune. I can spare you, *cara*, go have fun.'

'He likes to think I actually need to ask his permission before I have fun.'

People laughed and conversations started up, but under her own smile there was hope as she allowed herself to think that this was not all pretence.

CHAPTER ELEVEN

TO BEATRICE'S RELIEF the party did not drag on long after the meal. The guests of honour excused themselves relatively early and Dante took the opportunity to extract them at the same time.

As they walked through the doors into their private drawing room, he was tugging off his tie. A moment later the top buttons of his formal shirt were unfastened, and he gave a grunt of satisfaction before he flopped onto one of the deeply upholstered sofas that were arranged around the carved fireplace.

'That could have been worse.' He threw several cushions on the floor with a grimace of irritation before angling a glance at Beatrice. 'You don't agree?'

'Your father ignored me regally all evening.'

'I'd pay to have my father ignore me.'

She failed to fight off a smile.

'So what else?'

'I wanted to tell Lara that I was pregnant.'

'Then why didn't you?'

She slung him an exasperated look. 'I may know very little about royal protocols but I'm *pretty* sure telling a dinner guest I'm pregnant before the King and Queen know they are going to have a grandchild might break a couple.'

‘True…but you have made a friend?’

‘I like her,’ she said, ignoring the invitation when he patted the arm of the sofa beside him and choosing to sit instead opposite, with the long coffee table, with the tasteful stack of prerequisite coffee-table books that nobody was ever going to read, between them.

Her eyes went to the hand that still rested on the arm as she wondered uneasily if the gesture had been meant to remind her of another occasion when she had accepted the invitation only to find herself pulled down on top of him. She pushed away the images, but not before her core temperature had jumped several uncomfortable degrees.

‘Should I have told Lara that I’d join her book club?’

‘Why not? You make it sound as though you’ve signed your soul away. And it sounds more like a mother and baby group and you will fit right in. I have a list of the obstetricians I spoke of, if you’d like to look at them.’ He scanned her face. ‘We can tell my parents, if that would make you feel more comfortable.’

‘But what if something goes wrong?’ The words ‘like the last time’ hung unspoken in the airwaves between them. She shook her head, the imagined scenes of that eventuality lodged there, a nightmare mixture of their lost baby and the emotionally charged scenes that had followed her mum’s unsuccessful IVF attempts.

‘You cannot think that way. You need to enjoy this pregnancy and you won’t if you spend the entire time anticipating a problem.’ She could leave that to him, he decided as he experienced a swell of helplessness, a reminder of the way he had felt when the first pregnancy had tragically ended.

He hadn’t known what to do, what to say, and anything he had said had sounded trite and inadequate. He’d felt utterly helpless to lessen the grief she'd been feeling and unwilling to examine his own grief; his conditioning had kicked in and he'd taken refuge in work.

He knew he had failed her and was determined he would not again. He could keep her safe and he would.

'And if there is a problem?'

'Then we will deal with it together.'

It sounded good but it was the part he left out that made her look away. If anything went wrong with this pregnancy there would be no reason for her to be here.

'You know what would make you feel better?'

She forced a smile and tried to ease the sadness away. 'I'm pretty sure you're going to tell me.'

'You need to brush up on your lying skills, because you really are a terrible liar.'

'You make it sound like that is a bad thing.'

'A good lie gets you out of many a sticky situation, and sincerity,' he said, 'is a very bad thing, diplomatically speaking. Of course, if you can feign it—' He reached out and caught one of her shoes before it hit him in the face.

'I wasn't aiming at you.'

'Then you have real potential. That's better,' he approved when she lost her battle to contain her mirth.

'If you wore heels you'd know they are not a subject for jokes.'

'You don't need heels, and I already struggle with door frames,' he said, watching her wriggle her toes as she stretched out her legs towards the coffee table. He registered the tiny smile playing around the corners of her mouth before, tongue between her teeth, she nudged the neatly arranged books with her outstretched foot, spoiling their geometrical precision.

With effort he prised his eyes from the long length of

her endless smooth legs. It did nothing to ease the pulsing need that had settled like a hot stone in his groin.

'Feel better now?'

'A little.'

'Sometimes saying what you want to is a luxury.'

His voice held no discernible inflection but something in his expression made her wonder if they were still talking book clubs. She somehow doubted it; the gleam she could see through the dark mesh of his lashes confirmed it.

The slow, heavy pump of her heart got louder in her ears. It was something that would be reckless to pursue, better leave it be.

Sound advice.

'What do you want to say?'

Playing with fire, Bea.

For a long moment he said nothing. 'Do you really want to know?'

She swallowed, frustrated at having the ball thrown back in her court. If she wanted this to go to the next level, he was saying she had to take the conscious step to make it happen… She'd have no one to blame but herself.

This was exactly the sort of situation she had sworn to avoid and here she was virtually running after it, running after him. She could feel that reckless *let tomorrow take care of itself* feeling creeping up on her. Even from this distance she could hear him breathing like someone who had just crossed the marathon finish line, or was that her?

Without taking his eyes off her, he levered himself into a sitting position, leaned across the table that separated them and ran a hand down the instep of one of her bare feet.

She sucked in a fractured breath, opened her mouth to say— She would never know what, because the phone that lay in the small beaded evening bag she had dumped on the table rang.

'Leave it!' he growled out as the noise shattered the moment.

Yanked back to reality and her senses and not nearly as grateful as she ought to be for the fact, Beatrice shook her head, pulled her feet back, tucking them under her as she delved into the bag. Pulling her phone out, she glanced at the screen.

'It's Maya. I have to take it.'

Dante's jaw clenched, all of him clenched as frustration pumped through his veins in a steady stream. 'Of course you do.' He doubted Beatrice heard him as she was already sweeping into the direction of the bedroom, her phone pressed to her ear.

When she returned a few minutes later Beatrice wasn't sure if Dante would still be there, then she saw him looking tall and dangerous, prowling up and down the room like a caged tiger, glass of something amber in his hand and the lamplight shading his impossibly high carved cheekbones.

'Maya says hello.'

He flashed her a look. 'I'm quite sure that's not what she said, but hello, Maya.' He raised his glass in a salute.

Beatrice's lips compressed as she glared at him. His continued pacing was really beginning to wind her up. As if she weren't already tense enough, and *guilty*.

Maya had to have picked up that she couldn't wait to get off the phone. Her concerned sister, whose only crime was to have bad or good timing, depending on how you looked at it.

She winced as she replayed the short conversation in

her head. The gratitude she ought to have felt for being saved from basically herself was absent. The problem being she wasn't sure that she'd wanted to be saved.

Who was she kidding? She definitely hadn't wanted to be saved.

He halted his relentless pacing, drained his glass and set it down. It didn't take the taint of guilt and regret from his mouth. It seemed insane now that he had ever thought he could handle the scent of her perfume, the sound of her voice. It was all part of his personal agony. Wanting her was driving him out of his mind; the lust was all-consuming—it wiped out every other consideration.

He was still the same person; his own needs always would take priority.

'I can't say I blame her.'

Beatrice felt emotion swell in her chest. He sounded tired…and while you couldn't consider someone who was six feet five of solid bone and muscle vulnerable, his defences seemed to have lowered. Whatever internal battle he was fighting might have lowered his defences, but the dangerous explosive quality that was innate to him was much closer to the surface.

'Maya has nothing against you.'

His eyes lifted and he smiled; it held no humour. 'Of course she doesn't.'

'It's true, she is…protective, that's all.'

'I get that, and I admire her for it. I admire you. You are both there for each other,' he said broodingly.

She watched as he set his glass down with a thud and reached for the brandy.

'We're sisters, that's what it's like. You know that, you have a brother.'

The moment the words left her lips she knew she'd said the wrong thing.

She could almost smell the adrenalin coming off him as he stalked towards her, stopping a foot or so away. She couldn't take her eyes off the muscle clenching and unclenching in his hollow cheek.

'I was never there for my brother!' The words came out, acrid with self-loathing.

The confusion swirling in her head deepened. She took a step towards him and laid a hand on his forearm, conscious as she did so of the quivering coiled tension in the muscle that was iron hard.

It didn't cross her mind to be afraid or even nervous; she had never been afraid of Dante.

'But you are, Dante. You are doing all this.' She gestured to the room they stood in. 'For Carl, you walked away from your life and you never blamed him once.'

'You think I am noble…that is so far from the truth, *cara*, that it is almost funny. I had no idea that he was gay, let alone that he was so unhappy.'

'Perhaps he wasn't ready to share.'

'I should have known,' Dante persisted stubbornly. 'What sort of brother doesn't know his brother is hating his life, is so unhappy?'

'Oh, Dante, I'm so sorry. But that is not your fault.'

'If I'd been any sort of brother, he would have felt able to come to me. He couldn't, he didn't. What sort of brother, man, does that make me?' He glanced down, seeming to notice for the first time the small hand on his arm.

He pushed it away and Beatrice, the hand he had rejected pressed up to her chest, stood there, absorbing his words. Her heart twisting in her chest for him, she felt helpless to ease the haunted guilt she could see shining in his dark eyes, but she knew she had to try.

'It's not your fault he was unhappy, but you could never make the decision for him, Dante. He had to find the courage in himself to do that, and he did.'

'Oh, yeah, I was a really great person to confide in,' he sneered. 'My brother was crying out for help, a silent scream, but I was too busy with my own life. I did what all certified selfish bastards do. I looked after number one.'

His anguish felt like a dull blade in her heart.

This time when she laid a hand on his arm, he didn't shrug it off.

'Have you spoken to Carl about this?' she asked, wary of putting too much pressure on him. 'Asked him how he feels? Told him how *you* feel?' Her hand slid down his forearm until it covered his hand, her fingers sliding in between his.

She already knew the answer to that. Dante was not a man who spoke about feelings, which made her sure that it would not be long before he was regretting sharing this much with her.

'We don't talk about it,' he said, thinking of the email that remained on his phone. His brother had said all he needed in that, and neither of them had referred to it since.

'Maybe you should…' She paused, her heart aching as she saw the guilt that was eating him up. 'Talk? Maybe *we* should talk too?'

'I've always lived for myself. I can't be the man… your—'

'You are my man, my husband.'

'What are you doing, Bea?' The pupils of his eyes expanded dramatically as his glance rested on his own hand, now caught between both of hers, as she raised it to her mouth and touched his fingertips with her lips.

She felt muscles bunch in rejection and let go of his hand, but only in order to reach up and grab the back of his neck, dragging his face down to enable her to slant her lips across his.

She wanted to say, *Here is my heart, Dante, let me love you*, but instead she said, 'Make love to me, Dante.'

It was a fight he was always going to lose.

He had no idea how long it lasted before a groan that reverberated through his body was wrenched from his throat as he dragged her to him.

One hand behind the back of her head, he covered her mouth with his, the heat an explosion as their lips touched, their tongues tangled. The passion released burnt everything but raw need away.

The only cool he was aware of was the feel of her hands on his skin as she pushed her hands under the fabric of his shirt, across his chest and down over his belly, causing him to suck in gasps and then groans of encouragement as she fought with the zip of his trousers.

He kissed the smooth skin of her shoulder, and both shoulders were bared as her dress slithered to the floor and lay in a silk pool at her feet.

His hands on her waist, he pushed her away, far enough for him to see the complete picture she made. Smooth golden limbs and feminine curves concealed only by a strapless bra and a minuscule pair of matching knickers.

'You look like a goddess,' he rasped with throaty awe.

'I feel like a woman. You make me feel like a woman, Dante.'

Without a word he scooped her up. She laid her head

against his bare chest as he carried her through to the bedroom they had once shared, that they would share tonight, and if this was all they had then she would take it.

She knew with total certainty that any pain down the line was worth tonight. Tonight she needed him as much as he needed her. He might not love her the way she loved him but she would take what he had to give.

Dante was *very* giving; his touch set her alight and fed the relentless hunger inside her. As he paused to fight free of his shirt, she kissed his chest, tasting the salt on his skin, and when he bent back, his body arching over her as he knelt astride her supine body, he took her face between his hands, and kissed her like a man starved.

It wasn't until he lowered himself that she realised her bra was gone, even though she hadn't felt the loss until her sensitised breasts were crushed against the hard barrier of his chest.

Her legs parted to his touch, a low moan of pleasure fighting its way through her clenched teeth as he teased the sensitive moist folds with skilful fingers.

She was mindless with the need to feel him inside her, to feel him deep, feel him touch where no other man had. The relief when her agony communicated itself to him and he settled between her parted legs made her sob, as her legs wrapped around his waist, urging him deeper; she was frustrated by the teasing strokes until finally he sank deep, wringing a feral moan from her lips as her body arched up to meet him. As her nerve endings sang all the sensations merged into one glorious whole, they merged, they were one—*almost*.

As her climax came within reach Beatrice felt she was about to shatter into a thousand pieces. It was too much, too intense, then as it hit she was not broken, but miraculously whole again. She lost herself in the feeling as wave after wave of pleasure rippled along every individual nerve ending in her body.

After it ended, and he lay breathing hard on top of her, responding to a primal need to extend this intimacy, she wrapped her arms around his waist and whispered fiercely, *'Stay,'* against the damp skin of his neck.

He kissed her and pulled her head onto his chest and they lay, still joined, until she felt him stir inside her.

Her wide eyes flicked to his face so close to her own.

'You make me hungry, *cara*.'

'You make me greedy.'

Later that night they made love again, slower and with infinite tenderness, exploring each other's bodies with an endless fascination. The lightest touch of his hand and mouth made her body vibrate with pleasure. She sobbed with the intensity of it and every touch was heightened by the shattering depth, the sheer *intensity* of emotions that accompanied each brush of her skin.

When the deep release came it took her a long time to float back to earth.

Did she say, 'I love you,' over and over as she sobbed or was that part a dream?

Beatrice was not sure.

Dante did not sleep. Beatrice lay sleeping in his arms. His heart contracted when he looked at the perfect beauty of her face. It was hard feeling what he did when he looked at her, to hold on to the lie he told himself that what they shared was just sex, but it would never be *just* anything with Beatrice. He might try and deny it but deep down he had always known that. He felt a fool that he had ever imagined he could treat Beatrice like other women. She had always been different, she had always made him feel… Jaw clenched, he blocked the thought process before it led him to a place he was not ready to go, a truth he was not ready to see.

A man could change; she had made him believe that, because against all the odds she believed in him. As he looked down at the woman lying like a sleeping angel in his arms, he vowed to deserve her faith.

CHAPTER TWELVE

IT WAS STILL dark when Dante sliding away from her woke Beatrice. She stretched and stopped, the memories that explained the stiffness of her muscles flooding back. She reached out in the dark, her hand touching the smooth warm skin of his back.

Seated on the edge of the bed, he responded to her sleepy murmur of protest with a kiss that deepened as her lips softened beneath the pressure before he pulled away abruptly.

Suddenly cold even though the air was warm, she shivered.

'Who has a conference call in the middle of the night?' she complained, raising herself on one elbow and pushing the silky skein of hair from her sleepy eyes, desire ribboning through her and settling heavy and low in her abdomen as she smelt him on her skin.

'The half of the world that has been awake hours. It is what living in a global economy is all about, and it is not night…'

He heard her reach out for the lamp and covered her hand with his. 'No, leave it.' If he saw her, read the sultry invitation in her eyes and remembered feeling the aftershocks of her climax as they'd stayed joined as one, he was pretty sure that he would never get to that call.

She ignored him—of course she did.

She looked every bit as wanton and glorious as he had imagined as she sat there, her perfect breasts partially concealed by her hair.

She pouted. 'I don't want to be awake.' She didn't want the night to end; she knew it would, she just didn't want to think about it yet.

He slanted a kiss across her lips, the touch making her shiver, and flicked off the light.

'Then go back to sleep.'

It was a week later that Dante walked into the drawing room just as a young woman was walking out. This was the second time this week he had managed to arrange his day to include lunch with Beatrice.

On one level he couldn't believe he was trying to earn brownie points from his own wife, but amazingly he actually found that his new schedule made him more productive.

'Who was that?'

'My new PA.'

His eye-framing dark brows lifted. 'You are not letting the grass grow under your feet.'

'She came highly recommended.'

'By whom?'

'Jacintha.'

His brow furrowed as he loosened his tie. 'Who is Jacintha, again?'

'The maid. The one with the red hair and cool glasses.'

'You hired a PA on the say-so of a maid?'

'Should I have run it past you?' she challenged.

'Not at all.'

She smiled. 'Well, Jacintha's recommendation, and those of her previous employers.' She gave a small smug smile as she listed them, watching his eyes widen. 'I know working for me does seem like a step down, but she wants to come home because her mother has a heart condition. The best thing is she is not related even by marriage to any of *the* families.' It did not take long to figure out that most of the top positions in the palace were given to relatives or cronies of a handful of historically powerful San Macizan families.

'This will cause a storm in a champagne glass, you know that?' he mused, watching her face with a half-smile as he perched on the edge of the polished mahogany desk and began to leaf through the diary that lay open. 'Wow, you have hit the ground running,' he remarked as he skimmed through the entries written in her distinctive hand. 'Oh, leave Tuesday morning free. I've made an appointment with the obstetrician and—' He stopped and leaned in closer as he reread the most recent entry that had caught his attention before he stabbed it with his finger. 'What is this?'

'What is what?' she asked, not understanding the ice in his voice.

'"Fun run, five K, fancy dress optional",' he read out.

'Oh, that's Lara. She rang earlier. She is organising a fun run for the children's hospice. I agreed to take part.'

'That is out of the question.' The diary closed with a decisive click and he was on his feet looking tall, austere, and oozing simmering disapproval while inside his gut was churning with visceral fear.

She clung to her temper and reminded herself that this fragile peace between them required concessions on both sides. 'I don't have to wear fancy dress.'

'Running five K is a reckless risk in your condition.'

Her lips tightened as she pushed out her chin to an aggressive angle and, hands on her hips, stalked towards him, stopping a couple of feet away. 'There is nothing reckless about it. It is basically a fun jog or walk for a good cause, and I will enjoy it!'

'The risk is too great.'

Struggling to channel a calm she was not feeling, Beatrice held his stormy gaze. 'Do you really think that I would risk the life of our child on a whim?'

His eyes slid from her own, his chest lifting, before returning as he growled out reluctantly, 'No. The last time—'

The shadow of fear she glimpsed in this strong, seemingly invulnerable man's eyes drained the anger from her. She hurt for him because he couldn't own that fear, he couldn't reach out. 'I'm scared too, Dante,' she confessed, tears standing out in her eyes. 'But I can't…'

Nostrils flaring, he looked down into her face and felt the anger and frustration drain away. 'I'm your husband. Why won't you let me protect you?'

'Protect, not suffocate.' She took his silence as encouragement and added, 'And I'll make my own appointment, choose my own doctor.'

'Shall I come back later?'

Dante stepped back and gestured towards the table under the window embrasure. 'No, that's fine,' he said to the maid, without taking his eyes from Beatrice's face. 'Put it on the table.'

'Shall I fetch another cup?'

'No!' Beatrice supplied as the door closed silently behind the scared-looking young maid. 'So, I'll tell Lara, no, you won't come to cheer me on, shall I? She figured that would be worth double in sponsorship.'

He dragged a hand through his dark hair, the internal

struggle clear on the hard drawn lines on his handsome face. 'I will donate, and I'll come and support you.'

Her jaw dropped at the capitulation. 'You'll come.'

He shrugged. 'Someone has to make sure you don't decide to get competitive, but in return—'

'Return for what?' she began explosively before literally biting her tongue. 'In return what?'

'In return you go and see the doctor I made the appointment with. She is the best.'

Was it really a point worth making? She released a long hissing breath. 'All right.' She fixed him with a warning glance. 'But the next time you make a unilateral decision concerning me or the baby—don't!'

He gave a slow smile. 'I wouldn't dare.'

The walk through the private grounds calmed Beatrice after the confrontation. Gradually her pace slowed to a stroll as the healing of the quiet and solitude and nature's beauty seeped imperceptibly into her.

She remained, what? Wary, confused? Nobody in the universe made her *feel* as much as Dante did, and she couldn't get the fear she had seen in his eyes out of her head.

Instead of lunch with his wife, Dante spent a half hour pounding his body into submission in the private gym.

His mind remained another matter. Had he made the right decision? He knew that their marriage could not survive if they maintained a war of attrition. There had to be compromise even though it went against his instincts, and the idea of her running…falling… He threw himself into the next series of repetitions in the hope the pain in his muscles would drown out the torturous thought in his head.

Drenched with sweat, he was finally heading for the shower when he felt it.

Around him, weights in their cradles began to shake as the low distinctive subterranean growl of the earthquake built.

His first thought was Beatrice. He didn't pause. He grabbed his phone and got a low static buzz…and hit the ground running. Face set in grim lines, he was exiting the leisure facility when he encountered a uniformed figure who, without a word, fell into step beside him.

'We have set up a command centre in the old armoury to coordinate all rescue efforts.'

Dante nodded his approval. It made sense; the walls were ten feet thick and the building was cut into solid rock. 'Highness, we have choppers ready and waiting and the King and Queen will be evacuated as a priority. It's the communications that are the problem.'

'I'm on that…'

'My wife?'

'She left by the south-west door, heading in the direction of the sunken garden, twenty minutes ago.'

Lifting a finger in acknowledgement, Dante picked up his pace, leaving the military figure behind.

Bea dropped the flower she had just picked and froze, trying to figure out if she was having a dizzy spell or… The answer to her question came in the form of a deep primal subterranean roar that went on and on, it felt like for hours. She wasn't swaying but the ground was.

It stopped, and there was a total silence. Not even a bird sang or a bee buzzed, then, as if a switch had been flicked, individual sounds began to emerge from the silence. The noise built; there were cries from all directions mingling with the distant sound of sirens.

Beatrice hadn't moved; there'd just been an earthquake. What did she do, stay outside or go indoors? The sounds were mostly coming from the buildings.

She was still standing in frozen indecision when a familiar figure wearing running shorts and a gym vest appeared. She let out a sigh of relief. Dante was here; things would be all right. It might be illogical when you were dealing with the forces of nature, but she believed it. But he didn't know she was there.

Tears ran down her face as she tried to cry out, but nothing came, then, it was a miracle, just before he would have vanished from her eyeline, he turned.

A moment later he was racing towards her.

His name was lost in the warmth of his mouth as he grabbed her by the shoulders and dragged her into him. Crushing her as he kissed her with the hunger of a starving man.

When the kiss stopped, he lifted his head. 'Beatrice, you're safe…you're safe… Oh, God!' he groaned, dragging his hands down either side of her face, framing her delicate features, a mixture of frustration and fascination stamped on his face.

'I want…this is…' Teeth clenched, he set her away from him. 'We experienced an earthquake.' Unable to take his eyes off her, he ran his hands up and down her arms as he scanned her face. 'There may be aftershocks. You can't be here. Are you hurt?'

She shook her head. 'No, I'm fine. So that was an earthquake.'

'Yes.'

He sounded very calm and maybe it was catching

because she could breathe again without panting. 'I'm scared.'

'Yes.'

'I want to help…'

'No—no, you don't.'

Hands on her shoulders, he led her firmly back in the direction she had just come into the open green space of the gardens. He pushed her down on a stone bench and squatted down beside her.

'Listen carefully. I have to go,' he admitted, frustration etched in the strong lines of his face. 'But I won't be long. You stay here and if… There might be aftershocks and if there are, just get under this.' He patted the bench. 'You'll be safe, and I'll be back.'

She nodded. 'Be careful.'

Already feet away and jogging, he turned and grinned over his shoulder, waving a hand as though he were off for his morning run.

An hour later, Dante was relieved to see Bea sitting in the same place he had left her, but she seemed to have been joined by a dog.

The dog gave a warning growl when he approached, then licked his hand when he offered it. By the time he knelt beside Beatrice they were best friends.

'He just appeared,' she said, adding urgently, 'The earthquake, Dante?'

'So, right, first indications are it's not too bad.'

'Thank goodness!' She hadn't really been conscious of how high her tension levels were until they lowered, leaving her knees literally shaking as she reached out to stroke the fawning dog.

'What does not too bad mean?' she pressed cautiously as he pulled himself to his feet. It was weird that she loved the fluid grace of his movements, even at a time like this.

'Riota had the worse of it.'

She nodded, knowing that the only things on the uninhabited rocky outcrop a mile off the coast were the native tough sheep who, it had been explained, were ferried out there each breeding season and brought back after lambing.

'The damage is concentrated on the east coast.'

She released another little gusty sigh. It was another area where the rugged terrain meant there were no settlements.

'There was a landslip so the coast road is blocked, which is causing some problems. As far as I can tell from reports, the damage to outlying areas is minimal and, though there have been a few minor injuries, nothing significant so far. Except, of course, I'm sure it feels significant for the people involved. I need to get to Mentsa. The emergency services are coping but there is some panic. The church tower there has fallen.

'We're still assessing the airport, but the helicopter that dropped Carl off has already taken my parents to the mainland, and a few essential—'

At the mention of his parents, she shook her head.

'I get it,' she said, struggling not to judge, but it was hard when you compared the powerful couple's apparent response to their son's. Dante's instinct was to protect his people and theirs was to protect themselves.

She struggled to subdue her anger—this was not the time or the place—but she was determined to point it out the next time they criticised anything Dante did—always assuming that she would be here to say anything.

The abrupt realisation brought with it a wave of desolation as, still playing mental catch-up, she dragged her wandering thoughts back to the present.

'Carl is here?'

'He was on the mainland.' He slid his foot into his boot and looked up, meeting her eyes. 'I followed your advice and we were going to meet up and talk in person. He jumped in a chopper as soon as he heard. He's persuaded Grandfather to evacuate, along with you and some of the—'

Well, good luck with that, she thought. 'Along with me?' she interrupted.

Dante bent his head to tighten the belt on the trousers he had exchanged for his shorts. Nobody had produced a shirt; he still wore the vest that clung to the contours of his muscled chest and exposed the powerful musculature of his arms. He flashed her an impatient look.

'Don't be difficult,' he pleaded.

'I thought you said there is no danger.'

'There isn't.'

She gave an eloquent shrug and stood her ground.

'I'll just have someone gather a few essentials for you and be ready in five minutes. Someone will—'

'I've only just got back. I'm not going anywhere.' This was so frustrating; she had so much she needed to say. 'Are *you* leaving?'

He stood with his phone half raised to his ear. 'I'll be fine.'

'I have no doubt,' she countered coolly. 'That wasn't what I asked.'

'Me leave!'

He looked so offended by the mere suggestion and for a moment the surge of warmth and love she felt for this man swamped everything else she was feeling.

'That would hardly send out the right message. Panic

is the problem. My presence will hopefully help keep a lid on things. What are you doing? The helicopters are waiting. You need to get going and I need…' *You*, he thought and shooed the thought away.

She swallowed. 'You're hurt.' She walked up to him and touched the graze on his cheek that was seeping blood.

He moved back from her touch, a spasm of dismissal twisting his lips; he could not afford any distractions. 'It is nothing. You need to hurry.' He caught her wrists and looked down at her, allowing himself the indulgence for a moment of drinking in her lovely face.

'Your grandfather isn't going to go quietly.' Yet another worry for his already overburdened, though very broad, shoulders to bear.

Dante fought the reluctance to release her wrists and stepped back. 'He's a stubborn old— But don't worry,' he added, moderating his tone. 'We'll make sure he's all right.'

'Yes, I know you will,' she said, shaking back her hair and gathering it in one hand with a practised double twist of her wrist, then securing it in a haphazard ponytail on the base of her neck. 'So, what do you want me to do?'

He stared at her as though she were talking a foreign language. 'What are you talking about, Beatrice? I really don't have the time for you to— How am I supposed to focus if I'm worried about you?'

'I'm not going.'

'Beatrice…!'

'How about I trust you to take care of yourself, and you trust me? I can absolutely promise you that I have no intention of putting myself in harm's way,' she said, standing there with a protective hand pressed to her stomach.

After a moment of silence, she saw the flash of something in his eyes before he tipped his head in silent acknowledgement.

'I haven't got time for this.'

'That's what I was counting on,' she admitted and drew a grin that briefly lightened the sombre cast of his expression.

'All right. I'm staying, you're staying. But if you—'

She waved her hand in a gesture of impatience. 'Get under your feet? Faint? I get it. As always, your opinion of me is flattering,' she observed drily. 'Just go do your stuff, Dante.'

He stood there, his body clenched as duty warred with instinct. His instinct was telling him to carry her, kicking and screaming if necessary, to safety. His duty was to keep everybody safe, but how could he do that if he didn't know Beatrice was safe? His normal ability to compartmentalise deserted him in the moment as he looked down at her. Despite his terror at the thought of her and their child coming to harm, a terror that only increased when he imagined not being there for her, his eyes glowed with admiration.

The next time anyone said anything about genes he would tell the bastards that his wife knew more about the meaning of service and duty than the rest of his family put together!

Still he hesitated, unwilling, unable, to leave her, all his instincts telling him it was his job to protect her.

'Is that my protection detail?' she said, as three uniformed figures appeared on the horizon.

He nodded. 'Do as they tell you.'

'I will.'

She saw him exchange words with the approaching detail as their paths crossed, but they were too distant for her to hear what was said.

All three of the tough-looking military types, not seeming breathless even though they'd been running, paused with brief formality to bow when they reached her.

One stepped up. 'Highness, we are—' He broke off and, one hand pressed to his earpiece, turned away, listening.

'Is there a problem?' Beatrice asked anxiously.

The men exchanged glances, as though asking each other if it was appropriate to respond.

'My husband…?'

'His Highness will have received the information. It is confirmation that the palace has escaped any real structural damage, so it is safe to return. Actually the first reports suggest that there is very little structural damage at all, but there has been a partial wall collapse.'

'Inside the palace?' Beatrice asked.

He nodded. 'The nursery.'

The fine muscles around her mouth quivered. There were still wisps of panic floating through her head, but she was able to speak like a relatively calm person even if inside felt a lot less confident of her ability to cope.

'Are there casualties?' she asked, her thoughts quickly moving past her insecurities to the children she had seen on a visit earlier that week. She felt her eyes fill and blinked away the moisture as she pushed the now poignant memories away.

Tears were not going to help. Tears were for later, hopefully along with smiles. Right now she needed to focus.

'By some miracle it seems not.'

The tears she had tried to suppress spilled out, along with a laugh of sheer relief.

'Apparently they were all in the playground. There are scrapes and cuts, all minor, and a hell of a lot of hysterical parents arriving. The emergency services are having a lot of trouble. We need to keep them in one place. They need to take a headcount, but it's like—and I quote—*"herding cats"*, which makes it really hard for them to assess the situation.'

'The headmistress struck me as pretty competent. Is she still there?'

'She is concussed and has been hospitalised, so the main priority is to move the children and parents out of the immediate area without losing track of any children, so that we can secure the building against any potential aftershocks. It sounds simpler than it is. It's pandemonium.'

'But someone is helping.'

'Us, once you are safe, Highness.'

She held up a hand and wished she possessed half the calm she was channelling. 'Why waste time? Take me with you.'

The military figure shook his head. 'Our instructions are to—'

'I'm giving you new instructions. What's the harm? You said it's safe.'

CHAPTER THIRTEEN

DANTE WAS ON the way to the airport, which luckily had suffered no damage, and he was speaking to his brother via speakerphone.

'I should get there before your flight leaves. Do you have to fly straight out?'

'I've got a meeting I can't get out of tomorrow.'

'Right. I should make it before your flight if there are no hold-ups.'

'Is your heroine wife with you?'

'Heroine… Beatrice, you mean?'

'You got any other wives? They are playing the video on the big screens and there's not a dry eye in the house. She had all the kids singing and she's carrying the little guy—'

Dante could feel the pressure build in his temples as he tried to speak. He managed to get the words past his clenched lips on the third attempt. 'Beatrice is at the nursery, the one where the wall collapsed?' The news of a successful evacuation had reached him but not that his wife was involved in the process.

'Well, she was earlier, but the parents are being interviewed now and all are singing her praises. You're going to have to name a park after her, or put up a statue or something.'

Dante, who did not connect with the amusement in his brother's voice, swore loud and fluently, cutting his brother off mid-flow. He brought the car around in a vicious one-hundred-and-eighty-degree turn that sent up a dust cloud of gravel, and floored the gas pedal.

Beatrice spent a luxurious half hour in a hot shower, washing off the accumulated dirt and grime. Dressed in a blue silk robe, her long wet hair wrapped in a towel twisted into a turban, she walked back into the bedroom. She had checked her phone sixty seconds ago but she checked it again. Nothing since the missed call earlier, but the mobile mast had been down for a good part of the day and there were numerous black spots on the island.

She sighed. At times like this a fertile imagination was not a friend. She knew that she wouldn't be able to relax until she had contact from Dante again.

She walked over to the mirror, untwisted the turban and began to pat her long hair dry. She had picked up a brush to complete the task when the door burst open.

Dante stood there, his tall, lean frame filling the doorway, wearing fatigue pants that clung to his narrow hips; the vest that might once have been white was stained with dust and dirt. His dark skin seemed liberally coated with the same debris.

Relief flooded through her as her face broke into a smile of dizzy relief. 'Dante!' She was halfway across the room when she realised that something was very wrong. 'Are you hurt? Has something happ—'

'Quite a lot, it seems.'

She stopped dead. She could hear the flame pushing against the ice in his voice, and literally feel the raw emotion pulsing off him.

'I asked you to stay safe, I asked you… You promised, and what do you do?' He advanced a step towards her and paused, close enough now for her to see the muscle throbbing in his lean cheek. 'I trusted you to take care of yourself and our baby and then what do I discover? That you decided to put yourself and…and our child straight in the path of danger, quite deliberately.'

She gulped. 'The nursery, you mean? There was no danger. It was just, just…herding cats, that was all.'

'You could have died,' he rasped hoarsely.

She looked at this strange, coldly furious Dante and fell back on defiance. 'You could die crossing the road.'

A hissing sound left his white clenched lips.

'I told you to stay safe.'

Her chin lifted. 'And I made my own judgement.'

'You put our child in danger.'

'How dare you?' she cried, surging towards him, her hands clenched into fists, not sure in the moment if the anger fizzing up inside her was directed at the insulting accusation or the fact he was confirming that that was what this was about. It wasn't her safety; it was the baby. It was always about the baby, this time and last time.

Suddenly she was angry with herself as much as him for wanting to believe differently, wanting to believe she was more than a means to an end, a person, not an incubator.

He watched as, hands outstretched, she backed away from him, her chest heaving.

'How dare you even suggest that?' she began, her low, intense voice building in volume with each successive syllable. 'You are the father. Does it make you a bad father for putting yourself in danger today? No, that makes you a man doing the right thing. Well, I did the right thing today too. Women do not stay at home waiting for the heroes' return and knitting socks these days…my child was never in any danger at any point!'

Unable to stop seeing her body crushed beneath a pile of rubble, her dead eyes looking up at him, the nightmare vision playing on a loop in his head, he barely registered what she was saying.

'If it wasn't for the baby…' *for me*, the voice in his head condemned '…you wouldn't even be here today.' In danger and it was all down to him. He hadn't been there for her; he had never been there for her.

Just as he'd never been there for Carl.

She flinched as though he had struck her. 'I am aware of that,' she said, hugging the crushing hurt to herself. Did he think she needed that pointed out?

'Things need to change. Your safety is all that matters. You must come first.'

She stood there, knowing he meant the baby, but letting herself imagine for a moment how it might feel if the fierce protective emotion in his dark eyes was really for her, and when the moment passed she felt flat and empty. 'Some things you can't change.' You couldn't make someone love you and it was about time she started dealing with facts.

'I have to go.'

'Of course you do,' she said flatly.

'To the airport to say…things I need to say to my brother.'

'Well, don't expect me to be here when you get back because I'm going to keep my baby safe and I don't feel safe here, with you.' Like arrows, she aimed the words at his broad back.

Did he flinch at the impact? She didn't know, but she hoped so.

* * *

Dante got out of the car in front of the airport terminal and realised he didn't remember driving there at all. *Now that couldn't be a good thing, could it?*

As he strode in he glanced at the departure board. He had just caught his brother. He dodged some airport officials bearing down on him and tried not to notice a group sharing their experiences with a camera crew.

He almost made it.

'And here we have the Crown Prince himself, who was in the thick of it,' an enterprising journalist said, shoving a microphone in his face. 'Would you say this has been a lucky escape, sir?' He started to trot as it became obvious that Dante was not slowing down. 'The buildings here are pretty robust.'

'And the people,' Dante responded, walking on.

'The rebuilding,' the guy called after him.

Rebuilding. Dante's pace slowed for the first time as the scene with Beatrice flashed before his eyes. He had not rebuilt; he had demolished the progress they had made in a matter of minutes.

Carl, who was scanning a laptop that lay across his knees, looked up when Dante entered, closing the door on his bodyguard who stood outside. He set aside the computer and got up, walking straight across to his brother, wrapping him in a brotherly hug, which Dante returned.

Carl stepped back and, though half a head shorter than his younger brother, retained his grip on Dante's shoulders.

'Thank you for this.'

Carl looked bemused by the warm words. 'For what?'

'For coming back. And I'm sorry. I should have said it before, but I am truly.'

Carl shook his head. 'I hate to repeat myself, but for what?'

'For not being there for you. I *should* have had your back.'

Carl looked astonished. 'But you did.'

'I didn't know.'

'You were my younger brother. I couldn't burden you with my problems, with the emphasis on *"my"*. It took me a long time to get to that point. I was either going to accept the status quo or take that leap of faith, and you know me, I'm not like you. I was never one to put my head over the parapet and risk having it knocked off. I was the "toe the line for a quiet life" son.'

Though Dante looked thoughtful as he listened to this ruthless self-assessment, his expression and emotions were locked firmly in self-condemnation mode.

'I should have known how unhappy you were.'

'It wasn't about being unhappy. I was always just a wrong fit. I could never inspire the way you do. It's true!' Carl exclaimed when Dante shook his head, looking patently uncomfortable.

'This was always my decision to make and for a long time I wasn't brave enough.' His hand fell from his brother's shoulders. 'I'm happy I've met someone. And you have Beatrice back. How is the heroine?'

'I love her,' Dante said in a driven voice. He looked shocked. 'I love her,' he repeated slowly. 'Is this how it feels?' he asked, a kind of wonder in his voice. 'Oh, hell, I've been such an idiot.'

'Have you told her any of this?'

'She deserves better.'

'Than what?'

'Me! I'm a selfish bastard.'

'I have to tell you, brother, I prefer you as a bastard

than a martyr. Maybe Beatrice does too,' he added slyly, and watched the hope flare in his brother's eyes.

'What are you doing?'

Beatrice gave a start and spun around, her blonde hair almost flaring out then settling in a silky curtain to her shoulder blades as she faced Dante, who stood with his broad shoulders propped against the wall beside the door.

Once she moved past the head-spinning blood rush of adrenalin that had her poised in 'deer in the headlights' mode, she realised that, though the anger he had been nursing earlier had gone, it had been replaced by an explosive quality. He made her think of a time bomb ticking down, every taut muscle and clenched sinew stretched to the limit.

'I've just been packing.'

'So, you're running away?'

She turned away as she felt her eyes fill. 'I'm moving rooms,' she contradicted. 'I'm not sure I could be termed essential travel. It's ironic. I can cope with the petty official and your family, but, you're right, I am leaving because I can't stay with a man who doesn't trust me. You're not wrapping me in cotton wool, you're suffocating me!'

He flinched. 'I know I said some unforgivable things but when I knew that you had been… I just went like ice inside. I felt terror, real gut-freezing terror. I haven't felt that way since you lost the baby. I felt so bloody helpless.'

Her eyes fluttered wide with shock.

'I could see the pain in your eyes and I didn't know what to say. I couldn't help you. It was the worst feeling of my entire life, seeing you hurt. And being the emotionally crippled mess-up I am, I had no words…' He made a sound of boiling frustration between his clenched teeth as she grabbed his head in both hands. 'I should have been able to make you feel better. I should have kept you safe. I failed you and this time… I cannot *bear* to see you go through that again.' He swallowed hard, and captured her eyes with his agonised gaze. 'I swore to myself that I'd keep you safe but all I've ended up doing is pushing you away—*again*!'

'I'm still here.'

He extended his hands towards her and after a moment she took them. 'Don't leave me, Beatrice. Stay with me.'

'I'm frightened too,' she whispered.

'But you are no coward. You are the bravest person I know, and now the world knows too. I am proud of you and even if there was no baby, I would love you.'

Her lips quivered as she looked up at him, drinking in the details of his marvellous face. 'I love you, Dante.'

He bent his head, the ferocious hunger of his kiss leaving her limp and ludicrously happy as he trailed a finger down the curve of her cheek. 'I adore you. I am half a man without you but—'

She pressed a finger to his lips; she was not interested in buts. She had heard all she needed to. 'I love you, Dante. I always have and I always will.'

He caught her hand, his eyes not leaving her face as he pressed it to his lips. 'I love you, Beatrice. I thought loving you meant letting you go free, but now I know that I can't make that choice for you. It is yours to make.'

Raising herself on tiptoes, she took his face between her hands. 'I choose love.' She kissed him. 'I choose you.' She kissed him. 'I choose staying…say that again,' she said fiercely.

'What part?'

'The only part that matters, idiot. Say you love me!'

'I love you, Beatrice!'

She wound her arms around his neck, her feet leaving the floor as he kissed her back.

The kisses took them to the bed where, when they finally came up for air, they lay face to face, thigh to thigh, gazing into each other's eyes.

'I love your mouth,' she husked, exploring the individual dust-engrained lines on his face slowly, as if memorising them.

'Did Carl catch his flight?'

Dante nodded, unable to take his eyes off her face.

'And you two, are you okay?'

She was relieved when he nodded again.

'I'm glad.'

'So am I.'

'So what time is your parents' flight back?'

'They've delayed until tomorrow.' A sardonic smile twisted his lips. 'So the dust will literally have settled.' He slid a hand down her thigh and pulled it up and across his waist, dragging her in closer.

'This would be much better with no clothes.'

'It will be, but there is no hurry.'

She sighed and gave a sinuous wriggle closer, loving the hard lines of his body.

'I have a message for you from them.'

'Oh, don't spoil it!'

'They have asked me to inform you that it makes them very happy that you've returned. They are talking about a renewal of our vows.'

She felt her jaw drop. 'Is that some sort of joke?'

'No joke, they tell me you are *trending…*'

Her eyes flew wide. *'What?'*

'A photo of you has gone viral.'

He rolled far enough away to pull his phone from his pocket and scrolled to the photo that showed a golden-haired, jeans-clad Beatrice against a background of billowing dust, surrounded by a group of children who were all caught in the moment, looking up at her, while two of the smallest ones were thrown one over each shoulder. Dust particles caught by a ray of light made it seem as though she were surrounded by a shimmering golden glow.

After a slight hesitation she rolled forward, anchoring her hair from her face with her forearm. It afforded him a view of her face while she scanned the image that was the sort guaranteed to make a photographer's career.

It was no surprise to him that online fame did not seem to thrill her.

'Oh, God!'

'You don't look thrilled at the fame—*hashtag heroineprincess*.'

It took her a moment to recognise the moment someone had captured in an idealised version. The reality had involved dust and noise and a gut-wrenching sense of urgency as, afraid she would lose one of her charges, she'd tried to get them out of the exclusion zone around the unstable wall.

'It's embarrassing,' she countered, 'and I was not being brave. I was at my wits' end. It *was* like herding cats.'

'My parents are very impressed. They believe that you are an asset to the family, and, yes, that is a direct quote.'

Suddenly she was so angry she could barely breathe, let alone speak. When she finally made her vocal cords work, what her voice lacked in force it made up for in throbbing, furious sincerity. 'It really has nothing to do with them!'

'This is something I pointed out.'

She huffed out a tiny breath. 'Good!'

'They then informed me that it was my duty to save my marriage.'

'I hope you told them to stuff their duty!' she exploded.

'I did not use those words precisely, but that was the sentiment behind my response. I hate my life without you in it. It's a life with no heartbeat, no soul. I love you.' His gaze sank to the pulse pumping at the base of her throat. Her neck extended as he bent to kiss the pulse spot, his mouth moist against her hot skin.

'Because I'm an asset? Did they really say that? Should we tell them about the baby, do you think?'

The tentative question was lost on Dante. She was smiling into his eyes and he had never seen anything so beautiful in his life.

'I can't tell if I can hear your heartbeat or mine.'

'We have one, we are one. I love you, Beatrice. Being without you made me realise how much. Life without you is not a whole life. I'm not whole. I have a Beatrice-sized empty space inside me. When we married, I didn't know what love was,' he admitted. 'But you taught me how to love, and I know I will never love another woman. It isn't possible—we are two halves that make a whole.'

There were tears glimmering like diamonds in her eyes by the time he finished. 'I choose, I choose to be with you, always.'

'I love you, Beatrice. Stay with me, be my wife and

let me be *me* with you, even if I have to be royal for the world.'

She flung her arms around his neck, grinning as tears streamed down her face. 'You'll never get rid of me, Dante, not now, not ever.'

Several moments later a maid walked in; her eyes flew wide as she saw the couple locked in a passionate embrace.

Within thirty minutes the entire palace knew the Princess they loved was home for good; there was a collective sigh of relief. They knew the couple was their future.

EPILOGUE

'CAN I HOLD HER?' Rachel Monk whispered.

Standing beside the open French doors that led onto a flower-filled balcony, Beatrice smiled at her mother, who stood there looking too young to be a grandmother in her bold emerald green dress coat, a jaunty hat and heels that showed off her great legs.

Carefully she gave the sleeping baby to her mother.

'Not much point being quiet with that lot down there.' The christening party was still in full swing.

'You know I am so proud of you, don't you… Bea?'

'And I'm proud of you.' Her mum's work with the charity for women in abusive relationships had won more than her own admiration.

They had both moved on from the past.

'I wish your father was here.'

'Oh, I think he is—have you seen that chin, the dimple?' she said, looking down fondly at her daughter's face. Everything else about Sabina Elsa was pure Dante. Her daughter was going to be a beauty.

'She is a miracle.'

Beatrice turned her head. 'What are you doing, creeping up on us like that?' she asked, looking up at her tall, gorgeous husband with smiling eyes. 'She *is* a miracle,' she added softly.

They would always grieve for their lost baby, but it was balanced by the joy that his or her sister had brought into their lives. They both knew how lucky they were; they told each other so every day.

'Say cheese!'

They both turned as Maya, dressed in a bright orange minidress, appeared, camera in hand. 'Wow,' she said, looking at the results on her phone screen. 'That kid, sorry, my god-daughter, is a natural. Your mum takes a good photo too, Dante. This one of her pinching one of the waiters' bottoms is classic.'

'Oh, God, Maya, delete that right now,' Beatrice gasped.

Her sister twisted away as Beatrice went to grab her phone.

'We said no phones.'

'I'm exempt, and, anyway, Carl made me do it and he's royal.'

'You're impossible.'

Dante came up behind her and slid his arms around her waist, pulling her into him until he could rest his chin on the top of her glossy head. '*This* is my family and all that I need. A tabloid would pay good money for that snap, Maya.'

'Now he tells me.'

Grinning, Dante bent and whispered something in his wife's ear.

He laughed, loving that she could blush…loving her.

'You know, I used to think this place was a prison, but you opened the doors, let in the light that made me love you and set me free.'

'Oh, get a room!' Carl exclaimed, walking in.

It was a palace—they had a lot to choose from!

* * * * *

HER HARD TO RESIST HUSBAND

TINA BECKETT

To my husband, who stands beside me
through thick and thin.

And to my editor, Suzy, for making me
dig deeper than I ever thought I could.

CHAPTER ONE

TRACY HINTON DIDN'T faint.

Her stomach squirmed and threatened to give way as the scent of death flooded her nostrils, but she somehow held it together. Calming herself with slow, controlled breaths was out of the question, because breathing was the last thing she wanted to do right now.

"How many are there?" She fitted the protective mask over her nose and mouth.

"Six deaths so far, but most of the town is affected." Pedro, one of her mobile clinic workers, nodded towards the simple clay-brick house to his left, where an eerily still figure was curled in a fetal position on the porch. Another body lay a few yards away on the ground. "They've been dead for a few days. Whatever it was, it hit fast. They didn't even try to make it to a hospital."

"They were probably too sick. Besides, the nearest hospital is twenty miles away."

Piauí, one of the poorest of the Brazilian states, was more vulnerable to catastrophic infections than the wealthier regions, and many of these outlying townships relied on bicycles or their own two feet for transportation. It was hard enough to make a twenty-mile trek even when one was young and healthy, which these poor souls had not been. And cars were a luxury most couldn't afford.

She wouldn't know for sure what had caused the deaths

until she examined the bodies and gathered some specimens. The nearest diagnostic hospital was a good hundred miles from here. In any case, she'd have to report the possibility of an epidemic to the proper authorities.

Which meant she'd have to deal with Ben.

Pedro shook his head. "Dengue, you think?"

"Not this time. There's some blood on the front of the man's shirt, but nothing else that I can see from this distance." She stared at the crude corral where several pigs squealed out a protest at the lack of food. "I'm thinking lepto."

Pedro frowned. "Leptospirosis? Rainy season's already over."

The area around the house consisted of a few desiccated twigs and hard-packed clay, confirming her colleague's words. The sweltering heat sucked any remaining moisture from the air and squeezed around her, making her nausea that much worse. Situated close to the equator, the temperature of this part of Brazil rarely dipped below the hundred-degree mark during the dry season. The deadly heat would only grow worse, until the rains finally returned.

"They have pigs." She used her forearm to push sticky tendrils of hair from her forehead.

"I saw that, but lepto doesn't normally cause hemorrhaging."

"It did in *Bahia*."

Pedro's brows went up. "You think it's the pulmonary version?"

"I don't know. Maybe."

"Do you want to take samples? Or head for one of the other houses?"

Reaching into the back pocket of her jeans, she eased out her cellphone and glanced hopefully at the display. No bars. What worked in São Paulo obviously didn't work here. "Is your phone working?"

"Nope."

She sighed, trying to figure out what to do. "The tissue samples will have to wait until we come back, I don't want to risk contaminating any live patients. And maybe we'll come within range of a cellphone tower once we hit higher ground."

Benjamin Almeida pressed his eye to the lens of the microscope and twisted the fine focus until the image sharpened, making the pink stain clearly visible. Gram negative bacteria. Removing the slide, he ran it through the digital microscope and recorded the results.

"Um, Ben?" His assistant's hesitant voice came from the doorway.

He held up a finger as he waited for the computer to signal it had sent his report to the attending physician at the tropical disease institute of *Piauí*. The man's office was fifteen steps away in the main hospital building, but Ben couldn't take the time to walk over there right now. Dragging the latex gloves from his hands and flicking them into the garbage can to his right, he reached for the hand sanitizer and squirted a generous amount onto his palm.

"Yep, what is it?" He glanced up, his twelve-hour shift beginning to catch up with him. There were two more slides he needed to process before he could call it a day.

"Someone's here to see you." Mandy shifted out of the doorway, the apology in her cultured Portuguese tones unmistakable.

"If it's Dr. Mendosa, tell him I just emailed the report. It's a bacterial infection, not a parasite."

A woman appeared next to Mandy, and Ben couldn't stop his quick intake of breath. Shock wheeled through him, and he forced himself to remain seated on his stool, thankful his legs weren't in charge of supporting his weight at that moment.

Inky-dark hair, pulled back in its usual clip, exposed high cheekbones and a long slender neck. Green eyes—right now filled with worry—met his without hesitation, her chin tilting slightly higher as they stared at each other.

What the hell was *she* doing here?

The newcomer adjusted the strap of a blue insulated bag on her shoulder and took a small step closer. "Ben, I need your help."

His jaw tensed. Those were almost the exact words she'd used four years ago. Right before she'd walked out of his life. He gave a quick swallow, hoping his voice wouldn't betray his thoughts. "With what?"

"Something's happening in São João dos Rios." She patted the bag at her side, words tumbling out at breakneck speed. "I brought samples I need you to analyze. The sooner the better, because I have to know why people are suddenly—"

"Slow down. I have no idea what you're talking about."

She bit her lip, and he watched her try to collect her thoughts. "There's an outbreak in São João dos Rios. Six people are dead so far. The military police are already on their way to lock down the town." She held her hand out. "I wouldn't have come if this wasn't important. Really important."

That much he knew was true. The last time he'd seen her, she had been heading out the door of their house, never to return.

He shouldn't be surprised she was still roving the country, stamping out infectious fires wherever she went. Nothing had been able to stop her. Not him. Not the thought of a home and family. Not the life she'd carried inside her.

Against his better judgement, he yanked on a fresh pair of gloves. "Do I need a respirator?"

"I don't think so. We used surgical masks to collect the samples."

He nodded, pulling one on and handing another to her, grateful that its presence would hide those soft pink lips he'd never tired of kissing. Ben's attention swiveled back to her eyes, and he cursed the fact that the vivid green still had the power to make his pulse pound in his chest even after all this time.

He cleared his throat. "Symptoms?"

"The commonality seems to be pulmonary hemorrhage, maybe from some type of pneumonia." She passed him the bag. "The bodies have already been cremated, unfortunately."

"Without autopsies?" Something in his stomach twisted in warning.

"The military let me collect a few samples before they carted the bodies away, and the government took another set to do its own studies. I have to document that I've destroyed everything once you're done." She lowered her voice. "There's a guard in your reception area whose job it is to make sure that order is carried out. Help me out here. You're the best epidemiologist around these parts."

He glanced at the doorway, noting for the first time the armed member of the *Polícia Militar* leaning against the wall in the other room. "That wasn't one of my most endearing features, once upon a time."

He remembered all too well the heated arguments they'd had over which was more important: individual rights or the public good.

Biting her lip, she hesitated. "Because you went behind my back and used your job as a weapon against me."

Yes, he had. And not even that had stopped her.

His assistant, who'd been watching from the doorway, pulled on a mask and moved to stand beside him, her head tilting as she glanced nervously at the guard. Her English wasn't the best, and Ben wasn't sure how much of their conversation she'd grasped. "Is he going to let us leave?" she asked in Portuguese.

Tracy switched to the native language. "If it turns out the illness is just a common strain of pneumonia, it won't be a problem."

"And if it isn't?"

Ben's lips compressed as he contemplated spending an unknown amount of time confined to his tiny office.

With Tracy.

He had a foldable cot in a back closet, but it was narrow. Certainly not large enough for…

"If it isn't, then it looks like we might be here for a while." He went to the door and addressed the official. "We haven't opened the tissue samples yet. My assistant has a family. I'd like her to go home before we begin."

Ben had insisted his office be housed in a separate building from the main hospital for just this reason. It was small enough that the whole thing could be sealed off in the event of an airborne epidemic. And just like the microbial test he'd completed for a colleague moments earlier, any results could be sent off via computer.

Safety was his number-one priority. Mandy knew the risks of working for him, but she'd been exposed to nothing, as far as he could tell. Not like when Tracy had rushed headlong into a yellow fever epidemic four years ago that had forced him to call in the military authorities.

The guard in the doorway tapped his foot for a second, as if considering Ben's request. He then turned away and spoke to someone through his walkie-talkie. When he was done, he faced them. "We'll have someone escort her home, but she'll have to remain there until we know what the illness is. As for you two…" he motioned to Ben and Tracy "…once the samples are uncapped you'll have to stay in this building until we determine the risks."

Mandy sent Ben a panicked look. "Are you sure it's safe

for me to leave? My baby…" She shut her eyes. "I need to call my husband."

"Have Sergio take the baby to your mother's house, where she'll be safe. just in case. I'll call you as soon as I know something, okay?"

His assistant nodded and left to make her call.

"I'm sorry." Tracy's face softened. "I thought you'd be alone in the lab. I didn't realize you'd gotten an assistant."

"It's not your fault. She's worried about the risks to her baby." His eyes came up to meet hers, and he couldn't resist the dig. "Just as any woman with children would be."

He mentally kicked himself when the compassion in Tracy's eyes dissolved, and anger took its place.

"I *was* concerned. But it was never enough for you, was it?" Her chest rose as she took a deep breath. "I'm heading back to São João dos Rios as soon as you give me some answers. If I'm going to be quarantined, I'm going to do it where I can make a difference. That doesn't include sitting in a lab, staring at rows of test tubes."

He knew he'd struck a nerve, but it didn't stop an old hurt from creeping up his spine. "Says the woman who came to *my* lab, asking for help," he said quietly.

"I didn't mean it like that."

"Sure you did."

They stared at each other then the corners of her eyes crinkled. She pulled down her mask, letting it dangle around her neck. "Okay, maybe I did…a little. But at least I admitted that I need you. That has to count for something."

It did. But that kind of need was a far cry from what they'd once had together. Those days were long gone, and no matter how hard Ben had tried to hold onto her back then, she'd drifted further and further away, until the gulf between them had been too huge to span.

Bellyaching about the past won't get you anywhere.

Ben shook off the thoughts and set the insulated bag on

an empty metal table. He nodded towards the aluminum glove dispenser hanging on the far wall. “Suit up and don’t touch anything in the lab, just in case.”

She dug into her handbag instead and pulled out her own box of gloves. “I came prepared.”

Of course she had. It was part of who she was. This was a woman who was always on the move—who never took a weekend off. Tracy had thrown herself into her work without restraint…until there had been nothing left for herself. Or for him.

He’d thought she’d stop once the pregnancy tests went from blue to pink. She hadn’t. And Ben hadn’t been able to face any child of his going through what he had as a kid.

Gritting his teeth in frustration, he glanced around the lab, eyeing the centrifuges and other equipment. They’d have to work in the tiny glassed-off cubicle in the corner that he’d set up for occasions like this.

Keeping his day-to-day work space absolutely separate from Tracy’s samples was not only smart, it was non-negotiable. If they weren’t careful, the government could end up quarantining his whole lab, meaning years of work would be tossed into the incinerator. He tensed. Although if their findings turned up a microbe that was airborne, he’d willingly burn everything himself. He wouldn’t risk setting loose an epidemic.

Not even for Tracy. She should know that by now.

“I have a clean room set up over there. Once we get things squared away with Mandy, we can start.”

Tracy peered towards the door where the phone conversation between his assistant and her husband was growing more heated by the second. “I was really careful about keeping everything as sterile as I could. I don’t think she’s been exposed to anything.”

“I’m sure it’ll be fine. I’m going to take your bagged

samples into the other area. Can you wipe down the table where they were with disinfectant?"

As soon as Ben picked up the insulated bag, the guard appeared, his hand resting on the butt of his gun. "Where are you going with that?"

Ben motioned towards the clean room. "The samples can't infect anyone else if they're kept enclosed. You can see everything we do from the reception doorway. It'll be safer if you keep your distance once we've started testing, though."

The guard backed up a couple of paces. "How long will it take? I have no wish to stay here any longer than I have to."

"I have no idea. It depends on what we're dealing with."

Putting the bag in the cubicle, he gathered the equipment he'd need and arranged it on the set of metal shelves perched above a stainless-steel table. He blew out a breath. The eight-by-eight-foot area was going to be cramped once he and Tracy were both inside.

An air handler filtered any particles floating in and out of the clean room, but there was no safe way to pump air-conditioning into the space. They'd have to rely on the wheezy window unit in the main lab and hope it kept them from baking. He could offer to send Tracy on her way before he got the results—but he was pretty sure he knew how that suggestion would be met, despite her waspish words earlier.

You couldn't coax—or force—Tracy to do anything she didn't want to do. He knew that from experience.

Mandy appeared in the doorway to the reception area just as Ben turned on the air filter and closed the door on the samples.

"It's all arranged. Sergio called my mom and asked if she'd care for the baby overnight. He's not happy about staying home from work, but he doesn't want me to stay here either."

"I don't blame him. But look on the bright side. At least you can go home." He smiled. "Tell Sergio he should count his lucky stars I haven't stolen you away from him."

Mandy laughed. "You've already told him that yourself. Many times."

Tracy spun away from them and stalked over to the metal table she'd previously sanitized and began scrubbing it all over again. She kept her head down, not looking at either of them.

"Is the guard going to take you home?" He forced the words to remain cheerful.

"They're sending another policeman. He should be here soon."

"Good." He had Mandy go back and wait in the reception area, so there'd be no question of her being anywhere near those samples. Returning to the sealed cubicle, he slid the insulated bag into a small refrigerator he kept for just this purpose. The air was already growing close inside the room, but he'd worked under worse conditions many times before. Both he and Tracy had.

He could still picture one such occasion—their very first meeting—Tracy had stepped off the *Projeto Vida* medical boat and stalked into the village he had been surveying, demanding to know what he was doing about the malaria outbreak twenty miles downriver. He'd been exhausted, and she'd looked like a gorgeous avenging angel, silky black hair flowing behind her in the breeze, ready to slay him if he said one wrong word.

They'd barely lasted two days before they'd fallen into bed together.

Something he'd rather not remember at the moment. Especially as he was trying to avoid any and all physical contact with her.

She might be immune, but he wasn't. Not judging from the way his heart had taken off at a sprint when he'd seen her standing in that doorway.

Tracy dumped her paper towel into the hazardous waste receptacle and crossed over to him. "I just want to say thank you for agreeing to help. You could have told me to get lost." She gave a hard laugh. "I wouldn't have blamed you if you had."

"I'm not always an ogre, you know."

Her teeth caught the right corner of her bottom lip in a way that made his chest tighten. "I know. And I'm sorry for dragging you into this, but I didn't know where else to go. The military didn't want me to take the samples out of São João dos Rios. They only agreed to let me come here because you've worked with them before…and even then they made me bring a guard. I honestly didn't think anyone else would be affected other than us."

"It's not your fault, Trace." He started to reach out to touch her cheek, but checked himself. "The government is probably right to keep this as contained as possible. If I thought there was any chance of contamination, I'd be the first one to say Mandy needs to stay here at the lab with us."

He smiled. "If I know you, though, not one microbe survived on that bag before you carried it out of that town."

"I hope not. There are still several ill people waiting on us for answers. I left a colleague behind to make sure the military didn't do anything rash, but he's not a doctor, and I don't want to risk his health either." She blew out a breath. "Those people need help. But there's nothing I can do until I know what we're dealing with."

And then she'd be on her way to the next available crisis. Just like she always was.

His smile faded. "Let's get to work, then."

The guard stuck his head into the room. "They're sending someone for your friend. They'll keep her at home until the danger has passed."

Ben nodded. "I understand. Thank you."

When he went to the doorway to say goodbye to Mandy, she kissed his cheek, her arms circling his neck and hugging him close. When she finally let go, her eyes shimmered with unshed tears. "I'm so grateful. I can't imagine not being able to tuck my Jenny into bed tonight, but at least I'll be closer to her than I would be if I stayed here."

His heart clenched. Here was a woman whose baby meant the world to her—who didn't need to jet off to distant places to find fulfillment. Unlike his parents.

Unlike Tracy.

"We'll work as quickly as we can. Once things are clear, make sure you give her a kiss and a hug from her uncle Ben."

"I will." She wiped a spot of lipstick from his cheek with her thumb. "Be careful, okay? I've just gotten used to your crazy ways. I don't want to break someone else in."

Ben laughed and took off one of his latex gloves, laying his hand on her shoulder. "You're not getting rid of me any time soon, so go and enjoy your mini-vacation. You'll be back to the same old grind before you know it."

Mandy's escort arrived, and as soon as she exited the building, he turned back to find Tracy observing him with a puzzled frown.

"What?" he asked.

She shrugged. "Nothing. I'm just surprised you haven't found a woman who'd be thrilled to stick close to the house and give you all those kids you said you wanted."

"That would be impossible, given the circumstances."

"Oh?" Her brows arched. "And why is that?"

He laughed, the sound harsh in the quiet room. "Do you really have to ask?"

"I just did."

Grabbing her left hand, he held it up, forcing her eyes to the outline of the plain gold band visible beneath her latex glove. "For the same reason you're wearing this." He stared into her face. "Have you forgotten, *Mrs. Almeida*? You may not go by your married name any more, but in the eyes of the law…we're still husband and wife."

CHAPTER TWO

SHE'D FORGOTTEN NOTHING.

And she'd tried to see about getting a divorce, but being overseas made everything a hundred times more complicated. Both of the Brazilian lawyers she'd contacted had said that as an American citizen, she should return to the States and start the proceedings there, as she and Ben had been married in New York. But asking him to accompany her had been out of the question. Even if he'd been willing, she wasn't. She hadn't wanted to be anywhere near him, too raw from everything that had transpired in the month before she'd left *Teresina*—and him—for ever.

Staying married probably hadn't been the wisest move on her part but she'd thrown herself into her work afterwards, far too busy with *Projeto Vida*, her aid organization's floating clinic, to set the ugly wheels in motion. Besides, a wedding ring tended to scare away any man who ventured too close. Not that there'd been many. Her *caution-do-not-touch* vibes must be coming through loud and clear. She'd never get married again—to anyone—so keeping her wedding ring and her license made keeping that promise a whole lot easier.

Too bad she hadn't remembered to take the ring off before asking Ben for help.

She realized he was still waiting for a response so she lifted her chin, praying he wouldn't notice the slight tremble. "We're not married any more. Not by any stretch of the imagination. You made sure of that."

"Right." Ben turned away and gathered a few more pieces of equipment.

Her thumb instinctively rubbed back and forth across the ring, a gesture she'd found oddly comforting during some of the tougher periods of her life—like now.

Strange how most of those times had found her wearing surgical gloves.

Studying Ben as he worked, Tracy was surprised by the slight dusting of grey in his thick brown hair. She gave herself a mental shake. The man was thirty-eight, and she hadn't set eyes on him in four years. Change was inevitable. What hadn't changed, however, were the electric blue eyes, compliments of his American mother, or how they provided the perfect counterpoint for tanned skin, high cheekbones and a straight, autocratic nose—all legacies from his Brazilian father. Neither had he lost any of that intense focus she'd once found so intimidating.

And irresistible.

Snap out of it, Tracy.

She donned the scrubs, booties and surgical gear Ben had left out for her and moved into the glassed-in cubicle where he was busy setting up.

"Close the door, please, so I can seal it off."

"Seal it off?" Swallowing hard, she hesitated then did as he asked.

"Just with this." He held up a roll of clear packing tape. "Is your claustrophobia going to be a problem?"

She hoped not, but feeling trapped had always set off a rolling sense of panic that could quickly snowball if she wasn't careful. It didn't matter whether the confinement was physical or emotional, the fear was the same. Glancing through the door to the reception area, she noted the exit to the outside world was plainly visible even from where she stood. “As long as I know there’s a door right through there, I should be fine. The room being made of glass helps.”

“Good.”

Ben taped the edges of the door, before removing the insulated bag from the fridge and examining the labels on each tube inside. Selecting two of them, he put the rest back in cold storage.

“What do you want me to do?” Tracy asked.

“Set up some slides. We’re going to work our way from simple to complex.”

He turned one of the tubes to the side and read her label out loud. “Daniel, male, twelve years.” He paused. “Living?”

“Yes.” Her heart twisted when she thought of the preteen boy staring at her with terrified eyes. But at least he was alive. As was his younger sister Cleo. Their mother, however, hadn’t been so lucky. Hers had been one of the first bodies they’d found in the village. “Febrile. No skin lesions visible.”

“Signs of pneumonia?”

“Not yet, which is why this seemed so strange. Most of the dead had complained to relatives of coughs along with fever and malaise.”

“Liver enlargement in the dead?”

She swallowed. “No autopsies, remember? The military destroyed everything.” Her voice cracked.

Ben’s gloved hand covered hers, and even through the layers of latex the familiar warmth of his touch comforted her in a way no one else ever could. “Why don’t you get those slides ready, while I set up the centrifuge?”

Glad to have something to take her mind off the horrific scene she and Pedro had stumbled on in São João dos Rios, she pulled several clean slides from the box and spread them across the table. Then, carefully taking the cotton swab from Ben's outstretched hand, she smeared a thin layer of material on the smooth glass surface. "What are you looking for?"

"Anything. Everything." The tense muscle in his jaw made her wonder if he already had a theory. "You'll need to heat-set the slides as you smear them."

He lit a small burner and showed her how to pass the slide across the flame to dry it and affix the specimen to the glass.

The sound of a throat clearing in the outer doorway made them both look up. Their guard cupped his hands over his mouth and said in a loud voice, "Your assistant has arrived safely at her home."

Ben flashed a thumbs-up sign. "Thanks for letting me know."

Tracy's fingers tensed on the slide at the mention of Ben's assistant, which was ridiculous. Yes, the woman had kissed him, but Brazilians kissed everyone—it was a kind of unspoken rule in these parts. Besides, the woman had a family. A new baby.

Her throat tightened, a sense of loss sweeping over her. Ben had wanted children so badly. So had she. When she'd fallen pregnant, they'd both been elated. Until she'd had a devastating piece of news that had set her back on her heels. She'd thrown herself into her work, angering Ben, even as she'd tried to figure out a way to tell him.

That had all changed when he'd sent the military in to force her out of a stricken village during a yellow fever outbreak. She knew he'd been trying to protect her and the baby—not from the disease itself, as she'd already been vaccinated the previous year, but from anything that had taken her out of his sight. She hadn't need protecting, though. She'd needed to work. It had been her lifeline in a time of turmoil and confusion, and his interference had damaged her trust. She'd miscarried a week later, and the rift that had opened between them during their disagreement over the military had grown deeper, with accusations flying fast and furious on both sides.

In the end she'd opted to keep her secret to herself. Telling him would have changed nothing, not when she'd already decided to leave.

Work was still her number-one priority. Still her lifeline. And she needed to get her mind back on what she was doing.

Tracy took the long cotton swab and dipped it into another of her sample jars, laying a thin coating of the material on a second glass slide, heat-setting it, like she'd done with the first. "Do you need me to apply a stain?"

"Let's see what we've got on these first."

"There were pigs in a corral at one of the victims' homes. Could it be leptospirosis?"

"Possibly." He switched on the microscope's light. "If I can't find anything on the slides, we'll need to do some cultures. Lepto will show up there."

He didn't say it, but they both knew cultures would take several days, if not longer, to grow.

Tracy sent a nervous glance towards the reception area, where the guard lounged in a white plastic chair in full view. He twirled what looked like a toothpick between his thumb and forefinger. For the moment his attention wasn't focused on them. And he was far enough away that he shouldn't be able to hear soft voices through the glass partition.

"That could be a problem."

Ben turned toward her, watchful eyes moving over her face. "How so?"

"I told the military police you'd have an answer for them today."

"You did *what*?" His hand clenched on the edge of the table. "Of all the irresponsible—"

"I know, I know. I didn't have a choice. It was either that or leave São João dos Rios empty-handed."

He closed his eyes for a few seconds before looking at her again. "You're still hauling around that savior complex, aren't you, Tracy? Don't you get tired of being the one who swoops in to save the day?"

"I thought that was *your* role. Taking charge even when it's not your decision to make." She tossed her head. "Maybe if you'd stopped thinking about yourself for once..." As soon as the ugly words spurted out she gritted her teeth, staunching the flow. "I'm sorry. That was uncalled for."

"Yes. It was." He took the slide from her and set it down with an audible *crack*.

The guard was on his feet in an instant, his casual manner gone. *"O que foi?"*

Ben held up the slide. "Sorry. Just dropped it." Although he said the words loudly enough for the guard to hear them, he kept his tone calm and even. Even so, the tension in his white-knuckled grip was unmistakable.

The guard rolled his eyes, his face relaxing. "I'm going to the cafeteria. Do you want something?"

How exactly did the man expect to get the food past the sealed doorway? Besides, she wouldn't be able to eat if her life depended on it. "I'm good. Thanks."

"Same here," said Ben.

The guard shrugged and then checked the front door. He palmed the old-fashioned key he found in the lock before reinserting it again, this time on the outside of the door.

He meant to lock them in!

"No, wait!" Tracy stood, not exactly sure how she could stop him.

"Sorry, but I have my orders. Neither of you leaves until those samples are destroyed."

She started to argue further, but Ben touched her shoulder. “Don’t,” he said in a low voice.

Holding her tongue, she watched helplessly as the door swung shut, a menacing snick of the lock telling her the guard had indeed imprisoned them inside the room. A familiar sting of panic went up her spine. “What if he doesn’t come back? What if we’re trapped?”

Stripping off one of his gloves, he reached into his pocket. “I have a spare. I know you don’t like being confined.”

Sagging in relief, she managed a shaky laugh. “You learned that the hard way, didn’t you?”

The vivid image of Ben playfully pinning her hands above her head while they’d tussled on the bed sprang to her mind. The love play had been fun. At first. Then a wave of terror had washed over her unexpectedly, and though she’d known her panic had been illogical, she’d begun to struggle in earnest.

A frightened plea had caught in her throat, and as hard as she’d tried to say something, her voice had seemed as frozen as her senses. Ben had only realized she was no longer playing when she succeeded in freeing one of her hands and raked her nails down his face. He’d reeled backwards, while she’d lain there, her chest heaving, tears of relief spilling from her eyes. Understanding had dawned on his face and he’d gathered her into his arms, murmuring how sorry he was. From that moment forward he’d been careful to avoid anything that might make her feel trapped.

A little too careful.

His lovemaking had become less intense and more controlled. Only it had been a different kind of control than what they’d previously enjoyed, when Ben’s take-charge demeanor in the bedroom had been a huge turn-on. That had all changed. Tracy had mourned the loss of passion, even as she’d appreciated his reasons for keeping a little more space between them. Her inability to explain where the line between confinement and intimacy lay had driven the first wedge between them.

That wedge had widened later, when he'd tried to limit her movements during her pregnancy, giving rise to the same sensation of being suffocated. She'd clawed at him just as hard then, the marks invisible but causing just as much damage to their marriage.

The Ben of the present fingered the side of his face and gave her a smile. "No permanent damage done."

Yeah, there had been. And it seemed that one patch of bad luck had spiraled into another.

"I always felt terrible about that," she said.

"I should have realized you were scared."

"You couldn't have known."

Even her father hadn't realized their play sessions could change without warning. There'd always been laughter, but the sound of hers had often turned shrill with overtones of panic. A gentle soul, her father would have never hurt her in a million years. It didn't help that her older sister had been a tough-as-nails tomboy who'd feared nothing and had given as good as she'd got. Then Tracy had come along—always fearful, always more cautious. Her father had never quite known what to do with her.

She was still fearful. Still flinched away from situations that made her feel trapped and out of control.

And now her mom and her sister were both gone. Her mom, the victim of a menacing villain who'd stalked its prey relentlessly—turning the delicate strands of a person's DNA into the enemy. Passed from mother to daughter. Tracy had been running from its specter ever since.

Ben donned a fresh glove and picked up the slide he'd smacked against the table, checking it for cracks. Without glancing up at her, he said, "You look tired. I put the folding cot in the corner in case we needed to sleep in shifts. If I know you, you didn't get much rest last night."

"I'm okay." He was right. She was exhausted, but no way would she let him know how easily he could still read her. Or how the touch of concern in his voice made her heart skip a beat. "It's just warm in here."

"I know. The air-conditioner in the lab is ancient, and the filter doesn't let much of it through, anyway."

Even as he said it, a tiny trickle of sweat coursed down her back. "It's fine."

He pushed the slide beneath the viewer of the microscope and focused on the smear. "How old are the samples?"

"Just a couple of hours."

He swore softly as he continued to peer through the lens, evidently seeing something he didn't like. He took the second slide and repeated the process, his right hand shifting a knob on the side of the instrument repeatedly. Sitting up, he dabbed at perspiration that had gathered around his eye with the sleeve of his lab coat then leaned back in for another look.

"What is it?" She felt her own blood rushing through her ears as she awaited the verdict.

It didn't take long. He lifted his head and fastened his eyes on hers. "If I'm not mistaken, it's pneumonic plague, Tracy." Shifting his attention to the test tube in her hand, he continued, "And if you're the one who took these samples, you've already been exposed."

CHAPTER THREE

TRACY SAGGED AND swallowed hard, trying to process what he'd said through her own fear. "Are you sure?"

"Here." He moved aside so she could look at the slide.

Putting her eye to the viewfinder, she squinted into the machine. "What am I looking for?"

"See the little dots grouped into chains?"

"Yes." There were several of them.

"That's what we're dealing with. I want to look at another sample and do a culture, just in case, but I'm sure. It's *Yersinia pestis*, the same bacterium that causes bubonic plague. I recognize the shape." He rolled his shoulders as if relieving an ache. "Bubonic plague normally spreads from infected rats through the bite of a flea, but if the bacteria migrate to a person's lungs, it becomes even more deadly, spreading rapidly from person to person by way of a cough or bodily fluids. When that happens, the disease no longer needs a flea. We'll want to put you on a strong dose of streptomycin immediately."

"What about you?"

"I'll start on them as well, but just as a precaution." Ben dripped a staining solution on another slide. "Most of the people who work in the lab are vaccinated against the plague, including Mandy. But I assume you haven't been."

"No, which means neither has… Oh, God." She rested her head against Ben's shoulder for a second as a wave of nausea rolled over her. “That town. I have to get back there. They’ve all been exposed. So has Pedro.”

“Pedro?”

“*My* assistant.”

Just as he pushed the slide back under the microscope, the lock to the outer door clicked open before Tracy had a chance to figure out how to proceed.

The guard pushed his way inside, glancing from one to the other, his eyes narrowing in on her face. She sat up straighter.

“Problema?” he asked.

Instead of lunch, he only held a coffee cup in his hand.

A tug on the back of her shirt sent a warning Tracy read loud and clear, *Don’t tell him anything until I’ve taken another look.* The gesture surprised her, as he’d always been buddy-buddy with the military, at least from what she’d seen over the course of their marriage.

Still holding one of the slides, he casually laid it on the table. “We need to run a few more tests before we know anything for sure.”

“No need. Our doctors have isolated the infection and will take the appropriate containment measures.”

Containment? What exactly did that mean?

Her brows lifted in challenge. “What is the illness, then?” Maybe he was bluffing.

“I’m not at liberty to say. But my commander would like to speak with Dr. Almeida over the phone.” He gave Tracy a pointed stare. “Alone.”

A shiver went over her. Alone. Why?

What if the government doctors had come to a different conclusion than Ben had? What if they were assuming it was something other than the plague? People could still die…still pass it on to neighboring towns. And São João dos Rios was poor. How many people would lose loved ones due to lack of information?

Just like she had. She knew the pain of that firsthand.

She'd lost her mother. Her grandmother. Her sister—although Vickie's illness hadn't been related to a genetic defect. The most devastating loss of all, however, had been her unborn child. Ben's baby.

All had died far too young. And Tracy had decided she wasn't going to waste a second of her time on earth waiting around for what-ifs. Movement, in her eyes, equaled life. So she'd lived that life with a ferocity that others couldn't begin to understand.

Including Ben.

Genetic code might not be written in stone, but its deadly possibility loomed in front of her, as did a decision she might someday choose to make. But until then she was determined to make a difference in the lives of those around her.

Or maybe you're simply running away.

Like she had with Ben? No, their break-up had been for entirely different reasons.

Had it?

She pushed the voice in her head aside. "Why does he want to talk to Dr. Almeida alone?"

"That's not for me to say." The guard nodded towards the bag. "Those samples must be destroyed."

"We'll take care of it." Her husband's voice was calm. Soothing. Just as Zen-like as ever. Just as she imagined it would have been had she told him about the life-changing decision she was wrestling with.

And his icy unflappability drove her just as crazy now as it had during their last fight.

How could he take everything in his stride?

Because it was part of who he was. He'd grown up in Brazil…was more Brazilian than American in a lot of ways.

As Ben stripped the tape from around the door and

sanitized his hands before stepping into the hallway with the guard, Tracy sighed. She never knew what he was thinking. Even during their marriage he'd been tight-lipped about a lot of things. But as aloof as he'd been at times, she'd sensed something in him yearning for what he hadn't had when growing up: the closeness of a family.

It still hurt that she hadn't been able to give that to him. That even as she was driven to work harder and harder by the loss of her baby and by whatever time bomb might be ticking inside her, she was gradually becoming the very thing he despised in his parents.

Her sister had died never knowing whether or not she carried the defective gene. It hadn't been cancer that had claimed Vickie's life but dengue fever—a disease that was endemic in Brazil. She'd been pregnant at the time of her death. Her husband had been devastated at losing both of them. As had she. But at least Vickie had been spared the agonizing uncertainty over whether or not she'd passed a cancer gene down to her child.

As much as Tracy had feared doing just that during her pregnancy, she'd never in her weakest moments wished harm to come to her unborn child. And yet she'd lost the baby anyway, as if even the fates knew what a bad idea it was for her to reproduce.

Her vision suddenly went blurry, and she blinked in an effort to clear her head from those painful thoughts. As she did, she realized Ben and the guard had come back into the room and were now staring at her.

"What?" she asked, mentally daring him to say anything about her moist eyes.

Ben's gaze sharpened, but he said nothing. "I need to leave for São João dos Rios. Do you want me to drop you off at the airport on my way out of town?"

"Excuse me?"

Why would she need to go to the airport? Unless…

No way!

Her hands went to her hips. “I’m going with you.”

Both Ben and the guard spoke at once, their voices jumbled. She caught the gist of it, however. Evidently Ben had been invited to go but she hadn’t been.

Outrage crowded her chest. “I’m the one who took the samples. I’ve already been out there.”

“And exposed yourself to the plague in the process.”

“Exactly.” Her hands dropped back to her sides, palms out. “I’ve already been exposed. And I’m a doctor, Ben. I’ve spent my life fighting outbreaks like this one. I should be there.”

His voice cooled. “It’s not up to me this time.”

“*This* time. Unlike the time you sent your goons into that village with orders to send me packing?” She almost spit the words at him. “My assistant is still in São João dos Rios. I am not leaving him out there alone.”

Stepping around Ben, she focused on the guard. “I’d like to speak with your superior.”

The man blinked several times, as if he couldn’t believe she was daring to defy whatever orders he’d received. “I’m afraid that’s not possible—”

Ben’s fingers went around her upper arm and squeezed. “Let me talk to her for a minute.”

Practically dragging her to the other side of the room, his stony gaze fastened on her face. “What are you doing?”

“I already told you. I’m doing my job.”

“The military wants to handle this their way. They’ll go in and treat those who aren’t too far gone and make sure this doesn’t spread beyond São João dos Rios.”

“Those who aren’t too far gone? My God, stop and listen to yourself for a minute. We’re talking about human beings—about children like Daniel and Cleo, who are now orphans. They deserve someone there who will fight for them.”

"You think I don't care about those children? I was the one who wanted you to slow down during your pregnancy, to…" He paused for several long seconds then lowered his voice. "I care just as much about those villagers as you do."

His surgeon's scalpel cut deep. She could guess what he'd been about to say before he'd checked himself. He still thought her actions had cost the life of their child. And the worst thing was that she couldn't say with any certainty that he was wrong. She'd worked herself harder than ever after she'd had the results back from the genetic testing—struggling to beat back the familiar sensation of being trapped. But that wasn't something she wanted to get into right now.

"Let me go with you." She twisted out of his grasp so she could turn and face him. "Please. You have pull with these guys, I know you do. Call the commander back, whoever he is, and tell him you need me."

He dragged a hand through his hair then shook his head. "I'm asking you to walk away, Tracy. Just this once. You don't know how bad things might get before it's over."

"I do know. That's why I need to be there. Those two kids have already lost their mother. I want to help make sure they don't lose their lives as well."

She was not going to let some government bureaucrat—or even Ben—decide they were a lost cause. "I'll take antibiotics while I'm there. I'll do whatever the government people tell me to do. Besides, like I said before, my assistant is still in the middle of it."

She couldn't explain to him that she really did need to be there. This was part of what being alive meant—fighting battles for others that she might not be able to fight for herself. She took a deep breath. "Please, don't make me beg."

A brief flicker of something went across his face then was gone. "Listen, I know—" Before he could finish the guard appeared in front of them, tapping his hat against his thigh, clearly impatient to be gone. "We need to leave."

Tracy kept her pleading gaze focused on Ben. *He had to let her go. He just had to.*

Ben swore and then broke eye contact. "Call General Gutierrez and tell him we're on our way. Both of us."

The man didn't bat an eyelid. "I'll let him know."

Exactly how much influence did Ben have with these officials? She knew his salary came from the government, but to say something like that and expect it to be accepted without question…

She swallowed. "Thank you."

Jaw tight, Ben ignored her and addressed the guard again. "We'll follow you out to the village once I've destroyed the samples. We need to use my four-wheel drive to haul some equipment."

The guard swept his hat onto his head before relaying the message to his superiors. When he finished the call, he said, "My commander will have someone meet you at the town square and direct you to the triage area they've set up. But you must hurry."

Ben nodded. "Tell them we'll be there within three hours."

"*Vai com Deus.*"

The common "Go with God" farewell had an ominous ring to it—as if the man had crossed himself in an attempt to ward off evil. And pneumonic plague was all that and more. Its cousin had killed off large swaths of the world's population in the past.

Despite her misgivings about working with Ben again, a couple of muscles in her stomach relaxed. At least she wouldn't have to fight this particular battle on her own.

Ben would be there with her.

And if he found out the truth about the genetic testing she'd had done before their separation?

Then she would deal with it. Just as she'd dealt with the loss of her baby and her own uncertain prognosis.

Alone.

As they hurried to finish loading his vehicle, a streak of lightning darted across the sky, pausing to lick the trunk of a nearby tree before sliding back into the clouds. The smell of singed wood reached Ben a few seconds later, followed by an ominous rumble that made the ground tremble.

Tracy, who stood beside him, shuddered. "Only in *Teresina*."

He smiled. "Remember the city's nickname? *Chapada do corisco:* flash-lightning flatlands. If ever lightning was going to strike twice in the same spot, it would be here." He shut the back of the grey four-wheel-drive vehicle. "I'd rather not put that theory to the test, though, so, if you're ready to go, hop in."

She climbed into the SUV and buckled in, staring in the direction the jagged flash had come from. "That poor tree looks like it's lightning's favorite prom date, judging from the color."

Scarred from multiple strikes over the years, it stubbornly clung to life, clusters of green leaves scattered along its massive branches. Ben had no idea how it had survived so many direct hits.

Their marriage certainly hadn't been as lucky.

He got behind the wheel and started the car. "It'll eventually have to come down."

"Through no fault of its own," she murmured. "It's sad."

Was she thinking of what had happened between them? It had taken every ounce of strength he'd had after she'd left, but he'd forced himself to keep living. In reality, though, she had been gone long before she'd actually moved out of the house. He'd accepted it and moved forward.

Right.

That's why he was on his way to São João dos Rios right now, with Tracy in tow. He should have just shut her down and said no. General Gutierrez would have backed him in his decision. So why hadn't he?

"You sure you want to do this? The airport is on our way. We could still have you on a flight to São Paulo in a jiffy."

She jerked in her seat, gripping the webbing of the seat belt before shifting to look at him. "I can't just turn my back on the town. That's not how I operate."

Really? It had seemed all too easy for her to turn her back on him. But saying so wouldn't help anyone.

They reached the entrance to the highway, and Ben sighed when he saw metal barricades stretched across its width.

The four-lane road—long under construction—was still not finished.

He coasted down a steep incline to reach the so-called official detour, which consisted of a narrow dirt track running parallel to the road. It looked more like a gully from water run-off than an actual street. As far as the eye could see, where the highway should have been there was now a long stretch of hard-packed orange clay that was impassable. At the moment trucks seemed to be the only vehicles braving the washboard tract Ben and Tracy were forced to use. Then again, there was no other option. Most things, including food, were moved from city to city via semi-tractor-trailers. And with the current conditions of the highway it was no wonder things were so expensive in northeastern Brazil.

"How long have they been working on this?" Tracy asked.

"Do you really need to ask?"

"No. But it *was* paved the last time I was here."

They'd spent most of their marriage in *Teresina*, the capital of the state of *Piaui*. He'd rearranged his job so he could stay in one place. Ben thought Tracy had been willing to do the same. How wrong he'd been.

She *had* come off the medical boat and put someone else in her place, but that was about the only concession she'd made to their marriage. By the time he'd realized she was never going to slow down, he'd lost more than just his wife.

"Yes, it was paved, after a fashion." He grimaced. "I think the shoulder we're on is in better shape than the highway was back then."

Ben slowed to navigate a particularly bad stretch where torrential rains had worn a deep channel into the dirt. "Well, some parts of it, anyway."

"My car would never survive the trip."

He smiled. "Are you still driving that little tin can?"

"Rhonda gets great gas mileage."

His gut twisted. He could still remember the laughter they'd shared over Tracy's insistence on keeping her ragamuffin car when they'd got married, despite the hazardous stretches of road in Teresina. To his surprise, the little vehicle had been sturdier than it had appeared, bumping along the worst of the cobblestone streets with little more than an occasional hiccup. Like the bumper she'd lost on a visit to one of the neighboring *aldéias*. She'd come back with the thing strapped to the roof. He smiled. When he'd suggested it was time to trade the vehicle in, she'd refused, patting the bonnet and saying the car had seen her through some tough spots.

His smile faded. Funny how her loyalty to her car hadn't been mirrored in her marriage.

He cast around for a different subject, but Tracy got there first.

"How's Marcelo doing?"

Ben's brother was the new chief of neurosurgery over

at Teresina's main hospital. "He's fine. Still as opinionated as ever."

She smiled. "Translated to mean he's still single."

"Always will be, if he has his way." He glanced over at her. "What about you? How's *Projeto Vida* going?" The medical-aid ship that had brought them together was still Tracy's pet project.

"Wonderfully. Matt is back on the team and has a baby girl now."

Tracy's sister had died years ago, leaving her husband, Matt, heartbroken. "He remarried?"

"Yep. Two years ago." She paused. "Stevie...Stephani, actually, is great. She loves the job and fits right into the team."

"I'm glad. Matt seemed like a nice guy." Ben had met him on several occasions when they'd traveled to *Coari* to deliver supplies or check on the medical boat.

"He is. It's good to see him happy again."

Which was more than he could say about Tracy. Maybe it was the stress of what she'd been dealing with in São João dos Rios, but the dark circles under her green eyes worried him. He glanced to the side for a quick peek. The rest of her looked exactly as he remembered, though. Long, silky black hair that hung just below her shoulders. The soft fringe of bangs that fluttered whenever the flow from the air-conditioning vent caught the strands. Lean, tanned legs encased in khaki shorts.

And as much as he wished otherwise, being near her again made him long for family and normalcy all over again. He'd always thought she would bring stability to his life, help to counteract his tumultuous upbringing. His parents had drifted here and there, always searching for a new adventure while leaving their two young sons in the care of their housekeeper. In many ways, Ben had felt closer to Rosa than to his own mother, so much so that he'd kept her on at his house long after his parents had moved to the States on a permanent basis.

He'd thought life with Tracy would be different. That their children would have the close-knit family he'd always longed for as a kid. But Tracy, once the first blush of their marriage had faded, had started traveling again, always finding some new medical crisis to deal with, whether with *Projeto Vida* or somewhere else.

He could understand being married to your career—after all, he was pretty attached to his—but he'd learned to do it from one central location. Surely Tracy could have done the same.

Instead, with every month that had passed, the same feelings of abandonment he'd had as a kid had taken root and grown, as had his resentment. And once she'd fallen pregnant, she'd seemed more obsessed about work than ever, spending longer and longer periods away from home.

When he'd learned she was dealing with a yellow fever outbreak in one of the villages he'd finally snapped and called his old friend General Gutierrez—despite the fact that he knew Tracy been vaccinated against the disease. His ploy had worked. Tracy had come home. But their marriage had been over, even before she'd lost the baby.

So why hadn't he just settled down with someone else, like Tracy had suggested a few hours earlier? Marriage wasn't exactly a requirement these days. And why hadn't Tracy finally asked for a divorce and been done with it?

Questions he was better off not asking.

"What's the time frame for pneumonic plague?"

Her question jolted him back to the present. "From exposure to presentation of symptoms? Two days, on average. Although death can take anywhere from thirty-six hours after exposure to a week or more. It depends on whether or not other organ systems besides the lungs have been compromised."

"Oh, no."

"Speaking of which, I've brought packets of antibiotics in that black gym bag I threw in the back. Go ahead and dig through it and take a dose before we get there."

Tracy unhooked her seat belt and twisted until she could reach the backseat. She then pulled out one of the boxes of medicine and popped a pill from the protective foil. She downed it with a swig from her water bottle then shoved a couple of strands of hair back from her temple. "You have no idea how glad I am that you were able figure it out so quickly."

"I think I do." Surely she realized he was just as relieved as she was. "Not everyone has the equipment we do."

"Or the backing of the military."

He ignored the bitterness that colored her words. "Part of the reality of living in a developing country. We'll catch up with the rest of the world, eventually. Marcelo's hospital is a great example of that. It's completely funded by sources outside the government."

"So is *Projeto Vida*." She paused when they hit another rough patch of road, her hand scrabbling for the grip attached to the ceiling. "Speaking of funding, we'll need to check with the nearest pharmacist to make sure they have enough antibiotics on hand. I'll pay for more, if need be."

"I was already planning to help with the costs." He glanced over and their eyes caught for a second. When he turned his attention back to the road, her fingers slid over the hand he had resting on the emergency brake before retreating.

"Thank you, Ben," she said. "For letting me come. And for caring about what happens to those people."

He swallowed, her words and the warmth of her fingers

penetrating the icy wall he'd built up over the last four years.

It wasn't exactly the thing that peace treaties were made of, but he got the feeling that Tracy had just initiated talks.

And had thrown the ball squarely into his court.

CHAPTER FOUR

MILITARY VEHICLES BLOCKED the road to São João dos Rios—uniformed personnel, guns at the ready, stood beside the vehicles.

"They're not taking any chances," Ben muttered as he slowed the car on the dirt track.

"In this case, caution is probably a good thing." As much as Tracy worried about the presence of the Brazilian army, she also knew the country's military had helped ease Brazil's transition from a Portuguese colony to an independent nation. Not a drop of blood had been shed on either side. The two countries were still on good terms, in fact.

There was no reason to fear their presence. Not really. At least, that's what she told herself.

Ben powered down his window and flashed his residence card, identifying both of them. "General Gutierrez is expecting us."

The soldier checked a handwritten list on his clipboard and nodded. "You've been told what you're dealing with?"

No. They'd been told nothing other than Ben being asked to come, but Tracy wasn't sure how much this particular soldier knew. She didn't want to start a mass panic.

Ben nodded. "We're aware. We brought masks and equipment."

She didn't contradict him or try to add to his words. She knew he'd done quite a bit of work for the military and he'd probably identified many other pathogens for them in the past. They had also taken the time to track her down and challenge her work four years ago, when Ben had asked them to, something that still had the power to make her hackles rise.

The soldier nodded. "I'll need to search your vehicle. General Gutierrez said there were to be no exceptions. So if you'll both step out, please."

Ben glanced her way, before putting the car in neutral—leaving the engine running and nodding at her to get out. He handed her a mask and donned one himself as he climbed from the vehicle.

The soldier looked in the backseat. He then gave the dizzying array of equipment they were carrying a cursory glance but didn't open any of the boxes. He seemed to be looking for stowaways more than anything, which seemed crazy. Who would want to sneak into a plague-infested area? Then again, she'd heard of crazier things, and nobody wanted this disease to get out of the village and into one of the bigger cities. *Teresina* wasn't all that far away, when you thought about it.

Ben came to stand next to her, and she noticed he was careful not to touch her. She swallowed. Not that she wanted him to. She'd had no idea they'd be thrown together in a situation like the one they were currently facing. But despite the pain that seeing him again brought, she couldn't have asked for a better, or more qualified, work partner.

She heard her name being called and turned towards the sound. Pedro hurried toward them, only to be stopped by another soldier about fifty yards before he reached them. The man's point came across loud and clear. Once she and Ben crossed this particular line, there'd be no going back until it was all over. Who knew how long that could be?

"Ben, are you sure you want to do this? You can drop

me off and go back to Teresina. There's no reason to risk yourself and all your work."

A muscle spasmed in his jaw, his eyes on Pedro. "*My* name was the one on the dance card, remember?" He shoved his hands in his pockets. "Besides, this is part of my job. It's why I work at the institute."

"Yes, well..." She didn't know how to finish the statement, since her reasons for wanting him to go back to the safe confines of his office was nothing more than a bid to keep her distance. She'd used his invitation as a way to regain access to the town, but she was also smart enough to know they might need his expertise before this was all over. So she held her tongue.

She glanced back at the soldier, who was currently peering beneath the car at its chassis.

Really? The guy had been watching way too many TV shows.

"Can I go in while you keep looking? My assistant is motioning to me, and I want to start checking on the patients." Daniel and Cleo were in there somewhere.

The soldier waved her through, even as he switched on a flashlight and continued looking.

"Tracy..." Ben, forced to wait for his vehicle to pass inspection, gave her a warning growl, but she shrugged him off.

"I'll meet you once you get through the checkpoint. Don't let them confiscate the antibiotics."

And with that, she made her escape. Securing her mask and feeling guilty, she stepped around the line of military vehicles and met Pedro, pulling him a safe distance away from the soldier who'd stopped him.

"It's pneumonic plague," she whispered, switching to Portuguese while noting he was already wearing a mask. "You'll need to start on antibiotics immediately."

"I thought so. They're staying pretty tight-lipped about

the whole thing, but they've set up a quarantine area. Those who are ill have been kept separate from those who still appear healthy—which aren't many at this point."

"Any more deaths? How are Daniel and Cleo?"

"Who?"

"The two kids we found in the field."

Daniel, the boy she'd taken samples from, had been lying in a grassy area, too weak to stand and walk. His sister, showing signs of the illness as well, had refused to leave his side. They'd carried them back to an empty house, just as the military had shown up and taken over.

"No change in the boy, although there have been two more deaths."

"And Cleo?"

"She's definitely got it, but now that we know what we're dealing with, we can start them both on treatment." Pedro slung his arm around her and squeezed. "Can I say how glad I am to see you? These soldier boys are some scary dudes."

He said the last line in English, using his best American accent, which made Tracy smile. She glanced over at Ben, who was still glowering at her, and her smile died.

The soldiers weren't the only scary dudes.

Pedro continued, "The military docs have IVs going on some of the patients, but they wouldn't tell me what they injected into the lines."

"Strange." She glanced at one of the houses, which currently had a small contingent of guards at the doors and windows. "Did they say anything about antibiotics?"

"I think they're still trying to get a handle on things."

Ben joined them on foot, and she frowned at him. "Where's your car?"

"They're going to drive it in and park it in front of one of the houses. They've evidently got a research area already set up."

He glanced at Pedro, whose arm was still around her, obviously waiting for an introduction. Okay, this was going to be fun. She noticed Pedro also seemed to be assessing Ben, trying to figure out what his place was in all this. He'd never asked about her ring, and she'd never volunteered any information. Several people had assumed she was widowed, and she'd just let it ride. Maybe she could simply omit Ben's relationship to her.

Well, that would be easy enough, because there was no relationship.

"Ben, this is Pedro, my assistant." She hesitated. "Pedro, this is Ben, head epidemiologist at the *Centro de Doenças Tropicais* in Teresina. He's the one I went to see." Maybe no one would notice that she'd conveniently left out his last name. Not that she went by it any more.

Ben held out his hand. "Ben Almeida. Nice to meet you." He slid Tracy a smile that said he knew exactly what she'd done and why. "I also happen to be Tracy's husband."

The look of shock in her assistant's eyes was unmistakable, and he quickly removed his arm from around her shoulders. He shot her a look but dutifully shook hands and muttered something appropriate. She, on the other hand, sent Ben a death stare meant to cut him in two. Instead, he seemed totally unfazed by her ire.

Ben nodded. "I've heard Tracy's account of what happened here. Why don't you tell me what you've observed?"

It was said as if she was clueless. Pressure began building in the back of her head.

Her assistant knew better. "Well, she's probably told you more than I could. We've got about fifteen cases of… Tracy said it's pneumonic plague?"

"Yes." Ben's eyes followed the progress of some men in hazard gear as they went from one building to another. "And judging from the way they're treating it, they know what they're dealing with. Are they still burning the bodies?"

"Yes. Two more in the last couple of hours," Pedro said. "The boy whose sample I brought in—Daniel—is still alive, but he's pretty sick. His sister is as well."

She didn't need to say what else she knew: antibiotics needed to be started within twenty-four hours of the appearance of symptoms to be effective. Ben would already know that. The treatment window was narrow, but she wouldn't give up, no matter how sick the patient.

Tracy ached for the two children, their mother ripped from them without so much as a funeral service or a chance to say goodbye. Just thrown onto a flaming pyre to destroy any pathogens. How many other kids would watch helplessly as the same thing happened to their relatives? As much as she knew it had to be done, it still didn't make it any easier. How would she feel if the body being burned was Ben's?

No. Not Ben. She wouldn't let her mind go there.

"Where are they putting you up for the night?" she asked Pedro.

"They've got medical civilians in one house and military personnel in another. They post guards out front of both of them, though."

Ben's four-wheel drive pulled up beside them and the soldier poked his head out of the open window. "I'm taking your vehicle to the research center we've set up. Do you want a ride?"

"We'll follow on foot," Ben said. Tracy got the idea, he wanted to continue their conversation in private. "And if you could put Dr. Hinton in the same house as me, I'd appreciate it. I haven't seen my wife in quite a while and would like some alone time with her if possible." He quirked an eyebrow at the man, while reaching over and taking her hand in his and giving it a warning squeeze. The presumption of his move made the rising pressure in her head grow to dangerous levels.

Her poor assistant squirmed visibly.

If Pedro hadn't been beside them, she'd have made it plain how little contact—of any sort—she wanted with him. But she knew Ben well enough to know he didn't say or do anything without a good reason.

The driver grinned and promised to see what he could do.

But, oh, she was going to let Ben know she was *not* happy with that arrangement. She hadn't wanted anyone to know what their relationship was, and now everyone in town would be snickering behind their backs.

"Nice work," she hissed.

Pedro shifted from foot to foot. "I'm sorry, I had no idea you were… I just assumed you were…"

"Single?" Ben supplied, an edge to his voice.

Wow, was he actually doing this? He'd never expressed any hint of jealousy when they'd been together. And she didn't appreciate it now.

"No, not exactly. I just knew she didn't have anyone living with her."

Ben's brows lifted. "You knew that for a fact, did you?"

"Well, yes. W-we had staff meetings at her house on a regular basis."

Tracy took a closer look at her assistant's face. There was discomfiture and something else lurking in his brown eyes. Oh God. Surely he wasn't interested in her. She'd never given him any reason to think she might be remotely attracted to him.

At least, she hoped she hadn't. And yet Ben had automatically assumed Pedro might have his eye on her. Why would he even care?

She touched Pedro's arm. "Ben and I…well, it's complicated."

Complicated. It was. At least for her. And Ben had probably never forgiven her for walking away from their marriage without a word. But what could she have said, really?

Not only do I not want to get pregnant again, I might choose to have my non-cancerous breasts removed.

She could still explain, if she wanted to. But after the way he'd run roughshod over her four years ago, going behind her back and manipulating her into coming home, he'd pretty much snuffed out any feelings of guilt on her part.

Ben had been part of the reason she'd struggled with making a final decision about what to do about her test results. But now that he and the baby were no longer part of the equation, she'd put things on hold, choosing to make a difference in the lives of others instead.

Dragging her attention back to Pedro, she tried her best to finish her earlier statement. Putting more emphasis on the words than was strictly necessary, she wanted to make sure she got her point across to both of them.

"Ben and I are separated. We have been for quite some time. So anything that happens between us will be strictly business."

Now, if she could just convince herself of that, she should be good to go.

CHAPTER FIVE

THERE WAS A reason it was called the Black Death.

There was nothing pretty or romantic about the plague. And the pneumonic form of the disease was the most dangerous, rapidly killing those it touched.

Ben stepped into the tiny house where the patients were being housed, and he fought a wave of pure desolation as he looked over the place. Tracy seemed just as shocked, standing motionless in the doorway beside her assistant.

Simple green cots were packed into what used to be a living room, laid out in two rows with barely enough space between beds for doctors to work.

Ben counted silently. Fourteen patients. And not all of them had IVs started. In fact, when he looked closer, he saw that the wall over some of the cots had a crude "X" penned in black ink.

A chill went over him. Deathbeds.

His gaze moved further and he spotted two men he assumed were doctors, still wearing that hazard gear he'd spotted earlier. The pair stood on either side of a bed, assessing a woman who was wailing, the sound coming in fits and starts that were interrupted by coughing spasms. One of the men leaned past the patient and slashed a mark over the bed.

Just like that. Bile pumped into his stomach in a flood.

Tracy's gaze met his, her eyes reflecting pure horror. She reached out and gripped Pedro's sleeve. "So many."

The man nodded. "I know."

None of the trio had on the protective clothing worn by the other doctors, other than masks and latex gloves, but as Tracy was on antibiotics and Pedro had just been given his first dose, there was no need. He assumed the heavy gear worn by the other men would be done away with pretty soon.

Besides, it was stifling in the room, the number of bodies cranking up the temperatures to unbearable levels. There wasn't even a fan to move the air around, probably out of fear of microbes being carried outside the room. But none of these patients—even the ones without the fatal mark on the wall—would last long if they couldn't cool it down.

Ben decided that one of his first orders of business would be to set up some kind of misting system.

Tracy moved towards him and touched his arm, pointing to the left at a nearby patient. It was a boy who Ben assumed was the one she'd been so worried about. There was a black squiggle over his bed but it was incomplete, as if someone had started to cross him off the list of the living and had then changed his mind.

"I'm going to check on Daniel and Cleo."

Pedro made a move to follow then noticed Ben's frown and evidently thought better of it, shifting his attention to a patient on the other side of the room instead.

Why did he care if the man had a thing for Tracy? Unlike him, the assistant seemed to have no problem with her job. He probably traveled with her every chance he got.

A steady pain thumped on either side of his head, and he squeezed the bridge of his nose in an effort to interrupt the nerve impulses.

While Tracy checked on the boy, he made his way to

the suited pair across the room. He identified himself and flashed his ID card, causing one of the men's brows to lift. "You're the *epidemiologista* General Gutierrez sent for?"

Ben nodded. "Are you marking these beds on his orders?"

"Well, no. He won't be here until tomorrow." They glanced quickly at each other. "But we can't take care of fourteen patients on our own, so we've been…" The words trailed away, but Ben understood. They were deciding who was worth their care and who was beyond saving.

"Well, Dr. Hinton and myself will be joining you, so let's set up a rotating schedule. Between all of us I'm sure we can make an effort to see *all* the patients." He let his emphasis hang in the air.

"But some of them won't last a day."

"And some of them might," he countered. "Why don't you explain to me who you've assessed, and we'll divide the room into critical care and non-critical, just like you would for field triage. It'll help us divide our efforts."

Neither man looked happy to be challenged, but they didn't contradict him either. If he knew General Gutierrez, the man had told them to follow his recommendations. The doctors gave him a quick rundown and Ben made a list, marking "TI"—for *tratamento intensivo*—next to those patients who were in critical condition and needed extra care. Not one "X" went next to anyone's name.

Ben moved over to the older woman who'd cried out as the men had marked her bed and found she was indeed critical, with red staining around her mouth that signaled she was producing bloody sputum. He laid a gloved hand on her forehead and spoke softly to her, her glassy eyes coming up to meet his, even as her breath rasped in and out, breathing labored. "We're going to take good care of you, okay?"

She blinked at him, not even making an effort to speak.

Ben called out to Tracy. "I want IVs started on all the patients who don't currently have one. We're going to push antibiotics into them. All of them." Then he turned to one of the men and nodded towards the radio on his hip. "Can you get me General Gutierrez? He and I need to have a little chat."

She didn't know what he'd done, but Ben had obviously spoken to someone in authority and asked for some changes. The cots—with the help of other soldiers—had been rearranged according to how ill each patient was. Daniel and Cleo had ended up on opposite sides of the room.

Heart aching, she moved from the boy to another patient, trying not to think about his prospects as she quickly filled a syringe from a vial of antibiotics and inserted it into the injection port of the IV line, marking the time and amounts in a small spiral-bound notebook they'd made up for each patient.

She caught Pedro's eye from across the room and smiled.

"You doing okay?" she mouthed, receiving a thumbs-up in return. Although not a doctor, Pedro had accompanied her on many of her forays into villages and had helped enough that she knew he could hold his own in an emergency. She also trusted him enough to know he'd ask for help if something was beyond his capabilities.

Her shirt was soaked with sweat and she'd gone through masks at an alarming rate. She hoped Ben had brought a big supply. He'd mentioned setting up a rudimentary misting system to help cool off the room.

Right now, though, he was seeing to the unloading of his car, and she refused to think about where they were going to sleep tonight. Ben had said the same "house"… not the same "room" when he'd made his request. But he'd also made it plain that they were married, so she had no doubt they'd be placed together. What was he thinking? Surely he had no more desire to be with her than she had to be with him?

Okay, maybe "desire" was the wrong word to use. Because put them in a room alone together and they tended to combust at frightening speed. She remembered her fury as she'd walked into that village to confront him on their first meeting. She'd heard there was an epidemiologist heading her way down the river but that he was taking his sweet time.

Unwilling to wait for him to stop at every village and sample the local cuisine, she'd powered back upriver and stomped her way to the heart of the village. He'd been standing in the middle of a group of men, a big smile on his face. She'd opened her mouth to throw a vile accusation his way, only to have the words stop in her throat the second their eyes had met.

He'd stared at her for several long seconds then one eyebrow had quirked upwards. "Are you here for me?"

"I…I…" Realizing she'd looked like a fool, she'd drawn herself up to her full height and let him have it.

She'd let him have it again two days later. In an entirely different way.

Oh, God. She could *not* be in a room alone with the man if she could help it. So what was she going to do?

Stay with her patients as much as possible, that's what. She'd already been here for almost eight hours. And it was now a few minutes past the end of her shift. If she knew Ben, he would make them all stick to the schedule he'd drawn up—whether they wanted to or not.

Even as she thought it, she reached Cleo's bed and leaned over her. The girl gave her a tremulous smile, which she returned.

"Hey, how are you doing?"

"Sleepy, and my head hurts." Cleo's voice was a thread of sound.

"I know." Headaches were one of the symptoms of the plague, but Cleo's episode didn't seem to be progressing as rapidly as Daniel's had. "You need to rest. I'm sure—"

Something cool and moist hit her left ankle and swept up the back of her leg until it reached the bottom of her shorts. Stifling a scream, she straightened and spun around to find empty air. She lowered her gaze and spied Ben, on his haunches, about a foot away, a spray bottle in his hand. Half-thought words bubbled on her tongue but didn't find an exit.

He got two more squirts in before she found her voice. "What do you think you're doing?"

Holding the pump bottle up, he said. "We have a room full of sick people. All we need is to have a dengue outbreak on top of everything."

Repellant. Ah. She got it.

But why was he the one spraying it on her? He could have just handed her the bottle and ordered her to put it on.

"You were busy," he said, as if reading her thoughts. "And sometimes with you it's easier to act than to argue."

Like their first kiss? When he'd dragged her to him and planted his lips on hers without so much as a "May I?"

She swallowed, hoping he couldn't read the direction of her thoughts. Or the fact that seeing him kneeling in front of her reminded her of other times when he'd done just that.

Before she could grab the bottle out of his hand he went back to work and sprayed the front of her legs. "Turn around."

"Are you going to personally spray Pedro and the other workers, too? Or just me?"

"They're not wearing shorts." His brows went up. "Didn't think it was as urgent."

She couldn't stop the smile or the roll of her eyes, but

she obediently turned around. In reality the chill of the spray against her super-heated skin was heavenly as he slowly misted the back of her right leg. Looking down, she found Cleo looking up at her.

"He's bossy," the little girl said. Her voice was weak but there was a ghost of a smile on her face.

Tracy couldn't stop the laugh that bubbled out, her heart lightening at Cleo's ability to joke. "Oh, honey, you have no idea."

Ben's bossiness had a tendency to come out in all kinds of ways. Some of those she was better off not thinking about right now.

The spraying stopped and Tracy glanced behind her to find Ben staring up at her. Standing abruptly, he shoved the repellant bottle into her hands. "I'll let you finish up the rest. Give it to the other workers after you're done. And make sure you stay protected while you're here."

With that he walked away without a backward glance.

Stay protected? With him in the immediate vicinity?

She gave a huge sigh.

It would take a whole lot more than a bottle of repellent to do that.

CHAPTER SIX

HE WAS A masochist.

Ben stared at the figure sleeping in the hammock—her back to him—and wondered what on earth he'd been thinking by demanding they sleep in the same room. He obviously hadn't been thinking at all, but the sight of Tracy standing next to Pedro had sent a shaft of what could only be described as jealousy through him.

Why?

She could have been sleeping with twenty men a day after she'd left, and he'd have been none the wiser.

Yeah, but he hadn't had to stand there and witness it.

Even as he tried to convince himself that was the reason, he knew it went deeper than that. Deeper than the desire that churned to life as he stared at the sexy curve of hip flowing into a narrow waist. A waist that hadn't even had time to expand much before their baby had been lost.

She'd gotten off work two hours ahead of him, just as his schedule had dictated, which was a relief because she'd obviously come right back to the room and gone straight to sleep.

Which was exactly what he should be doing.

Tomorrow was going to be just as difficult as today.

Having Tracy here brought up all the tangled emotions he thought he'd already unraveled and put to bed. Sighing, he toed off his shoes, glad he'd donned a pair of athletic shorts to sleep in, because there was no way he was sleeping in just his boxers.

He slid into his hammock, trying to keep the creaking of the ropes to a minimum as he settled into place.

Someone like Pedro would have been ideal husband material for Tracy. He obviously didn't mind her vagabond spirit. In fact, he traveled with her on a regular basis, if appearances were anything to go by.

But then again, Pedro wasn't married to her. He hadn't had to sit at home wondering why she wanted to be anywhere else but with him. Wondering if, once their child was born, the baby would be dumped in the care of his housekeeper, just as he'd been when he'd been little.

Anger churned in his chest at the thought.

So why had seeing her bending over that little girl's bed, shapely bottom facing him, made the saliva pool in his mouth? And when she'd leaned further over, the long, lean muscles in her calves bunching as she'd gone on tiptoe to adjust the sheet on the far side of the cot, his body had roared to life. There hadn't been a drop of anger in sight.

He'd wanted her. Just as much as he always had.

He'd meant to hand her the bottle of repellent with a brusque order to put some on, but he'd been desperate to erase the images cascading through his mind. Squirting a healthy dose of cold liquid on her had seemed like the ideal way to shock her into moving—and shock his own body back to normal. Like a virtual defibrillator, halting a deadly spiral of electrical impulses before they'd overwhelmed his system.

His actions had backfired, though.

She'd turned around, just like he'd hoped, only his senses hadn't righted themselves, they'd gone berserk. And when he'd heard that low, throaty laugh at something her young patient had said, his stomach had turned inside out, drilling him with the reality of how stupid his move had been.

Besides, he'd had other things he needed to attend to.

Like going out and dunking his head in a bucket of water.

Which he'd done. Literally.

When he'd gone back inside, Tracy had already finished spraying herself down, the shine from the repellant glinting off the tip of her upturned nose, making his gut twist all over again.

He'd spent the rest of the day hanging mosquito netting around all of the patients' beds and caring for the ones who were the farthest away from his ex-wife.

Now, if he could just convince himself she really was his ex, he'd be just peachy.

Only two days into the outbreak and she was dog-tired. And hot.

So terribly hot. And now they were up to twenty patients, rather than fourteen.

The tiny house was still stifling, although Ben had figured out a way to combine fans with periodic jets of fine mist that reminded Tracy of the produce sections she'd seen at US supermarkets. It did help, but still…the place could never be deemed "cool."

Then again, it never really cooled off in this part of the world. Tracy had become soft, working in São Paulo for much of the year. The sticky heat that blanketed the equator—a place where seasons didn't exist—was unrelenting, reaching into every nook and cranny.

It had to be just as hard for Ben, who worked in an air-conditioned office nowadays, rather than doing fieldwork like he'd done when they'd met.

They'd administered a therapeutic dose of antibiotics into all their patients, but they were already seeing the truth of that narrow window of treatment. The patients who'd been diagnosed after help arrived and given antibiotics immediately were doing better than those who had already been ill when they'd arrived.

The statistics held true, with the sickest of their patients continuing their downward spiral. Still, they had to keep trying, so they stayed their course, using either IV antibiotics, intramuscular injections or, for those who could tolerate it, oral doses. Two more had died since their arrival, but at least Ben had ordered those awful marks above the beds to be scrubbed clean.

Amazingly, Daniel—although gravely ill—was still hanging in there.

She glanced over at Ben, who was injecting his next patient, squeezing the woman's hand and offering her an encouraging smile that she couldn't actually see—because of his mask—but the crinkling at the corners of his eyes gave him away. Oh, how Tracy had loved seeing those happy little lines go to work.

He put the syringe into the medical waste container they'd set up, and Tracy reminded herself to check on the supply of disposable needles. He caught her looking at him from her place beside Daniel's bed and made his way over to her. She tensed, just as she'd done every time they'd had to interact.

"Why don't you take a quick nap?"

She shook her head. "I'm okay. Besides, I've had more sleep than you have."

Something she would know, as she'd heard him get up in the middle of the night and leave their room both nights they'd been in there. Maybe he was as restless as she was.

Well, whose fault was that? He'd been the one who'd insisted they stay together, which had made things incredibly awkward with Pedro.

And there were no real beds, so it wasn't a matter of

her getting the bed while he slept on a pallet on the floor. No, all the workers had been assigned military hammocks, the residents' original hammocks having been confiscated, along with most of their fabric or upholstered possessions. Once some of the patients recovered, they'd have the added hardship of knowing many of their household clothes and belongings were long gone. Destroyed for the good of the village.

Tracy, for once, had agreed with the decision when Ben told her about it.

In addition to the bed situation, there wasn't much privacy to be had anywhere in the town. Showers had been set up in a clearing and the stinging smell of strong disinfectant soap had become an all-too-familiar fragrance around the compound. But even that couldn't totally vanquish the warm masculine scent that greeted her each night from the neighboring hammock where Ben lay.

Hanging side by side, the two hammocks were slung on three hooks, sharing one at the lower end, while the two upper ends branched apart onto two separate hooks, so that the hammocks formed a V. Knowing their feet were almost touching each and every night had been part of the reason for her sleeplessness.

So she'd lain awake for hours, despite her growing fatigue, until Ben—like he'd done the previous two nights—had slipped from his bed and out of the room. Only then had she finally been able to close her eyes and relax.

Ben looked like he was about to press his point about her taking a nap when the front door to the house banged open and a fierce argument carried through to where they were standing.

What in the name of...?

Both she and Ben moved quickly into the hallway, not wanting someone to be inadvertently exposed to the sickroom. They found one of the military police who'd been assigned to enforcing the quarantine arguing with a young girl who was around six years old. Tear tracks marked the dust on either side of the child's face, and her feet—clad only in flip-flops—were caked with dirt.

"What's going on?" Ben asked in Portuguese.

"She insists on speaking with a doctor, even though I've explained she can't go in there."

Tracy moved forward. "It's okay. I'll go outside with her."

"Tracy." Ben put a hand on her arm, stopping her.

She sent him a look that she hoped conveyed her irritation. "Someone has to talk to her. Better me than them." She aimed a thumb at the poor soldier.

"You need to at least take off your gear before you go out there."

"I will." She spoke softly to the child, telling her it was okay, that she'd be out in a minute. The girl nodded, the wobbling of her chin as she turned to go wrenching at Tracy's heart.

Ben caught the eye of one of the military doctors and told him they'd be back in a few minutes. They both stripped off their protective gear in the clean area and scrubbed with antibiotic soap. Tracy used her forearm to swipe at her damp forehead, frowning when Ben lifted a hand toward her. She took a quick step back.

"You have suds." He pointed to his own forehead.

She reached up and dabbed it away herself, avoiding his eyes, then pushed through the screen door at the back of the house. They made their way round to the front and the little girl rushed toward them. Ben stepped in front of Tracy, causing her to give a sigh of exasperation. "Ben, please. She's not going to hurt anyone."

Moving around him, she knelt in front of the child. "What's your name?"

"Miriam."

Tracy wanted to gently wipe a smudge on the little girl's forehead, much as Ben had tried to do with her a second ago, but she was too afraid of spreading germs at this point to touch anyone outside the village. "Okay, Miriam. What did you want to tell us?"

"You are doctors?"

"Yes. We both are. It's okay. Is someone sick?"

The girl clasped her hands in front of her and nodded. "My *mami*. She has been ill for two days, but told me not to tell anyone. But now..." Her voice broke on a low sob. "But now she does not wake up, even when I try to feed her broth."

"Where is she?"

"At my house. But it is a long way from here."

The first twinge of alarm filtered up her back. "How far?"

"The next village."

Horrified, Tracy stood in a rush and grabbed Ben's hand, her wide eyes on his. "Could it have spread beyond São João dos Rios?"

No! They'd been so careful, no one had been allowed to leave the village once the military had arrived.

But before that?"

His fingers closed around hers, giving them a quick squeeze, then addressed the child, whose small forehead was now scrunched in distress. "Was your mother coughing?"

"Yes. She said it was just a cold, but I am afraid..." She motioned around the quarantined village. "We have heard what happened here. They say the military is shooting anyone who is sick. I had to sneak past them to find you."

Tracy's heart clenched. She knew how suspicious some of these towns were of government officials. But those fears only helped spread sickness and disease. Because people who were afraid tended to hide things from those who could help them.

Like Tracy had when she'd left Ben four years ago?

No, it wasn't the same thing at all. She forced a smile to her lips, knowing it probably looked anything but reassuring. "No one is shooting anyone."

"Will you come and help my mother, then?"

Tracy glanced at the house, where one of the military police watched them closely. Would they let her travel to the village or would they insist on sending someone else? It was a tough call. She didn't want to risk spreading anything, but the more people involved, the more places the disease could be carried. "Yes, honey, I will."

When she tried to move towards the guard, Ben clamped down on her hand. "What do you think you're doing, Tracy?" he murmured, sending a whisper of air across her cheek that made her shiver.

"You heard her. Her mother is sick."

"You could end up making things worse for everyone."

The shiver turned to ice in her veins. Those words were too close to the message he'd sent with the military four years ago. Her brows went up and she looked pointedly at the guard behind them. "I'm going, whether you approve or not. You could always send your little friends after me. You seem to be quite good at doing that."

"Come on, Tracy. You know why I sent them. You were carrying our child."

She did know—and maybe she'd been foolish to travel alone, but she'd been just six weeks along and she'd already had her yellow fever shot. She also knew her reason for taking off that week had had little to do with the village and everything to do with the results of her test. Even so, the blinding humiliation of seeing those uniformed officials set foot on that beach—and knowing her husband had been behind their presence—still stung.

They glared at each other. The last thing she needed to do right now was antagonize him further. She forced her voice to soften. "Please, try to understand. I *have* to check on her mother. My job is part of what keeps me going."

"Keeps you going?"

That last phrase had slipped out before she realized it. Leave it to Ben to catch it as it flew by.

"I mean, my job is important to me, that's all."

His gaze raked her face, and she held her breath, hoping the raw fear that slithered up her throat wasn't visible. Breaking eye contact, he glanced down at the girl, whose terror was much more on the surface. "Fine. We'll both go. But we need to take precautions. We're on antibiotics, so I'm not worried about us, but I also don't want us carrying anything back that way."

Was that why he'd been worried? Maybe she'd misjudged him.

"What about Miriam?" She kept her voice just as low, switching to English to make it harder for the little girl to understand what she was saying. "They may not let her leave São João dos Rios, now that she's been exposed."

"I know. I'll talk to the guard and get her started on antibiotics."

Poor girl, she had no idea that by trying to get help for her mother she might become a virtual prisoner. And if the worst came to the worst, and her mother had the deadly disease, she might never see her again.

A familiar pang went through Tracy's chest. Her mother had died while Tracy had been here in Brazil. Six months after she and Ben had married, in fact. Her mother had had no idea she was sick during the wedding rehearsal or as they'd planned what should have been a happy occasion. But then she'd been diagnosed a few weeks after the ceremony. She'd died months later.

Squaring her shoulders, she went through the motions

of going with Ben to talk to the guard, who in turn had to make a phone call up his chain of command. An hour later, she, Ben, and four military personnel were on their way to the next village. Ben had his arm around her in the backseat of the four-wheel drive to help steady her as they hit pothole after pothole, the scarred tract rarely seeing much in the way of motor vehicles.

Loaded to the gills with medical equipment, as well as Ben's lab stuff, she leaned against him, allowing him to pull her even closer as she prayed that whatever they found would not be as bad as she feared.

"Bronchitis," Ben declared.

Tracy almost laughed aloud as a giddy sense of relief swept over her. "Are you sure?"

Ben sat behind the house on a low three-legged stool, studying the last of the slides through his microscope.

"I don't see any sign of plague bacteria. And she's awake now. No fever or symptoms other than some thick congestion in her chest." He leaned back and looked at her. "She probably kept going until she was literally worn out, which was why Miriam couldn't wake her up. Regardless, we don't have a case of the plague here."

"Thank God." Her legs threatened to give out, and she had to put a hand on Ben's shoulder to brace herself.

He glanced up at her, concern in his eyes. "Hey, sit down before you fall down." Before she realized what he was doing, he'd pulled her onto his left knee.

"Sorry," he murmured. "There's nowhere else to sit."

She nodded. "I'm sorry about what I said earlier. About you sending the military after me."

"Don't worry about it. You were upset."

She blinked. He'd just given her absolution. Whether it was for sins of the past or sins of the present was immaterial right now—not when the blood was thickening in her veins, the air around her turning crystal clear with secret knowledge.

The sudden sound of his breath being let out and the way his arm tightened around her back were her undoing. All she could think about was that she owed him a huge "thank you." Before she could stop herself, she looped her arms around his neck and leaned forward to kiss him.

CHAPTER SEVEN

HER LIPS GRAZED his cheek.

Ben wasn't at all sure how it happened. First she was apologizing then her mouth was on his skin. The instant it happened, something from the past surged inside him, and he brushed aside the gesture in favor of something a little more personal. If she was going to kiss him, he was going to make damned sure it counted. Using his free hand to cup her head, he eased her round until she faced him.

He stared at her for a long moment, taking in the parted lips, glittering eyes…an expression he knew all too well. He lowered his head, an inner shout of exultation going off in his skull when she didn't flinch away but met him halfway.

Their lips connected, and it was as if a match had been struck in the presence of gasoline fumes. They both went up in flames.

A low moan slid between them. One that most certainly hadn't come from him. Taking that as a signal to continue, his fingers lifted and tunneled deep into her hair, the damp moisture of her scalp feeling cool against his overheated skin.

Ignoring the microscope and slides, he shifted her legs sideways until they rested between his, without breaking contact with her mouth for even a second.

The change in position pressed her thigh against his

already tightening flesh, which was pure torture—made him want to push back to increase the contact. He forced himself to remain still instead, although it just about killed him. It had been four years since he'd held this woman in his arms, and he wasn't about to blow it by doing anything that would have her leaping from his lap in a panic. Realistically, he knew they weren't going to have sex behind the house of an ill woman, but he could take a minute or two to drink his fill of her.

Only, he'd never really get his fill. Would always want more than she was willing to give.

He licked along the seam of her mouth, asking for permission. She granted it without a word, opening to him. He went deep, his hand tightening in her hair as he tipped her head sideways seeking to find the best angle possible. She wiggled closer, taking him almost to the brink before he got himself back under control.

He gave a hard swallow. *Slow.*

Exploring the heat and warmth he found between her lips, he tried to rememorize everything and realized he didn't need to. Because he'd forgotten nothing. Not the taste of her, not the shivers he could wring from her by using his teeth in addition to his tongue.

And when he could no longer contain his low groan, her fingers came up and tangled in his hair. He could feel the battle going on within her and fought against his own need to control the situation, letting her lead instead.

Unfortunately, she took that as a signal to pull back, her breath coming in husky snatches of sound that he found erotic beyond belief.

She took a couple more quick gulps before attempting to talk.

"Ben," she whispered, her mouth still against his. "What are we doing here?"

In spite of himself, he smiled. “I thought that was fairly obvious.”

“Mmm.” The hum of sound drove him crazy, just like it always had. “This is a mistake. You know it is.”

“I know.” He bit her lower lip, sucking on the soft flesh before releasing it with a growl. “Doesn’t mean I didn’t enjoy it, though. Or that you didn’t either.”

“I know.” No arguments, no denying that she felt the same. Just an acknowledgement of what was obvious to both of them.

It had been an incredibly long week, and all he wanted to do was wrap his arms around her, make slow, satisfying love and then go to sleep still trapped inside her. Just like they used to.

But he knew that was the exhaustion talking. Not to mention that thing wedged against her hip, which was busy shouting out commands he was doing his best to ignore.

Sorry, bud. You’re out of luck.

Tracy leaned her forehead against his and gave a drawn-out sigh. “We need to get back to the other village if this one is in the clear.”

She heaved one more sigh, before climbing to her feet, looking anywhere but at his lap, which was probably smart. “I’m sure we’re both so tired we’re not thinking straight. We’ll regret this once we’ve had some sleep.”

She might, but he wouldn’t. Not even if he slept as long as Rip Van Winkle. He’d still wake up and want to kiss her all over again.

He closed his eyes for a long moment then started undoing his equipment without a word.

She laid a hand on his shoulder. “If it’s any consolation, you’re right. I enjoyed it too. You always were a great kisser.”

Some of the tension in his spine seeped away. Questions from four years ago resurfaced and he couldn’t keep himself from asking, "Then why were you always in such a hurry to leave?"

"Please, don't, Ben. Not right now."

And her response was exactly the same as it had been back then. She hadn't wanted to talk about it—had just wanted to head off on her next adventure.

There was nothing left to say, then. "I'll get some medicine out of the car and explain the dosage."

She nodded. "I'm sure they'll even let Miriam come home as there's no evidence of pneumonic plague here. We'll put her on the prophylactic dosage of antibiotics and she should be fine."

Stowing his equipment in a large box and carefully stacking his microscope on top, all he could do was wish for a prophylactic dose of something that would cut through his current jumble of emotions and put him back on the road to normalcy.

Normalcy. Wow. If he ever found a pill that would restore that, he'd end up a very rich man.

Tracy could have kicked herself. She'd let him kiss her. *On the mouth.* Worse, she'd kissed him back. Crazily. As if she couldn't get enough of him.

Her chaste little gesture of thanks had flared to inferno proportions in a nanosecond.

The chemistry between them was just as potent as ever. Something she never should've doubted. Something she should have been braced for and never allowed to happen.

And why on earth had she let herself be drawn into an argument about the past? Because she was trying to keep her distance emotionally? You sure couldn't tell it from where she stood. Because the only message she'd been sending while perched on his lap had been more along the lines of throw-me-on-my-back-and-take-me-hard.

To allow that to happen, though, would only make

things more complicated. Especially now. She could admit that she still cared about him, but it didn't mean they could—or should—be together. If she thought there was a chance, she might try to explain what had happened all those years ago. But it wouldn't do any good at this point. And the last thing she needed was Ben's pity. Hanging onto the anger from the past might be best for both of them right now, because in another week or so they'd be heading in opposite directions.

Lying in her hammock, hours from the time they'd finally climbed into Ben's SUV and headed back to town, she still longed to reach across the space and take his hand. Touch his face. Kiss his lips.

Why? None of it made any sense.

There were less than two feet separating them. Less at the foot end of the hammocks. And she'd never been more keenly aware of that fact than she was now. The village was still and quiet. The military doctors had taken up the night shift, leaving Tracy and Ben to get five or six hours of sleep, which was what she should be doing right now, rather than lying here staring at the ceiling. Luckily, Ben was facing away from her and couldn't see her restless movements. He'd fallen asleep almost as soon as his body had hit the hammock, while she'd pretended to do the same. Was still pretending, in fact.

Just like she'd pretended that kiss today was the result of exhaustion and stress.

He turned unexpectedly, and Tracy clamped her eyelids shut, trying to breathe slowly and deeply, even though her heart was pounding out a crazy tattoo. The sound of a throat clearing, some more rustling and then a low, exasperated curse met her ears. She felt a rush of air against her and the movement of his hammock disturbing hers where they intersected at the bottom.

Soft footsteps. Another oath. Then the sound of a door quietly opening and closing. Just like the last three nights.

She waited for several seconds before she got up the courage to open her eyes again and peek.

Yep. He was gone. Where was he disappearing to each night? The restroom? If so, that meant he'd be back in a matter of minutes—which he never was. She pushed her fingers through the open-weave fabric of her hammock in irritation, squeezing the fibers tight. Instead of wondering where he was, she should be using this time to try to go to sleep.

Fat chance of that now.

She continued to lie very still, waiting, staring at the closed door on the other side of the tiny room.

But fifteen minutes later there was still no sign of him, just like on previous nights. Had he decided he couldn't sleep? Yes, it was hot in the room—the fan doing nothing more than fluffing the balmy air—but it would be just as hot no matter where he went.

Did this have something to do with their kiss, earlier? If that were the case, then what was his excuse on the other nights?

Crossing her arms over her chest, she closed her eyes again and tried for the umpteenth time to go to sleep. Morning was going to come, and with it a whole new day of struggles and trials as they tried to care for their remaining patients.

Seven more days. That's how long Ben figured it would take to get the epidemic under control.

And that's how long she had to kick this stupid attraction to the curb and keep herself out of Ben's bed.

Seven, very long days.

CHAPTER EIGHT

"CLEO'S RIGHT HERE, honey."

Gently placing a moist cloth across Daniel's feverish brow, Tracy nodded at the neighboring cot, where Ben was adjusting the IV pole.

The boy had finally regained consciousness, four days after being found in the field. His first words had been to ask about his sister. The plea had remained throughout the day, sometimes interrupted by bouts of coughing, sometimes gasped between harsh breaths, but he never relented. The question was there each time he rallied for a few moments. And it made Tracy's heart squeeze. It was as if, even in his precarious state, he refused to believe Cleo was alive unless he saw it for himself.

Ben had finally relented and offered to shuffle patients around so that the brother and sister could remain close to each other's sides, despite the fact that he'd wanted patients placed according to severity of illness. Daniel was still gravely ill, whereas Cleo's sickness had not ravaged her young body as much as those of some of their other patients. She said her head still ached, but she hadn't worsened.

Daniel's glassy eyes swiveled to the right. "Clee," he whispered, shaky fingers reaching across the space and then dropping before he succeeded in reaching the other bed.

"She's here, Daniel, but she's asleep right now. We have to let her rest so she can be strong and healthy again." Her gloved fingers brushed back a moist lock of hair, a rush of emotion clogging her throat. “You need to do the same. She’ll still be here when you wake up.”

If you wake up.

She immediately dismissed the thought. Daniel’s vitals had slowly grown weaker over the last couple of days, but he continued to fight harder than anyone she’d ever seen. And so would she. She’d come here to fight for these kids, against the military’s wishes…against Ben’s wishes. And she was going to damn well keep on fighting.

Maybe there was a message for her in there somewhere. But she was too tired to dig for it right now. Maybe later.

As if he sensed the direction of her thoughts, Ben came to stand beside her. “You need to get some rest as well. You look exhausted.”

“We’re all tired.” She reached up to wipe a trickle of perspiration from her temple only to have Ben beat her to it, using one of the dry compresses to blot her forehead. She gave him a weak grin. “You’d think after almost a week I’d be used to the heat. I travel down the Amazon all the time.”

They both froze, and Tracy wondered if he was remembering that last fateful trip.

Ben had accused her of neglecting their marriage, of being careless with their baby’s health. Had she? Had her own plight so blinded her that she’d taken unnecessary chances?

She’d never know. And there was nothing she could do to go back and change things anyway.

Guilt gnawed at her, just as strong now as it had been back then.

“You’re good with them, you know.”

The change in subject made her blink. “With who?”

He nodded toward the kids. “These two.”

“I care about all my patients.”

"I wasn't accusing you of anything, Tracy. Just making a statement."

She considered that for a moment. The anger had been so strong at the end of their marriage that it was hard to hear anything he said without the filters of the past. Maybe she should start trying to take his words at face value. Maybe he could start doing the same.

She perched on the side of Cleo's bed, her fingers feathering through the girl's hair. A low sigh came from the child's throat, and she snuggled into her hand.

Tears pricked very close to the surface but she ignored them as best she could. "I can't imagine how they're going to feel when they wake up and realize their mother is gone. For ever."

Well, she took that back. She knew how that felt but she'd at least had her mom with her until she was a grown woman. These kids would never know how that felt. She wished there was some way she could take that pain from them.

"Sometimes a parent doesn't have to die to be gone," Ben murmured.

She glanced up at him, but he was staring through the dusty window across from them.

"Are you talking about your mom and dad?" Ben and Marcelo's parents hadn't been around much as they'd been growing up and both men carried some resentment about that. That resentment had carried over to Ben's marriage.

Her traveling had been a constant source of arguments almost from the moment they'd both said, "I do."

But Ben had been just as gung ho about his job when they'd met. She hadn't understood exactly why he'd wanted to give all that up. Well, that wasn't quite true either. When she'd found out she was pregnant, she'd been all set to let her office take over a lot of *Projeto Vida's* off-site calls. Then things had changed.

And Ben had reacted badly to her need for space…for time to think. In reality, she probably should have told him sooner, but she'd still been reeling from the news and grieving over her mother's and sisters' deaths.

Ben's eyes refocused on her. "No. Just talking in generalities."

He was lying. But it was easier to let this particular subject go. "I forgot to ask. How's Rosa?"

"Fine. Still at the house."

She wasn't surprised. The old housekeeper—who'd been widowed at a young age and had never remarried—had practically raised Ben and Marcelo. Of course Ben would keep her on. It was another thing they'd argued about.

Oh, not about Rosa still living there—Tracy loved her almost as much as Ben—but that he wouldn't hear of the housekeeper having any part in raising their child. The early elation of finding out she was pregnant hadn't lasted long.

When he'd asked about her plans for her job once the baby was born, she'd flippantly responded that Rosa would be thrilled to help during her absences—that she'd already asked her, in fact. Her words had been met with stony silence. Seconds later Ben had stalked from the room and slammed through the front door of the house.

Only afterwards had she realized how her comment might have sounded. She'd apologized and tried to explain once he'd come home, but she'd got the feeling Ben had heard little or nothing of what she'd said.

She sighed. "I miss Rosa."

"I'm sure she misses you as well."

Her heart aching, a silent question echoeing inside her head: *And what about you, Ben? Do you ever miss me?*

"Don't move too quickly. You're still weak."

Tracy put her shoulder beneath Daniel's arm and, with Pedro on his other side, they helped him walk slowly around the clearing in front of the house in an effort to ward off the possibility of deep vein thromboses from all his time in bed. Day five, and the patient who'd set off the frantic race to save a village seemed to have turned a corner—against all odds. Just yesterday they'd wondered if he would even make it. Somehow the twelve-year-old's body was fighting off the disease when by most medical journals' estimations he should be dead.

"M-my sister?" His voice was thin and raspy.

"Cleo is at the cafeteria. You have some catching up to do, you know," she teased. "Do you think you can handle the thought of sipping some broth?"

"I'd rather have *beijú*."

The local flatbread made from cassava flour was typical up here in the northeastern part of the country. Tracy had missed the gummy bread in São Paulo, although she could still find it on occasion.

Pedro shook his head. "I think we'd better stick to broth for today, like Tracy said."

Daniel made a face. "Not even beans and rice?"

"Soon," Tracy said with a smile. "Maybe in another day or two, okay?"

His already thin shoulders slumped, but he didn't argue as they led him over to the temporary mess hall the military had set up. The tent was divided into sides. Medical personnel and healthy villagers on one side and those with active infections on the other. Donning her mask, she ducked beneath the canvas door flap to deliver her patient.

Four long tables with wooden benches were mostly empty. There weren't very many patients at the moment who were well enough to actually walk the short distance from their beds. Huge fans sucked heat from the inside and blew it out, keeping the place from turning into an inferno as the sun baked the canvas roof. In fact, more of the flaps were open today, a sign the military knew things were looking up for the stricken town.

A wave from across the space caught her eye.

Cleo, seated at a front table, smiled, her dark eyes lighting up as she saw them come in. "Daniel, you're awake!" She motioned him over.

Tracy delivered their charge to the table and brother and sister were reunited—outside the sickroom—for the first time in over a week. Cleo's smile wavered and then she wrapped her arms around Daniel's neck and sobbed quietly. Tracy was forced to separate them gently when she grew concerned about the boy's system being overloaded. Before she could ask the person in charge of meals for a cup of broth, one magically appeared on the table in front of them.

Cleo, who'd begun to recover more quickly than Daniel, had black beans and rice on her plate—and Tracy could swear that was a piece of fried banana as well. Her own mouth watered, so she could only imagine how Daniel felt. But he dutifully picked up his spoon and gave a tentative taste of the contents of his cup. Despite the liquid diet, he closed his eyes as if it were the finest caviar.

"Good?" she asked.

He nodded, taking another sip.

Pedro glanced at the serving area. "I'm going to head over and get in line before it closes. What do you want?"

"I already have Tracy's food."

The voice came from behind them just as a tray was plonked down in front of her. A creamy-white *beijú*, slathered in butter, was folded in half and propped up on a neat mound of rice and beans. And, oh! A *whole* fried banana.

"Not fair," muttered Daniel, who looked longingly at the plate and sucked down another spoonful of his broth.

She glanced to the side and saw Ben, his eyes on Pedro as he set down a second tray beside hers. She gave her assistant an apologetic shrug. “Get something before they run out. I’ll see you later, okay?”

Ben waited for her to sit before joining her. Irritated, she realized she’d been looking for him all day.

“You’re supposed to be on the doctors’ side of the tent, you know,” she said, cringing as the words left her mouth. Great. No “Thank you” for the food. No “How are you?” Just a veiled accusation.

“Hmm. Well, so should you. I saw you come in and thought you might like an update on our situation.”

Our situation?

Oh, he meant here in town. He wasn’t referring to that disastrous kiss.

“Is that where you’ve been? With the military?”

“The guys in charge wanted me to fill them in. General Gutierrez is here and heard most of the news from his own doctors, but he wanted to make sure it matched the civilian report. The military’s reputation tends to be a touchy subject.”

“Since when?” As soon as the words were out of her mouth she wished she could call them back. “Sorry. That hadn’t come out right.”

He ignored her and leaned around her back to lay a hand on Daniel’s shoulder, smiling at the boy. “I’m surprised to see you out of bed.”

Cleo blinked at him with huge brown eyes. “What about me? Are you surprised to see me, too?”

“Definitely. But very glad.” He then ruffled Cleo’s hair, which caused the seven-year-old to giggle. The happy sound made Tracy’s heart contract. The man was a natural with children. He should have lots of them. All swarming around him like a litter of cute puppies.

“I haven’t heard a peep about any so-called meetings. Why didn’t someone call me?” She wasn’t really peeved but needed to get her mind off Ben and his future children.

Because it hurt too much to think about it. Not when she'd decided her previous pregnancy would probably be her last.

He glanced away. "I wanted to let you sleep in a little while longer. It's been a difficult week."

Come to think of it, no one *had* come to wake her up for her normal seven a.m. shift. Had that been Ben's doing as well? Her heart tightened further.

He was a good man. He'd deserved so much better than what she'd given him.

She cleared her throat, trying to get rid of the lump that clogged it. "Thank you. You weren't there when I woke up."

Turning to look at her, he lifted a shoulder. "I'm an early riser. Always have been."

Yes, he had been. But he hadn't normally left their bed in the middle of the night and not returned. A thought came to her. Maybe he'd found somewhere else to hole up. A streak of something white hot went through her. She had noticed a couple of female soldiers eyeing him. But surely…

Daniel lifted the last spoonful of broth and leaned back with a tired sigh.

She wanted to know what had been said during the meeting but she also needed to take care of her patients' needs. "Are you guys ready to go back to your room?"

Ben frowned down at her untouched tray, while Daniel shook his head. "Can I please stay here for a little while longer? I'm tired of lying in bed, and I want to talk to Cleo."

There was a sad note in the words, and Tracy had a feeling she knew what he wanted to talk to her about. What were these kids going to do when this was all over? A thought that had plagued her repeatedly over the past couple of days.

She nodded. "We'll move to another table and give you

some time alone, okay? If you need me, just wave, and I'll see you."

She and Ben picked up their trays. She noticed he headed for a different table than Pedro's. Thankfully her assistant was busy talking to one of the military doctors. Maybe he wouldn't notice.

She realized she wasn't the only one who hadn't touched her plate. "Eat. Then I want to hear about what went on at the meeting."

He lifted his brows. "I'll eat if you will."

Her lips curled into a reluctant smile, and she realized how little of that she'd done over the last week. "Deal."

The next fifteen minutes were spent in relative silence as she enjoyed her first quiet meal since they'd arrived. When she bit into her *beijú* she couldn't stop a low groan of pleasure. Ben remembered exactly how much butter she liked on it. And even though the bread was no longer warm, it was still as good as she remembered. "I have to take some cassava flour back with me so I can make this at home."

Ben didn't respond, and she only realized how that sounded when she noticed a muscle working in his jaw. Surely he knew she'd have to go back to São Paulo soon. Their life together was over, no matter how much she might wish otherwise.

Shaking off her regrets, she forced her back to straighten. "So, how did things go this morning?"

Cutting a chunk of fried banana and popping it into her mouth, she waited for him to fill her in.

"Tell me something," he said instead.

Her whole body went on alert. Because it was he who was supposed to be telling *her* something, not the other way around. And if he asked her about her reasons for leaving, she had no idea what she was going to say. Because for all her raging about Ben's ridiculous actions in sending in the cavalry when she hadn't been in any real danger, she knew it was only a symptom of an underlying problem.

Yes, he'd betrayed her. Yes, he should have come himself, instead of pretending the military had other reasons for her not being in that village. But her reasons for leaving were way more complex than that. Because in the same way the townsfolk's coughs were only a symptom of a raging wildfire burning below the surface, so were her issues.

"I thought we were going to talk about your meeting."

If she thought she could change the subject that easily, she was wrong.

"Why haven't you filed for divorce? Surely you could meet someone who loves your job just as much as you do." His glance went to the table where Pedro sat.

"I—I told you. It's hard to get a divorce from inside Brazil."

"And you mean to tell me that after four years there's been no one you've wanted to spend your life with?"

"If you're talking about Pedro, we're just coworkers." After Ben, she'd wanted no one. "I just haven't had the time to file the paperwork. It would mean a trip to New York."

She tried to turn the conversation back to him. And realized she really did want to know. "What about you?"

"I have no desire to go down that road again."

A spike of guilt went through her heart. Had she done that to him? Been such an awful wife that he'd never consider marrying again? She'd just assumed he'd be happier once she was out of his life, that he'd find someone who could give him what she didn't seem able to. "I see. But surely someday..."

"I don't think so." He dropped his utensils onto his plate with a clatter.

Surely he couldn't kiss her like he'd done a few days ago and not want that with someone else.

"You'd have eventually hated me, Ben. We both know

that. It was better that I left." Defective gene or no defective gene, she and Ben had never seen eye to eye on her job.

But would she have traveled as much without that fear prodding her from behind?

He turned to face her. "I never hated you, Tracy. But I deserved better than a letter left on my desk."

He was right. She'd left him an ugly, anger-filled missive detailing everything about their marriage she found unbearable, ending with the military invasion of the village that had ended in her expulsion. Part of that rage had been due to feelings of helplessness over her test results. Part of it had been caused by grief over the loss of her child. But the biggest part of it had been guilt at having failed him so terribly. She'd been too much of a coward to stick around and tell him to his face that it was over.

"You're right, Ben. It won't help, but I was dealing with something more than my pregnancy at that time."

"Something about your job?"

"No." It was on the tip of her tongue to tell him when Daniel waved from across the room. She realized this was neither the time nor the place to dredge up issues from the past. Not when there were lives in the balance and patients who needed her. "I have to go. I can't change the way things played out, Ben. All I can say is I'm sorry."

"Yeah, well, so am I." Before she could even get up from her place, Ben was already on his feet—had already picked up both their trays and was striding towards the front of the tent where the trashcans were located.

As she went over to Daniel's table, she realized Ben had never told her what the meeting this morning had been about.

And right now she didn't care.

CHAPTER NINE

THEY'D LOST ANOTHER patient during the night, and now this.

A flash of anger went through Tracy's eyes. "We have to stay for a week *after* the last patient recovers? You've got to be kidding. I can't be gone from my job for that long."

Her job. That's what it always came down to.

Unless it was more than that. She'd talked about dealing with other issues during their marriage that had nothing to do with her job. Or her pregnancy. He'd racked his brains, thinking back over every last detail he could remember.

And had come up blank.

Except for a vivid image of that kiss in the neighboring town a few days ago. He couldn't seem to get it out of his head.

In fact, the memory haunted him night after night and infected his dreams. The dreams that drove him from his bed and into the narrow hallway just outside the door. His back was killing him, but it was better than the other part of his body that was also killing him.

"The army is worried about keeping the disease contained, so they're upping the quarantine time." He frowned. "And because we traveled to that neighboring village, they want to keep tabs on it as well and make sure no one starts exhibiting symptoms."

She glanced around the sickroom at the dwindling number of patients. "We'll be sitting here alone, twiddling our thumbs, by that time, and you know it."

More than half of the surviving patients had gone on to recover, and the ones who'd shown no symptoms at all were still on doses of antibiotics and would be for several more days. She was right, though. Once the remaining cases were under control, there'd be no more risk of person-to-person contamination. And they'd be stuck here for a week with nothing to do.

Tracy walked over to one of the patients and checked the IV bag, making sure it didn't need changing. "We wore masks while we were at the other village, Ben."

"Not the whole time."

He saw from the change in her expression that she knew exactly when they'd gone without wearing their protective masks. Right before—and during—that deadly kiss.

She lowered her voice, even though she was speaking in English and no one would understand her. "No one saw us."

"Someone did." He nodded when her eyes widened. "And they reported it to the general."

"I thought you guys were big buddies."

"We're friends. But he's also a stickler for the rules."

"I found that out the hard way." Her eyes narrowed. "Listen, I can't stay here for ever. I have no cellphone reception, and there's no way I can get word back to *Projeto Vida* that I'll be delayed even longer. They need to at least let Pedro head back to the office."

He sighed. They hadn't seen much of Tracy's assistant since lunch the other day, and he wondered if the other man was actively avoiding them. Then again, why would he? Ben's lack of sleep was obviously catching up with him.

"They're not letting anyone out, and I wouldn't try to press the issue, if I were you."

"Did you set this up?"

"Get over yourself, Trace. This has nothing to do with you. Or me, for that matter."

She closed her eyes for a second. "You're right. Sorry."

He thought she actually might be. "Maybe I can ask him to get in touch with your office. I'm sure they must have a satellite phone or something they're using for communication."

Moving over to stand beside her, he touched her hand. "Listen, I know this hasn't been easy. Maybe I shouldn't have let you come in the first place, I don't know. But I'm really not trying to manipulate the situation or make things more difficult than they have to be. It's just as inconvenient for me to be stuck here as it is for you. I have my lab—my own responsibilities. Mandy can't hold down the fort for ever."

Her gaze softened. "Don't think I don't appreciate being able to come, Ben. I do." She hesitated then wrapped her fingers around his. "It just feels…awkward. And I know this is just as hard for you as it is for me. I really am sorry."

When she started to withdraw, he tightened his fingers, holding her in place. "Whatever else happens, it's been good seeing you again." The words had come out before he could stop them, and he could tell by her sharp intake of breath they'd taken her by surprise.

"You too."

Then what were those other issues you mentioned?

He somehow succeeded in keeping the question confined inside his skull. Because he already knew he wouldn't get an answer. Not until she was good and ready to tell him—if she ever was.

The woman was hiding something. But he had no idea what it was.

The last thing he wanted to do, though, was to fall for her all over again, and then stand around cooling his heels, hoping each time she left that when she returned, she'd be back to stay. He might be a glutton for punishment, but he was no fool.

So what did he do?

For a start, he could act like the scientist he was—examine the evidence without her realizing what he was doing. Just like he found various ways to look at the same specimens in his lab—using dyes, centrifuges, and cultures, until they revealed all their secrets.

He was trained to study things from different angles. His fingers continued to grip hers as he glanced down into those deep green eyes. That's what he had to do. Probe, study, examine—kiss.

Whatever it took.

Until she gave up every last secret. And then he could put his crazy emotions to rest once and for all.

Pure heaven.

Tracy sank into the fragrant bubbles, finding the water cool and inviting. Anything warmer would have been unbearable with the sizzling temperatures outside today. She remembered they hadn't even needed a hot-water heater for their showers in Teresina—the water coming from the taps had been plenty warm enough for almost everything.

She sighed and leaned her head back against the rim of the tub. She had no idea how Ben had arranged to have one of the large blue water tanks brought in and set up behind the house, but he had. He'd also had folding screens erected all around it for privacy.

The tanks were normally installed on residential rooftops as a way to increase water pressure. She'd never heard of bathing in one, but as it was the size of a normal hot tub, it was the perfect depth, really. He'd even managed to rustle up some scented shampoo that had probably come from the local market—although the store hadn't been open since the outbreak had begun.

She hadn't dared strip completely naked, but even clad in her black bra and panties the experience still felt unbelievably decadent. Better yet, Ben had stationed himself outside the screened-off area, making sure no one came upon her unexpectedly—not that they could see much through the thick layer of bubbles.

Why had he done it? Yes, they'd both been exhausted and, yes, despite her tepid showers, her muscles ached with fatigue from turning patients and making sure she moved their arms and legs in an effort to keep blood clots from forming.

Where had he even gotten the tank? It looked new, not like it had been drained and taken off someone's house. Well, once she was done, she'd let him have a turn. Only the bubbles would be gone by then and he'd be getting used water—unless they took the time to refill the thing. And she knew Ben was concerned enough about the environment that he wouldn't want to double their water usage.

Or… She pushed up out of the water and stared down at her chest. Her bra was solid black, so nothing showed through. In fact, her underwear was less revealing than what you'd find on most Brazilian beaches. So maybe he could just join her.

A faint danger signal went off in her head, its low buzz making her blink as she sank back into the water.

What? She wasn't naked. Far from it.

Ben had already seen her with a lot fewer clothes. And it wasn't like anyone was going to venture behind the house. The property itself was walled off with an eight-foot-high concrete fence—which was typical in Brazil. The screens were merely an added layer of protection.

If *she'd* been hot and sweaty when he'd unveiled his surprise, then he had to be positively baking. Especially as he was now standing guard in the sun just beyond the screens. And the water really did feel amazing.

"Ben?" His name came out a little softer than necessary. She figured if he didn't hear her, she could just pretend she hadn't said anything.

"Yep?"

Okay, so she was either going to have to suck it up and ask him if he wanted to join her or just make up some random question.

"Um…I was wondering if you wanted to— I mean the water isn't going to be as fresh once I get out, so do you want to…?" Her throat squeezed off the last of the words.

Ben's face appeared around the side of one of the screens. "Excuse me?"

"As long as we both have some clothes on, we can share the water." She couldn't stop a sigh as she curled a hand around the rim of the tank and peered over the top. "I know you won't pour a new bath for yourself."

"I'm okay." There was definite tension in his jaw, which should serve as an additional warning, but now he was making her feel guilty on top of everything else. Especially when she spied a rivulet of sweat running down the side of his neck, and he lifted a hand to dash it away.

"Come on. Stop being a martyr. You've earned a break. Besides, it'll help cool you off."

"That, I doubt." The words were so low she wasn't sure she'd heard them correctly but, still, he moved into the space, hands low on his hips.

He was soaked, his face red from the heat.

"Look at your shirt, Ben. You're practically steaming." She wouldn't mention the fact that seeing her husband layered in sweat had always been a huge turn-on. Maybe this *was* a mistake. But there was no way she was going to call back her words now. He'd think she was chicken.

So...should you stand up and cluck now...or wait until later?

He mumbled something under his breath that sounded weirdly like, "You're a scientist. Examine, probe..."

The rest of the sentence faded away to nothing.

"Come on, Ben. You're making me feel guilty."

His lips turned up at the edges. "And are you going to make *me* feel guilty if I refuse?"

"Yes." She realized once she'd answered him that his last phrase could have been taken more than one way. But then again she was hearing all kinds of strange stuff today.

When his hands went to the bottom of his shirt and hauled the thing up and over his head, her breath caught in her throat as glistening pecs and tight abs came into view—accompanied by a familiar narrow trail of hair that was every bit as bewitching as she remembered.

Okay, she had definitely not thought this through. For some reason, in her mind she'd pictured him clothed one second and in the tub the next. But then again, stripping outside the fenced area wouldn't help any, because he would still return *sans* most of his clothes.

His hands went to the button of his khaki cargo pants. "You sure about this?"

She gulped. "As long as you have something underneath that."

His smile widened. "It depends whether you're talking about clothing or something else."

Oh, man. She did remember he'd gone commando from time to time, just to drive her crazy. She'd never known when he'd peeled his jeans off at night what she'd find.

When his zip went down this time, however, she breathed a sigh of relief, followed by a glimmer of disappointment, when dark boxers came into view.

As if reading her thoughts, he said, "No reason to any more."

That little ache in her chest grew larger. He no longer had anyone to play those games with.

As he shoved his slacks the rest of the way down his hips and stepped out of them, she tried to avoid looking at him as she thought about how unfair life was. This was a man who should be in a monogamous, loving relationship. He'd been a great husband. A fantastic lover. And he would have made a terrific father.

"You do have clothes on under those bubbles, right?"

"A little late to be asking that now, don't you think?" She wrinkled her nose and snapped the black strap on her shoulder as evidence. "Of course I do. That invitation wouldn't have gone out otherwise."

His smile this time was a bit tight, but he stepped into the huge tub and slid beneath the water in a single quick motion. Too quick to see if the thought of them in this tank together was affecting him as much as it was her.

Oh, lord, she was an idiot. But as the water licked the curve of his biceps with the slightest movement of their bodies, she couldn't bring herself to be sorry she'd given the invitation.

"Nice?" she asked, making sure her bra-covered breasts were well below the waterline. Since it was almost up to her neck, they were nowhere to be seen.

He responded by sinking down further until his head ducked beneath the surface then rose again. A stream of bubble-laden water sluiced down his face, his neck…that strong chest of his… She only realized her eyes were tracking its progress when his voice drew her attention back up.

"Wish I'd thought of doing this days ago."

"Huh?"

He shook his head with a smile. "Nothing. Yeah. It's nice." He stretched his arms out along either side of the tub and watched her. "So, how was your day?"

Maybe this wasn't going to be so weird after all. "Tiring. Yours?"

"Interesting."

"Did General Gutierrez call another meeting?" If Ben had left her out of the loop again, she was going to be seriously miffed. Those were her patients as well. And she'd been first on the scene when the distress call had gone out.

"No, still the same game plan in place, from what I understand." He lowered his hands into the tub and cupped them, carrying the water to his face and splashing it. If he'd been trying to rinse away the remaining bubbles he'd failed because now they'd gathered like a thin goatee on his chin.

"Um..." She motioned to her own chin to let him know.

He scrubbed the offending body part with his shoulder, transferring the bubbles, then took up his position again, arms spread along the curved blue rim. She tried to make herself as small as possible.

"So, you said your day has been interesting. How so?" She kept her hands braced on the bottom of the tub to keep from slipping even further down into the water. Besides, the less of herself she exposed, the less...well, *exposed* she felt.

He shrugged. "Just doing some research."

"On our cases?"

"Our cases. That's exactly it."

She narrowed her eyes. Why did she get the feeling that the word "cases" was being thrown around rather loosely—at least on his side.

"Did you come to any conclusions?"

"Not yet. But I'm hoping to soon."

The look in his eyes was intense, as if he was expecting to see something reflected back at him.

She cleared her throat. "Daniel is almost better. A few

more days and he should be able to be released. Cleo is still complaining of a slight headache, though, and she isn't progressing as quickly as she was earlier."

"Hmm…I'll check her when I get back." His lips pursed. "I've been thinking about those two—Daniel and his sister, I mean. You're good with them."

Something in her stomach tightened. "Like I said earlier, I try to care for all my patients."

"I know you do."

"I feel terrible that their mother didn't…" The tightening spread to her throat, choking off the rest of her words.

"I know, Trace. I'm sorry." He shifted and one of his legs touched hers, his foot lying alongside her knee. She got the feeling the gesture was meant to comfort her because she was too far away for him to reach any other way. The tub was narrower at the bottom than it was at the top, and even though she knew why he'd done it, it still jolted her system to feel the heat of his skin against hers. She returned the pressure, though, to acknowledge what he'd done.

"Thanks," she said. "That means a lot to me."

She licked her lips, expecting him to move his leg away as soon as she said the words, but he didn't. Instead his gaze held hers. What he was expecting her to do, she wasn't quite sure. A shiver went over her when his foot slid along the side of her calf, as if he'd bent his knee beneath the water. Had he done that on purpose?

There was nothing in his expression to indicate he had.

Not only did he not move away, a second later she felt something slide against her other leg. She gulped. Now, that hadn't been an accident. Had it?

And the bubbles were starting to dissipate, popping at an alarming rate. Soon she'd be able to see beneath the water's surface. And so would Ben. So she either needed to wash her hair and get out fast or she needed to stay in and…

That was the question. Just how brave was she?

And exactly how far was she willing to let him go?

CHAPTER TEN

SHE DIDN'T KNOW what to do.

Ben watched the quicksilver shift of expressions cross her face the second his other leg touched hers—puzzlement, realization, concern and finally uncertainty.

"Tracy." He leaned forward and held out his hand to her, keeping his voice low and coaxing. "I know it hasn't been easy coming here—working with me. And I wasn't even sure I wanted you here. But it was the right thing to do."

The right thing to do.

And what about what he was doing now?

He had no idea if it was the right thing or not. But the second she'd invited him into the tub he'd wondered if this was where she'd been heading the whole time. Especially when he'd started shucking his clothes and he'd seen the slightest glimmer of hunger flash through her eyes. She'd quickly doused it, but not before it had registered for what it was. He'd seen that look many a time back when they'd been a couple.

The question was, should he push the boundaries? She was vulnerable. Tired—she'd admitted it herself. Wasn't he taking advantage of that?

He started to pull his hand back when she startled him by reaching out and placing hers within it, saying, "I know it was. So is this."

Without a word she held on tight and tugged, a movement that sent her sliding across the tub towards him. Her feet went up and over his thighs, hitting the curved plastic on either side of his hips. Her forward momentum came to a halt, and his libido took up where momentum left off.

Raw need raced through his system, replacing any ethical questions he'd had a few seconds ago. With a single gesture she'd admitted she wanted him. At least, he hoped that's what it meant.

"When do you need to be back to work?" he asked.

"I'm off until tomorrow." Still two feet away from each other, her gaze swept down his face, lingering on his mouth.

Until tomorrow. That meant he had all night. He forced himself to take a long, slow breath.

He smiled. "You know, we should have thought of putting a tub like this in our back yard. It's almost as big as a pool. The only problem with it is you're still much too far away."

"Am I?" Her thumb swept across the back of his hand beneath the water. "I've come halfway. Maybe it's your turn now."

"Maybe it is." He pushed himself across the space until, instead of being separated by feet, they were now inches apart. "Better?"

She smiled. "Yes, definitely." She released his hand and propped her fingers on his shoulders, smoothing across them and sending fire licking through his gut in the process.

He curled his legs around her backside and reeled her in the rest of the way, until they were breast to chest and she had to tip her head back to look at him.

"So, here we are," he murmured. "What do we do now?"

"Do you have to ask?"

His lips curved in a slow smile. "No, but I thought I should check to make sure we were on the same page."

"Same page of the very same book."

That was all the confirmation he needed. He cupped the back of her head and stared into her eyes before doing as she'd asked: meeting her halfway. More than halfway.

He swore, even as he kissed her, that he was still working on his plan. Still analyzing every piece of information. But that lasted all of two seconds before his baser instincts kicked in and robbed him of any type of higher brain function. He'd hoped to get an inkling of whether or not the old attractions were still there.

They were.

And at the moment that attraction was groveling and begging him not to screw this up by thinking too hard.

So he didn't. The fingers in her hair tightened, the silky strands growing taut between them. A tiny sound exited her throat that Ben definitely recognized. Tracy had always been turned on by control.

His over her. Or at least that's what she let herself believe.

In reality, though, she'd always wanted to control every aspect of her life, whereas he was happy to take things as they came. But in the bedroom it was a different story. Handing him the reins got her motor running, and right now Ben was more than happy to oblige.

Using his grip on her hair to hold her in place, he kissed along one of her gorgeous cheekbones, taking his time as he headed towards her ear.

"Ben."

His eyes closed at the sound of his name on her lips. Oh, yeah. It had been four long years since he'd heard that husky whisper—half plea, half groan. And it drove him just as crazy today as it had back then.

His teeth closed over her earlobe, while his free hand

trailed slowly down the curve of her neck, continuing down her spine in long feathery strokes, until the line of her bra interrupted him. He circled the clasp a time or two, his finger gliding over the lacy strap that transected her back. One snap and he had it undone.

A whimper escaped her throat, but she couldn't move, still held fast by his hand in her hair. He tugged her head back a bit further, exposing the line of her throat, and the vein beating madly beneath her ear. He licked it, pressed his tongue tight against that throbbing pulse point, glorying in the way those rhythmic waves traveled straight to his groin, making him harder than he ever remembered being. Unable to contain his need, he whispered, "I want you. Right here. Right now. Say yes."

She moistened her lips, but didn't keep him waiting long before responding. "Yes."

"Yes." He breathed in the word and released her hair, his hands going to the straps on her shoulders, peeling them down her arms and letting the piece of clothing sink to the bottom of the tank. He parted the bubbles on the surface of the water until her breasts came into full view.

"Beautiful." He cupped them. "Get up on your knees, honey."

She did as he asked, a water droplet clinging to the hard tip of her left nipple. Who could blame it? Certainly not him, because that was right where he wanted to be.

Lowering his head, he licked the drop off, her quick intake of breath telling him she liked the way he lingered, her fingers on the back of his head emphasizing her point.

He pulled away slightly, and looked up at her with hooded eyes. "Ask for it, Tracy."

Her lips parted, but she didn't utter a word, already knowing that wasn't what he was looking for. Instead, she kept her hands braced against his nape, and arched her back until the breast he'd been courting was back against his mouth. She slowly drew the erect nipple along his lower lip.

"That's it," he whispered against her skin. "I love it when you do that."

He opened his mouth, and she shifted closer. When his lips closed around her and sucked, her body went rigid, and she cried out softly. He gave her what she wanted, using his teeth, his tongue to give her the same pleasure she'd just given him. God, he loved knowing what she wanted and making her reach for it. His arms went around her back, his hands sliding beneath the band of her panties and cupping her butt. He slipped his fingers lower and encountered a slick moisture that had nothing to do with the water all around them. Raw need roared through him.

Knowing he was coming close to the edge of his own limits, he found her center and slid a finger deep inside her, then another, reveling in the way she lowered herself until they were fully embedded. He held her steady with one hand while his mouth and fingers swept her along remembered paths, her breathing picking up in time with his movements.

Not long now.

And he was ready for her. More than ready. He ached to be where his fingers were.

He clamped down with his teeth and at the same time applied steady pressure in the depths of her body, and just like in days past, she moaned loudly, her body stiffening as she trembled on the precipice before exploding around his fingers in a series of spasms that rocked his world. Within seconds he'd freed himself and lifted her onto his erection, sweeping aside the crotch of her panties as he thrust hard and deep.

Hell. His breath left his lungs as memories flooded back. Except everything was even better than he remembered, her still pulsing body exquisitely tight, her head thrown back, dark, glossy hair tumbling free around her bare shoulders as she rode him. Over and over, squeezing and releasing, until he could hold back no longer and with a sharp groan he joined her, falling right over the edge into paradise.

CHAPTER ELEVEN

A DISASTER. THAT'S what yesterday's session in the water tank had been.

Tracy stood in front of the tiny mirror in the bathroom and examined her bare breasts. Really looked at them for the first time in a long time. She'd spent the last several years avoiding everything they represented.

And yet they'd brought her such pleasure yesterday.

It was a paradox. One she'd tried to blank out by pretending they didn't exist. Only Ben had forced an awareness that was as uncomfortable as it was real. How much longer was she going to keep running away?

I'm not!

Tracy continued to stare at her reflection, her lips giving a wry twist. She'd believed those two words once, even as she'd scurried from one place to another. Now…? Well, now she wasn't so sure.

She should tell him. Now that the anger was gone, he should know the truth of what she'd been facing back then.

Why? What good could possibly come of it now that they were no longer together? Did she want him to feel guilty for what he'd done? For touching her there?

No. She wanted him to remember it the same way she did—as a pleasurable interlude that shouldn't be repeated.

She raised her hands and cupped herself, remembering

the way Ben's fingers had done the same—the way he'd brought his mouth slowly down…

Shaking her head, she let her arms fall back to her sides.

As great as their time together had been, retracing her steps and venturing back into an unhappy past was not a wise move. Ben had been miserable with her by the end of their marriage.

But how much of that had been her doing? Had been because of what she'd become? A phantom, too scared to sit in any one spot for too long—who had felt the walls of their house closing in around her any time she'd spent more than a couple of weeks there.

So how could she have let yesterday happen?

She had no idea.

Even though she could freely admit it had been a mistake, could even recite each and every reason it had been the wrong thing to do, she couldn't force herself to be sorry for those stolen moments. She'd always known what she'd felt for Ben was powerful—that she'd never feel the same way about another man—and being with him again had just driven that point home.

Which meant she couldn't let it happen again.

Reaching for her clothes, she hurriedly pulled them on, turning her back to the mirror like she always did and feeling like a fraud. It was one thing to admit her reasons for doing something. It was another thing entirely to change her behavior. Especially when that behavior had served her perfectly well for the past four years.

At least…until now.

By the time she made it to the makeshift hospital, Daniel was sitting in a chair next to his bed, his chin on his chest. His eyes were dry, but his arms were wrapped around his waist as if he was in pain.

She squatted next to him. "Daniel, what's wrong? Does something hurt?"

He shook his head, but didn't move from his slumped position.

"Then what is it?"

Several seconds went by before he answered her. "Where will we go?"

The question was so soft she had to lean forward to hear it, and even then she wasn't sure she'd caught his words.

"I'm sorry?"

Lifting his head, he glanced around the space. She twisted to do the same and noted several of the beds were newly empty—fresh sheets neatly pulled up and tucked in as if ready for new patients. Only there probably wouldn't be any.

There'd been no deaths in the last day or so, and the people who'd become ill after the teams had arrived had ended up with much less severe versions of the illness. It definitely made a case for early intervention.

"This is…was our living room…before my mom—before she…" He stopped and took a deep breath. "Once Cleo and I are well enough to leave here, where will we stay?"

Tracy's heart broke all over again. She'd been worrying over her little tryst with Ben when Daniel and Cleo were now facing life without the only parent they'd ever known. And because the two had no relatives that anyone knew of, and as their home was now being used as a temporary hospital, there was literally nowhere for the siblings to go once they were cleared of infection. Oh, the military would probably take them to a state-run orphanage once the quarantine period was lifted. But until then? No one was allowed in or out of the village.

Surely they could stay here in what had once been their home. But where? Every room was being used, whether to house soldiers or medical personnel. It was full. More than full. Even Pedro—whom she'd barely had a chance to speak to in recent days—had moved from where he'd been staying and was now bunking with members of the military unit assigned to São João dos Rios.

She thought for a minute. Ben kept talking about how much he cared about these kids. Maybe it was time to put that to the test. "We can ask to have two more hammocks put up in the room where Dr. Almeida and I sleep. At least until we figure something else out."

Once she'd said it she wondered if that wouldn't make the whole thing feel a little too much like a family for comfort. And she didn't want to give Daniel and Cleo the idea that they could stay together permanently. Because that wasn't on the cards.

Besides, she wasn't sure Ben would be thrilled about sharing his room with a preteen and a child, especially after the slow smile he'd given her that morning. The one that had her face heating despite her best efforts. He'd even stayed and slept in his own hammock last night—a first since they'd arrived. Was it because of what they'd done?

She must have thought so because it was what had set off the self-examination in the bathroom. She hadn't touched herself like that in a long time.

"Will the soldiers let us go with you?" Daniel gave her a hopeful smile.

No backing out now.

"I don't see why they wouldn't, but you'll have to get well first, which means you'll need to get some rest." What else could she say? They couldn't just let Daniel and Cleo wander the streets or sleep in one of the unoccupied houses. The pair had had a home and a family not three weeks ago. And now it was all gone.

She'd been there, done that. She could at least try to help these children as much as she could before she had to leave—be their temporary family, kind of like a foster-care situation. At least until they figured out something a little more permanent.

How was she supposed to do that before she headed back to São Paulo?

Something she didn't want to think about right now.

Just then, Ben walked into the room, his brow raised in question when he saw the two of them sitting together. She stood, glancing down at Daniel, and noted with horror he had a huge smile on his face.

Don't, Daniel. Not yet. Let me talk to him first.

But even as she thought it, the boy spoke up. "Tracy says Cleo and I can stay with you once we are well."

Ben's glance shot to her. "She did? When?"

"Just now. I explained we did not have any place to go, and she offered to let us stay with you. Cleo was scared." He blinked a couple of times as if that last statement had been hard for him to admit. "We both were…about what might happen. If they tried to take Cleo away from me…" He didn't finish the rest of his statement.

Ben's face grew stormy. "Tracy? Would you like to explain?"

"I, um… Well, I simply said we would figure something out…"

"Figure something out," he parroted.

Daniel's smile never wavered. He had no idea Ben's now icy glare was sucking the heat right out of the atmosphere.

Nodding, Daniel continued, "Yes, so Cleo and I wouldn't be alone—so we could stay together."

Oh, no! He'd obviously misunderstood her intentions—had thought she'd meant the living arrangements would continue even after they left the town. Ben was going to blow his top.

"Well, Daniel, I'm glad to hear she's making those kinds of plans." He moved toward her. "Can I borrow her for a minute?"

"Yes, I have to tell Cleo the good news, anyway. One of the doctors is helping her walk around the yard outside. She should be back in a minute."

Right on cue, Cleo and her companion came through the door and made their way slowly towards them.

"Tracy, do you mind?" Giving a sharp nod toward the door to indicate she should follow him, Ben stalked toward it.

Gulping back her own dismay, she forced a smile to her face. "I won't be long. Could you tell Cleo I'll be back to check on you both in a few minutes?"

As upset as Ben was, she couldn't help but feel a fierce sense of gratitude over the kids' steady improvement. From all indications, they were going to recover fully.

Two miracles in a sea of sorrows.

They'd lost fourteen patients in all. In such a tiny village it was a good percentage of the population. They'd have a hard time coming back from this without some type of government aid. Whether that meant sending them to another town and bulldozing these homes, or finding a way to get things up and running again, nothing would truly be the same again. They would not soon forget what had happened here.

Neither would she.

Pushing through the door, she saw that Ben was already striding down the hallway on his way out of the house. She hurried after him, knowing he must be furious. But once he heard her explanation, he'd understand that…

The second the bright noonday sun hit her retinas, a hand reached out and tugged her to the side, into the shadow of the house.

"Would you like to tell me what the hell that was all about? You expect those kids to stay with us once we leave here? Kind of hard, as we no longer live in the same house. Or even the same state."

"No. Of course not. He took my words the wrong way. I was only talking about here in the village. That they could stay in our room once they left the hospital." She reached out to squeeze his fingers then let go. "They have nowhere else to go. I didn't know what to say."

"So you said they could stay with us?" He swore softly. "Are you that worried about being alone with me, Tracy?"

She looked at him blankly for a second or two. "What are you talking about?"

"I'm talking about what happened between us yesterday." He propped his hands on his hips. "I think it's a little late to start worrying about your virtue—or reputation—or whatever you want to call it."

What a ridiculous thing for him to say. "You're wrong. This has nothing to do with what happened. Nothing."

"Then why?"

Was it her imagination, or was there a shadow of hurt behind his pale eyes?

"They have nowhere to go until the outbreak is over. This was their house, remember? Once they're released from care, they'll be expected to leave, just like our other patients have. They have no relatives here—or anywhere else, if what Daniel said was true."

Ben pivoted and leaned against the wall, dragging a hand through his hair, which was already damp from the heat of the day. "You're right. I thought…"

Since he didn't finish his sentence, she had no idea *what* he thought.

Maybe he was worried she was making a play for him. That she wanted to move back to their old house. No, that didn't make any sense. He'd given no hint he wanted to start things back up between them. For all she knew, he'd just needed to get laid, and she'd practically put up a neon sign saying she was ready, willing and able to take care of that need.

What had she been thinking, inviting him to get in the tub?

Well, it was over and done with. They were both adults. They *both* had needs—heaven knew, hers hadn't been met in quite some time. Four years, to be exact. She hadn't been with anyone since she'd left him.

To say that the experience yesterday had been cataclysmic was an understatement. A huge one.

"Maybe we can put up a curtain or something." She pressed her shoulder to the wall and looked up at him. "Can they stay with us? At least for a little while?"

"Of course they can." The words were soft, but he seemed distracted, almost as if his mind was already on something else entirely. "I'll check with General Gutierrez, and see what he can do about finding them a place to stay after the quarantine is lifted."

"Thank you." She leaned closer and stretched up to kiss his cheek, her hand going to his arm and lingering there. "And I'm sorry Daniel dropped it on you like that. He asked, and it was the only thing I could think of. I was hoping to talk to you alone before we made any decisions."

"What are you going to do about the other part? If he misunderstood, someone is going to have to talk to him."

"I know." She blew out a breath. "Let's give it a few days, though, okay? Until they're stronger and we see how things are going to play out here. Maybe someone in the town can take them in."

"That might pose a bit of a problem." He paused before covering her hand with his own. "I came by to tell you something is getting ready to happen."

Her internal radar went on high alert. "With the military?"

"Yes. I sat in on another meeting today." His jaw tightened. "The news wasn't good. And despite what you think, my opinion doesn't always hold that much sway."

Her skin grew clammy at the way he said it. "What are they going to do?"

Tracy had heard tell of things going on behind the scenes where the military police were concerned. Although many were honest, hard-working, family men, there were others who wouldn't think twice about asking for a bribe.

She'd also heard stories about other branches of the police colluding with the drug cartels that worked out of the *favelas*. The shanty towns were notorious for narcotics and illegal dealings. Many of the slums actually had armed thugs guarding the roads leading to the rickety housing developments. It was not only dangerous for the police to enter such places, it was often deadly. Only the corrupt cops could enter and leave with impunity.

"Nothing's been decided for sure. They're still discussing options with the central government."

The hair on the back of her neck rose at the quiet way he said it. She thought again about Daniel's words and the way she'd found him sitting in that chair. He'd seemed almost hopeless. An unsettling thought occurred to her.

"When Daniel mentioned having nowhere to go, I assumed he was talking about for the next several days. But you and he both jumped to the same conclusion about my offer. You both thought the offer was something more permanent."

"Yes."

"Why is that?" Her voice dropped to a whisper. "What's going to happen here, Ben?"

When she tried to drop her hand from his arm, he held on, fingers tightening around hers. "Remember I told you they were going to lift the quarantine in another week? That we—along with the rest of the medical and military personnel—would be allowed to leave once there were no new cases of the plague?"

"I remember."

"Have you looked around you lately? At the survivors?"

She tried to think. One young mother said her husband was trying to pack all their belongings. She'd assumed it was because they wanted to leave for a while to try to forget the horrors of what had happened here. But what if that was not the reason at all? "I know one couple is preparing to leave. So the military must be planning on lifting the quarantine for everyone at the same time."

"Oh they're lifting it all right. The people you mentioned aren't the only ones getting ready for a big move. There are signs of packing going on all over town. Windows being boarded up. *Acerolas* being bulk-harvested from trees."

She had noticed the berries being picked and put into baskets.

"So everyone is going to leave when this is over? They're going to board up the entire town?" If so, what did that mean for Daniel and Cleo?

"No, they're not going to board it up."

"What, then?"

He drew a deep breath then released it on a sigh. "They're planning to destroy the town once this is all over."

Her eyes widened. "Destroy it? How?"

"The same way they're destroying the bodies. They're going to torch everything, until nothing is left of this place but ashes."

CHAPTER TWELVE

A FAMILY. HE'D always wanted one, but not this way. Not at someone else's expense. And certainly not at the expense of an entire village.

He could still hear the pained cry Tracy had given when he'd told her the news.

Ben leaned against the wall as she helped Daniel attach one end of the hammock to the protective iron grating that covered the window. She gave the rope a tug to make sure it would hold. He'd offered to help, only to have her wave him off, saying Daniel needed something to do.

Maybe she did as well.

He tried to read her body language and the furtive glances she periodically threw his way. They hadn't had much of a chance to talk since she'd had to go back to work at the hospital, but her horror when he'd shared the military's plans had been obvious. They both knew it happened in various countries. Not just in Brazil. It could even happen in the United States, if there were ever a deadly enough epidemic. The same heartbreaking choice might have to be made: contain it, for the good of the general population.

In this case, he wasn't sure it *was* the only option. But in a poor state like *Piauí*, it was the easiest one. São João dos Rios was pretty far off the beaten path. It would be expensive for the military to come in and check the village periodically to make sure the outbreak didn't erupt again, as they still hadn't isolated the initial source of the infection. And if it did recur and spread to a place like *Teresina*—the state capital—it could affect hundreds of thousands of people. If he thought fourteen deaths were far too many, how would he feel if that number was multiplied tenfold?

Hopefully Tracy realized he'd been upset for another reason entirely when she'd explained about Daniel and Cleo sharing their room. And the spark that had lit in his gut when Daniel had talked about them all living together had been hard to contain once it had started burning, although he'd better find a way to extinguish it quickly, because Tracy had no intention of letting this arrangement become permanent.

Well, neither did he.

But he *had* been hoping to have Tracy to himself a little while longer before they went their separate ways. Why he wanted that, he wasn't sure. Maybe just to understand her reasons for inviting him into that tub. To say it had been unexpected would be an understatement.

That was the least of his worries right now, however. The folks in charge were concerned about this getting out to the press. Yeah, hearing that your own military had sluiced cans of gasoline over an entire village and set it ablaze would not be the most popular story. Which was why they were trying to go about it quietly and peacefully. They'd spread the word that stipends would be awarded to anyone who agreed to leave town after the quarantine was lifted.

If they could relocate all the townsfolk before the match was struck, no one would be the wiser—except Ben and a few other key people—until long after the fact. Telling Tracy had probably been a mistake, in fact. But given their history—and her distrust of the military—what else could he have done? Keeping this to himself would have given her one more reason to hate him.

As far as Ben was concerned, as long as no one was hurt, these were just buildings. But he knew Tracy would feel differently. It was one point they'd argued about in the past. He tended to see things with a scientific bent, rather than an emotional one. But it was also one of the things he'd loved about her. She was the balance to his cold, analytical stance, forcing him to see another side to issues. Which made his actions in the past seem childish and petty. If he'd waited until she'd gotten home to talk to her calmly and explained his concerns, would things have turned out differently?

Possibly. There was no way to know.

But it was another of the reasons he'd talked about the military's plans this time. Nothing good could come from discovering the truth from someone else. If she realized he'd kept the information to himself, she'd be furious. And that's the last thing he wanted. Especially after their time in that home-made hot tub—or cooling tub, in this case.

Daniel secured the last of the knots and tried to hop onto the hammock to check it out, but ended up being flipped back onto the floor instead. He lay there panting as if he was exhausted, which he probably was. He was still weak from his illness. Ben pushed away from the wall and reached the boy before Tracy did, holding out a hand. "Easy. You need to regain some strength before trying stuff like that. Besides, you've been on a cot for the last week and a half. You'll have to get used to sleeping in a hammock again."

Daniel let Ben help him up and then rubbed his backside with a rueful grin. "I feel so much better than before, so I forget." He glanced around the space, already cramped from three hammocks. "Where will Cleo sleep?"

"We'll string another hammock above yours. Kind of

like bunk beds. Only you're taller, so you'll sleep in the top one." Ben nodded at the bars on the windows. "They're strong enough to support both hammocks."

Tracy stood next to him. "Good idea. I was beginning to wonder how we were all going to fit."

He gave her a pained smile. "I could always put you up on top, but..." He let the words trail off, knowing she'd catch his implication.

True to form, pink stained both her cheeks, and she turned away to adjust the fan they'd brought in from one of the other rooms. "This will help keep the mosquitoes away, as most of nets are being used by the hospital."

"We never used them at home anyway," Daniel said.

Tracy's sister had died of dengue fever, so she was a little more paranoid about using the netting than many Brazilians. He couldn't blame her. He still remembered the day he'd come home to find the milky netting draped across their huge canopy bed. Despite the fact that her reasons for putting it up had had nothing to do with romance and everything to do with safety, he still found it incredibly intimate once they were both inside. And when he'd made love to her within the confines of the bed, there'd been a raw, primitive quality to Tracy that had shaken him to the core. She'd fallen pregnant that night.

A shaft of pain went through him.

Her eyes met his and she gave a rueful smile, her face growing even pinker. She was remembering those nights as well. He could at least be glad some of those memories made her smile, rather than filling her with bitterness.

And then there were these two kids. What was going to happen to them if the village really was burned down?

Something else he was better off not thinking about, because there wasn't a thing he could do about it.

Tracy says Cleo and I can stay with you once we are well.

If only it were that easy.

Wasn't it?

He swallowed, the words replaying in his head again and again. Evidently that "bath" had permanently messed something up in his skull. Was he actually thinking about taking on somebody else's kids?

He forced his mind back to the mosquito-net conversation between Tracy and Daniel, which was still going strong.

Interrupting her, he said, "We haven't been using nets either, Trace. It's not dengue season anyway."

"I know."

He sensed she wanted to say something further, maybe even about their current situation, but Daniel's presence made sharing any kind of confidences more complicated, if not impossible. And that went for any other kind of intimacies they might have shared in this room. Because with Daniel officially sprung from the infirmary, there was no possibility of that. But he would have liked to have talked to Tracy about…stuff.

Maybe even apologize for his actions four years ago.

"Will they still let me see Cleo?"

Surprisingly, Daniel had recovered faster than his sister, who would be in the infirmary for another day or so. And if he knew Tracy, she'd be sleeping in a chair next to the girl's bed, in case Daniel's absence made her jittery.

Tracy glanced at her watch. "I don't see why not. It's only seven o'clock. Curfew isn't for another three hours."

That was another thing. Yesterday, the military had suddenly instituted a curfew without warning. They'd said it was to prevent looting now that more people were recovering, but Ben had a feeling it had more to do with news being passed from person to person than anything else. Why prevent looting in a place they were planning to burn down?

No, it made no sense, other than the fact it was easier to keep an eye on folks during the daytime. If they imposed a curfew, they had more control over what went on after dark.

"Okay," Daniel said, then hesitated. "Do you need me to help with anything else?"

Tracy shook her head and smiled at him. "No, just be back by ten—tell Cleo I'll be there in a little while. And we'll try to rustle up a snack before bedtime, okay? We need to build up your strength."

The concern in her voice made Ben's heart ache. Tracy would have been a good mother had her job not consumed her every waking moment.

Job or no job, though, his own behavior back then wasn't something he was proud of.

It made him even more determined to set the record straight and see if they could make peace about the past. With Daniel sharing their room, he wasn't sure when he'd get the chance. But he intended to try. The sooner the better.

Tracy glanced at the door as it closed behind Daniel. She was still having trouble processing what Ben had told her. They were going to burn the town down? Without letting anyone have a say?

What would happen to Daniel and Cleo if that happened? She'd hoped maybe someone here would be willing to take on the kids since places like São João dos Rios tended to be close-knit communities. But if they all were forced to scatter in different directions, the kids might end up in a slum or an orphanage…or worse.

"What are those kids going to do now, Ben?" She pulled her hair up into a loose ponytail and used the elastic she wore around her wrist to secure it in place. Her neck felt moist and sticky, despite the gusts of warm air the fan pushed their way from time to time.

"I don't know." He leaned down to the tiny refrigerator he'd brought from his lab and opened the door. Tossing her a cold bottle of water, he took one out for himself, twisting the top and taking a long pull.

Tracy paused to press her bottle against her overheated face, welcoming the shock of cold as it hit her skin. Closing her eyes, she rolled the plastic container along her cheek until she reached her hairline, before repeating the action on the other side. Then she uncapped the bottle and sipped at it. "There's something to be said about cold water. Thanks."

"No problem. How long do you think he'll be?"

"Daniel?" She turned to look at him, suspicion flaring within her. "He'll probably be a while. He and Cleo are close."

"They certainly seem to be."

Surely he wasn't thinking about trying something in the boy's absence. "Why did you ask?"

"What Daniel said made me think about their future, and I thought we could try to figure something out, especially if the military's plans become a reality."

"What can we do?"

"I'm not sure." He scrubbed a hand across the back of his neck. "Maybe one of the villagers could take the kids with them when they leave."

"I thought about that as well, but I don't see how. The whole town will be uprooted and scattered. Most of them will have to live with other people for a while, until they get back on their feet. Adding two more mouths to the equation…?" She took a quick drink.

"You know how these things work, Ben. The people here are barely scraping by. To lose their homes, their livelihood? The last thing they'll be thinking about is two orphaned kids—no matter how well liked they are."

And how was she going to walk away from them when the time came? How could she bear to look those children in the eye with an apologetic shrug and then climb into Ben's car?

There was a long pause. Then Ben said in a low voice, "Ever since Daniel misunderstood what you meant, something's been rattling around in my head."

"Really? What?"

Before he could say anything, Daniel came skidding down the hallway, his face as white as the wall behind him. "Please, come. Cleo is sick. Really sick."

CHAPTER THIRTEEN

TRACY STROKED CLEO'S head, while Ben glanced at the read-out. "Almost three hundred. No wonder she's not feeling well."

Her blood-sugar levels were sky-high.

"She's mentioned having a headache on and off, but I thought it was because of the plague. I had no idea. Is she diabetic?"

"I don't know." He glanced at Pedro, who was standing near the head of the bed and had been the one to send Daniel to find them. "Did anyone notice her breath smelling off?"

A fruity smell was one sign of diabetes, and something one of them should have noticed.

Tracy bristled at his tone, however. "We've been fighting the plague for the last week and a half, Ben. We weren't looking for anything else."

"It wasn't a criticism. Just a question. Would you mind calling Daniel back into the room?"

Poor Daniel. He'd been banished as they'd tried to assess a thrashing Cleo, who not only had a headache but stomach cramps as well. It had seemed to take ages for Ben to get the finger-prick. They'd need to get a urine sample as well to make sure the child's body wasn't flooded with ketones. Without enough insulin to break down sugar, the body would begin converting fat into energy. That process resulted in ketones, which could quickly grow to toxic levels.

Cleo had quieted somewhat, but she was still restless on her cot, her head twisting back and forth on the pillow.

The second the boy came into the room, Ben asked him, "Does your sister have diabetes?"

"Diabetes?" A blank stare was all he received. "Is it from this sickness we had?"

Of course he wouldn't know anything about glucose levels or what too much sugar circulating in the bloodstream could lead to. Many of these people didn't get regular medical care. And what they did get was confined to emergencies or critical illnesses. Surely if the girl had type-one diabetes, though, someone would have figured it out. "Could her glucose levels have been affected by the plague?" Tracy asked.

"Possibly. Serious illnesses can wreak havoc on some of those balances. Or maybe her pancreas was affected. The plague isn't always confined the lungs. We'll pray the change is temporary, but in the meantime we need to get some insulin into her and monitor her blood-sugar levels."

"And if it's not temporary?"

"Let's take one thing at a time." Ben stripped off his gloves and tossed them, along with the test strip, into the wastebasket. "If the glucose doesn't stabilize on its own, we'll have to transport her somewhere so she can be diagnosed and treated."

"The hospital in *Teresina* is good."

Jotting something in a spiralbound notebook, he didn't even look up. "But she doesn't live in *Teresina*."

"She doesn't live anywhere. Not any more."

Unfortunately, she'd forgotten that Daniel was in the room. He immediately jumped on her statement. "But I thought we were going to live with you."

She threw Ben a panicked glance and was grateful when he stopped writing and came to the rescue.

"We're still hammering out the details."

Oh, Lord, how were they going to fix this? Hoping that one of the villagers would take the kids had already been a long shot. But if Cleo did have diabetes, it was doubtful if anyone from São João dos Rios would have the resources to take on her medical expenses.

She could offer to take the kids herself, but things in her life could change at any moment. Just that morning she'd faced that fact while staring in the mirror. She was going to have to do something about those test results—like sit down with a doctor and discuss her options. The more she thought about it, though, the more she was leaning toward a radical solution, a permanent one that would give her peace of mind once and for all. For the most part, anyway.

Maybe she could talk to Ben. Tell him what she was facing. And ask him if he would take the kids instead, at least on a temporary basis. Just until they figured out what was going on with Cleo.

And if he said no?

Then she had no idea what she was going to do. But one thing was for sure. She was not going to abandon Cleo. Not without doing everything in her power to make sure the girl was in good hands.

After they got a dose of insulin into her, they monitored her for the next two hours, until her blood-sugar levels began to decrease. An hour before curfew and knowing there would be little sleep to be had, Tracy asked Ben to walk with her to get a cup of coffee from the cafeteria, leaving Pedro and Daniel to stand watch. Several carafes were still on the buffet table, left over from the evening meal. Two of the pitchers even had some warm dregs left in them. Ben handed her a cup of the thick, black liquid and she spooned some sugar into hers to cut the bitter edge, while Ben drank his plain.

He made a face. "Not quite like I make at home."

Tracy smiled. "You always did make great coffee."

They wandered over to one of the tables at the back of the room. Ben waited for her to sit then joined her.

She nursed her cup for a moment before saying anything. "Do you think Cleo's blood sugar is going to drop back to normal once she's better?"

"I hope so."

"Ben…about what Daniel said…" She drew a deep breath and then blurted it out. "Maybe you could take them."

"Take them where? They don't have family that we know of."

Oh, boy. Something was about to hit that wheezy fan in the window behind her. But she had to ask. Had to try. "No, I mean maybe you could take them in for a while. Make sure Cleo gets the treatment she needs. It wouldn't have to be permanent."

Ben's brows drew together, and he stared at her for several long seconds. "What?"

Once the words were out, there was no retracting them, and they just seemed to keep tumbling from her mouth. "You always said you wanted kids. Well, this is the perfect solution—you won't even need a wife to birth them for you."

"I won't need a wife to…birth them?" His frown grew even stormier. "Is that how you felt about your pregnancy? That I was dooming you to be some type of brood mare? And our baby was just an inconvenience to be endured?"

"Oh, Ben, of course not. I wanted that baby as much as you did." She set her coffee down and wrapped her hands around the cup. "There were just circumstances that… Well, it doesn't matter now."

"What circumstances?"

"I don't want to talk about that. I want to figure out how to help these kids."

"And your way of doing that is by asking someone else to take them on?" He blew out an exasperated breath. "What are they supposed to do while I'm at work? Cleo can't monitor her own blood sugar."

"Daniel is practically a teen. And he's already displayed an enormous amount of responsibility. If she is diabetic, he could help." She plowed ahead. "You've seen how well behaved they are. They could—"

"I can't believe you're putting this all on me, Tracy." His fingers made angry tracks through his hair. "If you feel so strongly about it, why don't *you* take them?"

She knew it was an illogical thought, but if she ended up having surgery, who would watch the kids while she was recovering? It wasn't simply a matter of removing her breasts and being done with it. She wanted reconstruction afterwards. Each step of the process took time. Hospital time. Recovery time.

Both physical and emotional.

She decided to be honest as much as she could. "I can't take them, Ben. If I thought there was any way, believe me, I'd be the first to step up to the plate. They beat the odds and survived the outbreak—when none of us thought they could—so it just doesn't seem fair to abandon them to the system."

"Said as if it's a jail sentence."

"*Teresina* is poor. I've seen the orphanages, remember? I was one of the physicians who helped care for those children when I lived there."

"Let's go for a walk." He stood, collecting both of their half-empty cups. "I don't want Daniel to come in and find us arguing over his fate."

Fate. What a funny word to use. But it was true. What

Ben decided right here, right now, would determine those kids' futures. He could make sure Cleo got the treatment she needed. Even if this was a temporary setback, getting her glucose levels under control could take time.

Ben tossed the cups in the wastebasket and headed out the door, leaving Tracy to hurry to catch up with him.

"Won't you at least consider it?" she asked, turning sideways as she walked next to one of several abandoned houses.

He blew out a rough breath. "I don't know what you want me to say here, Tracy. I'll have to think about it. It would help to know why you're so dead set against taking them yourself."

"I travel a lot. My career—"

"Don't." The angry throbbing of a vein in his temple showed how touchy a subject this was. "Don't even play the travel card—you already know how I feel about that. Besides, I have a career too. So do millions of parents everywhere. But most of them at least want to spend a little time with their husbands and kids."

Shock roiled through her. Was that how he'd seen her? She'd known he hadn't like her traveling. Known it was because of how his parents had treated him and his brother, but hearing him say it outright hurt on a level it never had before.

"I did want to spend time with you." Her voice was quiet when it came out.

She should have told him the truth, long ago. But when he'd sent the military after her as she'd been trying to figure out how to tell him about the test results, she'd felt hurt and betrayed. And terribly, terribly angry. Angry at him, angry about her mother's death and angry that her future might not be the one she'd envisioned.

Maybe she'd turned a large part of that anger on Ben, somehow rationalizing that he didn't deserve to know the truth after what he'd done to her. Convinced herself that she didn't care what he thought—or that he might view her behavior through the lens of his childhood.

Abandoned by his parents. Abandoned by his wife.

What did that make her?

She closed her eyes, trying to block out the thought of Ben sitting alone at home night after night, while she'd tried to outrun her demons. "It's okay. If you can't take them, I'll find someone else."

"Who?"

"Pedro, maybe."

The frown was back. "You'd really ask your assistant to take two kids that you're not willing to take yourself?"

Her eyes filled with tears. "It's not that I'm not willing to. There are times I think about what our child might have looked like and I... Maybe I can take them for a while and then figure something else out." She bit her lip, unable to control the wobble of her chin.

Ben took a step forward so she was forced to look up at him then brushed wisps of hair from her temples. His hands slid around to cradle the back of her head. "I didn't say I wouldn't take them. I just said I needed to think about it. So give me a day or two, okay?"

She nodded, her heart thumping in her chest as his touch chased away the regret and did strange things to her equilibrium. "Okay."

"How do you do it?" He leaned down and slid his cheek across hers, the familiar coarseness of his stubble wrenching at her heart.

"Do what?"

"Talk me into doing crazy stuff."

"I—I don't."

"No?" His breath swept across her ear, sending a shiver over her. "How about talking me into getting in that tub?"

Oh. He was right. She had been the one who'd invited

him in. "Maybe it's not me. Maybe it's this climate. The heat messes with your brain."

"Oh, no. This is all you. *You* mess with my brain."

She didn't know if he thought she messed with it in a bad way or a good way. She suddenly hoped it was good. That he remembered their life together with some fondness, despite the heartache she'd caused him.

His lips touched her cheek then grazed along it as he continued to murmur softly to her. "Tell you what. The kids can come live at the house—temporarily, until Cleo is better and we can find something else."

She wasn't sure she'd heard him correctly. She pulled away to look at him, although the last thing she wanted was for his mouth to stop what it was doing. "You'll take them?"

"I think you missed the pronoun. I said 'we.'"

"What do you mean?"

"I'm not going to do this by myself. If Cleo's condition doesn't stabilize and this turns into full-blown diabetes, she'll need to be transported back and forth to a specialist. Her insulin levels will need to be monitored closely at first."

"Daniel—"

"Daniel is responsible, yes, but he's still just a kid. He's grieving the loss of his mother. I don't think it's fair to expect him to take on the bulk of Cleo's care."

"I agree."

"So the 'we' part of the equation means we share the load. You and me." His sly smile warned her of what was coming before his words had a chance to register. "Until *we* can arrange something else, you'll need to come back to Teresina. With me."

CHAPTER FOURTEEN

"WHAT?"

Ben had expected an angry outburst the second she realized what he was asking. What he didn't anticipate was the stricken pain that flooded her eyes instead.

Warning bells went off inside him.

"It won't be that hard. You can relocate for six months to a year—help the kids get through one school year. You'll be closer to the Amazon, anyway, if you're in *Teresina*, because *Projeto Vida's* medical boat operates out of *Manaus*."

She stopped walking and turned to face him. "Ben, I—I can't."

Something in her face took him aback. What was going on here?

"Why can't you? And if you mention the word 'travel,' the deal is off." He held his ground. "I want Cleo to get the best treatment available. In fact, I want that just as much as you do, but you've got to tell me why you can't sacrifice one year of your life to help make sure she does."

She turned away from him and crossed over to the trunk of a huge mango tree, fingering the bark.

Not about to let her off the hook, he followed her, putting his hands on her shoulders. She whirled round to face him.

"You want to know why I'm reluctant to commit to a

year in Teresina? Why I traveled so much while I was carrying our child?"

"Yes." He kept his eyes on hers, even as the first tears spilled over her lashes.

"Because I have the BRCA1 mutation. And I don't know when—or even if—that switch might suddenly flip on."

"BRCA..." His mind went blank for a second before his training kicked in. "One of the breast-cancer markers?"

A lot of information hit his system at once: Tracy's mother's early death from the disease, her grandmother's death. Next came shock. She'd been tested for the gene variation? There's no way she'd draw that kind of conclusion without some kind of definitive proof. "When did you find out?"

"A while ago." Her green eyes skipped away from his. "After my mother passed away."

An ugly suspicion went through his mind. Her mom had died not long after they'd married. A lot of things suddenly became clear. The frantic pace she'd kept. Her withdrawal a month or so before she'd finally walked out on him. "It was while you were pregnant, wasn't it?"

She nodded.

"You went through genetic testing and never said a word to me?"

"I didn't want to worry you. And then when the test came back positive..." She shook her head. "I was trying to think of a way to tell you. Before I could, you sent the military into that village. I was angry. Hurt. And then I lost the baby."

And then she'd lost the baby.

A streak of raw fury burst through his system closing off his throat and trapping all kinds of angry words inside as he remembered that time. She'd stood in his office a week and a half ago and accused him of going behind her back, and yet she'd traipsed around the country, carrying this huge secret.

Oh, no. That was where he drew the line.

"Yes, I did go behind your back, and I was wrong for doing that. But how is that any different than what you did? You went behind *my* back and had yourself tested for a gene that could impact your life…our future as a couple. How could you have kept that a secret?"

"You're right, Ben. I'm sorry." Her hands went to his, which had drawn up into tight fists as he'd talked. Her fingers curved around them. "At first I was just scared, wondering what it meant for our baby—and if it was a girl, if I would pass the gene to her. Then I worried about how this would affect us as a couple. I—I didn't want your pity."

"Believe me, pity is the last thing I'm feeling right now." At the top of the list was anger. Anger that she'd suffered in silence. Anger that she hadn't trusted him enough to say anything.

"I probably should have told you. I know that now."

"Probably? *Probably?* I cannot believe you just used that word."

She swallowed. "Okay, I *should* have told you."

"We were supposed to be a couple, Tracy. A team. I shared every part of my life with you. Didn't keep one thing from you."

"I know it doesn't seem right. But when you've had some time to think about it—"

"I don't need time to think."

When he started to pull away from her completely, she gripped his wrists, holding him in place. "Try to understand, Ben. My mom had died of cancer six months after we were married. We got pregnant sooner than we expected to, and I started to worry. Being tested was something I did on impulse, just to put my mind at ease. I didn't expect the results to come back the way they did."

"And yet you kept them to yourself. Even when they did."

"Yes."

The anger drained out of him, leaving him exhausted. "It explains everything."

And yet it explained nothing.

Not really. Millions of women faced these same kinds of decisions. And most of them didn't shut their loved ones out completely. Only Tracy had also been facing the loss of their child in addition to the test results. Not to mention what she'd viewed as a betrayal on his part.

He wrapped his arms around her and pulled her close, tucking her head against his shoulder.

"I'm sorry, Ben," she repeated. The low words were muffled by his shirt, but he heard them, sensed they were coming from her heart.

He didn't respond, just let the charged emotions crash over him until they were all spent.

Nothing could change what had happened back then. It was what it was. She'd made her decision, and now he had to make his. How he was going to handle this new-found knowledge?

"This is why you don't want to take Daniel and Cleo yourself."

"Yes."

Wow. He tried to find the right words but found him-self at a loss. Maybe like she'd been when she'd found out?

He gripped her upper arms and edged her back a little so he could look at her face. Fresh tear tracks had appeared, although she hadn't let out any kind of sound.

"This isn't a death sentence, Tracy." He wiped the moisture from her cheeks and eyes with the pad of his thumb. "Carrying the gene mutation doesn't mean you'll develop the disease."

"My mom and grandmother did."

"I know. But knowledge is power. You know to be vigilant."

"I know that I might have to take preventative measures."

Something she'd hinted at earlier. "Tamoxifen?" He'd heard that some of the chemo drugs were being used as a preventative measure nowadays, much like the antibiotics they'd used on those exposed to the plague in São João dos Rios. All in the hope of killing any cancer cells before they had a chance to develop and multiply.

"Some women choose to go that route, yes."

"But not you." It was a statement, because from her phrasing it was clear that she wasn't looking at that option. Or had looked at it and rejected it.

"No. Not me." She licked her lips. "I've been weighing the benefits of prophylactic surgery."

"Surgery..." He blinked as he realized exactly what she was saying. "You're thinking of having an elective mastectomy?" Against his will, his glance went to her chest and then back to her face.

"Yes. That's what I'm saying. I don't know the timing yet, but I realized not long ago that if I can head it off, that's what I'm going to do."

Shit.

He remembered their time in the tub and how he'd gently caressed her breasts. Kissed them. What had she been thinking as he'd brought her nipples to hard peaks? Even then, she hadn't said a word. Maybe she had been committing the sensations to memory.

Okay, now *his* vision was starting to go a little funny. He tightened his jaw. Tracy had said the last thing she wanted from him was pity. He needed to suck it up. Then again, she'd had a whole lot longer to process the information than he had. And ultimately she was right. It was her decision to make. He might disagree or object or even urge her to go ahead and do it, but he wasn't the one who'd have to live with the aftermath. Tracy was.

And he'd had no idea what she'd been facing all this time. He was surprised she hadn't chosen to have the surgery right after their break-up.

He decided not to say anything. Instead, he opted to go a completely different route.

But before he could, she spoke again. "So you see why I'm reluctant to say yes. I was planning to meet with a doctor when I got back to São Paulo."

"Give it some time, Tracy. Neither one of us should make any hard and fast decisions right on the heels of fighting this outbreak." He tucked a lock of hair behind one of her ears. "I'll be honest, though. I don't think I can commit to taking on Cleo's treatment on my own. And I'm not sure it would be fair to her or Daniel. I'm away a lot. Sometimes for days at a time."

"Kind of like I used to be." The words had a ring of challenge to them.

"The difference is I don't have a partner or children at home. Not any more."

She sighed. "And I did."

His thumb stroked her earlobe, watching as her pupils dilated at his touch. "Give me six months to a year of your time, Trace, and I'll take the kids on. I'm not asking you to renew our wedding vows or even get back together. We just have to…work as partners. For the sake of the kids, until Cleo is fully recovered and we can find a better place for them."

"I don't know. Give me a couple of days to make a decision, okay?"

"You've got it. But as for timeframes, we don't have that long, remember? São João dos Rios has less than a week. And then Cleo—and everyone else—will be escorted out."

CHAPTER FIFTEEN

INSULIN WAS A blessing and a curse.

A blessing because the change in Cleo had been almost immediate when they'd pushed the first dose into her. A curse, because this might be something she'd have to do for the rest of her life.

It explained why her body had taken so much longer to recuperate from the plague than that of her brother. She'd improve a little bit and then go back three steps for seemingly no reason. They'd assumed it was because she was one of the first victims. In reality it had been because the sugar had built up in her system like a toxin, infecting her tissue as surely as the plague had.

The insulin had worked. Today the little girl was well enough to walk the short distance from the village to a clearing to accompany Daniel, Ben and herself as they took care of some important business.

Just like a little family.

And that made her heart ache even more as they caught sight of the first of the cement markers on the other side of a small wooden fence.

"Will I see Mommy again?" Cleo's voice wobbled the tiniest bit.

"I think you will, honey. But only after you've had a long and healthy life."

Tracy wanted to do everything in her power to make sure that happened.

Even move back to *Teresina* for a while?

Ben stopped at an empty site beneath a tree, carrying a flat sandstone rock in one hand and a hammer and chisel he'd found in a neighbor's shed in the other. "How does this spot look?"

"Beautiful," Tracy said. "How about to you guys?"

Cleo nodded, but Daniel remained silent, his mouth set in a mutinous line, looking off to the left. He'd been silent since Cleo had asked if their mother would have a grave and a stone like their grandparents did. But when they'd given the boy a chance to remain behind, he'd trailed along at a distance, before steadily gaining ground until he'd been walking beside Ben.

"*O que foi*?" Cleo went over to Daniel and took his hand in hers, her concern obvious. "*Estás triste*?"

He shook his head. "*Vovô está por aí.*"

Ah, so that's why he was looking in that direction. His grandparents' graves were to the left. Cleo had assumed, like Tracy had, that Daniel was struggling with his grief. And maybe that was partially true. But he also wanted his mom's grave to be next to that of his grandparents.

"Can you show us where they are?" she asked.

Without a word, Daniel trudged to a spot about twenty yards to his left, where a weathered tombstone canted backwards.

Ben laid his tools on the ground and set to righting the stone as best he could, packing dirt into the furrow behind it. The names Louisa and Jorge were inscribed on the top, along with the surname Silva. Louisa had outlived Jorge by fifteen years.

Other than the leaning headstone, the graves were neat, with no weeds anywhere to be seen. They'd been well tended—probably by the mother of Cleo and Daniel. It made it all the more fitting that her grave be next to theirs.

"This is perfect," Tracy said.

Daniel gave a short nod, to which Cleo added her approval.

Kneeling on the packed ground next to her, Ben pulled out the sheet of paper that had the children's mother's full name on it and picked up his chisel and hammer. The first strike rang through the air like a shot, and Cleo flinched. Tracy put her arm around the girl and they stood quietly as the sound was repeated time and time again. A cadence of death…and hope.

Sweat poured down Ben's face and spots of moisture began to appear on his dark T-shirt, but still he continued, letter by letter, until the name of Maria Eugênia da Silva Costa appeared on the stone, along with the dates of her birth and death.

Cleo had stood quietly through the entire process, but when Ben glanced up at her with his brows raised, she knelt beside him. With tender fingers she traced the letters one by one while Daniel stayed where he was. He'd brushed his palm across his face as if chasing away sweat—but Tracy had a feeling a rogue tear or two might have been part of the mix.

Handing a bunch of wildflowers to the little girl, she watched as Cleo and Ben carefully placed the stone and cross, setting the tiny bouquet in front of the objects. Glancing at Ben, who'd slicked his hair back, she cleared her throat. "Would you mind saying a few words?"

Blotting a drizzle of perspiration with his shirt sleeve, he stood, lifting a brow. "It's been a while since I've gone to church."

"I'm sure you can think of something." Tracy knew she'd lose it if she tried to say anything.

Cleo rose as well and gripped her hand fiercely.

"Right." He put his hand on one of Cleo's shoulders and motioned Daniel over. The boy moved forward, his steps unsure as if he didn't want to face the reality of what was about to happen. Tracy knew just how he felt. Somehow seeing your mother's name carved into cold, hard stone made things seem unbearably permanent. Even more permanent than the granite itself.

As if aware of her thoughts, Ben started talking, his voice low and somber. "We want to remember Maria Eugênia and give thanks for her life. For the brave children she brought into this world and nurtured to be such fine, caring individuals." Ben's eyes met hers. "We leave this marker as a reminder of her time on this earth. A symbol that she was important. That she was loved. That she won't be forgotten. By any of us."

Cleo's hands went up to cover her face, her small shoulders shaking in silence, while Daniel stood unmoving. Ben knelt between them. One broad-shouldered man flanked by two grieving children.

Oh, God.

One of the tears she'd been blinking away for the last several minutes threatened to break free. But this was not the time. This wasn't about her. It was about these kids. About helping them through a terrible time in their lives. About helping Cleo get to the root of her medical problems.

She went over and gave Daniel a long hug. And then she knelt in front of Cleo, her eyes meeting Ben's as she brushed a strand of hair from the child's damp head and then dropped a kiss on top of it.

Suddenly she knew she wouldn't need a few days to decide. In the scheme of things, what was six months or a year when she could make a difference in these kids' lives for ever? Wasn't that what she'd come here to do? What she'd done even as she'd faced her test results? As impossibly hard as it might be to see Ben each and every day, she was going to *Teresina.* She was going to help make sure Daniel and Cleo were put in a situation where they could flourish and grow. And where Cleo—as Tracy had promised her—would have that chance at a long and healthy life.

Ben stood in the door of the sickroom and peered around one last time. Every bed was empty of patients, the IV poles disassembled and the military vehicles had headed out one by one, leaving only a small contingent to carry out General Gutierrez's final order. Ben had insisted on staying behind to make sure the last survivors had packed up and moved out of town, which they had.

Maybe it was the life-and-death struggle that had gone on here, maybe it was the unrelenting horror of what they'd seen, but most of the inhabitants had seemed only too happy to clear out. Most of them—except Cleo and Daniel—had relatives to turn to and those who didn't would have help from the government to start over, including jobs and subsidized housing, until they got back on their feet.

Several of the villagers, when they'd discovered what Ben had done for Daniel and Cleo's mother, had made similar monuments for their own loved ones and set them in various locations around the cemetery. Ben had wrung a promise from the general that the graveyard would remain untouched.

São João dos Rios was now a ghost town—already dead to all intents and purposes.

And soon his wife would be moving back into his house with a ready-made family in tow. He wasn't sure what had suddenly caused her to say yes. He only knew as the four of them had knelt in front of Maria Eugênia's grave, she'd met his eyes and given a single nod of her head.

He'd mouthed the words, "You'll go?"

Another slow nod.

There'd been no emotion on her face other than a mixture of grief and determination, and he'd wondered if he'd done the right thing in asking her to come. But he couldn't take on two kids by himself and do them justice. Daniel was a strong young man, a few years from adulthood, and Cleo a young girl whose body was still battling to adapt to diabetes, while her mind buckled under a load of grief and loss.

Right now, Tracy and the kids were going through Daniel and Cleo's house and collecting an assortment of sentimental items, and if he knew Tracy, she was making the case for each and every object with the soldier General Gutierrez had left in charge. His friend wasn't an unreasonable man, but he took his job seriously. He was not going to let this pathogen out of the city, if he could help it.

All clothing and linens had to be boiled before they were packed into crates and given a stamp of approval. The hours had run into days as people waited in line for their turn to sanitize their belongings.

A movement caught his eye and he frowned as he spotted Tracy's assistant heading over to the house. He hadn't realized the man was still here, although in the confusion of the last few hours he couldn't remember seeing him leave. Obviously, he wouldn't have without saying goodbye to his boss.

He turned, ready to follow, when Tracy came out of the house and met him. Pedro said something to her and she shrugged. But when the man laid his hands on her shoulders, a slow tide began to rise in Ben's head and he pushed off to see what was going on.

The first voice to reach his ears was Pedro's. "You can't be serious. *Projeto Vida* is your life. You can't just abandon it. What about the medical ship?"

Tracy shook her head and said something, but he couldn't quite make out her words. Ben moved a little faster.

"Why can't someone else deal with them?"

"Because there is no one else, Pedro. It's something I have to do. You and the rest of the crew can hold the fort until I get back."

Until she got back. Why did those four words make his gut churn?

Pedro evidently saw him coming and took his hands from her shoulders. It didn't stop him from continuing his tirade, though. "How long do you think that will that be?"

"Six months. Maybe a year." She glanced back at the door to the house. "Please, keep your voice down. We haven't talked to the kids about time frames."

"Why don't you just bring the kids down to São Paulo?"

"You know I can't do that. It wouldn't be fair to them or to you all. Our hours are all over the place and we're rarely in the office a week before we're off again."

The turning and shifting in Ben's gut increased in intensity. He hoped that didn't mean she was planning on keeping the same schedule once she got to Teresina. He expected her to be an active partner in Cleo's care, not an absentee parent.

He forced a smile as he addressed Tracy. "Is there a problem?"

She shook her head. "No, we're just working out some details about the office."

That's not what it sounded like to him.

Moistening her lips, she leaned forward to give Pedro a quick hug. "It's going to be all right. Give me a call when you get in. I should have cellphone service once I get on the road."

"Speaking of roads," Ben said, his eyes locked on Pedro, "we should all be heading in that direction. Do you need a ride anywhere?"

"Nope. I offered to help with the clean-up then I'll catch a ride to the airport."

Tracy smiled. "I thought you said the soldiers were 'scary dudes.'"

"They're not so bad once you get to know them. Other people…not so much."

Yeah, Ben could guess who that little jab was meant for. Luckily, his skin had grown pretty thick over the last several years. Not much got through.

Except maybe one hot-tub episode.

And a few hot tears that had splashed on his shoulder as Tracy had confessed her deepest, darkest secret. Oh, yeah, that had gotten through more than he cared to admit.

"I have a crate of embroidered linens that need to be boiled and then we can go."

Pedro, as if finally realizing she was serious about going to *Teresina*, spun on his heel and walked away.

Maybe he should give Tracy one more chance to walk away as well. But as much as he tried to summon up the strength, he couldn't. Not just yet.

He had two kids to worry about.

And maybe someday he could convince himself that was the real reason.

"Where are the beds?"

Ben found Daniel standing in the middle of his new room, the backpack with all his clothes still slung over one of his thin shoulders. At least the boy's cheeks had some color back in them. "It's right there against the wall."

And then he realized why the kid had asked that question. He'd probably never slept on a spring mattress in his life. The military had used canvas cots for sickbeds, while most of the houses in São João dos Rios contained *redes*…hammocks. Ben had nothing against sleeping in them. The things were pretty comfortable, in fact. And making love in one…

Yeah, better not to think about the times he and Tracy had shared one on various trips in their past.

Ben moved past Daniel and sat on the double-sized bed. "This is what we normally sleep on."

"But it's not hanging up. Doesn't it get hot?"

The kid had a point.

"That's why we have fans." He nodded at the ceiling fan that was slowly spinning above them. "It goes at different speeds."

"I don't know..." Daniel looked dubious.

Ben smiled. "Tell you what. Try it for a week or so and if you absolutely hate it, we'll go buy you a *rede*."

"My mom made mine herself. And Cleo's."

His throat tightening, Ben nodded. By now the military would have burned everything. Houses, most material possessions that could carry bacteria out of the city. That included Daniel and Cleo's hammocks. "I know. I wish we could have brought them, but there was no way to boil them."

They'd been able to sterilize a few of Maria Eugênia's aprons and embroidered towels, but hammocks had been too unwieldy. They'd been forced to leave so much behind.

"I understand." He looked around again. "Why is there only one bed, then?"

That was another thing. The siblings had shared a bedroom in their old house, but there were enough rooms here that they wouldn't need to any more. But how to explain that to a boy who'd never had a room of his own. "Cleo will have her own bed, in the room next door to this one."

Tracy was currently in there with the girl, making up the couch with sheets and pillows. He tried to look at his home through their eyes. He wasn't a wealthy man by American standards, but it would certainly seem that way to Cleo and Daniel. There was even an air-conditioner in each of the rooms for when things got unbearably hot.

But he didn't mention that right now. He wanted to give them some time to adjust to their new surroundings before springing too much on them.

The local government had been overwhelmed, dealing with the aftermath of the outbreak, so when Ben had asked permission to take the kids with them, they'd made copies of Ben's and Tracy's identity papers, called in a quick background check, then promised a formal interview in the coming weeks. He knew it would only be a formality. And maybe some long-lost relative would come forward in the meantime and claim the children.

He wasn't sure how he felt about that. In just two weeks Ben had grown fond of the kids. Too fond, in fact.

What had he been thinking, agreeing to this? And what had Tracy been thinking, saying yes?

A question that made something in his chest shimmy to life.

As if she knew he'd been thinking about her, Tracy showed up at the doorway with Cleo in tow. "We're all set up. How are you doing in here?"

Daniel looked up at the sign Rosa had hung on the bedroom wall when Ben had called to tell her the news.

Bem Vindo, Daniel!

There was a matching "welcome home" sign in Cleo's room, with her name on it.

Giving the first tentative smile Ben had witnessed since he'd known the boy, Daniel nodded. "I think we will do very well here."

"So do I."

The soft words came from Tracy, who also had a ghost of a smile on her face. She walked over and took one of his hands, giving it a quick squeeze before releasing it. Then she whispered the two most beautiful words he'd ever heard. "Thank you."

CHAPTER SIXTEEN

"I HAVE A surprise for you outside."

Ben had rounded them all up in the living room.

A surprise—anything, in fact—was better than Tracy trying to avoid looking into the bedroom she'd once shared with Ben. The one that seemed to call to her, no matter where she was in the house.

Tracy glanced at Rosa to see if she knew anything, but she just shrugged.

If the housekeeper was surprised to see Tracy back in *Teresina*, she didn't show it. She'd just engulfed her in a hug so tight it had squeezed the air from her lungs. She'd then dabbed the corners of her eyes with her apron before embracing each of the children.

"A surprise?" asked Cleo. "What is it?"

Giving Ben a puzzled look, Tracy wondered what kind of surprise he could possibly have. They'd only arrived a few hours ago. The kids hadn't even had a chance to explore properly yet.

"I bought a water tank," he said in English. "I thought we could convert it into a makeshift pool for the kids. Maybe even sink it partway into the ground to make it easier to climb into. I had it delivered when you agreed to come to *Teresina*."

Heat suffused her face as she processed this, ignoring the kids who were asking to know what he'd said. "Is it the one from São João dos Rios?" Lord, she hoped not. Those memories were even fresher than the ones from the bedroom down the hall.

"No. Bigger."

"We could have bought an inflatable pool."

"I figured this would be more permanent and less likely to rupture. I can't afford to have a built-in pool put in, but I figured the kids could help with the upkeep. It'll also give them a place to entertain any new friends they might make."

"That was nice, Ben." She refused to wonder what would happen to it once everyone went their separate ways. "I think they'll love it."

Tracy switched back to Portuguese and twitched her index finger back and forth at the kids' expectant glances. "I can't tell you what we said without spoiling the surprise."

Standing aside as Ben pushed the door open, she watched the kids lope into the back yard. A large oval water tank sat in a sandy area. Daniel's eyes touched it then skipped past, still looking for whatever the surprise was.

Ben was right, it was huge. The thing must hold a couple of thousand gallons. Why had they never thought of using one as a pool before? Perched on rooftops everywhere in Brazil, the blue fiberglass tanks came in various shapes and sizes. This one must have been meant for a commercial building.

Cleo seemed just as lost as Daniel was. "Where's the surprise?"

To them, evidently, a *caixa de água* was just that: a holding tank for water. They couldn't see the possibilities.

Ben walked over to it and put his hand on the curved rim. "This is it."

The way both kids' faces fell brought a laugh up from

Tracy's chest. "What? You don't think this is a good surprise?"

Cleo shook her head, and Daniel said, "It's fine. I'm sure you needed a new one."

"Oh, it's not for our roof." Ben motioned them round to the other side of the tank. They followed him, Tracy wondering what he'd hidden over there.

Taped to the outside edge was a glossy magazine ad showing a family playing in an above-ground pool, an inflatable raft bouncing on happy waves.

"This…" Ben patted the side of the tank "…is going to be a pool once we're done with it."

"A *piscina*?" Cleo's voice held a note of awe. "We're going to have a pool?"

"We're going to use the tank as a pool." He ran a hand over the top edge. "You're going to have to help me get it ready. And you'll have to help take care of it once it's set up. But, yes, we're going to have a pool."

"Beleza!" The happy shout came from Daniel, who now walked around the tank with a completely different mindset. "The water will be almost up to my neck."

"Yes, and you'll have to be careful with your sister," Ben said, "because it'll be over her head. I don't want you guys using this without supervision. In fact, I'm going to have a cover installed when it's not in use."

Cleo's fingers trailed over the image of the raft on top of the water.

Catching Ben's grin, Tracy could guess what was coming. "There's a bag on the far side of the tank, Cleo. Why don't you go and look inside?"

The little girl raced around to the other side. They soon heard a squeal. "A float. Just like in the picture. And there are two!"

"One for each of them," Tracy murmured to Ben. "You thought of everything, didn't you?"

"No. Not everything." Something in the words had her gaze swiveling back to him.

"I don't understand."

"I don't imagine you do, but it doesn't matter." He moved away from her before she could really look at him. She heard him talking to the kids then they all came around and walked across the yard behind the house, trying to decide on the best place for the pool. They finally came up with a spot near the *acerola* tree, where they'd at least get some shade during the heat of the day.

As soon as the kids had uncovered all the secrets of the soon-to-be pool, they went off to explore the rest of the backyard, leaving Ben and Tracy alone together.

When her eyes met his, the look was soft and fluid, reminding him of days gone by when he'd brought her flowers unexpectedly or had taken her on a long walk in the park.

Hell, he'd missed that look. Placing his hand out, palm up, he held his breath and waited to see if she'd take it. She did, her cool skin sliding across his. He closed his fingers, his gaze holding hers. "Are you okay with all this?"

"I am."

He'd felt the stab of guilt more than once since she'd agreed to come back with him. Especially after the way they'd parted four years ago.

With a sigh he opened his hand and released her. He'd never really known what she'd been thinking during those last dark days of their marriage. And he wasn't sure he wanted to. Maybe it would just make the rift between them that much deeper.

"I guess I'd better go help Rosa with dinner." She stepped up on tiptoe and gave him a soft kiss. "The kids love their surprise, I can tell. Thank you."

Tracy stood back with a smile, the corners of her eyes

crinkling. Oh, how he loved seeing that. The urge to kiss her came and went without incident. After screwing up so badly in the past, he didn't want to do anything that would send them spinning back to uglier times just when he was beginning to feel he'd made up some ground with her. Maybe with time they'd be able to move past those days and become friends again.

At least that was his hope.

Dr. Crista Morena gently palpated Cleo's abdomen, her brow furrowed in concern. "You know that type-one diabetes can occur at any age." She glanced up at them, and Ben could see the curiosity in her eyes. "You know nothing of her background, her medical history?"

"Just what we observed during the plague outbreak," he said. "Could her pancreas have been affected by the illness?"

She stood and straightened the stethoscope around her neck. "Some cases may be triggered by a viral infection—something in the enterovirus family—that causes an autoimmune response." She helped Cleo sit up. "I want to get some bloodwork done on her, but the finger prick we did when you first came in is right around two-twenty. We'll need to do another with her fasting. I'll send some testers home with you."

Tracy nodded. "Her glucose levels seem to fluctuate for no apparent reason, just like they did while she was sick, so her pancreas must be producing some insulin."

"If it's type one, she could be in the honeymoon phase. You administered insulin to bring her levels back down, right?"

"Yes."

"Doing that can sometimes give the organ a rest, stimulating those last remaining beta cells, which then pump out small quantities of the hormone." She looked at each of them. "If it's type one, the honeymoon phase is only a temporary reprieve. Those cells will eventually stop producing all together."

Ben swallowed. If that was true, Cleo would need constant monitoring for the rest of her life. Temporary would become permanent. He glanced at Tracy to see if she'd come to the same conclusion he had.

Yep. Her hands were clasped tightly in her lap, fingers twisting around each other. Well, taking the kids had been her idea in the first place.

But you agreed.

Besides, it had done him a world of good to hear Cleo's happy laugh when she'd realized what the water tank in the backyard meant. How her eyes had widened when she'd discovered she was getting a room of her own with a new pink bedspread—once the bed they'd ordered for her arrived. He wouldn't trade those moments for anything.

Ben helped Cleo hop off the exam table and motioned to the chair he'd occupied moments earlier. She chose to go to Tracy instead, who opened her arms and hauled the child onto her lap, hugging her close.

His throat tightened further. Tracy looked so right holding a child. Would she have cut back on her traveling if their baby had been born?

If the evidence he'd seen was any indication, the answer to that was no. She'd rushed to São João dos Rios during the outbreak, and Pedro had indicated they'd made quite a few trips during the year.

She saved lives by being in that city.

But at what cost to herself?

None, evidently.

Dr. Morena looked up from Cleo's chart and focused on Tracy. "I understand you practiced pediatric medicine in the past. We could use another doctor here at the clinic. Would you be interested?"

"How did you know that?" She shot him a glance that he couldn't read.

"Ben mentioned you were a doctor when he called to make the appointment."

His heart sped up as he waited to see her reaction. Although his slip had been unintentional, when Dr. Morena had mentioned an opening, he'd wondered if she'd say anything to Tracy.

"I haven't practiced pediatric medicine in quite a few years. I've been dealing more with indigenous tribes so—"

"You treat children in those tribes, don't you?"

"Of course."

Dr. Morena closed the cover of the chart with a soft snap. "It's like riding a bicycle. You never really forget how to deal with those little ones. And you obviously have a knack with them." She nodded at Cleo, who was now snuggled into Tracy's lap. "Give me a call if you're interested."

CHAPTER SEVENTEEN

It was like riding a bicycle.

Dr. Morena's words rang through her head a few days later as she stood in the doorway of her old bedroom.

Being with Ben in that water tank had been like that. Remembered responses and emotions bubbling up to the surface. She ventured a little further into the room, sliding her hand across the bedspread. The same silky beige-striped one they'd had years ago. She was surprised he hadn't bought a new set.

She glanced at the door and then, on impulse, lay across the old mattress and stared up at the ceiling. No one would know. Ben was safely at work right now, and Daniel had taken Cleo to explore the neighborhood. Even Rosa was off shopping for groceries, which meant she had a couple of hours to herself.

She wouldn't stay long, just enough to satisfy her curiosity. She'd passed this room for the last couple of days and had wanted to step inside, but she'd resisted the temptation.

Until now.

So, what does it feel like to lie here?

Just like riding a bicycle.

That thought was both terrifying and exhilarating.

The only thing lacking was Ben. And if he could see her now, he'd probably hit the roof. They'd patched together an uneasy truce since arriving in the city, and she was loath to do anything to rock that particular boat. But the open bedroom door had winked at her, inviting her to step through and relive the past.

Rolling onto her stomach, she grabbed the pillow and buried her face into it, sucking down a deep breath of air.

Yep, Ben still slept on the right side of the bed. His warm masculine scent was imprinted on the soft cotton cover, despite Rosa fluffing the pillows to within an inch of their lives. She'd have to make sure she left things exactly like she'd found them.

Being here felt dangerous…voyeuristic. And incredibly erotic. They'd made love in this bed many, many times. All kinds of positions. Her on top. Him. Her hands trapped above her head. His hands molding her body…making her cry out when the time came.

Just that memory made her tingle, her skin responding to the sudden flurry of images that flashed through her head. Oh, Lord. This was bad.

So bad.

Just like riding a bike.

Sitting on a bicycle was one thing. Putting your feet on the pedals and making them go round and round was another thing entirely.

She knew she should get up. Now. But the temptation to linger and let her imagination run wild—to remember one of their lovemaking sessions—was too great. The one that came to mind was when Tracy had been lying on the bed much like she was now. Only she'd been naked.

Waiting.

The covers pulled down so that Ben would find her just like this when he came home from work.

And he had.

Her nipples drew up tight as she recalled the quiet click of the front door closing. The sound of his indrawn breath as he'd stood in the doorway of this very room and spotted her. Without a word, warm lips had pressed against her neck. Just when she'd started to turn her head, eyelids fluttering open, she'd heard the low command, "Don't look.

She'd obeyed, letting him explore her body and whisper the things he wanted to do to her. His hands had slipped beneath her to cup her breasts, drawing a whimper from her when he'd found the sensitive peaks and gently squeezed.

Even now, Tracy couldn't stop her own hands from replaying the scene, burrowing between her body and the mattress.

"Mmm. Yes."

He'd touched her just like this. Her teeth had dug into her lower lip as she'd let the sensations spiral through her system. Just a hint of friction then more as he'd seemed to sense exactly what she was feeling.

"Ben." The whispered name was low, but in the silence of the house it carried. She let out another puff of breath between pursed lips, even as one hand trailed down her side, her legs opening just a bit.

It wouldn't take long. She was so turned on. Just a minute or two. And she'd relieve the ache that had been growing inside her since their time in the tub. She undid the button on her jeans and her fingers found the juncture at the top of her thighs, sweet, familiar heat rippling through her.

Maybe she should close the door. Just in case. Her head tilted in that direction.

Instead of empty space, her gaze met familiar broad shoulders, which now filled the doorway.

She yanked her hands from beneath her in the space of a nanosecond, molten lava rushing up her neck and scorching her face.

Oh, God! Had he heard her say his name?

"Wh-what are you doing here?"

"I would ask you the same thing, but I think it's fairly

obvious from where I'm standing." He took a step closer, his eyes never leaving hers. And the heat contained in them nearly burned her alive.

The door closed. The lock snicked.

"I was just taking a…" She rolled onto her back and propped herself up on her elbows, realizing her mistake when his gaze trailed to her chest and saw the truth for himself. Even she could feel the desperate press of her nipples against her thin shirt.

He stood at the foot of the bed. "Nap?" He gave her a slow smile. "Must have been having quite some dream, then."

Oh, it was no dream. More like a wish. And Ben had been at the heart of it.

"Wh-why did you just lock the door?" Sick anticipation began strumming through her, even though she already knew the answer.

His hands wrapped around her ankles and hauled her down to the foot of the bed, giving her all the confirmation she needed. "Isn't it obvious, Trace? *I* intend to be the one to finish what you started."

Ben wasn't sure what he'd expected when he'd come home early to spend the weekend with Tracy and the kids, but he certainly hadn't expected to find her in his bed…face buried in his pillow, her hands sliding down her own body.

Then, when she'd said his name, he'd known. She'd been fantasizing about him. About them. About the way they used to be.

He'd gone instantly erect, instantly ready for business. And then she'd turned and looked into his eyes, and he'd seen the fire that had once burned just for him. She still felt it. Just like he did.

It inflamed him. Enticed him.

And he wasn't above taking full advantage of it.

Leaning over the bed and planting his hands on either side of her shoulders, he stared down at her, hungry for the sight of her, hair in gorgeous disarray from being dragged down the bed, her slender body encased in snug jeans and a thin cami top. "Tell me you want me."

She licked her lips. "We shouldn't…"

"Maybe not. But I want to know. Was it me you were imagining?"

"Yes." The airy sigh was all he needed.

He bent down and closed his lips over the nipple he could see so clearly through her shirt, his teeth gripping, loving the tight heat of her against his tongue. She whimpered when he raised his head. "Did you imagine me here?" His knee parted her legs and moved to press tightly against her. "Here?"

Tracy's throat moved as she swallowed. "Yes."

His breath huffed out, and he moved up to whisper in her ear, "Let me, then. We'll sort all the other stuff out later."

She didn't say anything, and he wondered if she might refuse. Then her hands went to the back of his head and pulled him down to her lips, which instantly parted the second their mouths met. He groaned low and long as he accepted the invitation, pushing his tongue inside, tasting, remembering, pressing deep and then withdrawing…only to repeat the act all over again—a mounting heat growing in another part of his body.

Desperation spread through his veins, and he tried to rein in his need, knowing that soon kissing her would no longer be enough. The tiny sound she made in the back of her throat said she felt the exact same way.

This was how it had always been with them. The flames burned higher and faster than either of them wanted, until they were writhing against each other, fighting off the inevitable—knowing it would be over far too soon.

He pulled away, his breath rasping in his lungs. "Take off your shirt," he whispered. "I want to see you."

Tracy's hands went to the bottom of her cami without hesitation and lifted it over her head in a graceful movement that made him want to tear off the rest of her clothing and bury himself deep inside her. But he knew it was better if he didn't touch her for the next couple of minutes.

He nodded at her undergarment. "Bra next."

"Say please."

He swallowed, knowing she was teasing, but at this point he'd say anything she wanted. "Please."

She unclipped the front of the thing and shimmied it off her shoulders, the jiggle of her breasts making his mouth water. God, he wanted her.

He drank in the sight and, just like she always had, she took his breath away. "Touch them. Like you were when I came in." He gave her a wolfish grin as he added, "Please."

Her face turned pink, and this time he wondered if she might leap off the bed and stomp out of the room, but her hands went to her breasts and covered them, her head falling back as she gently massaged them.

This woman got to him like no other ever had. He slid his hand into the tangle of her hair and kissed her long and deep, drinking in everything he could.

He stood again, watching her eyes open and meet his. "Slide your thumbs over your nipples. Slowly. Just like I'm aching to do."

Again she hesitated, but then her hands shifted, the pads of her thumbs skimming over the tight buds in perfect synchrony. She repeated the motion, her gaze never leaving his. "Like this?"

"Oh, exactly like that." His voice had gone slightly hoarse, and he knew no amount of clearing his throat would chase it away. "Don't stop."

Her low moan sent heat skimming down his stomach and beyond.

"Where are the kids?"

"Outside. Rosa's shopping."

"Ah, so that's why you were in here." He stepped between her legs, which were still dangling over the side of the bed. He slowly spread them wider with his stance. "You thought you wouldn't get caught."

"I—I didn't plan it."

"But the second you got on that bed you felt it, didn't you? The things we used to do. Imagined me right here—just like this."

"Ben—"

"Shh. Don't talk. We're alone. We both want this." His fingers moved down to the waistband of her jeans. Her teeth sank into her bottom lip, her hands going completely still. "Uh-uh. I didn't tell you you could stop." He placed his hands over hers and showed her how he wanted her to stroke her breasts.

She moaned again, her hips shifting restlessly on the bed. "I want *you* to do it. Please?"

"Soon." His fingers returned to her jeans and dragged them down her thighs, stepping back so he could tug them the rest of the way off. "I don't want to waste a second of this time."

"The kids—"

"Will find the door locked." He smiled at her. "And you're sleeping. You need your rest."

Her panties were black, just like her lacy bra had been. His hand glided down her sternum, past her bellybutton and stopped, fingers trailing along the line formed by her underwear. He wanted to watch her do that too.

"Tracy." His eyes met hers, and he took her hands in his, running both sets down her stomach until he reached the satin band. "Take them off."

She hooked her thumbs around the elastic and eased them down her hips, over the curve of her butt. When she'd pushed them as far as she could go without sitting up, Ben slid them off the rest of the way.

She was naked. His hands curled around her thighs and pushed them apart, his thumbs caressing the soft inner surfaces, then shifted higher, watching her eyes darken with each excruciating inch he gained. When he reached her center, he found her wet…open. He delved inside, still holding her thighs apart. A low whimper erupted from her throat when he applied pressure to the inner surface, right at the spot she liked best.

Her flesh tightened around his thumb, and she raised her hips stroking herself on him.

"Please, Ben. Now."

He didn't want to. Not yet. But he couldn't hold off much longer. He was already shaking with need.

With one hand he reached for his zipper and yanked it down, freeing himself. They could take it slowly later. Gripping her thighs again, he pulled her closer before filling his hands with her luscious butt and lifting it off the bed. He sank into her, watching as she took him in inch by inch.

Buried inside her, he savored the tight heat, trying his best not to move for several seconds. Tracy had other ideas. She wrapped her legs around him, planting her heels against his lower back and pulled him closer, using the leverage to lift her hips up then let them slide back down, setting up a sensual circular rhythm that wouldn't let up. The result was that, although he held perfectly still, his flesh was gripped by her body, massaged and squeezed and rubbed and…

He gritted his teeth and tried desperately to hold on, but it was no use. Nothing could stop the avalanche once it began.

With a hoarse groan he grabbed her hips and thrust hard into her, riding her wildly, feeling her explode around him with an answering cry even as he emptied himself inside her.

Heart pounding in his chest, he continued to move until there was nothing left and his legs turned to jelly. Slowly lowering her to the bed, he followed her down, pulling her onto her side and gathering her close.

Her breath rasped past his cheek, slowing gradually.

The moment of truth. Was she going to bolt? Or accept what had happened between them?

He took a minute or two to get his bearings then kissed her forehead. "Was it as good as you imagined?"

"Better." Her soft laugh warmed his heart. "Only you had your clothes off in my imagination."

"We'll have to work on that."

"Mmm." She sighed against his throat then licked the moisture that had collected there. "Someone will be coming pretty soon."

"Exactly."

"I meant coming *home*."

Something in Ben's throat tightened at the sound of that word on her tongue. *Home.*

Was that what she considered this place? Or would she take off again the second she had the opportunity?

He'd better tread carefully. Not let himself get too comfortable. Because she considered this a temporary arrangement. And if not for the kids, Tracy wouldn't even be here right now. The fact that she hadn't automatically expected to share his bed spoke volumes. She hadn't planned on returning to their old relationship, no matter how good their little interlude in the water tank had been. Or how much she'd seemed to enjoy their time in this bed.

And she had enjoyed it.

Seeing her pleasuring herself on his bed…*their* bed…

had done a number on his heart. As had her admission of fantasizing about him…not about Pedro or some other faceless man as she'd touched her body.

Yeah. He'd liked that a little too much.

Well, somehow he'd better drag himself back from the edge of insanity and grab hold of reality. Because it wasn't likely Tracy was going to change her mind about staying with him for ever. And, unfortunately, with each day that passed he found that's exactly what he wanted.

CHAPTER EIGHTEEN

TRACY DREW THE insulin into the syringe and gave Cleo a reassuring smile. "You're becoming a pro at these."

This was Cleo's tenth shot, but her glucose levels were still fluctuating all over the place. Whether it was the honeymoon phase that Dr. Morena had mentioned or whether her pancreas would again start pumping out its own supply of insulin was the big question. One no one could seem to answer.

"It still hurts."

"I know. It always will. But sometimes we have to be brave and do what we know is best—even if it hurts."

Like leaving had been four years ago? Because that had hurt more than anything else ever had—that and her miscarriage. Looking back, she knew all kinds of things had led to her flight from *Teresina*. Anger, grief, shock. If Ben hadn't done what he had, she might have stuck it out and tried to make things work. But his actions had been the proverbial last straw…her whole world had collapsed around her, unable to keep functioning under the load she'd placed on it.

And now?

She and Ben hadn't talked about what had happened between them two days ago. There was still a part of her that was mortified that he'd caught her on his bed, but the result had been something beyond her wildest dreams.

He'd been arrogant—and sexy as hell—standing there at the foot of the bed, ordering her to touch herself.

If the front door hadn't clicked open and then shut again, they might have started all over again. But the second the sound had registered, there had been a mad dash of yanking on clothing interspersed with panicked giggles as they'd snuck out of his room to face Rosa and her armloads of groceries.

Ben had been a whole lot better at feigning nonchalance than she had as he'd taken the canvas sacks from the housekeeper and helped her put things away. But the burning glances he'd thrown her from time to time had told her he'd rather be right back in that bed with her.

Heat washed over her as she tried to corral her thoughts and keep them from straying any further down that dangerous path.

Tracy rolled up Cleo's shorts. "Ready?"

"I—I think so."

With a quick jab that was designed to cause as little pain as possible, she pushed the needle home and injected the medicine. Other than the quick intake of breath, the little girl didn't make a sound. As soon as Tracy withdrew and capped the syringe, she tossed the instrument into the mini medical waste container they'd set up.

Cleo's voice came from the stool where she was still seated. "Are you going to work for Dr. Morena?"

Ah, so she had heard the doctor as she'd talked to them in the exam room. Tracy didn't have an answer today any more than she'd had one for Ben when he'd asked her much the same question after making love.

They hadn't been together again since that night but he'd gotten into the habit of dropping a kiss on her cheek before he left for work each day. She probably should have moved away the first time he'd done it, but this morning she'd found herself lifting her cheek to him in anticipation.

At this rate, she'd be puckering up and laying one right on his lips very soon.

Probably not a smart idea.

She'd never fooled herself into thinking she didn't love Ben. Of course she did. She'd never stopped. She had been furious with him after the yellow fever incident and had needed time to think about how to deal with everything that had been going on in her life. Only she'd taken too much time, and hiding her condition had become second nature—and had seemed easier than returning to *Teresina* to tell him the truth.

During all those years she'd been gone he'd never called her, never begged her to change her mind. Although she couldn't imagine Ben ever doing that. He was strong, stoic. He'd had to be self-sufficient as a child in order to cope, since his parents had rarely been there for him.

She hadn't been there for him either.

But now he knew why. Didn't that change everything? Wasn't that what those little pecks on the cheek had meant?

She could say she hoped so, but in reality she had no idea. He'd barely had any time to process the information, but how would he feel once he had? She knew she was more than just the sum of her parts, but Ben loved her breasts. That much had been obvious from the heat in his eyes as her hands had cupped them. Stroked over the tips.

And, yep…her mind was right back in the gutter, despite her best efforts.

With a start she realized she was still standing in front of the cabinet, and that Cleo was now frowning up at her with a look of concern. Oh, she'd asked about Dr. Morena and whether she was going to work for her.

"How do you feel about what the doctor said? About me working at the clinic?"

Cleo hopped down from the stool and unrolled the leg

of the shorts. "Does that mean we'll keep on staying with you?"

Afraid to get the girl's hopes up too high, she said, "Why don't you leave the worrying about that to us, okay?" She dropped a quick kiss on her head. "Just know that you are loved."

Ben pushed through the front door, stopping short when the sounds of screaming came from the backyard. Dropping his briefcase on the floor, he yelled for Tracy, but other than those distant shouts his call was met by silence. A sense of weird *déjà vu* settled over him. This was much like the day he'd come home to find Tracy gone.

Except there'd been no shouting that day. Speaking of which…

Moving to the back of the house, he threw open the door that led to the patio. There, in the pool, were three bodies. Only they were very much alive.

In fact, it looked like he'd arrived in the middle of some kind of battle from the looks of the water guns in each person's hands. He walked up the steps to the top of the deck, which was still under construction, and all three pairs of eyes turned to him in a synchronized fashion. Too late, he realized his mistake when Daniel shouted, "*Atire-nele*!"

They all took aim and squeezed their triggers. Water came at him from three different angles, soaking his blue dress shirt and plastering it to his chest. "Hey! Enough already!"

No one listened, but then Tracy, clad in a cherry-red bikini that held his eyes prisoner for several long seconds, ran out of water first. As she was dunking her gun to reload, he pounced, going over the side of the water tank in one smooth move and capturing her gun hand as he hit the water—before she had time to bring it back up. She gave a startled scream when he wrapped his arms around her and took her with him beneath the water. Out of sight of the kids, who were bobbing around him, he planted his lips on Tracy's, a stream of bubbles rising as she laughed against her will. He let her up, where she coughed and spluttered. "Not fair!"

He slicked his hair out of his face, brows lifted. "And shooting me without any warning was?"

"You saw the water guns. We figured that was all the warning you deserved."

Ben stood there, dress shoes lying at the bottom of the pool, obviously ruined by now.

But he wouldn't change this scene for anything in the world. This was what he'd always dreamed of. Except in his daydreams Tracy had stayed by his side for ever. For a minute or two he allowed himself to mourn what might never be. But Tracy was here, right now. And all he wanted to do was pull the loose end on that bikini and see what happened. Only they weren't alone.

But at least she was playing. Laughing at his attempt to kiss her beneath the water. Maybe it was enough for now. He could wait and see how things went. If he didn't get his hopes up too high, they couldn't be dashed. Right?

"So. You planned to ambush me the minute I arrived, did you?"

Daniel gave him another squirt—which hit him squarely in the eye. "Ow!"

Another laugh from Tracy. When was the last time he'd heard her laugh with abandon? Far too long ago.

Her gun was still on the bottom of the pool. Diving beneath the water, he retrieved it and came back up, his head just barely above the surface as he let water fill the reservoir. Then he went on the attack, giving back as good as he got. Tracy stayed well out of the line of fire this time, double checking her bikini to make sure she was still in it. The act distracted him for a second and both the kids got him again.

He glared at his wife, mimicking her earlier words. “Not fair.”

“Oh, but you know what they say. All’s fair in…” Her voice trailed away, her smile dying with it.

He cursed himself, even though he knew it wasn’t his fault. Instead, he waved the kids off for a minute and jogged over to her. Draping an arm around her waist, he whispered in her ear. “Let’s just take it a day at a time, okay? No expectations.”

The smile she gave him was tremulous. “I feel awful, Ben.”

“Don’t.” He kissed her cheek. “Although I think you owe me a new pair of shoes.”

“Done.” She slid back beneath the water and leaned against the side. “This was a great idea. The kids love it. I’m thinking of enrolling Cleo in swimming lessons. Did you know she doesn’t swim?”

Tracy had switched to English so the kids wouldn’t understand her. He glanced at Cleo, who was hanging onto the side of the tank with one hand while maneuvering the water gun with the other. He answered her back in the same language. “She definitely needs to learn if the pool is going to stay up year round. How about Daniel?”

“He had lessons in school, but he’s never had a place to practice. So it might not be a bad idea for him to brush up on his skills as well.”

“Right.” He leaned back beside her, stretching his legs out beneath the water. Tracy’s limbs looked pale next to the black fabric of his slacks. “Did you put sunscreen on?”

“SPF sixty. The kids have some on as well.”

He touched her nose, which, despite her sun protection, was slightly pink. “How long have you guys been in the water?”

"About an hour. We were making a list of recipes that the kids' mother used to fix, and I felt like we needed to do something fun afterwards. I don't want every memory of their mom to end on a sad note."

"Smart." Ben paused, wondering how to ask the question that had been bothering him for the last couple of days. His timing tended to suck, so why worry about that now? "Listen, I've been meaning to ask. About the other night…"

She tensed beside him. "I don't think now is the best time to talk about this."

"I haven't exactly been able to get you alone." Whether that had been on purpose or not, only Tracy could say. "I'll say it in English, so no one else will understand. Are you okay?"

"Okay?"

"Are you upset with me for the way I…?"

He didn't know how else to ask it. And he wasn't sure if he was asking if Tracy was okay, or if "they" were okay.

She shook her head, eyes softening. "No. Of course I'm not upset."

"You've been acting a little funny."

"This whole situation is a little funny." She sighed. "I never expected to be back in *Teresina*."

"Are you sorry you came?"

Ben wasn't sure why he was pushing so hard for reassurance, but he felt like he was slipping and sliding around, searching for something that might or might not be there.

"No. But I was going to tell you something later today. I made a phone call and talked to my old doctor here. She got me an appointment with a surgeon on Monday."

He froze, then a million and one questions immediately came to mind. She gave a quick nod at the kids, who, Ben realized, were both looking at them, trying to figure out what was being said. "Okay. Let's discuss it after dinner, okay?"

"Thank you." She switched back to Portuguese. "Is the military still monitoring your movements?"

He'd mentioned an unmarked vehicle parked in the lot at the hospital since they'd gotten back to *Teresina*. He hadn't recognized it and the driver was always the same person. It was either the military or a terrorist, Ben had told her with a rueful smile. The latter wasn't very likely in Brazil, since it was a pacifist country.

"The car hasn't been in the lot for the last two days so hopefully, if it was the General's doing, they've decided I'm too boring to keep tabs on." He pulled a face at the kids.

Tracy laughed. "Those guys don't know you very well, then, do they, Dr. Almeida? You're quite unpredictable."

The way she said it warmed his heart, despite the chill he'd felt when she'd mentioned the word "surgeon."

He planted a hand on his chest as if wounded and winked at Cleo. "You think I'm a pretty boring guy, don't you?"

The little girl giggled then shook her head.

"What about you?" he asked Daniel.

The boy scratched his head with the tip of his water gun. "I guess you're okay. Not too boring."

Tracy grinned then shot Ben a smug look. "See? Told you."

They were throwing playful barbs at each other again. His spine relaxed. How good it felt to be back on solid footing, instead of crashing around in a scary place where you couldn't see the bottom for the muck.

At least for today. Monday might bring something altogether different.

Ben had knocked on her door that night around midnight. She'd been half expecting him to come and see her out of earshot of the kids. What she hadn't expected was for him to push the door shut with his foot and stand there, staring at her.

Then he'd swept her in his arms and kissed her as if there was no tomorrow. They'd made love on her bed, and it had been as fresh and new as the other two times they'd been together. Afterwards, he'd held her in his arms.

"Whatever happens on Monday, we'll face it together, okay?"

A little sliver of doubt went through her chest. "Are you saying you want to go with me?"

"Would that be okay?"

Tracy had to decide to let him in completely or shut him out. "What about your work?"

"I can take off for a couple of hours." Ben caught a strand of her hair, rubbing it between his fingertips.

"Okay." Whew. Why did that feel so huge? "I won't make any firm decisions until Cleo's diabetes is under control, but I just need to see where I am. I've been neglecting my tests and want to get caught up with them."

"Why now?"

"I don't know. Maybe I've been running away from making a decision one way or the other."

He nodded and wrapped the lock of hair around his finger. "If I asked you to start sleeping in our old bed again, would you say yes?"

"Tonight? Or…?"

"Not just tonight. From now on."

Wow. This had gone from talking about her appointment to Ben asking her to make their marriage a real one. At least that's what she thought he was asking. "I assume by sleeping, you don't actually mean closing our eyes."

The right side of his mouth quirked up. "I definitely think there might be some eye closing going on, but it would take place well before any actual sleeping."

Tracy's body quickened despite having just made love

with this man fifteen minutes ago. She tilted her head as if in deep thought. "Hmm. I don't know. Do you snore?"

"Interesting question. I do make sounds from time to time, but I don't know if I'd call them snoring." His fingers tunneled into her hair, massaging her head in tiny circles that made her shiver.

"I think I remember those sounds. I kind of liked them."

"Did you, now?" His thumb trailed down the side of her throat, stroking the spot where her pulse was beginning to pick up speed in response to his words and his touch.

"Mmm."

He leaned over and kissed the side of her jaw. "And I kind of like the little sound you just made."

"I'm glad, because if you keep that up, I'm going to be making a lot more of— Oh!" Her breath caught as his teeth nipped the crook of her neck, sucking the blood to the surface and then licking over it with his warm tongue.

"Say yes," he whispered.

"Yes." She wasn't sure what she was agreeing to, but it didn't really matter at this point. She wasn't about to hold anything back, and she trusted him enough to know he wouldn't ask her for more than she could give.

He moved to her lips. "Yes to sleeping in my bed?"

"I thought we'd already decided that."

"No, you were still questioning whether or not I snored." His tongue slowly licked across her mouth.

"No snoring. Just sounds." As she said each word, his tongue delved into her mouth before finally cutting off her speech altogether.

I didn't matter, though, because Tracy was already beyond rational thought, her arms winding around his neck.

She was ready to lose herself to him all over again—for as long as he wanted her.

CHAPTER NINETEEN

BEN WAS STILL groggy with sleep when he reached across the bed and realized Tracy was no longer there. He could hear her talking softly from somewhere nearby, and he woke up the rest of the way in a flash.

"But I have a doctor's appointment on Monday." There was a pause. "I suppose I could. It's not urgent."

Ben sat up in bed, looking for her. She must be in the bathroom.

He wasn't purposely trying to eavesdrop, but something about the way she kept her voice hushed said she wasn't anxious for anyone to hear the conversation.

"I don't want to be gone long. Cleo's still getting her shots regulated."

Climbing out of bed and reaching for his boxers, he padded to the door. "Pedro, I can't leave right this second. No, I know. I'm sure Rosa won't mind watching them while Ben is at work. She used to watch him when his parents were gone. I'd have to teach her how to give Cleo her insulin shots, though."

Rosa won't mind watching them.

The soft warmth he'd felt during the night evaporated. Why would Rosa need to watch the kids? Or give Cleo her shots?

Unless Tracy was planning to be gone for a while.

And why was she talking to Pedro in the bathroom, unless she was keeping something from him?

It wouldn't be the first time.

They'd been home less than a week, and she was already off somewhere?

A jumble of emotions spun up inside him like a tornado, anger being the first to reach the top.

No. He was not heading down this path again. He turned the knob and pushed the door open.

Tracy's mouth rounded in a perfect "O" that had looked incredibly sexy last night. But all he saw this morning was betrayal.

"Pedro, hold on just a second."

She put her hand over the phone, but Ben beat her to the punch. "You're leaving."

Licking her lips, she nodded. "Just for a few days. The medical boat docked at a flooded village. There are five cases of cholera and there's certain to be dozens more, as they've all been drinking from the same water source."

"Send someone else." His voice was cold and hard, but that's how he felt inside. "Let Pedro deal with it."

"He's not a doctor, Ben. I am. Matt called him, they're expecting to be overwhelmed by—"

"You're *a* doctor. Not the only doctor in the whole country. You have responsibilities here."

"Rosa can—"

Fury washed over him. "Rosa practically raised my brother and me. These kids need a steady presence in their lives, not be pushed off on someone else every time your assistant has a runny nose. You promised me at least six months."

"It's only this one time."

He closed his eyes for a second, his hand squeezing the doorknob for all he was worth. Then he took a deep breath. "I'm going to lay it out for you, Tracy. Either you let someone else handle this, and we start looking toward a future. Together. Or I'm filing for divorce. Even if I have to go all the way to New York to do it."

Every ounce of color drained from her face. "Wh-what about Daniel and Cleo? You said you couldn't do this alone."

"It doesn't look like I have much of a choice." He shot her a glance. "*I* made a promise that I intend to keep. Besides, I've been through the same rinse-and-spin cycle a couple of times already. I'm sure I can figure things out."

Just before he pulled the door shut he added, "Finish your conversation, then let me know what you decide."

Tracy draped a moist cloth over the forehead of the woman she was treating then used a gloved hand to check her vitals. They were through the worst of the cholera outbreak. There were several army doctors among their group, but this time they hadn't been sent at the request of her husband but were instead digging drain fields and latrines in an effort to prevent a recurrence.

Ben wouldn't send anyone for her this time, because he was through with her. He'd said as much.

She wasn't sure why Pedro's call had spurred her to action. Maybe her instincts were programmed to bolt at the first sign of trouble.

Like having an actual appointment with a doctor? Was she still running…still having to move and work to feel alive?

No, she'd felt alive with Ben as well. And this trip felt hollow. It didn't fulfill her the way it might have a few years ago. She missed the kids. Missed Ben.

Matt's wife sat down beside her on an intricately woven mat. "How are you holding up?"

Stevie had been with *Projeto Vida* for two years, working alongside her husband. They had a daughter as well, but she was confined to the boat this trip. Neither Matt nor Stevie wanted to run the risk of her becoming ill.

"As well as anyone."

Stevie gave her a keen look. "Are you sure about that?"

"We're all tired. I came here to help."

"And you have." Stevie touched her gloved hand to Tracy's. "How's Ben?"

She flashed the other woman a startled look. Word evidently traveled fast. "I wouldn't know. I won't be heading back there."

"I'm sorry."

"Me too." She gave her patient's shoulder a gentle squeeze and murmured that someone would check on her in just a little while then she stood with a sigh. "How do you do it?"

Stevie got to her feet as well. "What do you mean?"

"How do you keep your marriage together and travel on the boat?"

"We both believe in what we do." She stripped her gloves off and motioned for Tracy to follow her. Once outside the tent she leaned against a tree. "Sometimes I just need a breath of fresh air, you know?"

Tracy did know. The smells of illness got to you after a while.

Letting her head bump the bark of the tree trunk, Stevie swiveled her head toward her. "Matt wasn't sure he wanted to come back to Brazil after losing so much here. If he'd chosen to stay in the States, I would have stayed with him. Because that's the only important thing—that we're together."

"So you're saying I shouldn't have come."

"No." Stevie gave her a soft smile. "Only you know what's right…what's in your heart."

"I don't know any more. Ben never liked me traveling."

"I'm sure he missed you very much when you were gone."

"Yes, I suppose he did. But other wives travel."

"As much as you do?" Stevie paused for a moment or two. "I think you have to examine your heart and decide what it is you want out of life. Why you're so driven to do what you do."

Because she didn't have to think about anything else when she was helping people?

In the past she'd worked herself to exhaustion day after day—had fallen into bed at night, her eyes closing as soon as her head had hit the pillow.

Movement equaled life.

But was this really living? Was she doing this because she believed in her work or because she was afraid to stay in one place, where she might start feeling trapped—claustrophobic?

She'd missed her doctor's appointment to be here. Could she not have delayed her flight for a few hours? In reality, despite Pedro's dire predictions, there'd been enough hands to fight the cholera outbreak, even if she hadn't been here. She'd been living her whole life as if she were single with no commitments. Yes, she'd had this job before she'd met Ben. But in choosing it over him time and time again she'd been sending the message that he meant no more to her than he'd meant to his parents.

Lord, she'd made such a mess of things. Such a mess of her life.

And in staying so incredibly busy, she'd not only risked her long-term health but she'd also lost sight of the person she loved most: Ben.

Maybe it was time to start pulling away. Let someone else take the helm of her organization—Pedro maybe—and go back to practicing medicine in a clinic. She might not be able to help whole swaths of people but she could help them one at a time.

Which path was more valuable in the long run? Maybe it wasn't a question of either/or. Maybe each had its own place in the grand scheme of things. And there were two children who'd trusted her to be there for them.

She turned and hugged her friend. "Thank you. I think I've just realized where I should be."

"In *Teresina*?"

She nodded. "I don't know why I didn't see it before now."

"Maybe because 'now' was when you needed to see it." With a secretive smile Stevie waved to her husband, who was working off in the distance. He winked back.

And Tracy did what she should have done four years ago: she walked to the nearest soldier and asked if she could hitch a ride on the next boat out of the Amazon.

Ben sucked down a mouthful of tepid coffee and grimaced before going back to his microscope and glaring down at the slide beneath the lens. He had no business being here today. He'd had no business here all week.

Why had he drawn that ridiculous line in the sand and dared her to cross it? Maybe because he'd never forgiven his parents for withholding their affection when he'd been a child?

Yeah, well, he was an adult now. Well past the age of holding grudges.

He hadn't heard from Tracy since she'd left, and he'd cursed himself repeatedly for not being more sensitive the last time they'd talked…for not trying to really listen to what she'd been saying.

He wasn't the only one who was upset.

Rosa had chewed his butt up one side and down the other when she'd found out Tracy wasn't coming home.

"I used to think I raised you to be a smart boy, Benjamin Almeida. Now I'm not so sure."

"You shouldn't have had to raise me at all."

"Was it so bad? Your childhood?"

He thought back. No, his parents had been gone for months at a time, but when they had been there there'd been laughter…and then, when they'd left again there'd been tears. But through it all Rosa had been there. How many children grew up not even having a Rosa in their lives?

If he thought about it, he was damned lucky.

And if he'd given Tracy a little more time to settle in before jumping to conclusions at the first phone call she'd got from the office, maybe he could have done a better job at being a husband this time.

He rummaged around in his desk until he came up with an old tattered business card that he'd saved for years. Staring at the familiar name on the front, he turned it over and over between his fingers, battling with indecision. He knew from their time in São João dos Rios that the phone number was still the same. Finally, before he could change his mind, he dialed and swiveled around in his chair to face out the window.

Did she even have cellphone reception wherever she was?

He heard the phone ring through the handset, but there was something weird about it. Almost as if it was ringing in two places at once—inside his ear and somewhere off in the distance. On the second ring the sound outside his ear grew louder in steady increments, and he frowned, trying to figure out if he was just imagining it. On the third ring her voice came through. "Hello?"

Ben's breath seized in his lungs as he realized the greeting came not only from the handset pressed to his ear but from right behind him. He slowly swiveled and met sea-green eyes. They crinkled at the corners as they looked back at him.

Keeping the phone pressed to his ear, he gazed at her in disbelief, while she kept her phone against her own ear as well.

"Tracy?"

"Yes."

God, he could just jump up and crush her to him. But he didn't. He said the words he'd been rehearsing for the last half-hour. "I've missed you. Please come home."

Tears shimmered in her eyes, her throat moving in a quick jerking motion. "I've missed you too. I'll be there soon."

With that she clicked her phone shut and moved towards him. When she stood before his chair, he reached up and pulled her down onto his lap. "You're home."

"I am. I'm home." She wrapped her arms around his neck and pulled him against her. "And this time I'm here to stay."

One year later

Ben strode down the hallway of Einstein Hospital in São Paulo, Brazil, until he reached the surgical wing. Tracy's dad was already in the waiting room. He stood as he saw Ben heading his way. The two men shook hands, Sam taking it one step further and embracing his son-in-law.

Ben said, "I'm glad you were able to come, sir."

"How is she?"

"Still in surgery."

The months since Tracy had stood in his office and they'd shared declarations of love had passed in a flurry of medical tests for both Cleo and Tracy. Cleo's initial diagnosis of diabetes had been confirmed, but it was now under control. They'd even been granted custody of both children.

Tracy's mammogram had come back with an area of concern and whether it was cancer or not, they both knew it was time. They'd made this decision together soon after she'd come home. She'd shed tears while Ben had reassured her that he'd love her with breasts or without.

Nodding to the chair Sam had vacated, they both sat down.

"She did it, then," his father-in-law said.

"Yes." Ben leaned forward, elbows on his knees, clasped hands dangling between them. "She wanted to be proactive."

Tracy's dad nodded. "If her mother had known she carried this gene, I know in my heart she would have done the same thing. And I would have stood beside her." He dragged a forearm across his eyes, which Ben pretended he didn't see. "How long will she be back there?"

"Two to four hours." He glanced at his watch. "It's going on three hours now. We should be hearing something fairly soon."

Two to four hours. Such a short time. And yet it seemed like for ever.

Unable to sit still, he settled for pacing while Sam remained in his seat. Ben had already made all kinds of deals with God, so many he wasn't sure he'd be able to keep track. But Tracy had been so sure of this, so at peace with her decision in the past week.

A green-suited man came around the corner, a surgical mask dangling around his neck. "Mr. Almeida?"

Ben moved towards him, Sam following close behind. The surgeon frowned, but Ben nodded. "This is Tracy's dad. He's just arrived in town."

The man nodded. "The surgery went fine. I didn't see

any definite areas of malignancy, but I'm sending everything off to pathology for testing just in case."

"Tracy's okay, then?" Ben didn't want to hear about malignancies or what they had or hadn't found.

"She's fine." The man hesitated. "Reconstruction shouldn't be a problem. We'd like to keep her here for a day or two to observe her, however. Will she have someone to help her at home afterwards?"

"Yes." Ben's and Sam's answers came on top of the other, causing all of them to smile.

Ben finished. "We'll make sure she gets everything she needs." He knew the kids would both be beside themselves, desperate for a chance to talk to Tracy. But he'd left them in *Teresina*, in Rosa's care—though he'd realized the irony of it. Kids survived. And these two kids had survived more than most…more than he'd ever had to, even on his worst days.

"Good," the surgeon said. "Give us a few minutes to get her settled then someone will come and get you. Please, don't stay long, though. She needs to rest."

Ben held out a hand. "Thank you. For everything."

The surgeon nodded then shook each of their hands and headed back in the direction from which he'd come. Before he rounded the corner, though, he turned and came back. "I wanted to tell you what a brave young woman Tracy is. I don't know how much you've talked about everything, but whether you agree with her decision or not it was ultimately up to her. Support her in it."

"Absolutely." Ben wasn't planning on doing anything else. He'd spend the rest of his days supporting whatever decisions she made. He was just grateful to have her back.

"Thanks again."

"You're welcome. Take care." This time the surgeon didn't look back but disappeared around the corner.

"Why don't you go back and see her first?" Ben told Sam.

"My face is not the one she'll want to see when she wakes up. There's plenty of time."

Yes, there was. Ben swallowed. "Thank you. I'll tell her you're here."

Sleep.

That's all Tracy wanted to do, but something warm curled around her hand and gave a soft squeeze. Someone said her name in a low, gravelly voice she should recognize.

Did recognize.

"Trace."

There it was again. Her heart warmed despite the long shivers taking hold of her body. She was cold. Freezing. Her body fought back, shuddering against the sensation.

Something settled over her. A blanket?

She focused on her eyelids, trying to convince them to part—wanted to put a hand to her chest to see if they were still there.

Oh, God. Moisture flared behind still closed lids and leaked out the sides.

"Tracy." Warm fingers threaded through her own. "You're okay. Safe. I'm here."

She wanted to believe. But she was afraid the last year had all been a dream. At least the blanket was starting to warm her just a bit.

Her throat ached. From the tube she'd had down her throat.

Wait. Tube?

Yes, from the surgery. Ben was here. Somewhere. He promised to be here when she woke up.

So why was she even doubting she'd heard his voice?

Okay. Moment of truth.

Eyelids...open.

As if by magic, they parted and the first thing she saw

was the face. The gorgeous face that matched that low, sexy voice. Broad shoulders stretched wide against the fabric of his shirt. Ruffled brown hair that looked like he'd shoved fingers through it repeatedly, a piece in the back sticking straight up.

Long, dark lashes. Strong throat. Gentle hands.

Her husband.

"Ben?" The sound rasped out of her throat as if coated by rough sandpaper—and feeling like it as well.

"I'm here."

Yes, it was Ben. He was here. Crying?

Oh, God. He was crying because she no longer had breasts. No, that wasn't it. They'd made this decision together. Had they found something during the surgery?

She tried to glance down at herself, but everything was buried under a thick layer of blankets. But there was no pain. Could the surgeon not have taken them?

"Are they…?"

"Shh. You're fine."

Closing her eyes, she tried to clear her fuzzy head. "The kids?"

"I spoke to Rosa a few minutes ago. They're fine. They miss you."

I miss you.

Her lips curved as she remembered Ben saying those very words as she'd stood in the doorway of his office a year ago. That he'd actually called her—wanted her to come home—was a memory she'd treasure for ever.

Where was the pain? Shouldn't it hurt to have something sliced off your body?

"I miss the kids, too."

He smiled and smoothed strands of hair back from her face. "Your dad's here. They'll only let one of us in at a time, and he insisted you'd want to see me first."

"He was right."

Lifting her hand to his lips, he kissed the top of it. His touch was as warm as his voice. "I love you, Tracy. And I'm going to spend the rest of my life showing you how much."

She closed her eyes, only to have to force them open again. "I like the sound of that."

One of the nurses appeared in the doorway, leaning against the frame. "We probably need to let Mrs. Almeida get some sleep."

"Mrs. Almeida." Tracy murmured the words as her eyelids once again began to flicker shut. She loved having his name.

Almost as much as she loved the man who'd given it to her.

EPILOGUE

THE SUNRISE WAS gorgeous, a blazing red ball of fire tossed just above the horizon by the hand of God.

Today promised to be a scorcher—just like most days in *Teresina.* And she relished each and every one of them. Curling her hands around the railing of the deck off their bedroom, Tracy let the warmth of the wood sink into her palms and gave a quiet sigh of contentment. She loved these kinds of mornings.

Five years since her surgery and no sign of cancer.

Tracy was thrilled to be a part of Crista Morena's thriving pediatric practice. And twice a year she and Ben took a trip along the Amazon to do relief work. Together. Something that might have been impossible in the past.

A pair of arms wrapped around her from behind, sliding beneath the hem of her white camisole and tickling the skin of her tummy. She made a quiet sound, putting her hands over his and holding him close. Leaning her head against her husband's chest, she thought about how truly blessed she was.

Except for one thing.

"I miss Daniel." The wistfulness in her heart came through in her voice.

Their adopted son had left for college in the States last month and was busy studying to be a doctor—hoping to return to Brazil and help people in communities like São

João dos Rios. His mother would be so very proud of the man her son had become. The four of them had made several trips back to the kids' home town, and although the razed village was sad testament to what had happened there, it was also a place of joy. A place of new beginnings.

They'd had a permanent stone marker made and had placed it on Maria Eugênia's grave—although both Daniel and Cleo had decided the crude rock Ben had carved should remain there as well.

They'd also made a pact to go back once a year to put flowers on her grave.

Cleo, now thirteen, was growing into a beautiful young woman who was sensitive and wise beyond her years. All too soon she'd be grown as well, leaving them to start a life of her own.

"We can always phone Daniel later this afternoon." Ben planted cool lips on her neck.

"We'll wait for Cleo to get home from school. I can't believe how fast time has gone by."

"I'm grateful for every moment." His lips continued to glide up her neck until he reached her earlobe, biting gently.

She shivered, her body reacting instantly, the way it always did for this man. "So am I."

A thin cry came from the back of the house. Tracy squinched her nose and sighed. "So is someone else."

Their baby girl, just three months old, was letting them know she was hungry. Although she would never replace the baby they'd lost all those years ago, trying to have another child had seemed the right thing to do. Tracy was grateful for second chances, no matter how they came.

Ben had taken a little more coaxing—a year to be exact. He'd been worried about the ramifications to her health, but in the end he'd agreed. And Grace Elizabeth Almeida had come into the world kicking and screaming.

Someone ready to take on the universe and everything it held.

"I guess we'd better go feed her before she gets really wound up." Ben turned her in his arms and nipped her lower lip. "Although I was hoping we might get a little alone time. Just this once."

"Don't worry, Ben. We have plenty of time. Our whole lives, in fact."

Tracy sighed, her happiness complete. She had everything she could possibly want out of life. She and Ben had found their middle ground, despite seemingly impossible odds. And she'd discovered there was more than one path to happiness, as long as the man she loved was by her side. And as her three children had taught her, there was definitely more than one way to make a family.

* * * * *

ONE LAST KISS

JESSICA LEMMON

For those of you who believe in second chances.

Prologue

Five and a half years ago, New Year's Eve

"Daddy," Gia Knox said from between clenched teeth. But her father, busy bragging on her as per his usual, wouldn't be dissuaded. His current brag was her graduating the Massachusetts Institute of Technology with honors, and the impressive work she would soon do at the family company, ThomKnox.

"She inherited her brains from me, of course." Jack Knox gave his only daughter a wink and wrapped an arm around her.

"Don't be silly, Jack," Gia's mother, Macy, interjected. "Everyone knows our daughter inherited her intelligence from me. Let's leave these kids alone. We're ruining their fun."

Macy whisked Jack away so suddenly, Gia was left alone with one of the most talented web designers in the company. She shuffled her feet as best she could in black Louboutins, clasping her hands in front of her black glittery skirt. By the time she was fiddling with her long beaded necklace over her sequined top, she realized she was having a rare awkward moment.

“Sorry about that,” she muttered to the man before her. “They’re proud. Anyway, it’s great to meet you, Jayson.”

“Cooper,” he said, the deep timbre of his voice glancing off each one of her ribs. “No one calls me Jayson.”

“Well, then I definitely won’t call you Cooper. I pride myself in being unique.” She’d meant the quip to be a cute conversation salve to the embarrassing display by her dad, but it came out sounding flirty. And Jayson responded.

“You, Gia Knox, are definitely unique.” His smile twitched beneath a trimmed neat goatee before vanishing. That half smile was completely attractive. Disarmingly so. All of him was. He had broad shoulders and wore a suit well. She’d surreptitiously checked him out more than once while her father was rattling off her GPA.

Jayson’s thick wavy dark hair was cut professionally and close, but his facial hair lent him an air of mystery. And those eyes. Blue and piercing, she’d bet they didn’t miss a thing.

“Well, then, Jay,” she said, testing the new nickname and receiving an eyebrow arch in response, “you’ll either be enchanted or disappointed to hear I’m joining the tech team.”

“Enchanted,” he answered without hesitation. “Definitely enchanted.”

“Sixty seconds!” Her brother Brannon called out, blowing into a noisemaker and earning a round of cheers and applause. Nearly every employee of ThomKnox was present at the New Year’s Eve celebration, including Gia’s family since they *were* ThomKnox.

Partygoers followed Bran’s lead and pressed in toward the center of the ballroom, leaving Jay and Gia to watch them go.

"The moment we've all been waiting for," she said as the crowd began a sloppy midnight countdown at the thirty-second mark. "A bunch of employees making out at the stroke of the new year."

This time when her gaze clashed with Jayson's, it stuck. She found herself unable to look away. The moment his eyes left hers they took an inventory of her mouth.

She felt the brush of his gaze the way she might have felt his hand. Or his lips. It was intimate. It was heady. He had her thoroughly distracted and totally off-kilter. She'd had one glass of champagne, no more, but felt as if she'd polished off a bottle and then someone had hit her over the head with it.

Had she ever met a guy and felt this much *longing*? And what was it about *him*—but she knew. Jayson was as charmed by her as she'd been by him. Rarely was attraction ever that equal.

At that second—and the three that followed—she imagined satisfying her longing and kissing Jayson Cooper. Lifting to her toes and pressing her mouth to his. He smelled good from where she stood, and she'd bet he was absolutely intoxicating close up.

There's only one way to find out.

Jayson, his gaze trickling back up to hers, leaned forward the slightest bit.

Then a red-haired woman who was even shorter than Gia and wearing a skirt that was a lot tighter than Gia's, crashed into him.

"Cooper, come *on*! We'll miss the countdown!" The redhead bounced as she wrapped both her arms around one of his. Her headband bobbed, the words *Happy New Year* waving. "Hi," she chirped. "I'm Shelly."

"Gia Knox." Gia shook the other woman's hand, feeling the loss of Jayson's attention when he rigidly looped his arm around his date's waist.

As if summoned, Gia's boyfriend, Tom, approached. "There you are."

Tom leaned in to kiss her cheek and she pasted on a plastic smile.

"It was nice to meet you, Jay," Gia called as Tom pulled her toward the crowd. Jayson nodded, his frown slight but visible, as Shelly towed him to the middle of the room.

Gia and Jay watched each other as the countdown continued, as more and more distance separated them and more and more people came between them.

Three.

Two.

One.

"Happy New Year!" the crowd shouted as silver and gold confetti rained down on the ballroom.

"Happy New Year, baby," Tom said to Gia and then captured her mouth in a kiss. She pushed aside the inconvenient—and possibly insane—attraction she felt toward Jayson and focused on her date. But Tom's kiss barely registered on her *oh, baby* scale. Her heart wasn't racing the way it was a moment ago. Her stomach wasn't clenched in delicious anticipation as it had been a moment ago.

She leaned into the kiss, determined to bury that errant blip of lust. She was soon going to be working with Jayson Cooper, and indulging in anything, especially a fantasy, wasn't a great start to her career at ThomKnox.

That night became a night she never ever forgot. Not because of Tom or the party or the tepid New Year's kiss. No, the most memorable part of that night was meeting a handsome, blue-eyed stranger that, little did she know at the time, would soon become her husband…and soon after that, become her *ex*-husband.

One

The technology department was a big, open bullpen-style seating area with Jayson Cooper in the mix with his brethren. Gia, who'd worked in tech for years, had recently had a title update. She'd taken over as chief marketing officer after she and Jayson divorced. Her office was still on this floor, off to the side, with windows so she could look out on all of them.

Jayson didn't used to mind her being nearby.

Now, though, he *minded.*

It was closing in on a year and a half since their divorce. Moving on was difficult when the woman you were to move on *from* was directly in your line of vision day after day.

He was being looked after by a woman who'd refused to let him look after her during their entire marriage. What good was a husband whose wife refused to let him care for her?

No good, that's what.

He and Gia worked well together for their sakes as

much as the sakes of their coworkers. They gave each other crap—the good-natured kind—at work and made sure to always end the day on a positive note. It'd been working… for a while.

He thought he knew how to protect and love a woman, but when it came to Gia Knox-Cooper, he'd been at sea. She was independent and headstrong and rarely if ever met him halfway. He'd known that about her going into their marriage but had expected things to change after the "I dos." Each of them had only grown further apart. Which was why their divorce had been a blessing. He understood now that were better separate.

Taylor Thompson, soon to be Taylor Knox as she was the fiancée of Royce Knox, swept into the department and past Jayson's desk.

"Coop, can you pop into Gia's office with me for a second?"

"Sure thing." He rose and followed Taylor, who was dressed smartly in a no-nonsense black dress, her dark blond hair pinned at the back of her head. She was second in charge as COO of the company, professional and spunky and exactly what Gia's oldest, most rigid brother had needed in his life. She'd sprung a pregnancy announcement on Royce last year, and now those two were to be wed. With better results, Jayson hoped, than his marriage to Gia.

Anyway, their wedding ceremony would likely include their daughter, born right after Addison and Brannon Knox's wedding six months ago. Or, as Jayson liked to think of it, the night when he *nearly* lost his damn mind and slept with his ex-wife.

In her office, Gia was leaning back in her leather executive chair, her long dark hair spilling over her petite shoulders. Her red dress one that would make Jessica Rabbit weep with envy.

Gia was petite, curvy and hiding a beautiful body beneath that frock. It was a body he'd brought to the pinnacle of euphoria time and time again. If physical compatibility equaled a successful marriage, they'd still be together.

Taylor slapped two cream-colored notecards onto the desk and two pens on top of them. "Fill these out. Each of you."

Gia and Jayson exchanged glances before Gia picked up one of the cards to examine it more closely. "It's filled out, Tay."

"So's mine," Jayson said, picking up the other card. His name was right there. *Jayson Cooper* and beneath it, the box "attending" was marked with an X.

Taylor snatched the card from him and pointed at the blank area beneath it. "This reads 'Plus-one, yes or no' and there is a line there for a name for the seating chart."

Taylor handed the card back to him. "Yes," she said and then snapped her gaze to Gia. "Or no. This isn't twenty questions. It's *one*. I don't care what the answer is, but I need a final headcount for the caterer."

He narrowed his eyes at Gia and she mimicked his reaction.

"I'm a yes," she answered cheerily, marking the box with a flourish. "But as my date's a celebrity, he'd rather not have the catering staff know his name." She handed over the card, her smile forced, Jayson guessed, for his benefit.

"Really?" Taylor asked, proving this was news to her. "We'll talk later. What about you, Coop?"

"Same situation," he answered, marking the yes box. "Ironically."

Gia crinkled her nose, but he kept his gaze trained on Taylor.

"There. Now was that so hard?" Taylor offered a saccharine-sweet smile and then spun on one heel and left the office.

"Holy Bridezilla," Gia said once she was gone. "She's

my best friend and I love her, but *yikes*." Then she looked at him. "I didn't know you had a date."

"I didn't know you had a date, either." Going for casual, he tucked his hands in his pockets and waited.

Silence invaded for a few uncomfortable seconds while she examined her fingernails.

"Well, I didn't want to attend my other brother's wedding and have a repeat of what happened at Bran's." She then fidgeted with a pen. "That was a mistake."

Her pulling him into a spare bedroom at the mansion and kissing him so hard he saw stars was a *big* mistake and she wasn't the only one who thought so. Since then he'd had trouble keeping his mind on work and keeping their aboveboard banter from crossing into sexual territory.

His mind returned again and again to the way she'd tasted that night—like champagne, and a woman he hadn't had a sampling of for too long. If there was one essence he was powerless against it was the rare and intoxicating flavor of his ex-wife.

They'd made out hot and heavy, hiding in the spare guest bedroom after the wedding. Her dress was rucked up to her waist while she plunged her hand down his pants. The memory of the heat, the *want* and the sheer high of being able to take her where she needed to go was a memory that hadn't faded for him in the least.

He clasped his hands in front of his crotch to hide his reaction, and forced his thoughts on what had interrupted them that night.

Taylor's going-into-labor screech.

There. Thinking of that helped quell the lust.

"I didn't realize you were seeing anyone," Gia said, obviously fishing for details. Details she wouldn't get since Jayson didn't actually have a date. He guessed now he'd have to find someone. A celebrity apparently, since he'd coat-tailed Gia's story with a story of his own. He sure as shit wasn't admitting he lied to save face.

"It's new," he answered. "I didn't realize you were seeing anyone either." He'd stayed similarly single. Work kept him busy, but even if it hadn't he had no interest in a relationship. Once bitten…

Last fall he'd attended Bran's wedding alone, not thinking a thing of it. Jayson was still considered family outside of the office. Bran and Royce were like brothers. That said, even if he'd had one, bringing a date to a Knox family gathering would have been strange for him and stranger for his date.

It hadn't occurred to him until now that Gia might have a date for *this* wedding. He'd assumed she was following the same unwritten rule: no bringing dates around the ex.

Guess not.

"The tablet update is nearing release," he said, guiding the conversation back to the safe, neutral ground of ThomKnox. Where he and Gia were concerned, work might well be the last frontier of neutral territory. They'd had their differences in the past—namely him working hard to make her happy and her resisting his every effort—but here they had the same goal.

ThomKnox was the number one priority in their lives. They'd always do what was best for the company.

And, in this case, he thought as he took a seat to tell her about the latest software update in detail, the best thing for the company was Gia and him getting along.

Together or not.

Two

Six months ago at Bran's wedding

This is crazy.

You're crazy.

We're both crazy!

But oh, did Jay taste good. Really damn good. After being without sex for so long, Gia was beginning to worry about ill effects. She'd gone on a few random dates over the summer, since not dating would be admitting she wasn't over her ex, but each of those dates had ended with a good-night kiss that had only made her think of Jayson Cooper. So while he was totally over her, evidently she was still affected by him.

Case in point.

His tongue, though. Who could deny how good he was with it? Either tangling with hers or gliding down her neck. He suckled on her pulse point while his fingers lifted her dress to do what he was best at: pleasure her.

Fingers in her panties, he slipped along her folds, driving her wild. She moaned into his mouth. He kissed her harder, trying to quiet her. Possibly the only part crazier than carrying on with him was doing it in her parents' vineyard mansion after her brother's wedding. When she saw the guests filtering outside, either to leave or enjoy cocktails around the fire, she'd rushed him into the nearest spare room.

No one had noticed them missing. Nor would they if she could keep her *moaning* to a minimum. A challenge, given his touch was sending her into an orgasmic stupor.

It didn't take long.

She gripped his shoulders hard, pulled her mouth from his and came. She allowed herself a breath or two before her hand was shakily finding its way to his pants. She had his belt undone, zipper down, and was cradling several inches of his budding erection when it happened.

A scream of pain shattered the air—coming from the back patio and from, she guessed, a very pregnant Taylor.

Jayson snapped his mouth from Gia's, blinking hard as if trying to focus. She held her breath and listened. A going-into-labor Taylor shouted again.

Talk about a buzzkill.

"Damn," he said, which is probably what Gia would have said had she been able to speak after her powerful release.

And, oh, was her orgasm a good one. She'd been in charge of her own pleasure since she and her ex went kaput. It was irksome to be reminded of what she'd been missing.

"Get dressed, G," he said, his raspy voice dancing along her nerve endings. He moved her hand out of his pants, flashed her a smile that made her knees weaker, and then kissed her palm.

"What did we do?" she muttered. There was no good end to this night if they slept together, intellectually she'd known that. Yet look how close they'd come to actually sealing the deal!

What was she thinking?

She *wasn't* thinking. Plain and simple…

Gia, chin in her palm, eyes unfocused and gazing into the distance, blinked back to reality.

Her blue cheese–stuffed-olive dirty martini was half gone, but then she'd arrived at the bar early on purpose. She hadn't intended on daydreaming about her ex-husband, or reminding herself that she'd been without an orgasm of that caliber in over six months. She'd arrived early and drunk down half a martini for one reason: she needed to bolster her confidence before meeting her celebrity date.

Blinking the bar into focus, she sucked in a breath and blew it out. Other couples dotted the room, drinks in front of them, the low candles on the table setting the tone: romantic. Why did she choose someplace this romantic? She should have invited him to coffee…

Denver "Pip" Pippen, skateboarding superstar and hot cult god, was about to be interviewed for the role of a lifetime: to be her date to Royce's and Taylor's wedding.

Not that he knew that.

No, she hadn't had a date when she'd marked the RSVP card. But, with Jayson standing there looking as gorgeous and distracting as ever, she realized that attending another wedding without a date could land her in the guest bedroom with him again.

That.

Could not.

Happen.

She'd found Pip's profile on Divinely Yours, a dating app for the wealthy and elite. Not quite A-listers, but not D either. The app was recommended to her about a year ago by a well-meaning friend. At the time she'd shrugged it off, too focused on the ThomKnox tablet launch to dream of throwing herself to the wolves on a dating app. But after filling out Taylor's RSVP card under duress, Gia decided that the dating app might not be the worst idea ever.

Tonight, she'd find out.

She spotted Denver the moment he breezed through the entrance. He carried with him a certain amount of charisma that turned more than her head. As the hostess walked him over, Gia tested her own reaction. She'd seen photos, and videos, online, but this was Denver Pippen in the flesh. That was always a different experience.

His longish dark blond hair was messy and wavy. He wore a baggy T-shirt and jeans—casual but designer, and Converse sneakers. He shot her a smile that took up most of his face in the most charming way imaginable.

Yes. He'd do nicely.

"You must be Pip," she said, offering her hand.

She hadn't expected a demure kiss to the hand and wasn't disappointed. Instead he said her first name, dragging it into a prolonged "Jee-ahh" and kissed her on the cheek.

When he backed away she noticed the silver scar on his eyebrow, and another on his upper lip. She knew from videos of his skateboarding stunts that Denver also had plenty of scars on his upper arms and calves. Somehow, on him, the messy hair and scar combo worked.

"Fancy place." His lazy speech was half surfer dude and half stoner.

"I ordered already. I'm terribly impatient." She fingered the stem of her martini.

"Rad." He flagged down a waitress and ordered a beer. He was polite and brought forth a genuine smile from the waitress. *Nice.* Had he been rude, Gia would have had to leave and gone back to square one. He was doing well so far.

"So, ThomKnox. Computers. Cell phones. All that techy stuff." He wiggled his fingers as if he were talking about sorcery instead.

"That's the gist of it."

"What's your jam over there?"

"I run the marketing department."

"Rad."

She sipped her martini, hiding a smile. *Rad*, indeed. She'd always thought that with her MIT degree she'd be *running* the tech team, but that position had gone to Jay.

Her father had assured her that Jayson was the right fit, and that he'd preferred Gia to be in a higher position, one of more prestige at ThomKnox. But when Jack's own CEO position had come up for grabs, Gia was content to let her brothers duke it out. Literally, as it were.

Newly divorced, she'd cashed in on another interest and opted to run Marketing instead. On good days she stood behind her decision to nurture her need to lie low. On bad days, she wished she'd insisted on taking over the department she loved.

Pip rapped his knuckles on their table to the beat of the music and drew her from her musings. With her eyes, she traced the scars on his hands.

"How did skateboarding become a passion?" she asked.

"My dad bought me a board when I was twelve. He used to do it. He was killer. Once I landed my first big jump, I was hooked." He held up one injured hand, where his middle finger bent at an unnatural angle. "Never deterred by danger."

"I guess not." From what she'd read on his Wikipedia page, Denver Pippen had broken bones. A lot of them. "Once I crashed, I'd be done. I'm not much of a risk taker."

She winced at the truth behind that admission, recalling the way she'd ducked out of the tech department after the divorce. She'd loved her job, but after she and Jayson split she couldn't bear to be "under" his authority another second. She needed space, and while she didn't have it in physical form, since her office was still on the tech floor, at least they weren't quibbling over who ran the weekly meetings.

"Why would you risk ruining those beautiful brains?" Denver flipped his palm over and motioned for her hand. Intrigued, she slipped her hand into his. Rough. Calloused. "I looked you up. MIT, smarty-pants. You're the prize Knox. So why'd you swipe on my mug on Divinely Yours?"

Good question. She'd waded through a sea of billionaires, millionaires, actors and video game creators. Pip was wildly different from someone she would normally choose—different from who anyone would choose for her. Pip was a guy who would be a good short-term solution to a problem. Since she wasn't ready to submerge herself entirely into the dating pool, she figured he'd be a perfectly good date to the wedding. He wouldn't have the wrong impression about how serious they were, and he'd likely walk away without looking back.

Instead of telling him he was a convenient solution, she went with a more palatable answer. "I liked your face."

He grinned. It was a handsome face.

"I like your face, too, *Jee-ahh.* So what's up? Drinks on a Monday at six o'clock? This screams trial." He drank from his beer glass. "What's the real gig?"

He was sharper than he wanted others to believe. And direct.

She lifted an eyebrow. "Now who's the smarty-pants?"

His laugh was a low, rolling chuckle.

She held on to the stem of her martini glass and told him the truth. "I need a date for my brother's wedding. It's next Saturday."

"And you thought of me?" Humor radiated off him. "You want to piss off your parents or make someone jealous?"

She wasn't trying to make Jayson jealous. Nor did she care if her parents were upset by her attending solo or with a date. What she did care about was the seemingly undeniable lure of her ex-husband.

The way Jay could look at her from across a room and make her heart skip a beat and her brain forget their checkered past. An innocent, polite dance at the last wedding reception had turned into more when his hand moved to her lower back and he'd laid his lips against her ear.

She couldn't let that happen again.

"A bit of both," she lied to her date.

"I'm your guy." Pip held up his beer glass in a toast.

He wasn't, not permanently, but he'd fill a much-needed void. Smiling, Gia tapped her glass with his.

Three

The woman lying in the sand was tall, given the way her limbs splayed attractively into a pose as she leered at the camera lens.

Gia's claim she was dating a celebrity had given Jayson an idea. He'd called his stepbrother, Mason, later that day and, as luck had it, learned that Mas had a photoshoot scheduled with a supermodel.

Cha-ching.

Mason squatted in the sand in front of the woman and gave her commands like "sultry, now sweet, give me a smile" while the shutter clicks from his camera fired.

Jayson had heard enough teasing over the years to last a lifetime. *Mason and Jayson, are you two twins or something?* The answer was obvious just by looking. Jayson had a wider, thicker build than his brother. Mason was tall and slim, with an added four inches of height. They'd both had goatees years ago, but Jayson had abandoned his. Now he either shaved or didn't and those were the only two options.

"Beautiful, Natasha," Mason praised the model as he lowered his camera. *Beautiful Natasha* was an apt nickname. The bikini-clad goddess with sand stuck to her boobs had graced many a magazine. She was on the cover of last year's *Sports Illustrated* swimsuit edition. This year she'd been replaced on the cover, but was still featured inside, and today she was shooting her own calendar.

Landing *the* Natasha Tovar was a big win for Mas. He'd started his career taking family portraits, made a brief foray as a wedding photographer—Jayson and Gia's wedding, actually—and then Mason had stumbled into shooting models, which was harder than one might imagine in California.

"We have it?" Natasha brushed sand from her supple body before slipping on a white "robe," for lack of a better term.

Jayson could see right through it and when the cups of her bikini top wet the robe, they were a pair of fluorescent orange globes he had trouble looking away from.

"Who's this?" She toweled her hair and walked every inch of her mostly legs body toward Jayson.

"This is my brother, Jayson Cooper. Goes by Cooper." Mason slanted a glance from Natasha to Jayson, his eyebrows winging upward as if to say *I told you she was perfect.*

"Nice to meet you, Cooper." She extended a hand, which he accepted. She left sand in his palm. She didn't introduce herself and Jayson figured it was because she didn't have to. He possessed a penis therefore he should know who she was. She excused herself and walked up the beach toward a trailer.

"She's putting that wiggle into her walk for you," Mason said. He thumbed through some of the shots on his Canon while the lighting guy left behind his umbrellas and reflector panels to seek out the food truck parked in front of the more populated part of the beach. "You hungry?"

"Always," Jayson said.

"That food truck sucks—" Mason tipped his head to indicate the direction his lighting guy went "—but I brought Chester's homemade tamales."

Jayson's stomach roared. Mason's husband made the best tamales on the planet. "I am not above eating half your lunch. Especially if Ches made it."

"He's a keeper." Mason smiled.

At eighteen years old, after he graduated high school, Mason had come out officially. Jayson's response? A nonchalant shrug. He couldn't have been less surprised.

Mason's father, Albert, was alarmed, which helped Jayson realize that his stepfather rarely paid attention to life outside of work. But, Albert was also a good man and, while it took him longer, he accepted that his son was gay. Jayson's mom, Julia, was as unsurprised as Jayson. She'd helped Albert realize the truth: Mason was still Mason, no matter who he loved.

Anyway, that was ancient history. Mason and Chester had wed two years ago and were now like any boring married couple. Or, what Jayson thought a boring married couple should be like. He and Gia hadn't made it to "boring."

The brothers split a pan of tamales—thankfully, Mason had two forks—while sitting on a piece of driftwood watching the waves crash on the shore. Not a bad way to spend an afternoon.

"Can't believe you drove all this way to meet her. You must be desperate," Mason said around a final bite.

Jayson tossed his fork on the empty pan and swiped his teeth with his tongue. How to respond to that? Mason knew Jay needed a wedding date—an impressive one—but Jay hadn't told him why.

He hadn't shared with his brother that he'd brought Gia to orgasm six months ago and since then she'd shut him out like it'd never happened. It wasn't unlike right before their divorce hearing, when they'd had car sex. Unplanned, mind-blowing car sex. Then, five days later, Gia showed up at court with ice in her veins like she hadn't felt the earth move.

But mind-blowing car sex could not a marriage save. Whenever they were arguing, and that became more and more often near the end, she claimed she couldn't be with someone who "controlled" her. Jayson, whose real father had controlled their household with fists and fear, never reacted well to that accusation.

"Want to tell me why you need a supermodel as your wedding date?" Mason asked.

Well. What the hell.

"Gia is bringing a date to her brother Royce's wedding. I'm not showing up alone."

"How mature."

"Gia and I almost had sex not that long ago, Mas." Jayson shook his head. "Could have set us back years. Plus, the guy's famous. I had to step up."

"Famous?"

"Denver Pippen," Jayson said through his teeth. Apparently, Gia had met him for cocktails and things went well. Not that Jayson had been lurking around the office, but okay, he'd been *sort of* lurking. And he'd heard Gia excitedly telling Taylor that her date was going to be none other than skateboarding legend, Denver "Pip" Pippen.

"He's hot," Mason said. "That sports drink commercial where he leaps those cars…"

"Not helping." Jayson stood, frustrated. "What could Gia possibly have in common with a guy who's broken nearly every bone in his body? She's all brains and he pounds his into the pavement."

"And you thought Natasha would make her as jealous as you are." Mason smirked.

"I'm not jealous of that joker-smile idiot." He frowned, considering. "But if I see him kiss Gia, I'm going to give him a new scar."

Mason laughed. "It's past time you *both* got out there, Coop. You've been out of the game for a while."

"Thanks for the reminder." He pushed a hand through his hair. "It's not easy to date when your ex-wife is in your social circles."

Mason gave his brother the side-eye. "You two *stay* in each other's circles. You still act married. Divorced people move on. You two moved sideways."

Jayson shook his head, but he wasn't committed to it. Mason had a point. It wasn't easy to move on when the wound was fresh.

"I'm moving on now," Jay said, simply because he needed to say it out loud.

"Good. I've been priming Natasha today about your arrival. Told her you were hot and single. Then I mentioned that you were going to the Knox family vineyard over the weekend and you should have seen her face." Mason reached for his camera. "Actually you *can* see her face. I snapped a few shots of her reaction."

"You did tell her I needed her to be a plus-one to a wedding, didn't you?"

"And do all the legwork for you? Absolutely not. Natasha!" Mason called over his shoulder.

Her trailer door opened a crack. "More photos?"

"No photos. Cooper has something to ask you." Mas slapped Jay's shoulder as Natasha came out of the trailer and wiggled her way across the sand. "No time like the present."

Mason vanished inside and shut the door behind him.

Natasha, still in her see-through robe, peered up at Jayson expectantly. “What’s up, Coop?”

Palming the back of his neck, Jayson smiled down at the supermodel. Here went nothing. “Are you busy on Saturday?”

Four

Denver drove separately to the wedding, which left Gia wringing her hands. She assumed he knew better than to wear a baggy T-shirt, jeans and Converse to a formal Knox event but...*did he?*

Her own attire was a blush pink bridesmaid's dress, short but flowy. The dress was higher in the front than the back, the spaghetti straps showing off her shoulders. The narrow bodice gave her a bit too much cleavage, but it wasn't as if she could help it.

Turned out there was no need to worry. Denver showed up for the wedding in head-to-toe Armani so it wasn't hard to forgive his windblown hair with sunglasses perched in it. He turned plenty of heads upon his arrival, mostly other men at the party who knew sports.

She hadn't spotted Jayson yet, but no matter. She'd achieved her goal. She was at Royce and Taylor's wedding with a date, which meant she wasn't going to trip over Jayson after she drank too much champagne and then try to take his pants off.

Denver made his way to the white folding chairs set up on the hill overlooking a stunning vineyard and Gia readied herself with the other bridesmaid, her very pregnant sister-in-law Addison.

Addi blew out a breath and gave Gia a steady smile. "I'm fine."

"It'd serve Taylor right if you went into labor right here, right now," Gia joked. After all it was Taylor who'd gone into labor after Addison's wedding.

"I'll see what I can do," Addi said with a laugh.

The violinist started playing. As maid of honor Gia began the procession of two. She stepped onto the white runner, smiling for the photographer. She winked at her brother Royce who looked uncharacteristically nervous, before her eyes tracked to Brannon who gave her a nod.

When her gaze naturally reached the final groomsman, her heart thundered. Of course she knew that Jayson was a groomsman and would be standing with her brothers, but she wasn't ready for the gut-punch vision of him at the end of an aisle she was walking. They'd been married outside as well, though their wedding was beachfront instead of among a backdrop of grapevines.

Her smile tightened along with her grip on the bouquet of lilacs. She could do this. She would. For her brother.

Positioned up front, she scanned the crowd for her date, finding Denver sitting in full man-spread in the second row. Before she could decide how she felt about that, Addison took her place next to Gia and Taylor began her descent.

Taylor made an ethereal bride in white, the short beaded train of her dress shimmering in the midday sunshine. Tears pricked Gia's eyes as she watched her best friend take Royce's hand, and they rolled down her cheeks as she considered that her best friend was about to become her *sister*.

Once Royce had kissed his bride, and Addison and Gia had gone through several tissues, the crowd cheered for the latest Mr. and Mrs. Knox. The exit music began, which meant Gia was officially off the hook.

Or so she thought.

Brannon bypassed her to take Addi's arm. "Sorry for the bait and switch, sis, but my wife needs me."

"You wish," Gia teased. Addison chuckled.

Addison, her hand bracing her very pregnant belly, beamed up at her husband before looping her arm in his. Bran mumbled something to her and she nodded, assuring him she was "still fine."

"Stuck with me, then," Jay commented as he offered Gia his arm.

"The sacrifices we make for those we love," she mumbled before pausing to smile for the photographer. "I didn't see your date."

"She's seated behind your date."

Gia turned her head to find her date leaning over a chair and chatting up a gorgeous brunette. She had to blink twice to be sure she was seeing correctly. "Is that—"

"Natasha Tovar. Supermodel."

Yes, that's what Gia thought. She let out a noncommittal hum. "Did Mason hook you up with Miss *Sports Illustrated*?"

"He introduced us. She likes my accent." He leaned down when he spoke. Whenever he was close, she had trouble thinking clearly.

"You don't have an accent."

"To Natasha I do. She's Russian."

"Good for her," Gia grumbled.

The guests meandered to the tent next and Gia and Jayson waited for their dates. As the supermodel approached, Gia felt her lip curl.

It'd have made her day if Natasha Tovar had been airbrushed within an inch of her life in her photos, but the gorgeous brunette was every bit as tantalizing in person as on a glossy magazine page. She was tall and leggy with high cheekbones and big eyes. Every other step she took revealed one supple thigh through the slit in her short black dress.

"What about your guy?" Jay rumbled, his voice low. "Does he own a hairbrush or is that how the kids are wearing it these days?"

Jerking her attention to Denver, who she honestly hadn't been watching, Gia retorted, "I admit, it's nice to date someone younger after having been with an older man for so long."

Jay smirked, his confidence unwavering. "Aged to perfection, sweetheart."

Goose bumps cropped up on her forearms the way they did whenever her ex-husband was accidentally sexy. Which happened more than she'd dare admit. Thankfully their dates reached them before he noticed her reaction.

"Dude, do you know who this is?" Denver asked Gia, his thumb pointing at Natasha.

"Ms. Tovar, is it?" Gia extended a hand. "It's lovely to meet you. I didn't know you were dating our Jayson."

"Coop and I met a few days ago and we hit it off. He's not gay like his brother so it worked out."

Gia pressed her lips together to smother a laugh and turned to Jayson. "Such high praise."

"Looks like Denver has all of his teeth," Jayson said under his breath. "Good for you."

Gia leered at him but he still wore that infuriatingly handsome smirk. He swept Natasha away and Gia groused in their wake, wishing they didn't look good together. They did. Dammit.

"She's hot," Denver put in as he placed his hand on her lower back.

"Not all of us are built like giraffes," she said, noting that she was being catty but not really caring.

"No, baby, not you." Denver bent his knees to come eye to eye with her, his hands gripping her biceps while he looked straight into her eyes. "You are gorgeous in another way. A different league. Beneath this package of curvaceous goodness, you deliver a totally gnarly experience."

Judging by his smile that was a compliment. "Um. Thanks?"

"You're welcome. Let's find some grub." She and Denver walked to the reception tent overlooking the vineyard. Where Addi and Bran's wedding had been contained to the immediate backyard, Taylor and Royce's was more sprawling. There were easily three times the number of guests here than at Bran and Addi's. Maybe Gia would be lucky and she wouldn't run into Jayson and Natasha again tonight.

Alas, when Denver and Gia approached the bar, Jayson was there, handing off a slim glass of clear bubbly liquid with a lime wedge in it to Natasha.

"What do you think, baby? Shots?" Denver asked Gia. Jayson turned and frowned. No, not a frown. There was an entire lightning storm forming behind his eyes.

Ignoring them both, she ordered for herself. "Dirty martini, up with three olives. Blue cheese stuffed if you have them."

"Shot of rum and a bitter IPA. Something local if ya got it." Denver seemed none the wiser to Jayson's disapproving presence.

Well, her ex could just deal with it. She didn't like his date any more than he liked hers.

The bartender made their drinks and Jayson, one hand wrapped around a glass of red wine, the other around Natasha's waist, gestured to a table.

"Dirty martini," Natasha laughed before she walked off with Jayson.

"What the hell was that supposed to mean?" Gia whispered to herself.

"It means she knows you got it going on, baby," her date answered.

"Gia," she snapped, shooting lasers from her eyes at Denver. "My name is Gia."

"Jee-ahh." His grin widened.

She sighed. She guessed that was better than "baby."

Five

"The guest rooms are on the second floor," Gia was saying to Denver as they crested the stairs. It was getting late, most of the guests filtering off. As part of the bridal party, it was her duty to oversee that the guests who were staying the night had everything they needed.

"Cool. I'll grab my stuff." He dropped a kiss on her mouth—one that startled her since they hadn't kissed yet. The night they'd enjoyed their first drink together had ended the way it'd started: with a demure brush of his lips on her cheek. "Yo, Natasha," Denver called before jogging up the stairs.

Gia's eyes sank closed. *Of course* the Russian goddess had witnessed that kiss. She turned, unsurprised to find Jayson there as well.

"We are staying, too," Natasha informed Gia.

"Yippee."

"Yes, it's very exciting," Natasha said, missing Gia's sarcasm. "I'll freshen up, but not done yet. More dancing." She gave Jayson a limp shove on the chest and then glided up the stairs.

"Enjoying yourselves?" Gia asked him, her tone flat.

"I love a good wedding." He pushed his hands into his pants pockets. He'd lost the jacket and bowtie from earlier, which left him in a white button-down shirt with the sleeves pushed to his elbows.

He looked good.

He rarely didn't.

He cleared his throat. "Where's your room?"

"Far end of the hallway." Denver's room was catty-corner to hers, not that she volunteered that information. "What about yours?"

"We're in the middle." He shot her a heated look and she could've sworn it was because he was thinking of the room they'd stayed in when they'd last visited her parents' mansion. The master guest suite. At least neither of them had been stationed there tonight.

Still, the "we" niggled at her. "We" meant that he'd be crawling into bed with *Miss Russia* tonight.

"She's not your type." Gia worked to sound curious. To be fair, she *was* curious. She hadn't seen him with anyone since they divorced and then he came out of the gate with a thoroughbred.

His shrug was infuriatingly blasé. "I don't have a type."

Her type used to be broad, dark and handsome with a protective streak a mile and a half wide. Five o'clock shadow and short-cropped dark hair. Eyes so blue she'd felt as if her soul was being inspected by a fallen angel…

But that was when she was in love with Jayson. She wasn't in love with him anymore.

When she'd married him she thought he understood her; that he'd allow her to be herself and forge her own way. Instead he'd attempted to corral and protect her, a lot like her father and brothers had done.

She twisted her lips in thought. “I don’t have a type either.”

“Coop! I found these in our room!” Natasha jogged down the stairs waving a pair of maracas from a Knox family trip to Puerto Rico. A keepsake. Gia felt the slow burn of anger broil her hairline. This woman needed to learn keep her hands off what didn’t belong to her.

“Hey!” Gia lifted her voice, “Those are—”

“Going right back to where they came from.” Jayson removed the maracas from Natasha’s hands and gave them to Gia. As he walked off with his date, Gia heard him assure Natasha that they’d find some other way to entertain themselves on the dance floor.

And probably, Gia thought as she stomped upstairs, they’d find a way to entertain themselves in their shared bed, too.

Ugh.

“Cool digs.” Denver shut his bedroom door and met her in the hallway Then he rubbed his hands together. “What are those for?”

“Nothing.” Gia shoved the maracas into his chest and bypassed him to walk into his room. “Change of plans. We’re staying in my room.”

She exited carrying his duffel bag and opened the door to her room next. He followed behind her, a confused expression on his face.

“Together?” he asked.

“Yeah.” She dropped his bag onto the down comforter. “Together.”

Denver gave her one of his wide, carefree grins. “Sweet.”

“But dancing is my *favorite*.”

It wasn’t Natasha’s enunciation of favorite (fave-oh-right) that annoyed Jayson so much as the whine that accompanied it.

She was a beautiful woman with scads of confidence. She was educated and outgoing. She didn't drink alcohol. She was polite to everyone she met.

But.

She was needy and clingy and driving him up the wall. He'd danced with her. And danced. *And danced.*

He unwound his date's fingers from his forearm. "Natasha. No means no."

She thrust out her bottom lip. It didn't make her any less attractive.

He offered a tolerant smile and gentled his voice. "If I don't have a cigar with Brannon, he's going to kick my ass."

She let out a sharp gasp. "Cigars cannot touch this mouth."

"It's just one," he said, instead of *so, what?* There wasn't a single spark of attraction between them, though sleeping with her had crossed his mind. If for no other reason than to take his mind off his ex-wife, who was swishing around here in a short dress with enough cleavage to fall into.

He'd bet Denver noticed. Jayson sawed his teeth together.

"No kissing," Natasha hissed before she scampered off. The band played a fast song and she grabbed hold of a geriatric gentleman and started dancing with him. Jayson seemed to remember that guy from a board meeting. Anyway, the old guy looked happier than Jay was about the dancing, so they could have at it.

Outside, he found Bran standing in a half circle with a few other guys from work.

"There he is." Bran handed over a cigar and cutter. "Where's your supermodel date? Did she finally realize what a loser you were and ditch you?"

"She's dancing." *Some more.*

"Gia and Denver Pippen?" Bran asked around the cigar between his teeth. "What's that about?"

Jayson cut and lit his own cigar. He took a long puff and blew out his answer. "Wish I knew."

"Haven't seen them in a while. Did they leave?"

Jayson welded his back teeth together. "I think they're staying."

More like he *knew* they were staying. At the end of the hall. He saw her go upstairs earlier. If she'd met Denver in that room, Jayson had a good idea what they were doing right now.

He shouldn't care, but when it came to Gia, married or not, he'd always had the fierce desire to protect her. Denver seemed harmless—the sports star probably did more damage to himself than he'd ever do to another person—but she might need a reminder that she didn't have to wander that far down the evolutionary scale to rummage up a date.

"Huh." Bran sent a derisive look at the second floor of the house where a few bedroom lights were on. Gia's brother didn't go on a rant about her and Denver, and Jayson understood. Bran was close friends with Jay, had been for years, but if he had to choose sides, Bran would choose Gia. That was the way it should be.

"How's Addi? She holding on to that baby a while longer?" Jayson asked, segueing as seamlessly as possible.

"She's taking it easy tonight. Other than a few kicks to the beat of the music, she says the baby is content to wait." Bran's smile was contagious. "God, I can't wait to meet her. My daughter."

"Me too." Jay slapped him heartily on the shoulder. Brannon and Royce were family. Being divorced from Gia hadn't changed that. After they'd split, she'd insisted no one treat Jayson differently. The only one unable to follow that request was Gia herself. She'd been aloof and cool for the most part. Exception being at this very house about six months ago…

"Gentlemen," Royce greeted them upon his approach.

He was still dressed in his tux, the formality suiting him. Taylor, in her formfitting lace wedding gown, a scooped V in the front and back, wore a tired smile.

"Cigar?" Bran offered Taylor.

"Shut up." She gave her brother-in-law a playful slap before fussing with a drooping ring of flowers in her hair. "I'm falling apart."

"You're not," Jayson assured her.

"Thanks, Coop." She smiled genuinely before turning her attention to Bran. "Say the word and we'll delay the honeymoon. Royce and I want to be home when Addi has the baby."

Jayson was surprised to see Royce nod his agreement. "It's not a problem, Bran. Really."

"Go." Bran waved a hand. "The baby will be here when you come back."

"But I want to be there." Taylor appeared as unsatisfied by this decision as her new husband. "The *moment* it happens."

"Guys. Go to the Bahamas. Any excuse to delay and neither of you will ever go. You work too much."

Jayson regarded the ground and smiled to himself. Bran was as dedicated to their family's company as Royce and Taylor, even though he played down his commitment.

"He's right," Taylor told Royce. "Plus, if we stay here, your mom and dad will insist on keeping their granddaughter anyway. They've been looking forward to our honeymoon as much as we have."

"Not as much," Royce told his bride.

"We have things under control here," Jayson assured her. He was happy for them. Not every marriage ended in catastrophe.

Though a lot of them do, murmured the cynic inside.

"*Fine*. I'll go to the Bahamas," she said with a surly huff. "Where is Gia, anyway? I wanted to say goodbye."

This again? "I believe she went to bed."

"Oh." Taylor's brow crinkled. Jayson was an inch away from encouraging her to go upstairs and interrupt whatever might be happening, but he managed to keep that request to himself.

Progress. He was growing.

Royce shook Jayson's then Brannon's hands. "Call us the second Addi's in the hospital," he instructed his brother. "Day or night."

"Honeymoon, Royce," Bran told him. "You have to relax."

"I don't relax." Royce dipped his chin at Jayson, his tone firmer than before. "Coop. Keep an eye on our girl."

"What was that about?" Bran asked once they'd gone.

"No idea," Jayson lied, lifting his cigar to his lips.

Royce wasn't referring to his daughter, but Gia.

It wasn't so long ago that Gia's father, Jack Knox, had given Jayson a similar command. Her family had always wanted to protect her.

It'd taken Jayson a while to learn it, but he now knew what Gia wanted more than anything. And that was to take care of herself.

Six

Last January, the ThomKnox parking garage

"Thanks for the help," Gia said, chasing after Jayson. "Even though I told you I'd carry that."

"Not happening, G." Like he'd let her carry a thirty-six-inch screen from the executive floor down to the parking garage. "Why are you in the garage, anyway? You should be parked up front in the space with your name on it."

She beeped a key fob. "My interior is black leather. It'd soak up the heat from the sun and then when I climbed in I'd suffocate and die."

"Well, we can't have that." The black Mercedes Benz C-Class was a beauty. He should know. He'd picked it out. At the time he hadn't imagined he'd be leaving it with her because they were divorcing.

Five days from now they'd finalize their split on paper. Officially.

He'd already secured an apartment. Most of what he was

taking there was already in storage. He'd moved out gradually, thinking it would hurt less. Turned out there was no way for divorce to hurt less. It hurt. That's all there was to it.

He slid the large screen, in its factory box, into the trunk and shut it. She went around to the driver's seat and climbed inside, turning over the engine. The sound echoed in the garage. Not a soul was parked on the third level. Other than a guard and few brown-nosers, Jay guessed the first floor was just as empty.

Gia rolled down the window. "Guess I'll see you later."

He locked onto her brown eyes, stuck on what to say about any of it. All of the arguments he wished could have been simple misunderstandings. All of the accusations said in the heat of the moment that he should have taken back.

Too late now.

"I'm sorry," he said, the words exiting his throat like broken glass. Not because he didn't mean it. He was sorry, sorry that their marriage was ending in a stalemate.

"Don't be." Her smile was forced. "We did our best."

"Did we?"

She watched him, chewing on her lip. He hadn't meant to ask, but now that he had...*did they* do their best? Or were they giving up?

She shut off the engine and stepped out, folding her arms and leaning on the door. Eyes on his, she said, "Yes. We did."

"I'm not a quitter. Neither are you," he offered. "This feels like quitting."

"We can't change the past, Jay." She shrugged. "And the future is unknown. Besides, we're not quitting. We're deciding to be apart. Our love for this company, and my family, isn't going anywhere. The only difference in our lives will be that you no longer live in the house."

He rested a hand on the car's roof and hovered over her. "I'll also no longer be in your bed."

Heat warmed her caramel-colored eyes to deep, chocolate brown. He brushed her soft cheek with the back of his fingers.

"I'll no longer kiss these lips good-night." He touched her mouth with his thumb. That would be the hardest transition—for both of them, he'd bet.

"We have a few days," she whispered, arching her back and brushing her breasts against his chest.

He didn't need more of an invitation than that. Lowering his face, he captured her lips with his. She wrapped her arms around his neck and kissed him back.

Her entire body participated, from her fingernails scratching his scalp to her leg wrapping around his hip. Hand beneath her thigh, he hiked her leg higher and deepened their kiss. His erection raged as a contradicting voice inside yelled for him to both stop and go faster.

"Point of no return," he breathed into her ear before nipping her earlobe. If they slept together, it'd change everything. He knew it in his bones.

He wasn't sure if that was wise, or infinitely stupid.

She pulled away, her tongue swiping her bottom lip. When her teeth came down to capture it, he knew her answer.

"One more time," she answered.

He didn't think, he only acted.

Cigar enjoyed, time killed, Jayson trudged upstairs to his date.

He'd waited until the band packed up, sitting up and talking to Bran and a few of his friends to further stall the inevitable. He knew Gia was upstairs with Denver. Neither of them had reappeared. Jayson hadn't been in a big hurry to run upstairs and corroborate that suspicion.

He turned down the hallway to walk to his room when Denver clomped up the stairs behind him, a glass of brown liquid in hand. “One for the road, bro,” he said, his speech wobbly.

Jayson welded his jaw together as Denver disappeared into Gia’s room. Fists balled, he considered his options. Bust into the room and demand his ex-wife stay away from that harebrained, brick-headed dolt, or stand idly by.

There would be consequences if he banged on that door and checked up on her. She didn’t like him undermining her. That was the word she’d often used. *Undermining.* As if protecting someone he loved was an insult.

Then again, making sure she was safe was worth any consequence, big or small. He’d started toward the bedroom door when her laugh floated out from under it.

He froze in place, at once disgusted and resigned. She sounded fine. Happy, even.

That sucked.

On heavy legs he turned back toward his own room and walked in. Natasha was waiting for him.

“Fix it.” She pointed at the dresser, where one drawer was opened at a weird slant. “I can’t live like this.”

“Can’t have you roughing it,” he said, sarcasm thick, as he fixed the drawer with a quick wiggle. Forget that she was in a Knox mansion overlooking a vineyard, majestic mountains as a backdrop.

All he wanted to do was close his eyes and wake up in the morning.

“You are not nice,” she said. Arguably she was right. He hadn’t been very nice. “I am showering. Don’t join me.” She closed herself into the bathroom. And locked the door.

“No problem, lady.” He sat on the edge of the bed and scrubbed his face with both hands.

He was beat, but he couldn’t sleep knowing what was going on at the end of the hallway. He decided to head downstairs. The bar was closed, but he knew where Jack kept the good scotch. Jayson needed a nip after the day he'd had. Hell, he needed a *bottle*.

When he exited his room, Gia was tiptoeing out of hers. They shut the doors to their rooms simultaneously. He smiled and she smiled back at him, each amused by the unintentional choreography.

She'd changed from her bridesmaid's dress into a short pair of cutoff shorts and an oversize pink T-shirt. She looked cute. Relaxed. Warm and sleepy.

The thought of Denver touching her made Jayson want to howl.

She shoved her hands into her back pockets. "Hey."

"Hi." Still in his trousers and white shirt from the wedding, he was overdressed for this chance meeting. "Couldn't sleep."

"Yeah. My roommate is, ah, he finally fell asleep."

After what?

He didn't dare ask.

"Is the party winding down?" She folded her arms over her stomach and shifted on her feet. Fidgeting, the way she did when she was nervous.

"Royce and Taylor took off for the honeymoon. Addi and Bran are in their room. Your mom and dad left a little while ago with the baby. Just catering staff and house staff tidying up downstairs."

She nodded, glancing away before looking back at him. "I was going to grab a snack. Want to join me?"

"I was heading for the bar, but I never turn down a meal."

She joined him at the top of the stairs and they walked down side by side. "I didn't mean to take you from your *date*."

If it wasn't for the way she pronounced that hard *T*, he wouldn't have had any idea his ex-wife was jealous. He wasn't proud of it, but he liked knowing he wasn't the only one entertaining the green-eyed monster tonight.

Downstairs in the kitchen, she weaved between the house staff, greeting them by name while pulling out containers of leftovers from the fridge.

She handed him a large plate and filled it with a variety of salads and pasta, meats and cheeses, and on another plate served up a large slice of cake. When she started to put the containers back into the fridge, one of the house staff shooed her away.

She walked outside and on the way Jayson grabbed a pair of sparkling-water bottles. They stopped at a picnic table beneath a broad tree overlooking the vineyards. The house glowed warmly in the background, looking as homey as a thirty-something-room mansion could.

They dug into their shared snack in silence.

"Mmm. God. This is better than…" She trailed off before rephrasing her statement. "This is better than it was the first time."

"Did you do something to work up an appetite?" He narrowed his eyes.

She popped a square of cheese into her mouth and raised an eyebrow. "Did *you*?"

He reached for his water bottle and unscrewed the cap before taking a long guzzle. Not as good as scotch, but it would do. Patience shot, he said what was on his mind. "What the hell are you doing with that clown?"

"Excuse me?"

"Denver Pippen. *That's* who you're choosing to be seen with?"

"How is that any of your business?" She let out an incredulous laugh.

"I refuse to stand by while you waste your time with an idiot like Denver Pippen."

"Oh, you're one to talk! You brought a runway model to my brother's wedding."

"She's a *swimsuit* model."

Even in the dim light he could make out the redness of his ex-wife's cheeks. "You're a hypocrite. You're allowed to sleep with whoever you want, but I can't? Who the hell do you think you are?"

"I didn't sleep with Natasha," he blurted out before he thought better of it.

"Not yet," Gia said, but her voice was small. She hadn't expected him to say that.

"Not ever," he answered with finality.

Seven

Jayson took a bite of the cake and licked his fork. Gia crossed her legs beneath the table, memories of his mouth—and how good he was with it—assaulting her.

So he hadn't slept with Natasha? Gia had to chew on that for a while. She did so with a slice of brie.

He scooped up another large bite of leftover wedding cake. "Is it about sex? Is that the appeal?"

Unwilling to confess anything, she claimed her own fork and ate a bite of cake. She was still sort of in shock that Jayson hadn't slept with the beautiful woman he'd brought to the wedding.

"If it's about sex, you can do better," he pressed.

She met his eyes and in their blue depths recalled the way he used to look at her. Heated. Down to her very soul. Sex with Jayson had been exquisite. Unparalleled.

Too long ago.

"Who am I supposed to sleep with? *You*?" Her heart

thundered while she held her breath. Waiting. Daring him to answer. He didn't disappoint.

"Yes. If what you're after is a physical release, I'm a sure thing. But not with some random guy who isn't worthy of you." The words were gravel dragged over concrete. Jayson was pissed. Which also made him *hot*.

If temptation was a grain of sand, she'd be standing on an island. He could deliver on a physical release—tenfold. And if any proof was needed, she had it. Her body had come alive the second he'd said the word *yes*.

But they'd learned that lesson, hadn't they?

"We tried that already," she said. "We're good in bed but not outside of it. Look at us now. We should be in our separate rooms and yet..."

"And yet." He let the words hang.

She had a heart to protect. Unraveling her marriage had been the hardest thing she'd ever done in her life. Away from him she'd finally felt like an adult who was in charge of her own life. She loved her family, but they had a way of coddling her that she didn't appreciate. She understood that she was the youngest, but her reaching the pinnacle of adulthood should have quelled everyone's urge to protect her.

The freedom of being married was eye-opening...until she'd realized Jayson trying to take care of her much like her father and brothers.

There was a certain amount of freedom that came with being single. She could eat dinner whenever she liked without having to take a vote about whether to order out or dine in. She could stay up too late, fall asleep on the couch, enjoy the shower all to herself...

Although that part had its downsides.

Jayson had washed her back *and* her front when they'd lived together. In the moments she was romantic with herself, she used some of those memories as motivation.

But.

Going backward was never the best way forward. Wasn't that what all the memes on Pinterest said?

"It's too late." She stood from the picnic table.

He stood and blocked her path, hulking and dark, brooding and beautiful. "Too late for what?"

She put a hand on his chest to push him away but it settled there, content to touch him even as her brain urged against it. "It's too late to get back together."

He leaned in, the clean scent of his aftershave mingling with the crisp air from the vineyard. Lips close to hers, but still not touching, he muttered, "Who said anything about getting back together?"

Time stopped.

The only sounds came from the catering staff packing up the truck and the rustling of the leaves overhead. Chaotic thoughts dipped and weaved inside her head while she debated the very thing she shouldn't be debating.

Was she delaying the inevitable? Or was she too tired to think clearly?

Too *excited* to think clearly…

"You're right, G." He dragged in a sigh and blew it out, his breath dusting her cheek as he moved his lips to her cheek. "It's too late for this conversation."

She didn't know if he meant it was too late tonight or too late overall but either way she supposed he was right.

"Good night."

"Good night." She watched him go even though part of her wanted to chase after him. The stupid part of her that forgot what life was like when they'd been married.

He'd been opinionated and stubborn. He didn't listen when she spoke. He thought he knew best. He made decisions for her instead of with her. What made her think he'd changed?

Upstairs the light in his bedroom window turned on and

then off. He was in there now, with Natasha. He hadn't slept with her. Not yet. But like with their marriage, Gia was out of time. She'd had her chance to have him for herself. And it would have been amazing.

But then what?

Inside, a staff member rushed to take the dishes from her hands. Gia headed upstairs to her date, bypassing Jayson's bedroom door and doing her best to shut out what might or might not be happening beyond it.

Denver was sprawled out and snoring, where she'd left him. She crept through the darkness and bumped into his foot hanging off the end of the bed. Grabbing her pillow, she snagged a quilt off the footboard and went to the armchair in the corner.

Looked like she'd be sleeping here tonight while Prince Charming hogged the covers.

Natasha turned pouting into an art form.

Jayson had never seen anything like it. He'd gone back to the room last night and had tried to negotiate for one of the pillows. She'd kept all four. He could see the argument forming in midair between them, so he'd smiled and assured her he was good on the floor. Which was where he slept, his tuxedo balled up into a makeshift pillow while he slept in his shorts.

Now morning, he was feeling every inch of that hardwood floor on his aching lower back. He needed a cup of coffee more than a shark needed seawater. The outdoor patio was bustling with wedding guests who'd stayed over. They were making their way through the breakfast buffet and from the looks of it, the food supply was nearing depletion.

He squinted through the windows against the bright sunshine, his eyes adjusting and catching sight of Natasha in a royal blue dress. Her plate was piled with fruit and she was carrying a glass of green liquid.

Yeah, he'd skip socializing outside, thank you very much.

He tipped the last of the coffee into a mug, grateful not to have to mingle to acquire a much-needed caffeine fix. He couldn't talk to Natasha without at least being mildly alert. He raised the mug to his lips, but before the blessed moment that first hot drop hit his tongue, Gia appeared out of the ether.

"Is that the last cup?"

She wore the same cutoff frayed shorts and pink top from last night, only today she'd strapped on open-toed sandals. They added to her height, which brought her lips closer to his. At least the sandals were what he was blaming on his inability to look away from her mouth.

"You look like you slept better than me," he told her. She looked rested. Damned good. A little too rumpled for his pleasure, like Denver had slid his busted fingers through her hair this morning.

"There's more coffee outside." Jayson scowled and lifted the mug to his lips again. This time she wrapped her fingers around his at the handle.

"Then go outside and fetch yourself a cup. This is my house." A feral spark lit her dark eyes as she tugged on the mug.

"This is your *parents'* house. My employers. Plus, I was here first." He pulled up on the mug while she pulled down, each of them careful not to spill the precious liquid that would deliver morning pep.

"I can't go out there," she said with a frown.

"Why not?"

But then he turned his head and saw Denver lounging at the carafe, chatting to a couple Jayson didn't recognize.

"Did you two have a spat?" Jayson's smile was incurable at the idea.

"If by *spat* you mean did I sneak back into our shared room on tiptoes so I wouldn't have to wake him and have an awkward conversation this morning about how I wasn't going to sleep with him, then yes. We had a spat."

Shocked by that, he temporarily forgot to hold on to the mug. She easily removed it from his hand, doctored it with some half-and-half from the fridge and leaned on the wide, stainless steel doors. She took the first coveted sip, closed her eyes and hummed.

"You mean have an awkward conversation about how you weren't going to sleep with him *again*?" Jayson asked, fairly sure that's not what she meant. Sounded like she hadn't slept with Pip at all. If so, *that* was good news.

"I didn't sleep with him. Do you think I'd sleep with a guy on our first date or something?"

He tilted his head and watched her with his eyebrows raised.

Cheeks blushing, she mumbled at the edge of the mug, "You don't count."

"I don't?" Hand on her waist, he leaned over her to say into her ear, "As I recall it was right in this house." Her turn to be too shocked to hold on to the coffee. He reclaimed the mug and took a heavenly drink.

"That bathroom, if memory serves." He pointed across the hall at the staircase, beyond which was a half bath where they'd sneaked off after excusing themselves from the dinner table.

"That wasn't our first date. It was a work function." Her lips lifted at the corners. Good memory for both of them, that night.

"Tomato, potato."

Smiling, she shook her head at his bad joke.

"In all seriousness—" he moved the mug when she reached for it "—I'm glad you didn't sleep with him."

"I'm glad you didn't sleep with *her*." She snatched the mug. "You didn't, right?"

He shook his head. "I didn't."

"Good. She's too beautiful. It's unfair to us mortals."

Oh, Gia. He managed a sad smile. Tipping her chin, he peered down into her coffee-colored eyes, took in the riot of deep brown waves surrounding a face he'd stared at many a night while watching her sleep. Without makeup, freckles dotted the bridge of her nose—too faint to see unless you were really looking.

He was really looking.

"She's got nothin' on you, G."

They were in a holding pattern, her hands wrapped around the mug, and one of his hands on her face, the other flattened on the refrigerator next to her shoulder. The rest of the world might as well have crumbled to dust. All his reasons for not sleeping with her were harder to grasp when he was this close to her.

If they slept together she'd throw up a wall. They'd argue. This would end as badly, if not worse, than it had when they'd divorced.

And still…

"Jay…" She was poised to say something really undesirable. Maybe a "we can't" or "we shouldn't." She would have been right.

So he did what he had to do to prevent hearing it—and kissed her before she was able to speak.

Eight

Gia wasn't sure who leaned in first and erased the gap between them, but before she knew it, the sexual tension that had been roaring inside her like a five-alarm fire in the dry season *ignited.*

Jayson's warm lips pressed against hers as her back flattened on the cool steel door of the refrigerator.

His mouth was still fused with hers when he took the coffee mug from her hands and set it on the counter. He pulled her away from the fridge and, still kissing her, walked her out of the kitchen. Had anyone seen them? Had their dates seen them? She didn't know.

She didn't *care*.

When they reached the staircase, he came up for air and craned his neck toward the voices coming from the top.

There was a moment of hesitancy that gave her enough time to reconsider, but she only laughed. He took that as a yes, when in reality it was a *hell yes*, before eagerly steering her into the bathroom on the other side of the stairs.

Having sex back where it'd all started was risky territory, but by the time he shut them into the small room, she only cared that they were finally—*blessedly*—alone. He didn't bother with the switch, so the yellow glow of a night light barely illuminated the space—if it could even be called that. His big body added to the necessary bathroom accoutrements, the only place left for her was where he put her next.

On top of the sink.

"Oh!" Hand to her mouth, she stifled her surprised reaction as the people who owned those upstairs voices passed by the bathroom door. Once they were gone, Jay moved her hand away.

Mouth ravaging hers, his hands moved to her T-shirt and stripped it over her head. He didn't hesitate, didn't ask, didn't wait. He simply read her body language and right now—with her own hands pawing at his T-shirt—it was fairly obvious what she wanted.

Him.

Her fingertips raked over his abdominal muscles, still defined the way she remembered. So much of him was the way she remembered—which was both good and bad—but at the moment she focused on the parts of him she craved.

His seeking mouth over hers.

His diving tongue, hot and insistent.

His big hands, making her delicate by comparison.

She unbuttoned his jeans and slipped her hand inside. Both of them moaned their approval when she found what she was looking for. Long and broad, he was a sight to behold. She couldn't resist sneaking a peek of her stroking hand in the meager light.

"This is a bad idea," she couldn't help pointing out. She was out of breath from excitement, no longer able to call up *why* this was a bad idea. She only knew that it was.

"The worst," he agreed. "Some things never change."

A crooked, cocky smile crested his firm mouth, his eyes at half-mast while his erection was at full tilt. "That was verbatim what you said the last time we were in here about to do this for the first time."

"You remember that?" she asked as he divested her of her shorts. She had to let go of him to support herself on the edge of the sink but once her lower half was naked, she put her hands on him again.

"Are you kidding?" There was something tender in his voice, even as he wrestled with her shoes and shorts. Something about his tone reminded her of how in love they once were. Before he became the Fixer of All Things.

"I—I don't have a condom," she said since that was the first unromantic comment that popped into her head.

"I do." He frowned. "In my room."

She shook her head. "We're not risking that again."

Being busted by Addison at her wedding last year had been embarrassing. Gia had been walking around telling anyone who would listen that hers and Jay's split was amicable and that they were better off apart. And then she'd been caught with her pants down—well, not really. But when Addi had busted them, Jay's zipper was *open*.

Resting his forehead on hers while her hand worked on him, he blew out a slow breath. "I have to be inside you."

She gripped his face, feeling the stubble on his jaw. His next exhalation brushed over the tender skin on her neck. His desperation matched her own.

"Are you still on birth control?" he asked.

"Yes."

He lifted his head, his blue eyes going stormy gray with lust. With need. With want.

"No condom," she decided, because that was the only decision.

He wasted no time lining up her entrance with the swollen head of his cock, pulling her flush to the edge of the sink. She held his neck, her fingers eagerly bunching his T-shirt while he slid in deeper. *Deeper.*

Seated to the hilt, he blew out a tortured breath that fanned her hair and tickled her ear.

Against that delicate shell, he growled, "God *damn*."

No one had been inside her since he had, and sex in the Mercedes, while that back seat had been a tight fit, had been similar to this time. Out of control with want, they hadn't considered the future.

They hadn't considered the past, either. The years of arguing and misunderstandings. The sadness over their crumbling marriage with each of them helpless to stop it.

Now, though. Ahh, the blessed *now*.

Now was about the physical. About his ability to turn her on and know what she liked. He displayed that next, by tucking his wide palms around the globes of her ass and pulling her down on top of him. Impaling her while his arms shook with the effort of moving her on and off him. Her breath sawed from her lungs in soft high-pitched sighs.

This was Jayson Cooper at his best.

The first time they'd had sex had been in this very bathroom, in this *very* position. She'd joked then that she was going to marry him "if only to have sex like this on demand whenever I need it."

He must have noticed her mind wandering. He stopped long enough to remind her, "Stay with me. You have an orgasm for me. I know it."

An orgasm for me.

He'd always phrased it that way, as if her having an earth-shattering, bone-rending orgasm was a gift *to him*. Another reason she'd vowed to marry him.

She shut out all other thoughts and concentrated on the sensations in her body. On the soft rub of her nipples on her bra each time he pulled her flush against his chest. On the way he tasted on her tongue, the salt on his skin, the rough scrape of whiskers from where he hadn't shaved yet...

He gripped her hair, balling it in his fist while she explored his neck with her mouth. He loved that.

Scraping her teeth along his jugular, she suckled his earlobe next. "Did Natasha treat you this well, Jay?"

His agonized "no" made her believe that was true.

"Did your skateboarder friend handle you the way I do?"

"Never." She shook her head, feeling naughty that their dates were still here. Couldn't be helped. Jayson and Gia hadn't been great at avoiding each other even when they'd tried.

They exchanged grins briefly and then they stopped talking. The only sounds were the heated slap of their bodies interspersed with labored breaths until her orgasm rolled over her like a cresting wave, crashing down and taking her mind with it.

For this finite moment, any issues between them were nonexistent. There was only right now—only him coming, the growl in his throat, the stiffening of the muscles in his arms. He filled her, both with his essence and with the deep, guttural moan of completion in her ear.

Eventually, after they'd managed to calm their breathing, he pulled out of her and rested her limp body onto the sink. He braced the sides of the counter, his forehead conking onto her shoulder.

"That—" he said between a deep breath "—was better than the last time we had sex."

In the parking garage. Five days before their divorce.

He wasn't wrong. It *was* better, and on that long-ago day it had been pretty damned incredible.

"When you got it, you got it." She kissed his temple.

He raised his head and his smile nearly took her breath away—as if she needed any help with that. He lowered his mouth to hers for a kiss when the doorknob jiggled.

"Someone in there?" came Addison's voice from the other side of the door.

It occurred to Gia suddenly, alarmingly that she'd ducked into a bathroom to have sex with her ex at yet another wedding. Only this time, she'd succeeded.

And she'd done it with their dates outside. With the possibility of being caught, she felt more shamed than naughty. She and Jayson had no business carrying on with each other anywhere, let alone *here*, where she might have to explain their behavior to her sister-in-law…

"One second!" she called out then whispered to him, "I can't believe it. Addi's going to bust us *again*."

"Like I said—" He zipped and buttoned his jeans and laid a succinct kiss on her forehead "—some things never change."

Nine

"It's a good thing Royce and Taylor aren't here," Brannon said from the head of the conference room table.

"Agreed," Jayson said. Those two deserved to enjoy their honeymoon and their time together *without* worrying about problems at the office.

"We'll solve the issue before they come home," Gia chimed in from his left. Her eyes flashed quickly from Jayson to Brannon.

As Jayson had expected, she'd been as cool as a cliché cucumber this week. He'd seen her react that way before—after the car sex and the almost-sex last year. She'd let herself go with him, but when they were done, she acted like it'd never happened.

That morning after Royce and Taylor's wedding, Jayson exited the bathroom first with Gia behind him. Addison had given them a wide-eyed blink followed by a sideways smirk. There was no need to explain. He guessed Addison

Abrams had overheard enough to answer any lingering questions she might've had.

Natasha, on the other hand, hadn't noticed he was missing. He'd driven her home, admittedly awkward after their tense date, but she hadn't said much. Though she did make sure and tell him, "It was a nice wedding, but we will not be seeing each other again, Coop."

Fine by him.

He'd called Mason after the drop-off to apologize for potentially ruining his stepbrother's working relationship with Natasha, but Mason assured Jay that his prize supermodel was under contract.

That left Jayson to wonder what the hell he'd been thinking bringing a stranger to a Knox wedding. And further wondering why the hell Gia had done the same thing. But he knew. They'd been trying to fireproof from exactly what had ended up happening anyway.

Jayson couldn't regret it, even if Gia was still giving him the cold shoulder. He, for one, wanted to do it again. No sense in letting perfectly incredible sex rot on the vine.

He wasn't sure where she stood. If she was regretful or reliving the afternoon on a loop in her head the way he was. She was a good actor when she needed to be. And at ThomKnox, under the watching eyes of her brothers, she did some of her best work. He understood why she didn't want to broadcast what happened, but he saw no need in pretending. Addison knew what had happened, so there was a ninety-nine-point-nine percent chance that Brannon knew, too.

He glanced at his ex-wife while her brother pecked at the T13 tablet in his hand. She held Jayson's gaze for an extra beat, licking her top lip before pressing it against her bottom one.

He'd expected an unreadable expression, but hers wasn't

unreadable. Her eyes were heated and slightly vulnerable, and the way she jerked her gaze from his gave her away.

She wanted him again. He knew it in his balls. Not such a good actor after all, it seemed.

"I see what you mean." Brannon frowned at the tablet in his hands. "It shuts down."

"That's the bug," Jayson said, his mind returning to the task at hand. The tablet launch last year had been smooth and since then, the sales were above where they'd projected. The software update that was due to go out next month, however, was a hot wad of WTF. "It ran fine last week and now it's not. I have no idea what's transpired since then to screw it up."

Unless Jayson and Gia having sex caused a tear in space and the working part of the software was sucked into a black hole.

Unlikely.

"We'll find the glitch," she reassured all of them, her expression shifting back to calm and collected. "We have the best tech team is the country."

"Damn straight," Jayson agreed. He didn't realize that he and Gia were smiling at each other until Brannon cleared his throat.

"No need to mention this to Taylor or Royce until they're back to work. This issue could go away in a matter of hours." Bran handed the tablet back to Jayson.

Also unlikely. Jayson had complete faith in their tech team, himself included, but he wasn't sure this problem would be resolved that quickly.

"I'll clear my desk and make myself available," Gia said. "You could use the extra brainpower." She smirked at her brother and Jayson and then left the conference room.

"You two seem to be getting along well," Brannon said, his tone droll.

"Yeah." Jayson wasn't giving him any more than that, just in case.

"Guess her and Pip didn't work out."

"Guess not." Jayson smiled.

"How's it going with Natasha?"

"That didn't work out, either. Which I'm assuming you already know."

"It wasn't like you two pulled off a supersecret heist." Bran appeared more amused than angry. "What the hell were you thinking? Your dates were outside having coffee and you and Gia were—" He shook his head.

"My brain wasn't doing any of the thinking."

"I do *not* want to hear details. What Ad told me she heard outside that bathroom door was already too much information." Brannon pushed his hand through his hair.

"Is there an 'if you hurt my baby sister' speech forthcoming?"

"If anyone hurts you," he told Jayson, "it'll be Gia. She's been taking kickboxing, you know."

Jayson frowned. He hadn't known that, actually. He didn't know a lot about what she did outside of work these days.

"Probably to protect herself from the morons she's contented to date."

"Pip." Bran shook his head. "Why *did* she bring that halfwit to Royce's wedding, anyway?"

"Got me," Jayson said, though he suspected he knew.

"Clock's ticking. Find the mysterious bug that's killing our tablet before Royce returns from his honeymoon," Bran said, obviously glad to change the subject.

"We'll run at it with everything we have. I'll pair everyone up to run code."

"Let me know if you need any monetary support for the venture." Bran slapped Jayson's back as he exited the conference room.

Downstairs, Jayson entered his department and clapped his hands together to get his team's attention. Gia, standing in her office doorway, paused to listen.

"I have a project for you that's going to take precedence over whatever you're currently working on," he announced. The room fell silent as all eyes turned to him. "The good news is I'm paying for overtime and carryout."

"And the bad news?" Gia asked.

"There'll be a lot of both," Jayson answered with a smile.

Jayson stepped into Gia's office and shut the door. He was suited, his jacket in place and his tie knotted.

Each time she'd seen him since last weekend she was reminded of their midnight snack outside, the sexual tension that had been strung so tight she could have played it like a harp. Of course, they both knew where that'd led.

Even though she'd been trying for the last few days to pretend the morning in the bathroom hadn't happened. That she hadn't had sex with the last man on the planet she should've had sex with.

She wrinkled her nose and considered Denver Pippen.

Fine. Jayson was the *second to last* man on the planet she should have sex with.

She'd done a damn good job of keeping her attraction to him in the "There but Unacknowledged" category since they nearly tore each other's clothes off last year. Now she wasn't sure she was hiding it as well.

Shutting her office door behind him, he stalked toward her desk. "I need you."

Because she had sex on the brain, she imagined him throwing her onto her desk and searing her lips with his specific brand of kiss. Instead, he sank into the guest chair.

He crossed his legs ankle-to-knee style and rested one broad palm on his knee. His posture was strong and sure. Nothing new there, but now it served as a reminder that he'd made love to her while standing and supporting her weight using nothing but his arm strength.

"More accurately," he continued. "I need your hardware."

I need your hardware.

"Oh?" she said instead of what she was thinking, which was admittedly half as interesting.

"Big Ben," he answered.

Big Ben was her computer system at home—formerly hers and Jay's home. It had multiple screens, the newest, latest bells and whistles, plus an encrypted cloud back-up system and crazy-fast internet connection set up in the family room. Ben was the Ferrari of home computers. Of course Jay wanted to use it.

"And your software." He tapped his temple with one finger. "I paired everyone off to investigate the bug wreaking havoc on the update. Hell, there could be several bugs for all I know." His eyebrows jumped. "Winner gets a pizza party."

She chuckled. The winner would get more than that—whoever solved this conundrum would attain superhero status.

"If we can fix that bug, it will increase speed and update security on every ThomKnox tablet out there. Our reputation is at stake," he said, serious now.

She felt the same way he did. Despite the casual way he'd asked to borrow her hard-and software, they both knew that ThomKnox's future was nothing to laugh about. Could their company hang with the behemoths, or would ThomKnox forever be second in the technology world?

"Whatever you need," she answered.

"You're the most technically savvy human being in this company." He stood. "Apart from your father."

"And Jack's retired." She used to be shy about flaunting her brains or know-how until she went to college. Leaving for school had given her a freedom she hadn't been able to attain when she'd lived at home. College was the first time she could date without worrying about her father and brothers stating their opinions for the record. As she'd grown up, her family had loosened up, but at times she still felt like a little girl around them.

She'd say this for Jayson: For all his flaws and their incompatibility, he never let her play down her accomplishments. He'd always told her she was smart and to use that to her advantage. *Hell, G, abuse it,* he used to say.

What'd torn them apart ultimately, and a little at a time, was his overprotective nature and need to control every aspect of their shared lives. Now, though, while he was acutely focused on fixing the tablet issue, he didn't seem overbearing at all.

Was she seeing him through sex-colored glasses since their last encounter, or had he really changed?

She shook her head to jar loose that dangerous thought. Jayson had said it himself—they weren't getting back together. And if they weren't getting back together, then there was no reason to wonder if he had changed.

If she kept that front of mind, it would make being alone in the same house alone with him a lot easier. Anything could happen, true, but if they were on the same page, they could solve this issue swiftly and then be done with it. And with each other.

But when he stood and gripped the doorknob to leave, her gaze lingered on his capable hands and strong body.

"I'll bring Thai," he said.

"Okay," she said, even though she wasn't sure it was going to be.

Ten

It'd been a long day.

Gia left her hunchback of Notre Dame posture at the desk in her home office and walked to the sofa to collapse on it.

The square plastic black containers holding the remnants of their Thai dinner were strewn about the coffee table. They'd eaten before and during reviewing the complicated update code but somehow she was hungry again.

She reached for one of the containers and her plastic spoon, slumping back on the couch again. She scooped the tofu green curry on rice and vegetables into her mouth and chewed forlornly.

Jayson joined her, forking a bite of his leftover dinner, Thai Basil Beef, into his mouth. "I don't feel any closer to figuring it out," he said between mouthfuls.

"Me neither. I love lemongrass," she said before her next bite. No sense in talking about their abject failure.

"Someone at work could've had some luck." But they

knew better. If any of their team at ThomKnox had found the solution they'd have called Jay immediately. "We'll figure it out."

"Hell yes we will." She set aside her food and straightened her spine. She refused to be felled by one little error. The T13 had been wildly successful and the update would only improve its usage. She wouldn't—couldn't—let her team fail. Er, Jay's team. *Their* team.

The tech department was as close to having kids as they'd come.

"Don't despair." Food container empty, he rested his palm on her knee. Her bare knee thanks to her changing into shorts and a T-shirt. He still wore his pants from work, his sleeves shoved up, his top two buttons open and revealing the bit of dark chest hair she'd always liked. That masculine thatch reminded her that he was capable. And even an independent girl like herself could appreciate his trustworthy side.

Speaking of…

"I owe you for the food. We'll split it." She stood from the couch and walked to her purse, resting on a chair in the corner of the room.

"I got it."

"Jayson. I ate my weight in Thai food tonight."

"So?"

"So, I can pay for my own dinner." She dug some cash from her purse.

"ThomKnox is paying for dinner."

"Well…you picked it up." She waved the bills.

"*No.*" He enunciated the word slowly.

"It's important to have boundaries. And this is a good way to establish them."

"Boundaries? The sex on Saturday *established our boundaries.*"

"I thought we weren't going to bring that up."

"I thought you would have by now." He walked to where she stood and bracketed her hips with his hands. Before she could lecture herself about kissing him, he'd leaned temptingly close. "Why don't you want to have sex with me?"

She did, but damned if she would admit that. She choked on a laugh and said, "I can think of approximately a million reasons."

But really, there was just one.

Sex with Jayson made her remember being married to him and remembering being married to him made her remember divorcing him and that hurt.

When he lowered his lips to hers each of those million reasons disintegrated into a million pieces. He erased the inch and a half between them and kissed her gently.

She drank in his spicy kiss before she could argue with herself about it. He banded his arms around her waist like he did the last time they were together. When he'd lifted her into his strong arms and held her like she was the only woman on the planet who mattered.

A long time ago, she *was* the only woman who mattered to him. He had taken his duties as husband seriously. Some days too seriously. He'd ruled this house, or had tried anyway. So many of their arguments came from his inability to be flexible on a decision, or his tendency not to include her in the decision at all, and her own insistence that she could take care of herself without him.

Her urge to be independent was a constant refrain she'd grown tired of thinking about. Her whole life she'd been fighting for every inch of independence gained. By the time she was married to Jayson, a man who'd championed her more than any before him, she'd expected to have plenty of that much-needed space.

She pulled her lips from his. How could she expect space from a man who was constantly, and welcomingly, invading hers?

He was breathing heavy, his pupils wide and black. His eyes were her favorite shade of smoky blue. Judging by the state of his pants, he was as turned on as she was.

"We can't," she managed, half expecting him to lean in and prove her wrong.

He didn't.

"You always do this," he said instead. His nostrils flared.

"Do what?" Her blood pressure spiked at his tone, and at losing out on what they both wanted, and she didn't know what he was talking about yet.

"Retreat," he answered. "I don't rcmember you giving up this easily when we were married."

The reminder that they used to stand in this very room and argue about who knew what was a shadow she couldn't escape.

"Lucky for us we don't have to dig in our heels any longer, Cooper." She stuffed two twenty-dollar bills, now sweaty in her palm, into his shirt. "Thank you for dinner."

"What the hell did you call me?"

Since he'd just challenged her on retreating, she decided to stay for this battle.

"Everyone calls you Coop or Cooper," she said with a shrug.

His hulking dark presence was less intimidating than it was downright hot. "You're not everyone."

Like a stripper in reverse, he pulled the money from his shirt and dropped it onto the coffee table. "I don't need more reminders that you don't need me, Gia. You've made that perfectly clear."

She was frozen in shock until he turned to leave.

"You are so arrogant!" she called after him. "You only care about getting your way, don't you?"

"Getting my way? You think I'd rather leave than give you an orgasm with this mouth?"

He gestured to his mouth, tempting her since she still

felt the imprint of his kiss on her lips. Her knees literally went gooey. Jayson was good with his hands but he was very, very good with his mouth.

"I can take care of myself." But her response was automated. She'd been trying to convince everyone in her life of that for so long, the words came out robotic.

"No, you don't need anyone, do you? Least of all me." His tone was angry, but there was a dose of pain in those words—one she didn't like hearing. Part of her wanted to correct him. To tell him that she'd missed him when they'd split. That his presence in and around the house was what had made this pile of bricks and siding feel like home.

She'd missed him, but she hadn't known how to find her way back to him, either. Not when she'd said so many hurtful things she couldn't take back. She hadn't wanted Jayson's protection and service. She'd wanted to stand as his equal. To experience life with him, not apart from him.

But it was too late for those sorts of observations.

Their standoff lasted several seconds. He stood, silently daring her to give in to her wants—her *need.* But they'd already given in to the temptation and sex hadn't solved anything. Worse, their at-work conversations had been laced with hidden innuendo. Her mind wasn't on her work, it was in his pants. And as long as that was the case, they'd never fix this damned update.

"We have an important job to do," she said, leaning on her old friend, Pragmatism. "We shouldn't let ourselves be distracted."

"Yeah," was all he said before he gathered his bag and walked out of the room. She stood and listened to him go, closing her eyes against the finality of the front door quietly shutting.

Eleven

"I should let you two rest."

Jayson meant to hand back Addison and Brannon's daughter right away, but he delayed. Quinn Marie Knox was nestled in his arms and cooing up at him. A series of gurgles and grunts came from the precious bundle, her big eyes taking in as much of the world around her as they could. Tiny fingers clutched and released the air and he was fairly certain he'd lost his heart to her.

Finally, he was able to release baby Quinn in her mother's arms. "Sorry it took me so long to stop by."

Addison had gone into labor the night he and Gia had eaten Thai food and argued. The same night he'd kissed her and had hoped to end up in her bed, or hell, at least on the couch.

But, no.

In spite of the desire surging within and between them, Gia had retreated. Once again he'd found himself surrounding her with the protection and love he thought she needed, only to watch her retreat.

He stepped in, she stepped back. The dance continued. He wondered if he'd ever learn.

Addison adjusted her baby girl against her chest, who was nuzzling to be breastfed. "That's okay, Coop. I know you're busy."

"Say bye to Uncle Jayson." She waved her daughter's closed fist.

He smiled and waved back. Uncle Jayson. He liked that.

Family had always been important to him. Losing his marriage with Gia had been the ultimate failure. He didn't know what he would've done if he lost his work and his in-laws, too. The Knoxes stitched everyone into their family quilt—and once you were there, you didn't want to leave.

Jayson exited the sitting room and wandered through the kitchen. Bran was at the back door, pulling on a pair of boxing gloves. Once they were on, he punched them together. "Ready?"

"As I'll ever be." Jayson hadn't been through training Bran had, but he knew how to scrap. *Without* gloves. He'd gone a round or two with his own father and had lost. Badly. At age twelve he'd stepped between his abusive father and his mother, and had taken hits for her. He'd never been prouder of a black eye in his life.

Since then he'd developed a penchant for protecting those he loved, made easier when his mother remarried a good man and in turn gave Jayson a brother. He smiled as he considered Bran's and Addi's daughter. That little girl would never have to wonder if she was loved or safe a day in her life.

"She's great, your daughter," he told Bran.

"Those Knox genes." Bran grinned. "Although she inherited all the beauty from my wife."

Not all of it. Jayson found himself thinking of Gia. Again.

After stepping into the ring and receiving some basic instruction, Jayson was throwing punches comfortably at his ex-brother-in-law. Bran's backyard was lush with green grass and flowers and trees. It was a strange setup for trying to kick the other man's ass.

Not that there was any animosity lingering between them. Throwing punches at the middle Knox sibling was more about technique than working through a problem.

Jayson was frustrated with the way things *hadn't* gone with Gia, but there was no need for him to exercise that frustration physically. He preferred to funnel that irritation into his work—namely solving the problem with the tablet before Royce and Taylor arrived home from their honeymoon.

Jayson finally landed a hit on Bran's ribs and earned a satisfying grunt from his opponent. Bran caught his breath against the ropes, nodding that he was done.

"You're a fast learner," he praised as he and Jayson stepped from the ring.

A pair of loungers was set up in the grass, a cooler of ice-cold beer bottles between them.

"And I thought your daughter was beautiful. That cooler is a sight." Jayson accepted a beer and sat down, spinning off the cap and taking a long, refreshing slug.

Bran let out a beer commercial–worthy "Ahhhh."

After Bran reminded Jayson to keep his face protected in the ring, he paused, stared into his beer bottle and asked, "You and Gia avoiding each other?"

Here we go.

"Why?"

"You two arrive separately to meetings. I thought at first you were trying to make it look like you weren't dating by avoiding each other, but since Quinn was born, it seems like things went south."

"Well. Well. Look who's become observant."

"Very funny."

"I was being serious." This was the same man who, last year, hadn't had a single clue that Addison was madly in love with him. If it hadn't been for Bran and Addi's road trip to Lake Tahoe, Jayson wondered if Bran would have ever figured it out.

"So am I," Bran said, studying Jayson closely. "What's going on? Gia and Addi were talking when Gia was here yesterday, but Addi told me she's sworn to secrecy." Bran took a swig from his bottle. "Can you believe that?"

"Yeah, I believe it." Jayson sighed. "Nothing happened. Not really. We worked. She insisted on paying me for her half of dinner. We fell into old patterns of arguing like we did when we were married." He shrugged, unsure how else to explain it to someone who had been married for about two minutes. "It's hard after a while. The arguments become tiresome. And they're never about what they're about."

"Meaning Gia's paying for dinner was about more than money." Bran, his gaze unfocused on the yard, shook his head. "She always wanted to be treated like one of the guys. I suspect it's because of having two older brothers. And of course, we have this adorable kid sister who is a smart-ass, but loves so fiercely it's undeniable. All we wanted to do was protect her from anything—or anyone—that might make her cry."

Jayson stared at Bran's profile in deep thought. He could relate to that. How many times had he stepped in to protect Gia the way he'd stepped in to protect his mother? Only Gia hadn't really needed that sort of protection. There was no dragon to slay where his ex-wife was concerned.

But for the first time he considered how Bran and

Royce, and Jack, too, had handled Gia with kid gloves. She wouldn't have seen their efforts as protection, but as them stunting her growth. She'd wanted to flourish on her own, without their involvement.

And, he reasoned, without his as well.

"She's not weak," Jayson said, and wondered if his protectiveness made her feel like he thought she was. Then he remembered a bunch of other arguments that had ended with her accusing him of being "controlling" and he didn't have to wonder any longer.

"I overstepped," Jayson admitted for the first time in his life.

"By buying her dinner?" Bran asked, dubious.

"In the past. By telling her what she needs. By making decisions without her. By refusing to let her stand on her own two feet."

"You were trying to take care of her. We all saw that." Bran sipped his beer. "Plus you know how much she loves to win. She'll do anything to make you see her point of view."

"She stuffed the money down my shirt."

"'Course she did," Bran laughed. "Listen, whatever stuff you and G have going on is your business. I care about you both, but I also know you're capable of working things out. I just wanted to make sure I wasn't going to lose the dream team when it came to fixing this tablet issue."

"Gia and I are pros at dancing around each other," Jayson assured his friend.

That was the truth. They knew how to button down and focus on work. No matter what had happened between them since their divorce, they would prioritize ThomKnox and fix the tablet because nothing was more important than that.

Almost nothing… but there was no fixing what had been broken between him and Gia.

Twelve

The motivation to succeed was an attribute Jayson and Gia shared. Which was why they'd agreed that on Saturday, he'd return to the house and fire up Big Ben, and the three of them would make a decent bit of headway.

He'd been working for four hours straight without coming up for air when Gia interrupted.

"How's it going?" She was carrying her own T13 while his was being used as a coaster for his coffee cup. Without a solution for the update, "coaster" was the only purpose the tablet would serve. She moved the empty mug, clucking her tongue.

She didn't need to say anything. That small gesture spoke volumes.

It spoke of mini arguments about using a coaster or a napkin, about not resting his shoes on the coffee table. All insignificant, but they had a way of becoming bigger and bigger over time—the way individual grains of sand eventually became an island.

That's what he and Gia had between them. An island of misunderstandings and assumptions.

"I thought I had a breakthrough, but it turned out to be nothing." He might as well be talking about them. He'd had an inkling of the part he'd played in the deterioration of their marriage, but hell if he knew what to do about it now.

She seemed content to keep her distance. She'd worked by the pool today rather than inside the house, and when she did venture into the house, she grabbed whatever was fastest to eat before returning to the pool again.

"We'll find it." She sounded tired, as if she might not believe that.

He understood how hard it was to admit something was unfixable. Admitting as much about their marriage had been the most difficult thing he'd ever done.

"I'm going to run a few errands. I can't look at a screen any longer." She started to leave the room but he wasn't ready to let her go yet. In an attempt to keep her attention, he dealt a low blow.

"Finally met our niece," he said, receiving the smile he'd expected.

She crossed her arms over a simple sundress that looked anything but simple on his ex-wife. Her curves tantalizingly stretched every seam.

"I love that both Addison and Taylor have baby girls. Serves my male-dominated family right."

Remembering what Bran had told him, Jayson said, "They were overprotective."

"Men tend to treat me like fine china."

"Not a bad thing to be cared for." He still didn't fully understand why she didn't like her family looking out for her. He'd have given anything for a father who wanted to protect him at all costs.

"I had to run off to MIT for my brothers to admit I grew up. Jack didn't catch on ever, I don't think."

Yeah. Jayson didn't think so, either. Gia's father had stepped in time and again to make sure she was taken care of. Including with her husband. Whenever he thought of Jack's conversation with him before he and Gia married, Jayson bristled. Mistakes were definitely made.

"I'm not fragile," she stated now, and just stubbornly as she had in the past. "And I don't give up. On anything."

He thought of something else he and Bran talked about—how competitive she was, and suddenly had a great idea.

"Except you're going shopping. So you sort of are giving up."

She made a disgusted sound. "I'm taking a break. Breaks are good for the brain."

So was sex.

"I'll bet you I find and fix the bug before you do." She was smart, but so was he. "We've been stuck on this for far too long. Maybe what we need is a little friendly competition to motivate us."

"I'm plenty motivated." But her eyebrow arched high on her forehead, a sure sign she'd been properly provoked. "I know I'll find the problem before you do."

"If you're so sure, then why not bet?" he goaded.

"What do you have that I could possibly want?"

When he held out his arms, she rolled her eyes, but her smile was worth it. "Be serious."

"Okay." He thought for a second, and then landed on the one offer she couldn't refuse. "If you win, I'll cook for you."

She snorted.

"My grandmother's homemade pasta."

Her mouth dropped open.

He grinned, knowing he had her. He didn't make his grandmother's homemade pasta recipe often, but he had made it for Gia when they were married—for their anniversaries. Both of them.

"I can guess what you want if you win." She folded her arms. "I'm not having sex with you again."

"You're sure you'll win. What are you worried about?"

"Hmm. Well I *was* sure. You're pretty motivated by sex." Her smile held. She didn't hate this idea. Not even a little.

"I admit, that's a good motivator." Especially sex with her. "But this time we're not doing it on a bathroom counter. We'll be in bed."

He tipped his head and walked closer, daring her to say no. To admit that she was afraid of losing, and therefore sleeping with him. Or worse, to refuse the bet because she didn't *want* to sleep with him.

She did neither.

Because she'd sooner die than admit she didn't think she could win. Plus, as he'd suspected, she wanted to sleep with him again.

She folded her arms over her breasts. "This is bribery. I love that pasta more than anything."

"I know." He loved every second of this exchange. He slid by her and headed for the kitchen. "Have fun shopping. I'll be here toiling away on a solution."

"Shopping can wait," she said. "If I'm going to win, I may as well do it. Also, I expect the works for my meal. Candles. Music. I want to walk in and mistake my kitchen for a fancy Italian restaurant."

Yep. He had her. Now all he had to do was win.

"Sounds like you're taking the bet." He pulled open the refrigerator and pretended to search for something to eat.

"Okay, Jay." She faced him. "We have a deal."

She picked up her tablet and walked through the kitchen, sliding her sunglasses onto her nose. She took her place outside on the lounger by the pool.

The clock was officially ticking. He no longer cared

whether or not he found the problem before Royce and Taylor came home.

All he had to do was find it before Gia did.

Gia justified her decision not to shop since she had something to wear to her date tomorrow. Nothing new, but still.

She'd spent the remainder of the day hunched over her notes and her tablet, though sadly didn't feel much closer to the answer than before.

The stakes were high. Jayson's grandmother's pasta recipe was nothing to joke about. Plus, while sex with him was off the charts fantastic, she also knew the repercussions of falling into bed with him again.

She didn't need to feel any more for him than she already did. Letting her heart be involved after she'd put their marriage *and* divorce to bed could be disastrous. She was supposed to be moving on, but here she was a year and a half later and not only had she had sex with him already, he was inside their former shared house right now.

Which was why she didn't cancel her date.

She'd paused from her work by the pool to check her messages on the Divinely Yours app. She had several, including one from Denver Pippen. He mentioned he'd be out of the country for a skateboarding competition in Germany. He let her down easy, telling her know that while he'd had fun at the wedding, he didn't see them going further.

She agreed, but appreciated his candor. He could've ghosted her, but chose to lay out the facts. Pip wasn't a bad guy, he just wasn't right for her.

She'd scrolled down through a few seriously gross offers in her inbox before coming across a message from a name she recognized. Elias Hill.

Elias was the founder/owner of Hill Yacht Company.

He'd praised her work at ThomKnox and then invited her out on the maiden voyage of his latest model before it hit the showroom floor. He'd sealed the deal at the end: "No pressure, Gia. Just a day on the water."

She *so* needed a day without pressure.

She didn't expect a relationship to bloom from a yacht-date with Elias Hill. But if the unthinkable happened and Jayson won this bet, she could lean on the excuse of dating Elias and avoid going to bed with Jayson. That was cheating, she supposed, but didn't they say that all was fair in love and war?

Yawning, she gathered her things and headed inside. She was done for today and looking forward to curling up with a cup of tea and a good book. It was time for Jayson to head home, too. He'd been tireless, but he had to give up at some point.

Plus, she needed to tell him about the date—which he wouldn't like—and let him know that the house was off-limits while she was away. They could resume their investigation on Monday when they were both working.

But halfway through those thoughts, she found her ex-husband, the heels of his sneakers resting on the arm of the sofa, fast asleep.

"Jayson." A familiar frustration bubbled up at the sight of him sprawled out, his shoes on the furniture. Irritation was easy to come by when she spotted his empty coffee cup and a plate with crumbs on it left on the table.

And yet, she didn't have the heart to wake him. He had to be exhausted. He'd admitted earlier today that he hadn't slept well this week, too worried about this update fix. There was something so vulnerable about the way his long eyelashes shadowed his cheeks. And something so animal about the way his dark scruff decorated his jaw. She remembered the last time he'd kissed her, his whiskers abrading her chin. How hard it'd been to stop kissing him. To put up her guard and turn him down when her body had begged her to continue…

She tossed a blanket over him rather than wake him, reassured that the date tomorrow was exactly what she needed. There was a time when she would've kissed the corner of Jayson's mouth and told him it was time for bed. A time when he would've pulled her down into his arms and said, "Lie with me a while."

No longer.

Their passion and sexual need for each other was alive and well, but their ability to be vulnerable had vanished. She mourned that briefly as she flipped off the lamp. But by the time she locked the front and back doors and headed upstairs to bed, she justified that her mourning period was well and truly over.

Already she could feel herself softening toward her ex-husband, those old feelings lurking around in her head and, if she wasn't careful, in her heart.

That was one risk she wasn't willing to take.

Thirteen

Jayson exited the downstairs bathroom and wandered into the kitchen. He'd fallen asleep in his former house. Being here this early in the morning, and stumbling into the kitchen in search of coffee, was so familiar it was bizarre.

He didn't know if he was more surprised he'd slept through the night or that Gia had let him stay.

He could hear her moving around upstairs, but evidently she'd been in here earlier. Coffee was made, most of the pot gone. He poured what was left into a mug and took a long draw.

"Morning." Gia breezed into the kitchen dressed in a bright pair of shorts and a shimmery shirt. Her shoes were tall. Her toenails painted the same color pink as her shorts.

"You look nice," he said, unable to keep from running his eyes over those tanned, smooth legs. Her hair was wavy and draped over her shoulders, the way he liked it.

"Thanks," she replied.

"I'm making more coffee," he told her as she gathered

her purse and stuck a pair of sunglasses on top of her head. "Sorry I crashed on the couch. I was beat."

"No big deal." She flashed him a quick smile.

"Where are you off to?" Apparently, he was going to have to ask.

"Oh, I have a thing." She waved a hand like she wasn't going to say more but then she did. "A date."

"A date." What the hell?

"Yes. It's a casual day on a yacht."

"With who?"

"Jayson. This isn't any of your business."

He knew that. He forced a smile, hoping it'd gain him an inch. "Just curious if you and Pip ended up working everything out."

"No." She said it with enough finality that he believed her. "I met today's date on the same app where I met Denver, though. His name is Elias Hill."

"You're still on the dating app?" He blinked down at his coffee, wondering if he was still asleep. Or hallucinating. After what had happened between them at the wedding, he hadn't expected her to be *dating*.

She started for the front door and he chased after her, careful not to spill his coffee. "Is that safe?"

"Is what safe?" she asked, grabbing her keys.

"Going on a boat with a guy who could be a serial killer."

"Jay." She gave him a bland look. "Elias Hill is the CEO of a billion-dollar yacht company. I doubt he has murder on the high seas at the front of his mind."

Jealousy roared to life inside him at the same time he had the realization that even though this setup felt familiar—them waking up in the same house and chatting over coffee—there was one big difference.

They were no longer married.

If she wanted to go on a date, she could. Still, he couldn't help saying, "I don't like it."

"You don't have to." She patted his cheek with one hand.

Then she was out the door, leaving him in need of a shower, a second cup of coffee and an excuse to stick around. Any good friend would make sure she returned home safely from her date.

Elias Hill had been perfectly nice. Perfectly casual. Perfectly polite and perfectly suited for someone like her. He liked talking business but knew when to relax. He didn't have any dumb come-on lines and he didn't call her "baby" or "Jee-ahh" the way Denver Pippen had.

Elias was…well, perfect.

He was also perfectly *boring.*

By the time they'd had lunch, she was yawning behind her hand. She tried to convince herself it was because she'd stayed up late working. Because she'd had trouble sleeping knowing her ex-husband was downstairs—the man was majorly throwing off her chi. But all that line of thinking did was bring Jayson back to the forefront of her thoughts and then she'd ended up comparing him to Elias.

Elias's muscles beneath his white shirt looked nice enough, but he somehow lacked the roundness through the shoulders that Jayson had. His forearms were fine, but she doubted he had the strength to lift her up so she could wrap her ankles at his waist. His face was pleasant, but too clean-cut. His lips were too narrow. His hair, wavy in the breeze, was thinner than Jay's full, thick, but short locks.

Elias was as boring as his stale, white outfit—a literal blank slate—and his personality barely appeared. He spoke carefully and evenly, but his stories droned on, and the last one about the investors' party meandered and looped but in the end had no point.

He wasn't witty. He wasn't stubborn. He wasn't challenging.

He isn't Jayson, her mind offered and she told it promptly to shut up.

She didn't want Jayson. That was her mantra after they docked, after she'd allowed Elias to kiss her cheek and as she drove home. So intent on making that her new truth, she decided that working side by side with Jayson was probably a bad idea. Bet or no bet, she needed to put some distance between them.

When she stepped into the kitchen of her house and looked out the window, instead of finding peace in being alone she found Jayson Cooper in her pool.

He was naked save for a pair of board shorts, and floating on a yellow raft shaped like a lemon slice. He should have looked ridiculous, especially wearing a pair of pink sunglasses that belonged to her, but he didn't.

He looked damned tempting with a solid tan and a five o'clock shadow darkening his jaw. He was cradling a can of sparkling water in one hand, his head leaning back, showcasing the column of his strong neck. Beads of water danced along his body, glistening in the waning sun.

Her mouth watered.

How dare her body react to him? He ruined everything—including her date. If not for sleeping with Jayson so recently, she might have found Elias Hill perfectly pleasant.

Perfect. *Yuck.*

She replayed that dumb story about the family dog he'd told her and cringed. How was it that a billionaire yacht CEO wasn't more interesting?

"What the hell are you doing here?" she growled, tossing her beach bag onto an empty lounger. She was still wearing her new bikini beneath her shorts and top and had been planning on coming home and swimming off her frustration.

"You're back. Didn't expect you for a while." He finished off his water and crunched the can with one hand before tossing it to the side of the pool. "I was going to leave, but I was caught up in working and decided to take a dip. I was planning to be gone by the time you came home."

"Sure you were." But him being here didn't piss her off as much as she wanted it to.

Especially when concern leaked into his tone when he asked, "Didn't go well?"

She crossed her arms and shrugged.

A frown bisected his eyebrows. "What the hell did that bastard do?"

She dropped her arms. "Nothing. I'm not mad about my date. I'm mad because you're here and I want to swim."

"I have to leave so you can swim?" When he said it out loud it did sound silly.

"Whatever. It's hot and I'm frustrated and I'm coming in."

Hands in her hair, she pulled her waves into a ponytail and stripped out of her clothes. She was aware of Jayson watching her from behind those pink sunglasses. Especially since this bikini was gorgeous. The hot pink suit covered what it needed to, but the peekaboo mesh at the neckline hinted at what she was hiding.

She stepped to the zero-entry side and started down the ramp, the warm water lapping at her ankles, then calves, then knees. She commented about how the water was colder than she'd expected and he grinned.

"Don't." She warned, sealing her fate.

He was off the raft in a shot, tossing the sunglasses to the side of the pool and then…he was gone.

"I just washed my hair!" she shouted as he cut through the water. Before she could turn to walk up the ramp, he'd surfaced and scooped her into his arms like Swamp Thing.

"You know better than to tell me the water's cold, G," he said, his eyelids lowering ominously.

She kicked her legs uselessly and wiggled in his grip. “I take it back!” she said through breathless laughter.

“You can’t take it back.” He laid a hard kiss on her mouth and walked her toward the deep end. Before she could beg him not to throw her in, he’d already tossed her into the air.

Fourteen

What was more fun? Kissing and then throwing Gia into the deep end or watching her try and catch him while he swam left then right in a zigzag?

Kissing her, definitely. With or without the throwing. Though throwing her in had been fun, and something he'd done time and time again after they'd bought this house.

"Dammit, Jay!" she sputtered after she surfaced.

"You know better than to step into the water with me. You'll end up wet." Letting the double entendre hang, he gave her a wicked smile and added, "In *or* out of the water."

"You're an ass." She launched herself at him but this time he didn't move, catching her instead. He wrapped her legs around his waist and walked her into deeper water.

"I have a very nice ass. Or so I've been told."

She rolled her eyes. "Is that what *Natasha* told you?"

"Natasha didn't think of anyone but herself most of the time. Care to share about Elias?"

She pouted, but didn't move to escape his grip. "No comment."

"Were you trying to make me jealous by going on a date?"

"I was trying to take my mind off of you!" She jerked her gaze away like she hadn't meant to admit that.

"Oh, really." He gave her a squeeze. "Did it work?"

She tightened her arms around his neck. In this position every one of her curves lined up with his body perfectly. What he wouldn't give to have a taste of her mouth, or feel her ride him, those thighs locked tight...

"I'm not seeing Elias again."

That was evasive, but some damn good news.

"Why'd you go out with him in the first place?"

"Because sleeping with you is a really, really bad idea."

"Ouch." That hurt.

The divorce had been hard on both of them—he knew that. But he'd also figured out that they hadn't had their fill of each other yet. A marriage was more than attraction, but that didn't mean they couldn't have fun together while in each other's immediate proximity.

"You already slept with me."

She sighed. "I know. I don't think we should do it again."

He felt the corners of his mouth pull down. "Why the hell not?"

"How's this going to work, Jay? We give in to our physical attraction, and then what? Walk away?"

That was the gist. But she sounded as wounded as he felt at the idea.

"What's the alternative? You've made it clear you don't want me in your space permanently."

"That's not fair."

"No, but it's true."

She quirked her lips, and he guessed it was because he'd made a good point.

"We tried to repair our marriage and work together. We failed. I'm not sure much has changed since then."

They were the same people, he couldn't argue that. "Yes, but we know what it costs to be together. We know better than make the same mistakes we made before. That has to count for something."

She watched him and he watched her. The water lapped against his waist and her thighs, which were still cradled in his hands.

"Gia. If you don't want—"

She kissed him and cut off the offer he hadn't wanted to make. He'd been about to reassure her that if she didn't want to sleep with him, she didn't have to—bet or no bet.

Turned out she put his tongue to better use. Her mouth moved on his. Softly. *Slowly.* This was nothing like the day in her parents' vacation house kitchen—or the bathroom interlude that followed. They explored each other carefully, like neither of them wanted to spook the other away.

Her hand vanished into the water and next he felt her tender grip on his erection.

He grunted, hardly able to breathe now that she was handling him with long, even strokes. She smoothed her lips over his open mouth, tempting him, turning him on so much his brain wasn't operating at full capacity.

But he couldn't keep from replaying her words—and the wave of regret they'd arrived on.

He ended the kiss and looked his ex-wife in the eyes. "I don't want to fail with you again, G."

Damn. That was honest. More honest than he'd meant to be.

She released him, untwined her legs from his hips and swam for the ladder. He thought that was it, that she'd changed her mind and, hell, maybe that was for the better. For them to cut their losses and let go of the idea of *them* altogether.

But then she turned and looked over her shoulder before climbing out and said, "Well. Come on."

He followed obediently, his eyes feasting on the vision of his ex-wife climbing the ladder. She pulled herself from the water, her long, soaking hair arrowing down her back, a trickle of water flowing over her tanned skin. Her plush bottom in that hot pink bikini. God, he could take a bite out of her—she looked that damn delicious.

Even if this was a bad idea, he wasn't as future focused as Gia. He didn't give a damn what happened in a day or a week or a month from now. Whenever he was with her physically, the world was suddenly right. Everything made sense for the time they were together and that was enough for him.

She toweled off and he did the same, quickly. Unlike his apartment where everyone could see everyone, they didn't have to worry about privacy in this backyard.

The house was in a neighborhood but not the tightly packed suburbia that he'd grown up in. Here, the houses were spaced out enough that no one could peer over at them from an upstairs window. That fact, and the tall white privacy fence around the entire backyard, was probably why Gia let him take off her bikini top.

He released her gorgeous breasts into his hands, stroking the chilled buds. The sun was receding fast, the cooler air blowing in, but he didn't want to suggest they go inside. He was afraid she'd have second thoughts. They had momentum, and if they lost it, they might never find it again.

She shivered as she slipped her bikini bottoms off her legs. He followed suit, kicking off his shorts in record time. Then he stared.

He loved Gia's body. He always had. And now he was going to love her body from head to toe—for as long as she could stand it.

She'd always loved foreplay and he'd been more than

willing to take his time with her. They hadn't had the chance for foreplay the last time they were together. He intended on remedying that.

He backed her to the rattan chaise lounger and laid her down. "Are you—"

She hushed him with her finger against his lips. Clearly she didn't want to give herself a chance to have second thoughts either. She ran that same finger down his chest, belly button and lower as she sat on the lounger.

When she navigated his favorite part of his body into her mouth, whatever thoughts had been bouncing around in his head vanished. There was only the feel of her heated mouth suctioned onto him.

He rested his hand on the back of her head while she worked, admiring her grace and beauty while she took him on her tongue. She was the best. He hadn't been a saint while they were divorced, so he knew of what he spoke.

Gia blew his mind. Thoroughly. She didn't try to impress him; she simply enjoyed herself. Pleased with herself for pleasing him. So focused on him, she must not have noticed when he gently cupped her jaw to stop her. She took him to the hilt again, one long, slick slide that had him welding his molars together.

He forced himself from her mouth, bending at the waist while he waited for the spots to clear from his vision. He wanted to finish inside her tonight.

She peered up at him, eyes wide. When she licked the corner of her mouth, he worried he might come right then. He was a grown man, in charge of his faculties most of the time, but this was his weak point.

She was his weak point. His ultimate Achilles heel.

He was starting to see what she meant about this being a bad idea, but damned if he'd stop now. He tossed his beach towel on the concrete and lowered to his own knees in front of the lounger.

Pushing her shoulders, he encouraged her to lie back. He didn't have to convince her much. Propped up, arms draped over her head, she was a goddess. The purple-pink sky intensified the surreal moment, the water droplets still clinging to her skin sparkling in the fading light.

He bent and licked a drop off her nipple, then the side of her breast. He repeated the action on the other side, not wanting to give one breast an unfair amount of attention. Then he ran his tongue down her middle to her belly button while her hands sank into his hair and gave a little tug.

"Someone's excited," he murmured against her damp flesh.

"It's been a while," she breathed.

He liked hearing that way too much.

"I'll be down here awhile to make up for it."

Promise made, he tugged her so she was flat on her back, and then rested her knees on his shoulders. Her open before him was a gift. She trusted him with her pleasure. It hadn't been enough to save their marriage, but he was proud she was willing to give herself to him.

He kissed the insides of her knees and worked higher and higher up her thigh. Her breaths tightened, and he drank in her anticipation. It gave him strength to know that she needed this—not only the orgasm, but an orgasm that only he could deliver.

Wedging a space for his shoulders, he dipped his head and tasted her, dragging his tongue in one slow line.

She shivered.

He did it again, this time flattening his tongue.

She shuddered.

With a proud smile to himself, he renewed his efforts and dove in, this time not letting up until her cries of completion were echoing across the nighttime sky.

Fifteen

Julia and Albert Robinson's patio was a work of art. The built-in stone grill sat in the center, the matching tiled bar top wrapping around each side. It took up at least half the space available, the other half filled with an oversize square outdoor dining table and eight chairs. Overkill for their modest house, but his mom wouldn't let Jayson buy her a house. He had to be happy with what they'd accept—in this case a brand new back patio design for her for a Mother's Day gift. Next year he'd talk her into an in-ground pool.

His mother deserved to be spoiled, though he would admit his stepdad did a good job of spoiling her in all the ways he could. Albert had padded their retirement fund, made sure she felt safe and loved. But Albert couldn't afford the extras that Jayson could provide. Jay made a hell of a lot of money and without a family of his own to support, figured he could afford to spoil them.

The glass patio door slid open and Chester, Mason's

husband, stepped outside with a tray of burgers and brats, the vegetarian versions for himself. "Mas, hon, bring me a beer," he called over his shoulder.

"Can I help?" Jayson held out a hand.

"Yes, occupy your brother so he doesn't get in my way," Chester said with a good-natured eye roll.

While Chester and Albert decided what grill arrangement was optimum for the burgers and brats, being careful not to "contaminate" Chester's veggie fare, Mason and Jayson sat at the far side of the newly built bar. Their mother was inside finishing up her famous deviled potato salad.

"I like this dining set," Mason said before sipping his beer.

"Glad they let me do it."

"You're a good son. If you're trying to win, you've done it."

Jayson knew his brother was kidding. Mason was driven, ambitious—one didn't accidentally become a standout photographer in the fashion industry—but he was also laid-back. When the topic of conversation rounded to Natasha, Jayson shook his head.

"I should have warned you," Mason said. "She's a diva. Gorgeous, but a diva."

"Gia's prettier," Jayson muttered.

Mason's silence was deafening. He smirked. "What is going on?"

"Nothing's going on. It was just an observation." Jay took a swig of his own beer.

"I noticed you were in a better mood than usual and I couldn't figure out why. Now I know. Sex with the ex."

"Don't be crass," Chester called out before addressing Jayson. "I would love it if you two found your way back to each other."

"He's a romantic," Mason chided.

"Romance is a tall order for Gia and me," Jayson said,

meaning it. They'd tried the happily-ever-after route, went off-road and ended up in a ditch.

He considered Albert, and his mother who joined him at the grill, and Mason and Chester. Maybe romance wasn't a tall order for his family, but it seemed an insurmountable leap for Jayson.

"I'm going to check the garden." Jayson stood abruptly and left his family on the patio. He stepped around the side yard to where his mother kept a small herb garden. Over the fence, the neighbor's squatty bulldog barked hello.

"Hey, Ollie." He grinned down at the portly dog who wagged the entire back half of his body since his nub of a tail was incapable of the action. Jayson bent over the top half of the fence and gave Ollie a scratch before settling on the stone bench next to the garden.

He'd always wanted this sort of peace for his mother. This house, this neighborhood was a huge step up from where he'd grown up with a father who made their lives a living hell for far too long.

Only a boy at the time, Jayson had vowed to save his mom from the adult man who wasn't man enough to pick on someone his own size. Thankfully his mother had friends. The first—and only—time Eric Cooper had hit Jayson in the face, she'd left with Jayson in tow and had run straight to those friends.

By the time they'd returned home two days later, Eric was gone. Julia changed the locks and began looking for a new apartment immediately—even before the house was listed on the market.

She'd picked up a second job, and then a third, and Jayson grew up fending for himself. He'd seen his role as the protector, until Albert stepped into their lives and took over. Albert, a nerdy type who at first didn't seem capable of slaying a butterfly let alone a dragon, had been adamant about their boys being kids and not worrying about adult problems. He assigned household duties, relegating Jayson to trash duty and Mason to lawn mowing.

Jayson grew up the rest of the way like a normal kid, and would be forever grateful to Albert for giving him a good childhood. He hadn't known at the time that Albert was saving him, though. There'd been moments where he'd argued and yelled, but Albert seemed to understand that Jayson had been raised by a man with no boundaries. Boundaries that Albert set gently, but firmly.

Once grown, Jayson was determined to provide his mother and stepfather with the sorts of things they'd done without on their quest of raising two teenagers—one of them angry thanks in part to DNA and past trauma, the other struggling with his sexuality.

Jayson had been lucky. Some kids didn't make it out of a dark past as cleanly.

When he'd met Gia, his world had stopped. Honest to God, it'd been like a movie. He'd spotted her across the room, the soundtrack of a cheesy ballad playing in the background.

When he'd gone to her father to ask for his daughter's hand in marriage, Jack replied, "As long as you take care of her." Jack had gone on to explain that he knew he couldn't always be there for his daughter, and now that was Jayson's duty.

Jayson had taken that duty seriously. He knew how to take care of a woman, knew what she needed.

Or so he thought.

Each time he tried to do his *husbandly duty,* Gia had shut him down. Now that they were divorced she needed him less than ever.

In his efforts to be a good man, a good husband and nothing like his father, had he gone about being a husband the wrong way? He'd never laid a hand on Gia—he'd sooner die—but he'd strong-armed her in other ways, hadn't he?

He'd tried corralling her the way Jack had—protecting her the way Royce and Bran had. And like she'd done with each of those other men, she'd pulled away from Jayson, too.

Flubbing a marriage was a big failure for him. He'd never intended on divorcing. He'd planned on being married one time, for forever. But as their communication deteriorated, he found himself swallowing arguments instead of having them. He'd opted for silence over involvement. He should have told her what he was thinking. What he was *feeling*.

At the time he hadn't wanted to be wrong.

Stupid.

"You two aren't related, but you're a lot alike." Chester appeared around the corner, gave Ollie the bulldog a scratch on the head and then sat next to Jayson. "I have a thing for the strong, silent type. I can't help it. If you need to talk, I'm a good listener."

Jayson debated before giving in. He could use a second opinion on the thoughts ricocheting off the inside of his skull.

"Gia and I have a complicated past, but I think a future would be even more complicated."

"Possibly. It's hard not to go back to that familiarity, though. Been there. My ex before Mason." Chester shook his head. "It didn't end well, but we weren't anything like you and Gia."

Jayson turned his head. "Meaning?"

"You two are good for each other, but you're each holding on to your pride with both hands. Vulnerability is the key to any good relationship."

"Gia and I have been naked together, Ches. *Recently.* How much more vulnerable can you get?"

Chester patted Jayson's shoulder. "Jayson, Jayson. Sometime you should try admitting you made a mistake. That goes a long way."

“She’s the one pushing me away.” Jayson stood. It hurt to admit that out loud. He assumed that hurt was the vulnerability Ches had been referring to.

“I’ll stay out of it,” Chester vowed as he stood, also. “After I say one more thing.”

Jayson could have guessed his brother-in-law wouldn’t keep completely silent.

“Even if you don’t ride off into the sunset together, if spending time together helps you and Gia over a hump—no pun intended—then go for it.”

“That doesn’t exactly sound like you,” Jayson narrowed his eyes in suspicion. “I thought you were rooting for us to get back together.”

“Always.” Chester smoothed a finger over one manicured eyebrow. “I also recognize that you are happier when you’re talking about her, and I like seeing you happy. Don’t beat yourself up so much about the past. These things have a way of working themselves out.”

He patted Jayson’s leg and then walked off.

Jayson stood for a solid minute and watched a honeybee visit flower after flower at the edge of his mother’s garden.

He *was* happier with Gia in his life. He couldn’t argue that. He was happier sleeping with her, too. He thought about her happiness, then and wondered…

Had he prioritized his own happiness over hers in the past? Had she been telling him what she needed this whole time but he hadn’t listened?

Ollie barked, interrupting his thoughts.

“Yeah, yeah. I know,” he told the dog.

The answer was a resounding *yes*. To both.

Sixteen

"I've never been so tired in my life," Addison said, rocking the car seat on the chair next to her. "I'm not sure how it happened but she's completely nocturnal. Do you think Bran is secretly a vampire?"

Gia laughed. She invited Addi out of the house for lunch, knowing that Bran's wife was climbing the walls. Work was Addison's favorite pastime, which she'd swapped for staying home with her daughter during her maternity leave.

The day was sunny and beautiful so they'd opted to sit outside at the swanky café midway between their houses. Soft jazz music played in the background interspersed with the light tinkling of silverware on plates.

"At least Quinn sleeps when you're out of the house." Her niece's eyelashes cast shadows on her chubby cheeks, causing Gia to smile again. "And you know I can come over and help whenever you need me."

"I know. You're kind of awesome like that."

"Best aunt ever." Gia pressed her fingertips to her collarbone. She'd loved both her nieces on sight, couldn't get enough of them.

She and Jayson hadn't seriously discussed children when they were married. They were always waiting for work to slow down, or for things between them to settle. But now with two of the most beautiful babies on the planet in her immediate circle, she could admit she'd been thinking a lot more about the family she might have some day.

The problem was she couldn't picture a man in the role of father to her children—save one.

Guess who that was?

Now that they'd had slept together twice, she wasn't sure what she should be doing. Breaking up with him to search for Mr. Forever, who she was seriously doubting she'd find on that dating app? Or continuing with Jayson knowing that they wouldn't work permanently?

"I feel like Royce and Taylor have been on their honeymoon for a hundred years." Addison stopped rocking her daughter and ate a bite of her strawberry spinach salad.

"Right? He becomes CEO and then turns into a big slacker." Which wasn't true at all. Her oldest brother deserved a break.

"How is the tablet thing going?" Addi asked. "Have you and Jayson cracked the code?"

"Not yet. We've been working on it, though."

"Must be hard to work that closely with him and not want to strangle each other. Or, you know, have sex in the bathroom." Addi smirked.

Gia shook her head. "Knew that was coming."

"Come on! Give me something. You have sex for the first time since your divorce and you're not going to dish even a little?" Addi tilted her head. "Wait—that *was* the first time, wasn't it?"

"That was the first time," Gia confirmed, then offered

a coy smile. "Though we did do it in the car five days before the divorce."

Addi laughed, pure glee as she stabbed her salad.

"You're enjoying this."

"I really am. I haven't been out much," Addi said. "So, what else can you tell me? Now you're working together and having sex all over the house?"

Gia lifted one half of her club sandwich. "Only once. By the pool. And it wasn't a good idea. Especially after my date with Elias."

"You went on a date?" Addi gaped at her. "Who's Elias?"

"A guy I met on the app." Gia bit the corner of her sandwich. "He was..." *Not Jay.* "Nice but boring."

"Well, one thing's for sure. With you and Jayson, things are *never* boring."

Gia ate a french fry. Things between her and Jayson were never boring because they were unresolved. It was like there were arguments floating in the air between them. Things they'd never said as well as things that had been said way too much.

"I'm not sure what we're doing," Gia admitted. "Jayson and I. We've done this already—the whole shebang. Wedding. House."

"You don't have to figure that out now," Addi said practically. Quinn cooed and Addi rocked the car seat.

"No, but we'll have to figure things out eventually."

"This is where your big brain gets you into trouble. Sometimes you just have to go for it and see what happens next."

"You mean like you did with Bran." Gia folded her arms on the table and lifted one eyebrow. Addison had leaped before she looked with Bran and they'd suffered a setback because of it.

"Just like that." Addi nodded, surprising Gia with her reaction. "It worked out in the end. There's no right way to do what you're doing. And you don't have to protect yourself with Jayson. He's the safest bet you have."

Yes, in some ways he was safe. He wouldn't hurt her. He respected her. He'd give her the best time of her life in bed.

But he was also unsafe—because every time he was around her, she couldn't seem to separate the man who'd broken her heart while they were married from the man who'd won it early on.

She didn't want to dive in headfirst again only to discover they were still in the shallows. Any attempt at a long-term relationship could land them back in the same situation they were in before.

And she couldn't stomach ending things with him again. It hurt too much the first time.

The conversation with Addison looped in Gia's head when she returned to work, crashed into her when she climbed into her car to drive home, and arrived on a silver platter when Jayson showed up at her house twenty minutes later.

The front door opened and her heart zoomed to her toes. He walked in, a leather shoulder bag in his hand. "It's just me" might as well have been a "Honey, I'm home."

She was in the kitchen, the makings for a sandwich spread out on the countertop.

"No takeout tonight?" He examined the countertop: mayo jar, bakery-fresh whole wheat bread, leaf lettuce, a freshly sliced tomato, smoked turkey breast and a jar of pickles.

"You're welcome to have one."

"Thought you'd never ask." He hesitated, his eyes lingering on her mouth. She licked her lips self-consciously, knowing she shouldn't want the casual peck hello but wanting it anyway.

In the end, his mouth flinched into a tight smile and he leaned past her to pluck a pickle slice from the jar.

As homey as this scene felt, they were still separated. She'd do well to remember that.

He set his bag down on a bar chair and rubbed his hands together. "I need chips."

"On top of the fridge," she answered automatically. But he knew where the chips were in this house. He'd been the one to store them there to begin with. Why she'd kept them there when she had to grab a footstool to reach them was beyond her.

He was right. Some things never changed.

"Before you met me you crammed them into a cabinet and broke half the chips in the bag." He sliced open the bag with a pair of scissors from a drawer he was also familiar with. The entire scene was eerily familiar. As if they'd time-traveled back to when they were married and this was a typical day after work.

And yet it was utterly and totally different.

What was it that Jayson had said the last time they'd slept together? *I don't want to fail with you again.*

He hadn't said, "I don't want to fail you" nor had he said, "I don't want to fail." He'd said, "I don't want to fail *with* you," as if they'd both had blame in what happened between them.

She couldn't remember a time when he wasn't justifying his position and his actions. When he wasn't and expecting her to go along with what he'd decided should happen. He never listened, and she never felt heard.

Had he changed in the year and a half they were apart? Or was that dangerous and hopeful thinking?

They made their sandwiches side by side in silence.

"Why did we buy such a big house?" she asked as she traversed the wide layout of the kitchen to the trashcan.

"You love this house."

"I do but it's too much—" Especially now that it was just her.

He navigated a huge bite of his stacked turkey sandwich before speaking. "You loved it and I wanted you to have it."

Both true. She'd stepped into this very kitchen and had done a twirl reminiscent of *The Sound of Music* on the marble tile. "I did love it."

"You talked about huge Christmas dinners prepared in this oven," he reminded her. "And kids running through the halls. You wanted a dog at one point. Remember?"

A dog. That's right. She remembered.

Remembering hurt.

And now she couldn't begin to picture another man—like Denver or Elias—in the kitchen eating over the counter. One who didn't smash potato chips between his sandwich before taking a bite.

"We've had some pretty late nights." She needed to tell him what she'd been thinking. Establish some boundaries for both their sakes. "If you don't want to drive home, you don't have to."

His eyebrows lifted in interest. "Oh, yeah?"

"The pool house is all yours," she said, before he had the very wrong idea of what she was offering.

No matter what fun with Jayson she could have, Gia knew what was at stake. Being with him in this familiar environment was chipping away at her resolve. She didn't need the constant reminder of what they could have had—of what they'd once naively dreamed they could have.

"The pool house," he repeated, his tone flat.

"Sure. There's a lot of unused space out there. I still have that bed out there."

He watched her, his eyes darkening to navy blue. "I know that bed, G."

She couldn't look away even though she should. She knew that bed, too. While the house was filled with decorators for nearly a month, she and Jay had stayed in the pool house. They'd made love on that small double bed, woke to a view of the pool and their backyard. He would rise before her and make coffee in the cheap four-cup coffee maker and deliver her the first cup.

Simpler, better times.

It seemed no matter where she looked she couldn't escape memories of them together. How was she supposed to make a life on her own for herself when she couldn't leave *them* behind?

Seventeen

He'd nearly cracked the code by nightfall.

Gia had gone to bed before him, leaving him in the family room to work. He apparently now had two options. Drive home or sleep in the pool house.

It irritated him that she wanted to kick him out. They'd been close lately. Why the sudden line in the sand?

He shut down Big Ben and pulled his keys from his pocket, frowning down at them. He didn't want to go home. He wanted to stay here—and *not* in the damn pool house. He couldn't escape the idea that Gia needed him here, in the *actual* house.

Not to protect her—the gated community was safe. And the security system he'd insisted she install after he moved out was top-of-the-line. But to just…*be here*. She'd seemed sad after telling him he could stay in the pool house, and he didn't want her to be sad and alone.

So, he laid down on the couch anyway, his arm thrown over his head, eyes on the ceiling. He slept a little and thought a lot. About the arguments they'd had behind these walls. Those once impassioned disagreements that turned into apathetic silence, which then led them to split in the first place.

Around six thirty in the morning, he heard her shuffle into the kitchen. He was already at the desk, bleary-eyed and tired, since he'd thought a lot more than he'd slept.

"Morning," he croaked, to let her know he was there.

"Morning." Her dark hair was scooped into a topknot and she wore a short silk robe, white with big black flowers on it. She looked soft and approachable and adorable, and his hands itched to touch her.

"You're wearing glasses," he observed as he stood to stretch.

"They're new." She touched the frames. "I usually wear contacts at work."

"Oh." So much had changed, and yet whenever he was here he was somehow frozen in time.

She scooped coffee grounds into a filter basket. "Coffee?"

"Sure."

She pressed the button on the machine and propped her fist on her hip. She was cute and sleepy and damned sexy. Especially in those dark-framed glasses. "You didn't sleep in the pool house did you?"

"How did you—I didn't feel right leaving you." He lifted a hand to his hair, feeling strangely uncomfortable.

"And you in my house when I told you to leave felt *right*?"

"What are you trying to avoid by kicking me out, G?"

He could feel the sexual tension between them right now. She was likely trying to avoid this very situation. Them, together, wearing very little.

"You never listen. I have been sleeping alone for a while now. I don't need a guard downstairs."

He opened his mouth to tell her he wasn't guarding her, he wanted to be here for her in case she needed him. But old patterns threatened. If he said that, she'd tell him that he could let go of the need to take care of her since they were divorced.

He didn't want the conversation to go that way. Time to try something new.

Vulnerability.

Hadn't that been what Chester recommended?

Jayson didn't have a good track record with vulnerability. His father had seen it as a weakness to exploit, and his mother felt guilty that she'd caused Jay to feel unsafe. He'd shored up his emotions for a damn good reason—to protect himself and the people he loved. Only now he wondered if opening up to Gia might be the what they needed to bury their past once and for all. Still, opening up could be the ultimate humiliation for him if she rejected him—totally possible.

He needed her closer for this conversation. Tucking a finger into the silky belt at her waist, he pulled her to him. "You like to remind me how much you don't need me, which makes me feel rejected."

She blinked up at him. Now that he'd admitted what he was feeling, what he was *feeling* was exposed. Might as well have loaded a gun and handed it to her. Rather than backtrack, he decided to lean in a bit more. "When we were together I went about protecting you in the wrong way."

Her eyes widened. She stared as if shocked by his words. For good reason. He'd rarely if ever admitted as his mistakes in the past. He'd always thought he knew best.

"I care about you," he said. "I never meant to hobble or limit you. I never intended for you to feel like you were a child I was looking after. Despite not wanting to be like my dad, I guess I had a heavy hand after all."

No, he'd never physically harmed her, but trying to stifle

her when she should be wild and free hadn't been much better.

She reached up and placed her hand on his cheek. "No, Jayson. You're nothing like your father. I heard the stories from both you and your mom, and I believed then what I believe now."

He stayed silent, as if part of him knew how badly he needed to hear what came next.

"You're overprotective at times, but you're also kind. And sweet."

He grumbled.

She laughed and patted his cheek. "It's okay to be sweet. You're not your dad. You could never be that small of a man."

The moment called for a kiss, so he bent his head. She inclined her chin to meet him in the middle.

Maybe vulnerability had its merits.

She tasted like Gia. Like the woman he hadn't seen at this ungodly hour since he'd awoken next to her in the bed they shared. It was a bed he'd like to share with her again… say, right now.

She surprised him by reaching up and clinging to his neck, kissing him deeper. He untied her robe, slipping his palms over her warm skin. Beneath he found a simple white tank top and black panties. This outfit was one of his all-time favorites. No fancy lingerie needed, his ex-wife was sexiest when she wore cotton.

He sucked in a breath as he lifted the edge of her tank and tickled her skin. "So soft."

Her own breathing sped as her hands roamed over his T-shirt. "We have to go to work," she cautioned, but there was no conviction in her words.

"And if we don't?" He wrapped his arms around her and pulled her flush against him. He was already hard from that kiss. “When was the last time you did something you weren’t supposed to, Gia?”

She laughed, the sound husky and sexy, and turned those dark eyes up to him. Her grin held. “It’s been frequent since we’ve been hanging out more often.”

He liked that.

He lifted and deposited her on the countertop, content to use the momentum they had to spend some serious quality time with her. Just as his mouth stamped hers and his hand closed over her breast, a sharp knock came from the front door.

“It’s us!” Taylor Knox called out. She hadn’t made it into the kitchen yet, but she would soon enough.

“Crap! I forgot.” Gia shoved away from him and hopped off the counter.

“What the hell…?” He adjusted the part of himself that had recently become large enough to be a distraction.

“Royce and Taylor asked if they could swing by on the way to work today to drop off something.”

“What something?” It’d better be important, that was for damn sure.

She waved him off. “Go hide.”

“Hide?”

“Jayson, it’s seven in the morning and neither of us are dressed.”

“Last I checked we’re not teenagers. You have nothing to explain.” He folded his arms. He wasn’t going anywhere. “You’re a grown woman.” As a grown woman she could sleep with Jayson—or *almost* sleep with him—anytime she liked.

“At least act casual?” she pleaded.

“Casual went out the window with that kiss.”

She glared, a sure sign she agreed, and then walked out of sight.

A moment later, Taylor was chattering her way excitedly through the house. Royce's low murmur followed. Jayson poured himself a cup of coffee and leaned against the countertop. When Taylor entered the kitchen, her sentence trailed off into an ellipsis.

"Hi, Coop," she said carefully, exchanging glances with Royce before swapping a lengthier one with Gia.

"Morning." Jayson sipped his coffee.

"Cooper." Royce's expression was harder to read than his wife's.

"Coffee?" Jayson offered.

"No, thanks," Taylor said. "We brought a few souvenirs and I wanted to drop them off before Gia took off for work. We have something for you, too, but it didn't occur to me to bring it."

"For good reason," Royce murmured. "We didn't expect to find you here." He didn't often play the big, bad brother card with Jayson—or at least he hadn't in a while. If he thought he was intimidating… Hell, Jayson was older than Royce.

"Why don't we have our coffee outside," Royce added.

"I'll have mine right here, thanks, but you can go outside if you like." Jayson grinned.

Royce glowered for a beat before Taylor interrupted the short standoff.

"We should go. Don't you have to be in the office soon?" Taylor asked her husband.

"Nope."

"What's the matter, Royce? Afraid to admit your feelings in front of your sister? She's an adult, you know." Jayson informed him.

"Afraid has nothing to do with it." Royce faced his sister. "Are you being careful with him? In *every way imaginable*?"

"Royce!" Taylor shot him a peeved look.

"Gia knows what she wants," Jayson said. "She also

knows what she doesn't want. She'd never allow me, or anyone, to trample her wishes. You know that better than anyone. She's damned well capable of making decisions for herself regardless of what you or I want her to do."

Royce's nostrils flared.

Gia took a step closer to Jayson and he instantly realized what he'd done. He'd spoken for her instead of giving her the space to speak for herself. Dammit, would he ever learn?

"Thank you, Jayson."

Wait. Did she just *thank him*?

"I'm not interested in your advice when it comes to Jayson," she told her brother." She winked at Taylor. "Yours I'd consider."

"Aw, thanks, G." Taylor smiled. Royce did not. She gave her husband's arm a light slap. "Oh, stop being so overbearing. Jayson's right. Gia can take care of herself." Taylor set the gift bag on the counter before curling her arms around one of Royce's. "We'll be leaving now. See you at the office."

Once they'd gone, Jayson turned to his ex-wife. "Did I have a stroke or did both you and Taylor admit that I was right?"

"Don't ruin this moment by being arrogant." But Gia was smiling when she said it. She pulled the coffee cup from his hand and set it on the counter. "Now, where were we? We have a few minutes to continue what we started before going in to work."

He didn't hesitate, setting her on the countertop next to his coffee and kissing her.

They didn't end up having sex, but second base wasn't bad.

Eighteen

The moment Gia sat down at her desk later that morning and opened her laptop Taylor appeared as if a magician had *abracadabraed* her there.

"I leave for my honeymoon and apparently miss a really big development between you and Jayson! Did you not each bring your own dates—the first time I've ever seen that happen, by the way—to my wedding? Tell me everything. Every last thing." She dragged a chair over and sat, elbows propped on the desk's surface, chin in her hands.

"Well—"

"Addison told me you had sex after the wedding, but I thought she was mistaken. I mean it was the morning after and there were still guests mingling at the breakfast bar."

"Well—"

"I never believed you with that skateboarder for a second. Or Cooper with that model." Taylor rolled her eyes. "Give me a break."

"Yeah, um… Our dates weren't really doing it for us."

"So you did it to each other?" Taylor giggled at her own joke. "Sorry about busting in on you two this morning."

"It's okay. He wasn't supposed to be there, actually. I asked him to sleep in the pool house."

"Boundaries are important," Taylor said carefully.

About that... The second Taylor and Royce left, Gia happily made out with Jayson. He'd admitted he handled things poorly when they were married and then defended Gia to her brother. It was beyond sexy hearing him say she could handle herself. She'd wanted to see that change in him for so long. Now that she had, she was having trouble trusting it.

"Sex is a normal, natural thing," Taylor said. "If that's where you and Cooper are, enjoy it."

"You, too? Addi told me to go for it. It's not that easy, you know. Jayson and I are divorced."

"Yeah, and you're still human. Plus, you two have a very unique relationship, even with a marriage behind you. Mistakes are always made in relationships. Sometimes you have to grow and learn. Maybe your timing was off the first time around."

"Or maybe I'm going to lose my heart to the one man I should know better than to hand it to." Jayson was a wonderful person and hotter than Hades in the summertime but him admitting he'd overstepped one time wasn't going to fix everything.

"Oh, honey." Taylor patted her best friend's hand. "I love you. I wish you every happiness in life, whether you end up sharing a life with Jayson or not. But sometimes you have to take a leap of faith even if you're not sure it's going to work out. Look at me. After all the mistakes I made, I have Royce. I have Emmaline. Can't blame me for wanting you to have that same happiness."

"No. I can't blame you." Gia smiled. What Taylor and Royce had was beautiful and everlasting.

"It's okay to screw up." Taylor stood. "I know you think

you have to be bulletproof—to hold your own and make sure you do everything for yourself, but in the end it's not worth it. It's okay to admit you messed up. Messing up is a sign that you tried."

Gia *had* tried in her marriage, but she was haunted by the worry that she hadn't tried *enough.* If she and Jayson were to realize they'd made a mistake divorcing, would she ever be able to forgive herself for causing them so much pain? After all, she was the one who'd offered divorce as a solution.

Rather than say any of that, she nodded at her friend. "Thanks, Tay."

"You bet, doll." Taylor slipped out of Gia's office at the same time Jay passed by the door. He stopped and leaned in, both hands on the door frame. He looked good. Somehow better than he had a few hours ago. She was struck with the overwhelming need to touch him.

"Brainstorming sesh tonight at the house?" he asked.

The house. He'd worded that carefully. "Sure."

"Wine?"

Maybe she'd been overthinking—a hobby she was intimately familiar with. Maybe she should take her sisters-in-law's advice and enjoy the moment. "Sure."

"Red? White?"

"Chardonnay would be lovely."

"Consider it done." He tapped the door frame and walked away. She watched him go, admiring his strong, straight back, dark wavy hair and long legs.

That night Gia was propped up on her sofa, tablet in her lap. Jayson sat at the desk on the other side of the room.

She thought about her conversation with Taylor when she should have been focusing on solving the tablet issue. No one on their team had made headway. When she suggested to Jayson they should scrap the update, he nearly blew his stack.

We can't let this beat us, G. Those improvements are vital to the survival of this tablet. If we give up now, we're signing its death warrant.

That made her think of them, their marriage. Had they given up rather than improve?

The longer she sat in the same room with him, the more irresistible he became. That same old familiarity smacked between them, here in their former shared house. Even when they weren't having sex, she felt the sizzle of attraction. Even with the unromantic pizza box on the coffee table, what was left of their dinner having congealed into a rock-hard mass of cheese and olives.

It was important for her to define boundaries not only for Jay, but for herself. She shouldn't have continued kissing him this morning. She should have marched upstairs and dressed for work, and kept her cool. That lengthy physical interaction with him made it harder for her to bury those thoughts about their marriage and the mistakes that were made. In short, it'd made it harder for her to continue moving *forward.*

She was stuck. On the damn tablet issue, and on Jayson.

With a sigh, she restarted the tablet for the nine-hundredth time and began poking around. As expected, it powered down before she'd had a chance to—

"Oh my God," she muttered. While part of her mind had been turning over her current situation, the processing part had shoved two puzzle pieces together. She knew *exactly* what to do to fix this update.

Jay swiveled in his chair, barely reined-in excitement in his eyes. "That sounded promising."

She had to smile. He knew her *Eureka!* voice.

She rushed to the desk, physically moved his hand from the mouse, and clicked out of what he was working on. A few clicks and keystrokes later, she knew she had it. A zap of intuition told her that she'd tripped upon exactly the right code.

She was a superhero.

"That's it. The fix. I know it. I know it, I know it..." Heart racing, she stood over the desk staring down at Jayson, her chest rising and falling with each truncated breath.

"Why am I not surprised?" His slow blink communicated that he was proud. His approval, while dangerous to covet, was oh-so welcome.

"Hand it over. I'll update the software and we'll do a test. We'll see if you just won the bet. Or if I have another shot at winning it myself."

Right. The bet. She hadn't been thinking about that. Her thoughts had narrowed to fixating on him and finding the glitch.

What felt like years later, but was more like fifteen minutes, she chewed on the side of her thumb and paced from kitchen to living room.

Finally, she heard the telltale chime of the tablet firing up. She raced over to watch as his blunt fingers tapped from screen to screen. He powered down and glanced up at her, warmth in his blue eyes. While her breath stalled in her lungs, he powered up the tablet one more time and tapped on the screen.

"It didn't crash. *Yet.*" His lips curved. "The shutdown typically occurs immediately. Just to make sure, have at it." He handed over the tablet and instructed her to test it for herself. "I'll do the same with mine."

Jayson opened one webpage and another, and then another. He opened a social media app. He uploaded a game, played it for a few minutes, and then closed it and opened a documents file.

No crashing. Not a whisper that anything hadn't been operating before.

She did it. *She did it!*

He was thrilled and awed by her brilliant mind. He was also disappointed for not discovering the fix himself. Had it been his stroke of genius that fixed the tablet, they'd be naked by now, her under him, moaning his name.

Not that he was giving up.

"Anything bad happen yet?" he asked.

"Not yet." She showed him her screen. "Other than a new addiction to Candy Blaster. I'm on level thirteen already. You know what that means?"

"You can blast candy with the best of them?"

"Har-har. It *means* I am owed a homemade pasta dinner." Her grin was contagious. Once upon a time she'd called that recipe a "panty dropper."

No, he wasn't giving up on getting her into bed yet.

He rose and walked to the sofa. "You should be proud. An issue that stumped the best minds at ThomKnox didn't stand a chance against yours."

"Thanks." She gave him a sheepish smile. He loved her humility, even though he'd argued with her to own her smarts on more than one occasion.

"I'll let everyone know the race is over, then I'll head to the office." He grabbed his tablet and bag and slung it over his shoulder.

"Now?" She stood and fidgeted with her own tablet. "I mean. We should at least soak in the win."

She didn't want him to go? Interesting.

While he would be the first to admit that a celebration was in order, he also knew she'd been hard at work on this for long enough. Once the adrenaline wore off she was going to be exhausted and grouchy. He could handle both, but he wasn't sure she could handle both with him around.

"I don't want to wait another second to input this fix in

the system. Good job, Gia. Killed it." Rubbing her biceps with his palm, he leaned down to kiss her on the cheek. When he pulled back she turned her head, her dark eyes seeking his with so much want he could feel it in his bones.

He thought for a second she might kiss him. Thought that her lingering gaze might lead to more. If that was the case, he'd have a hard time making himself leave, no matter what needed to be done at work.

"Okay." She blinked, at that dash of errant lust dissipated. "You owe me dinner."

"I do," he agreed. One panty-dropper dinner, coming right up. Once upon a time he'd had his sights set on wooing her. How interesting to find himself back in that same boat now. "How's Saturday? Six o'clock?"

She nodded. "What do you want me to do?"

"Enjoy the spoils that come with winning." He headed for the door and she called out good-night. He glanced at his hand on the doorknob, all but forcing himself to leave the house and her behind tonight.

"Good night, G," he said to himself once he was outside.

Nineteen

Jayson sat on the corner of his desk in the center of the tech department, addressing his team. Everyone was sitting at their surrounding desks, eyes on him while he delivered the very good news that the software glitch had been *unglitched.*

Gia lingered at the threshold of her office, arms folded, hip propped on the doorway. In case anyone was watching her, she needed to appear both supportive and comfortable. The supportive part was easy. Jayson was amazingly adept at work and was a respected and admired leader.

The comfortable part took some doing.

Watching him sit there, one foot on the floor, the other dangling off the corner of the desk, his hands folded between the spread of his thick thighs made her want him. The way she'd wanted him last night.

He hadn't tried anything and she kept telling herself she was glad. After all she'd been trying to establish boundaries.

And now, voilà. *Boundaries.*

His team laughed at something he said and Jayson smiled. He had an easy way of wielding power. Like a gladiator in the ring who knew he was in charge of the crowd. Even the standard office attire of a gray-blue button-down shirt and dark tie, dark gray pants and leather shoes didn't distract from that power.

She had been surrounded by powerful men all her life. Men, this one included, who thought they knew what was best for her. She'd never been intimidated or afraid to stick up for herself. She'd never been afraid to speak her mind.

She recalled his moment of vulnerability, when he'd admitted he'd been heavy-handed while they were married. He had, but their problems weren't only caused by him. He'd been trying to help, which made her wonder… Had she been so concerned with asserting herself that she'd trampled on his efforts to care for her?

That was an uncomfortable thought. Almost as uncomfortable as her cheeks going warm the moment he turned his head and focused on her.

Oh, how she'd been tempted to keep him at the house a little longer. To talk him into a glass of wine and some kissing on the couch. It would have been playing with fire, she knew. So why was she so disappointed that he'd left instead?

He'd confused her lately.

She'd thought she knew him. Knew his tendency to steamroll her, and that he hadn't been the best listener, but lately she was beginning to think he'd changed. Not only had he admitted he didn't handle things best while they were married, but he'd also argued with Royce that she could handle things on her own.

She'd been unable to believe what she was hearing.

While she'd been hyperfocused on their *inability* to work things out in the past, she couldn't help thinking that fixing the unfixable tablet issue was a symbol of how much she and Jayson had grown since they'd divorced.

Her body wasn't helping matters.

Every nonsexual thing he said now grew wings and flapped low in her belly. The phrase *integrated software analysis* shouldn't make her want him.

"I appreciate the team's attention to detail," Jayson's voice dipped into an unintentionally sexy husk. "You should be proud of how hard you've worked. I know you've been sweating over the details in search of that magical sweet spot…"

As she absently twirled a few strands of her hair, her eyes feasted on the broadness of his chest. The hardness of his body. She'd stayed up past dark working up a different kind of sweat with him when they were married… And she recalled with clarity how tirelessly he'd searched for her magical sweet spot…

"Now the confession," he said, his gaze arrowing straight to her. "Gia solved the problem. We had a bet going, too. I lost."

After applause, and her demure curtsy, one of their tech gurus, Ric, called out, "What'd you lose, Coop?"

"I have to spend several hours in a hot kitchen making my grandmother's homemade pasta recipe." One eyebrow rose in an insanely sexy way. With a heated glance toward her he added, "If I would have won—"

"I would've had to cook for him," she blurted out. "Great work everyone. It was a team effort, no matter who found the glitch. Sometimes finding what doesn't work can be just as important as what does."

Jayson gave her an approving smile. "Well said, Gia." He turned back to the group. "We're going to celebrate with a party here at ThomKnox for our department. Champagne will flow, but not yet. First we have to finish the corrections that I started, coordinate our efforts with Marketing, and then put the update back on the calendar. Thanks, everyone. You know what to do."

The team turned around in their chairs, opened computers or laptops, reached for their tablets and did as Jayson asked. He stood from his desk and followed her inside her office.

"Champagne?" She asked when he shut the door. "That was nice of you."

"Nice, huh?" He took another step closer to her and she tightened her arms over her chest, refusing to let him in on the fact that her nipples were desperately trying to get his attention. "I didn't know you were going to cook for me if I won."

"Well… I couldn't tell them the truth," she whispered.

"Which was what, again?"

She ignored his devilish, tempting grin, which wasn't easy. "I have work to do too, you know."

"Yeah, yeah. So do I." Before he left, he turned. She felt his eyes raking over her black pencil skirt and red silk button-down shirt. "Proud of you, G. I mean it."

"Thank you." She meant that, too.

His lips pulled into a quick, tight-lipped smile, and then he left the office, and left her to wonder if maybe they had both changed over the last few years after all.

After promising champagne to the staff, Jayson considered that he and Gia hadn't yet properly celebrated their win. Yes, it was a team effort, blah, blah, blah, but she deserved to toast to her accomplishments in private, and without having to put on her work face.

Outside her house, he rang the doorbell, which felt odd considering he used to live here. But as they'd established recently, they were no longer the same people who used to live here. She'd changed since then, and so had he. Now they were somewhere in the middle, and he wasn't sure if that was a good or a bad thing.

The door opened and there stood his ex-wife, in that same scintillating red shirt that hugged her breasts. She'd kicked off her shoes in favor of bare feet, which he liked even more.

"Did I black out? Is it Saturday already?" Her eyes went to the champagne bottle, tied with a gold bow—the biggest one he'd been able to find at the convenience store. "What's this?"

"It's a bow." He flicked the fringed ribbon. "I was going to go with red to match your shirt, but this one matches the label." He spun the bottle to show her a familiar gold label.

"My favorite."

"It's the same brand I chose for the party for the team. It got me thinking that you and I never celebrated."

She chewed on her lip, considering.

"Can I come in?"

"Only because it's my favorite champagne and I could never turn it down. Which I'm sure you knew."

"Guilty." He smiled.

"*One* glass." She stepped aside for him to come in. There was a candle lit in the kitchen, soft music playing from a speaker in the living room.

"Feels different in here." Like it used to, he thought, but didn't say. She had a way of putting her feminine stamp on everything. He hadn't been able to achieve this sort of warm, welcoming vibe at his apartment. It still felt stale and drab.

"I had to air out the stench of defeat." She sent him a feisty smile as she reached for the handle on a tall cabinet. "You didn't have to give me credit for fixing the glitch, by the way." Her T-shirt rode up and exposed her flat, tan belly.

He set the champagne aside, the bottle sweating from

the ride over in the car, and placed a chilly hand on the side of her waist.

"Your hands are freezing!" she shrieked. She swatted him away but there was a playful glint in her eyes.

"Never could resist that move." He eased her to one side and pulled down the pair of fluted glasses.

"I could've done that," she mumbled.

"Yes, but I'm here so you didn't have to." He handed the stemware over, upside down. When she took them in her hands, she brushed his fingers. An innocent touch, but his heart mule-kicked his chest in response.

"They don't get a lot of use. That cabinet is high." That was her way of saying thank you, he guessed. Or avoiding mentioning that those were the very champagne flutes they'd toasted with at their wedding.

Had Gia been anyone else he might have been surprised that she hadn't thrown out every item that had anything to do with them, but she'd never been petty.

She rinsed out the glasses and took her time drying them while he unwrapped the foil from the neck of the bottle. When he moved to twist off the cork she stopped him with one hand.

"Wait! Don't you want to…" She gestured outside.

"Risky." He pretended to deliberate.

"Worth it," she said before dashing outside.

In the backyard, he angled the bottle so the cork would shoot into the privacy fence rather than into the sky—a mistake he'd made once before with near disastrous consequences. He twisted the cork so that it was halfway out and then popped it with his thumb. It sailed over the pool and hit the privacy fence with a soft *thump.*

"I love that noise. Smart aim," she praised. "Remember that time when you shot the cork over the fence? It must've gone a mile."

"How could I forget? It was the shot of a lifetime. If I was trying to hit Neil's lit grill, I never could have done it."

"Not for a million dollars," she agreed with a laugh. He laughed with her, enjoying the memory and the ease between them—a rarity over the last couple of years. "Guess it wasn't all bad. Our marriage."

"No. It wasn't." She took the bottle from his hand and tilted it to her mouth, swallowing a fizzy mouthful of the very expensive champagne. He followed her lead, taking a slug from the bottle next before settling onto the chaise lounger. He patted the cushion next to him, remembering what they'd done the last time they were on this piece of furniture.

"No funny business," she warned as she sat down, proving her memory was as good as his.

"Just an innocent bottle of champagne shared between two ex-spouses. What could possibly go wrong?"

She took a drink, this time holding on to the bottle while she stared off into the distance.

He wondered if, like him, her mind returned to the last bottle of champagne they'd shared out here.

It was one of the worst nights of his life...

Twenty

Two months before the divorce

"I thought you'd be happy," Jayson growled, equal parts confused and pissed off.

Making Gia happy was a target he couldn't hit. God knew he'd tried. It made him feel like a failure when she was unhappy and lately that'd been more often than not.

"Happy?" she asked, her tone filled with accusation.

"Yes." He glugged a few inches of champagne into her glass and then into his. "You had a problem. I fixed it."

She threw her hands up. "Without talking to me!"

"What was there to talk about?"

She snatched the bottle from him, nearly knocking over her glass. He snatched the glass before it hit the newly installed ceramic tile, sloshing champagne onto his hand in the process.

"Unbelievable," she grumbled, sliding the patio door aside and stomping outside.

With a sigh, he followed.

"You making a decision without me, on something as large as a vehicle parked in our shared garage does *not* make me happy. You should have asked my opinion."

"All you do is complain about my truck!" He'd bought the exact Mercedes she'd cooed over when they saw it advertised the other day. "You wanted something classier. You said so yourself."

"I didn't mean I wanted you to go out and buy it for me!"

"Why? Because you can buy it for yourself? I am aware of the Knox family fortune you're sitting on, Gia. You don't have to rub my nose in it."

She set the champagne bottle on the ground next to her and crossed her arms over her chest. "You're never going to understand, Jay."

He was beginning to think she was right.

"I love the car," she said. Cryptically. "But I would rather you have included me in the decision to buy it. Stop assuming you know what I want and *ask me*."

Blinded by anger, and embarrassment, he didn't hear what she was really saying. So, of course, he continued to defend himself. "All I do is cater to what you want. It'd be nice if you appreciated it once in a while."

"You want me to *thank you* for bypassing me and doing what you feel is best?"

He'd dug in then, a mistake, but he was too pissed off to change course. "That'd be a nice change of pace."

Jayson sat next to her now on the lounge, the starry sky black above them, the water in the pool still and dark.

He hadn't handled that night well. He hadn't handled much well when they were married. He constantly felt insulted. Like a failure. He'd been trying to be her hero. How was a guy like him supposed to out-hero Jack and Brannon and Royce Knox, the three giants in her life?

He couldn't.

And so, he'd attempted to prove himself over and over. But he hadn't known what she'd wanted. Finally, he thought he knew what that was.

She wanted to be heard. To be considered.

That night's argument wasn't about the Mercedes. It was about her wanting to be included in the decisions and choices in their shared marriage. He saw that now. As crystal clear as the glassware they didn't bother using.

"You're thinking about the night you bought the car," she said.

"Yes."

"So am I."

"It was the last time I saw you drink champagne from the bottle."

"It was the last time I did it." She took another swig and then handed him the bottle.

He set the champagne aside and rested his elbows on his knees, watching the water on the surface of the pool ripple in the evening breeze. "I should have talked to you before I bought it."

He sensed more than saw her shake her head. "I should've accepted it for what it was. A gift. Instead I accused you of making choices for me."

"That evening didn't go the way I wanted," he said, remembering what came next. She'd been the one to point out that if they couldn't relate on a basic level they were better off apart. He'd asked her if she cared to clarify that, and she'd said divorce wasn't out of the question.

"I told you that night I'd be better off without you." She winced.

"No, you didn't. You said we'd be better off apart. Where we couldn't hurt each other any longer. That was my opportunity to promise you I wouldn't hurt you again. Instead, I refused to back down."

He'd agreed with her. Said that if she wanted a divorce, that was fine by him. He'd been hurt, his pride bruised. His ego had taken a beating. "I thought I couldn't please you."

"In your defense, I can be difficult," she said now, but with a kind smile.

"You were being *you*. Which is exactly why I fell in love with you in the first place." He reached for her hand and intertwined their fingers. As he'd realized previously, vulnerability wasn't his strong suit—or hers. The inability for them to let their guard down with each other was probably to blame for their splitting more than anything. "It'd be so easy to lean in and kiss you."

She licked her lips and dipped her chin. Not a nod exactly, but she leaned the slightest bit closer and peered up at him. Tenderly, he stroked her jaw with his thumb. Once he saw his future in those deep brown eyes. Now he only saw his past.

A past littered with failure and regret. A past he couldn't undo.

"But I promised no funny stuff," he murmured.

Time to stop doing what he wanted, or what he decided was right for her. Gia had gone on not one date but two in order to put distance between them. It was time for him to stop pushing so damn hard.

Pulling his hand away, he stood. She watched him, longing emanating from her like heat off the desert floor. Then she armored up.

"Drive safe." She plucked up the bottle as she stood. "Thank you for the champagne."

That's my girl.

"You're welcome."

He walked inside and she followed, abandoning the bottle in the kitchen to see him to the door. He fought the urge to turn and kiss her one last time. That would've felt too final. Like admitting he couldn't live without her.

And he could.

He'd been doing it for years.

Twenty-One

Saturday afternoon came and he showed up at the house, apron in hand. No, really. The black canvas apron read "Pasta la Vista, baby" in bold stencil print.

Gia bought it for him last Christmas. Got a big kick out of herself for being so clever. But amidst the joking and ribbing, she also went on and on about how he'd made the best homemade pasta she'd ever eaten. And that even the best local Italian place in River Grove, Garlíc, couldn't best his skills. It'd made him proud, truth be told.

He'd gone home that night and made pasta by hand, no pasta maker to be seen since he'd left that piece of equipment with Gia. He'd made enough to feed an army but hadn't taken her any of the leftovers. It seemed too personal. Too much of a throwback to the last time he'd made her pasta—on their wedding anniversary. And after they'd nearly slept together at Addison and Brannon's wedding, he hadn't wanted to risk sending the wrong message.

He found said pasta maker now, an item his ex-wife had

insisted having on the gift registry, exactly where they'd put it after they moved in. Bottom cabinet on the island and all the way in the back. As he wrestled it from behind baking dishes and a large stand mixer, he wondered if she'd forgotten about it or if she kept it on purpose. If she'd been planning on learning to make pasta herself—unlikely—or if she couldn't part with the piece of machinery because it reminded her of him.

That seemed even more unlikely.

He'd ask her why she kept it, but she wasn't home. She'd told him to let himself in, that she had errands to run.

The last time she'd left him on his own, she'd gone on a date with a billionaire yacht owner. It still chapped Jayson's ass, even though he supposed it shouldn't. She was as single as he was and allowed to date whomever she chose. Lately that'd been a bitter pill to swallow.

She didn't disclose where she was going or who she was going with so those feelings of jealousy threatened to rise. He ignored them as he piled flour and dug a well, hand mixed in eggs and slowly folded that into a dough.

He was beginning to see that letting go was an art. One he hadn't mastered yet, but he hadn't been trying until now. Not really.

Over the last eighteen months he'd seen and talked to Gia almost every day. She was part of the fabric of his existence. That he no longer climbed into bed with her was a disappointment he'd managed because he had to. Then the morning after Royce's and Taylor's wedding, he'd realized something important.

Gia wanted him, too.

In the heat of the moment, they'd been caught up, time traveling back to their very first encounter, in the same damn bathroom. Which wasn't that surprising given how lackluster their wedding dates had been. But expecting to be able to continue forward without repercussions or emotions was a fool's dream.

When he'd brought the champagne over, he'd learned just how much of that baggage existed for both of them. The memories, the arguments. Sex—even really great sex *twice*—wasn't going to be the magic wand that erased their past.

He'd admitted his faults to her, but that was also too little too late. If he'd been a man who'd recognized in the moment what she needed, maybe they'd still be together.

He punched the dough, more frustrated with himself for being a dumbass than anything and decided that while he couldn't change the past, he could change the future.

Jayson and Gia weren't going to live happily-ever-after, but they could find joy together right now. Even briefly.

"Hey, Siri," he called to his phone. She answered, in an Australian accent, because why not, and he requested what he'd nicknamed his "Badass" playlist. His favorite song, and Gia's for that matter, was the theme song for *Rocky*.

The drumbeats started playing, those initial first few beats reminding him who he was and what he was capable of. He was going to move forward from here, as he was in this moment. He knew how to treat Gia and what she liked, and regardless of the future—whether they had one or not—they had this moment.

And this moment was what mattered.

After a shopping excursion that had yielded zero shopping bags, Gia walked into her foyer and into a wall of music. Jayson's singing voice was on point. She'd always admired his ability to carry a tune, her own talent having ended up somewhere between Brannon and Royce. Bran was an abysmal singer and Royce wasn't half-bad. She guessed that made her about a quarter good.

Jay must not have heard her walk in. Lingering at the

mouth of the living room/kitchen area she watched as he shook his ass at the stove. A black apron was tied at his waist—the one she'd bought for him last Christmas, she'd bet.

A drum solo lifted on the air and he raised the wooden spoon in his hand and pounded the invisible drum set. Upon spinning around, presumably for a final cymbal crash, he spotted her.

"Hey." He dropped his arms, wooden spoon still in hand, steaming pot behind him on the stove. "I didn't hear you come in."

"You don't say." She allowed herself a laugh, because how charmingly taken aback was he, and stepped into the kitchen. Her senses went wild. "Oh my God, it smells incredible in here."

Looked pretty incredible too: her hunky ex-husband, forearms bared, scruff decorating his jaw, wearing that silly apron.

"Homemade sauce." He gestured to a pot on the back of the stove, lid on, and then to the pot he'd been stirring. "Pasta's almost done. Made-from-scratch garlic bread is in the oven."

"You went all out." She was touched. The last time he'd done that they were celebrating an anniversary. Their last, as it turned out.

"I lost fair and square. You didn't expect a jar of Prego sauce and a box of frozen garlic rolls, did you?"

"No. I didn't." His attention to detail was one of the main reasons she'd fallen in love with him. He didn't miss a thing. And he'd wanted to give her *everything*. When they were married, his attention felt smothering. Once he'd moved out, she thought she'd feel free. Instead she found herself struggling to befriend the man she'd vowed to love until the end of time.

Since that thought was a touch heavy for this homey

scene, she decided to lighten the mood. "You know if you'd have cooked like this more often…"

"Don't say it," he warned, pointing at her with the wooden spoon before giving his pasta another swirl.

"I was going to say I'd be a lot fatter."

"That is not what you were going to say." Sliding her a glance, his mouth hitched into a half smile, he set the spoon aside. He grabbed an open bottle of red wine and the empty glass next to his half-full one, and sloshed in a few inches of wine before handing it to her. "Unless you'd rather chug it out of the bottle."

"Us being apart certainly didn't make you any funnier."

He grinned—full out—and she thought to herself that while he hadn't become funnier, he'd somehow become *sexier.* She eyed his backside as she sipped the fruity, deep-colored wine, recognizing it the moment the flavors burst onto her tongue.

"Is this—"

"One and the same. I wasn't going to, but then I remembered that whenever I made pasta we had this vintage."

The same wine they'd drunk on their anniversary, and their favorite from their trip to wine country that first Christmas they'd spent together. She hadn't had it in too long, fearing bad memories. But here they were, and the wine was delicious, her ex-husband was in her house shaking his great ass, and she didn't have any bad memories. Only good ones.

She'd been overthinking the night he'd delivered her champagne. She should have leaned in and kissed him—even if they'd ended up in bed together, it would have been better than soaking in the tub by herself, wishing he was there.

Regardless of the consequences.

It wasn't as if they'd end up *accidentally* remarried. They each knew the score. Their marriage didn't work because of their needs to guard their own space. They couldn't be together while also being apart.

She'd loved him, but that hadn't made them bulletproof. Admiration, friendship and sexual compatibility was one thing. Wedded bliss? Another altogether.

He lifted a noodle from the pot with a pair of tongs and gingerly ate it. Nodding, he lifted his eyebrows before slurping the rest of the noodle down and Gia pressed her thighs together. *Soooo. Sexy.*

"Done," he announced with a nod.

"I'll go change."

"Why? You look great."

She supposed her dark blue skirt and red-striped tank and flats were suitable for a dinner at home, but she wanted to honor his efforts by stepping it up.

"I just want to. You're dressed up." she told him.

"Am I?" He glanced down at his charcoal gray pants and short-sleeved gray utility shirt—the one she'd always liked, with the black buttons.

"Give me five minutes."

"Okay." He held her eyes for a prolonged beat. His gaze was a touch daring, more playful than aloof, almost… tender. Open.

Shutting out thoughts about how she wished he would have been this open and irresistible when they were married, she climbed the stairs to change for her dinner date.

Twenty-Two

Jayson wished she wouldn't have changed. Seeing her in the low-cut navy blue dress that showcased her gorgeous breasts was torture. Also, *incredible*. He was gifted an eyeful whenever she bent over her plate.

Plus, she moaned while she ate.

Literally. *Moaned.*

He'd already been distracted by her bare legs and a pair of sexy high-heeled shoes. When she reentered the kitchen he'd nearly fumbled the bread basket. The moaning thing? Not helping matters.

"You should've been a chef," she proclaimed before taking a giant bite out of a wedge of toasted garlic bread. He'd mixed minced garlic and fresh herbs with butter and slathered it onto the bread before baking. The result?

"Ohhhhh, God." Her eyes slid shut and she tilted her head back.

Orgasmic. That was the result.

He adjusted his pants and drank down more wine.

Maybe if he was super drunk he'd pass out and not be tempted to sleep with his ex-wife.

Again.

"If I were a chef, who would run your tech department?" Work. Talking about work wasn't sexy.

She swiped her mouth with a cloth napkin. "Duh. Me."

"Then who would run Marketing?" Fork hovering, he waited for her to answer but instead she twisted her lips to one side.

"We'd find someone." She shrugged one petite bare shoulder. A shoulder he wanted to kiss.

"Someone better than you?"

"I'd rather be in tech, anyway."

"You were. Before we split."

"You were there first," she argued.

She'd left the department—while not *physically* leaving the department. Her office was the same as it'd been back then. He'd originally given her the space since he felt as if he'd taken the job that should have been hers.

He wound pasta on his fork. "I would have thought you'd jump at the chance to be CEO when your father retired."

"I was too busy putting out marketing fires to even think about it."

He knew that. She worked hard.

"And now?" He leaned in, interested to hear her plans.

"I'm happy for Royce. And I'm relieved that the position of CEO didn't come between him and Brannon."

"What about you, G? What do you want?"

She blinked at him as if she was stunned that he'd asked. Had he ever asked her? Had anyone?

Damn. He'd been an ass.

"I want world peace." She gave him a disingenuous smile and then ate a bite of garlic bread. "What's wrong, do you want me out of your department?"

"You know I don't." He liked her there. "I need your brains."

"Finally, a man who loves me for my brains." She chuckled before going quiet. Probably because she'd mentioned the *L*-word. Love seemed to be tangled up between them and whatever they were to each other now. It was easier to compartmentalize before they'd had sex. Before he'd been sleeping over. Before he'd made her pasta and brought anniversary wine.

"I always appreciated how smart you were," he admitted. "I also appreciate how kind you are. How giving. Admit it, you wanted to kick my ass out of the tech department but you didn't want me to be exiled."

"My family never would have let that happen." A dodge for sure, but he felt justified that he was right.

"But you're doing well without me," he said.

"Without you! You won't leave!"

"You went on a date after we slept together, G. I can take a hint."

"This again?" She dropped her fork. "Elias and I didn't connect. He was as boring as plain oatmeal."

Jayson sat up taller. He liked hearing that.

"Plus you can't be mad about it since I returned home and had sex with you right away."

"You were the one who stripped down to a bikini."

"And you were powerless to stop yourself?" Her smile held and he didn't look away this time. Despite her trying to be blasé about this entire interaction, sexual tension was strung between them, power cable thick.

"I can stop myself." His voice was a low growl. "What do you think I'm doing right now?"

"What if…" She lifted and dropped one shoulder and studied her plate. "I don't want you to stop yourself? What if…" She met his gaze and batted her thick dark eyelashes. "I want to cut dinner short and take you upstairs?"

His entire body screamed *yes*, from his head to his lap. His grip on his fork tightened. He said nothing. Seemed the wisest course of action since he wasn't sure if he was being pranked.

"What if—" she stood from her chair and reached behind her to unzip her dress "—I want to have sex with you right now? On the kitchen floor." She dropped the front of her dress and exposed a strapless bra, the cups pushing her breasts up and together. That's what had been teasing him during dinner. That damn bra.

"I'd say no," he bit out.

She pushed out her bottom lip into a pout and he nearly let loose the feral grin he'd been hiding. Standing from his chair he reached her in two steps and crushed her body against his. With one hand he gripped the material of her dress and tugged it down until it was on the floor.

"Upstairs. In bed. With the lights *on*."

Excitement crowded out the worry in her eyes. "Sounds good to me."

Wasting no time, he lifted her into the cradle of his arms and carried her upstairs. With every step he ascended he stomped out the warnings in his head. They were crossing a lot of very dangerous lines. This time when she retreated, would she avoid him for good?

He didn't know.

But if this was their last time, he was going to make sure she never forgot it.

She kissed his neck when he crested the top of the stairs. Softly. Gently. Her lips on his skin caused his blood to heat.

"Which room is it again?" He smiled down at her before kissing her briefly on that beautiful mouth. So precious, his Gia.

No. Not precious. Just satisfy her needs and yours.

He'd make tonight worth it for both of them.

In the room he deposited her not-so-gracefully onto the rumpled blankets.

"Still don't make your bed?" he asked as he unbuttoned his shirt.

She sat on her knees, those luscious breasts spilling over her bra and giving him a peek of nipple. "Why bother? When I'll only mess it up again?"

She reached for his belt and while she worked at unbuckling it, he took off her bra and thumbed each of her nipples until she was squirming where she sat. She let out a moan.

"Thought you only made that sound while you ate pasta."

"Pasta and sex." She shoved his pants past his hips and he left her to kick off the remainder of his clothes.

"The two things I'm good for," he said, to let her know that he knew the score tonight. He knew she wasn't asking for a reunion. She didn't want to relive anniversaries past.

Tonight was about physical need. Sex for sex's sake.

Knee to the bed, he positioned himself over her. One side of her mouth lifted as she touched his chest and scooted herself back to accommodate him. He liked being accommodated. By this woman especially.

"Kiss me, Jayson Cooper."

"You got it, Gia Knox-Cooper." The air grew suddenly heavy. As he tasted her mouth and she wrapped her arms around his neck, he pushed out any thoughts about how she used to be his—how she still had his name. How he'd blown it over and over again and this could be yet another in a great line of mistakes he'd made with her.

Instead he focused on the tight, high breaths coming from her throat. On the feel of her fingernails tracing the lines of his back while he stroked into her. On the nip of her teeth on his earlobe.

Soon, to the crescendo of her hoarse cries in his ears, he followed her over.

And his world went blissfully black.

* * *

Unwilling to move from her spot on the bed, Gia stretched like a languid cat before curling into a ball again. Jayson had come out of the bathroom and stepped into their formerly shared walk-in closet, rummaging for what he called "those sexy gold shoes."

He was talking about a pair of Greek goddess, strappy heels she'd purchased for a Cleopatra costume one Halloween. She'd kept them, even though they were the most impractical purchase ever, because that night he requested that she wear *only* the shoes. They'd had fantastic sex, which was apparently par for course, and she'd fallen asleep wearing those shoes. She woken with strap marks crisscrossing up her legs. He'd removed her shoes and kissed every inch of her body before bringing her a very strong cup of coffee while she was still in bed.

That'd been a great morning.

He emerged with a white shoebox and shook it. "What's this?"

"I don't know. What is it?" But as he came closer and began digging through the box, she knew exactly what was in it. He lowered himself to the edge of the bed and she sat up and pulled the sheets over her naked body to peer inside.

He held up a birthday card with a dog holding a pair of false teeth in his mouth. "You kept this?"

"I like it." She snatched the card and read the inside. The inscription read "Love you, wife. J."

"The front is funny," she amended, tossing it back into the box. She stuck her hand in and came out with a refrigerator magnet from their trip to wine country that read "Let it merlot, let it merlot, let it merlot."

"I should put this on the fridge." She set it aside.

"You have a lot of random things in here." He held up a new pair of shoe strings that were knotted together.

“They were the extra pair that came with my Sauconys. I don’t have those shoes anymore.”

Jayson plucked out a laminated tag. “My old ID badge from the office.”

“You look like a serial killer in that photo.” His hair was longer, and messy, and he had that goatee. His expression was bland and morose.

“Must have been a bad day.” He held the badge next to his face and mimicked his old self. “Before. After.”

“After is better.” She snatched the tag and studied the slightly out-of-focus mug shot. “I liked that goatee though. Why’d you shave it?”

“I got lazy.”

She scraped a fingernail along his cheek. “I like it now though. Sometimes scruffy. Sometimes smooth. You keep me guessing.”

“So do you.” He held her eyes for an uncomfortable beat, one that reminded her more of their past than this shoebox of paraphernalia.

“You rose through the ranks faster than anyone I’d ever seen,” she said to change the subject.

“Oh yeah?” he said distractedly, pulling out her old gym pass.

“Yeah. Even Royce didn’t become chief financial officer as quickly as you became chief technology officer.” She’d never thought about that, actually. One minute Jayson was a web designer with talent to burn and the next running the entire technology department. It’d impressed her. She’d been so elated over his raise, she’d wanted to throw a party but he wouldn’t let her.

She’d forgotten that until now.

He was frowning, sifting through the random collectibles. She took the box from his hands and set it aside, wrapping her arms around his neck.

"Guess I forgot how talented you are outside of the bedroom and kitchen."

His cocky smirk returned. "Is this your way of asking for seconds?"

"Do you mean of pasta?" She tried to sound innocent.

"I mean sex. Are you kicking me out tonight?"

She bit her lip, considering. She'd sort of forgotten about that part—the leaving part.

"I mean, whatever you want," she hedged.

"Are you asking me to stay?" He cocked his head. "Or saying I don't have to leave?"

"Is there a difference?" Her smile shook. There was a *big* difference.

"Let's discuss it at length after." He removed the sheet covering her breasts and kissed a path down to her belly.

"After what?"

"Don't play dumb with me. You and I both know you're not."

She sighed and fell back into bed, the shoebox forgotten as well as the discussion about him staying or leaving.

The next morning, she woke to find him next to her. They never had discussed it. And she tried not to think about how much she liked rolling over and bumping into his solid, warm back.

Twenty-Three

Gia had planned the pool party with her family a month ago and since she didn't have the heart to disinvite Jayson, he was in attendance as well. Not that anyone present batted an eyelid. Her ex was part of the crew.

Only after the night he'd cooked for her, made love to her multiple times, and slept over, she was regretting him being there, and not because she wanted him out of her life.

She was beginning to want him back *in* and that was infinitely more dangerous.

Despite her trying not to soften around him, somehow he'd wedged into her heart.

She'd loved him when they were married, but now she loved him in a different way. What she felt for him was deep with understanding and nothing she could shrug off easily. They'd grown since their divorce, and she was fairly certain them splitting had a lot to do with that growth.

There were only so many flippant responses and sarcastic jokes she could trot out before the truth was evident to her—and everyone in her family.

She'd fallen in love with her ex-husband.

Doomed. That's what she was. *Doomed.*

How could she be brave enough to try again? After she'd failed so completely the first time? And after he'd summarily dismissed her the morning after he'd cooked for her and made love to her. He'd left, calm, cool and collected. As if he *hadn't* felt the earth shake the night before.

"I know what this was, G," he said, lingering at the front door. She had dressed in her robe and panties while he'd pulled on his trousers and shirt from last night. When she'd asked him to stay for coffee, he'd refused.

"Oh?" Her heart pounded. She was afraid to ask what he meant and afraid not to. She couldn't very well tell him she loved him, could she?

"There is a lot between us that is unforgivable. I know that a few good moments aren't enough to erase the past. Reconnecting with you was worth whatever happens next."

"Jay—"

"Hear me out. I have zero regrets on my end. I don't want you to have any on yours." He leaned down and kissed her. It felt final. Too final. "You don't have to find ways to avoid me, either. I won't come around unless asked."

Then he'd walked out the door and she hadn't seen him until they were both at work, their office faces on. When Bran had asked Jayson if he'd see him at the pool party this weekend, the three of them had been standing in her office. To avoid awkwardness, Jayson had swiftly agreed. Once Bran left, Jayson told her that he didn't have to come, but she'd lapsed into her "no big deal" self and told him to show up anyway.

Now he was here and splashing in the pool with her niece and Gia feared she'd made a colossal mistake.

"Meeting in the kitchen," Taylor announced. They were

seated around the patio table, snacks in the center. Bran and Jayson were in the water with Quinn while Jack and Royce were enjoying a beer on the loungers.

"Girls only," Taylor added as she handed over baby Emmaline to Royce and gestured for Addi to follow. She nodded at Gia and then at Gia's mother. "You too, Macy."

Gia, feeling as if there was a boulder in the pit of her stomach, followed her sisters-in-law and mother into the house. They stood around the kitchen island and every pair of eyes homed in on her.

"What?" Gia asked, growing more nervous.

"Did something happen?" Taylor asked.

"Like what?"

"Like you're madly in love with Jayson?" Addison filled in.

"Honey, it's all over your face." Macy, apparently, hadn't missed a thing.

"Did you tell him? Did he shoot you down? Did you two break up?" Taylor asked.

"No and no. And…not really."

Taylor, unsatisfied with those answers, narrowed her eyes.

"After we—" Gia's gaze trickled over to her mom and decided to be vague "—*ate pasta*, he said he didn't expect anything from me."

"Only because you run like a startled deer each and every time he gets close," Addi said. "Sorry. I know it's not my business, and I don't want to argue with you, but I'm right."

Taylor and Macy nodded in agreement.

Unable to defend herself when she was outnumbered, Gia threw up her hands. "Fine! I love him. What am I supposed to do about it?"

"Go out there and tell him!" Taylor whisper-shouted.

"We're tired of you guys skirting each other. Just lay it out there. Let 'er rip."

"How much sangria have you had?" Gia asked.

"A lot," Taylor said, "but that doesn't mean I'm wrong."

"I have so much to lose," Gia announced miserably. She could be shot down. And then her carefully constructed façade that she'd erected—the one where she pretended not to miss him and that she'd moved on with her life—would come tumbling down. Only this time she had a feeling she'd be buried beneath the rubble.

"Hell yeah you do," Taylor agreed. "But he might surprise you. We're going to leave soon. You should talk to him once we're gone."

"So are we. Quinn needs a nap and so does her mom." Addison smiled warmly. "Go for it, Gia. If the worst happens, we'll be there for you."

"I'll corral your father out of here, too," Macy promised.

A second later, Gia was enveloped into a hug from all three women. Feeling excited, nervous and…yeah, mostly nervous, she wondered what Jayson would say. She wondered what she *wanted* him to say.

She wasn't expecting a proposal, but was it too much to hope for a reunion? Even one where they continued on the path they were on would be better than nothing. Though she was risking *nothing* as well, wasn't she?

Admitting to him that she loved him could push him away completely. He seemed so *done* the other morning when he'd pragmatically explained she didn't need to worry about him being in her space. And when Bran had asked if he'd be at the pool party, Jayson had been quick to tell her she could disinvite him.

He could revert to form and tell her how she *should* feel. But she held out hope that he'd listen to her this time around. That he'd be the man she continued to want and need.

The what-ifs were killing her. There was no way to know for sure which outcome to expect… She'd just have to confess, and hope for the best.

The next hour passed easily. Her family made no more mention of love or whether or not Gia talked to Jayson yet. As promised, Taylor and Royce filtered out, Addi and Bran right behind them.

Macy still hadn't managed to corral Gia's dad, but everyone knew that Jack Knox was almost as hard to corral as his daughter.

"I'm not leaving until I have ice cream cake," he declared with a white-toothed smile.

"I'll get it," Jayson offered but Macy pushed him back onto the lounger.

"You keep Jack company. Gia and I will get it."

Gia found herself back in the kitchen at the same countertop, facing a similar firing squad as before, only now there was only one gunner.

"How are you? Are you losing your nerve?" Macy asked as she pulled the cake from the freezer and opened the box.

"There's a lot at stake, Mom."

"Marriage isn't easy. Whether you've tried it once or four times."

"How would you know if you're in the *once* club?" Gia pulled a knife from the drawer and began cutting the cake.

"Because husbands and wives change each decade so it feels like multiple marriages," her mom joked. "Everyone makes mistakes. Jayson has made his, you've made yours. The trick is being able to admit them and forgive each other."

"He's different," Gia said, thinking of how Jayson had behaved lately. "He talks differently. I know it's dangerous to think people change, but—"

"But they do. That means you've changed, too. Have you

been honest with yourself about that? Have you showed *him* you're different?"

Gia felt the sting of tears in her nose. "Of course not. It's all his fault, remember?"

"Don't be glib with me, Gia Knox-Cooper. You have been gracious and poised about this divorce. You've also been an insufferable smart-ass."

"Mom."

"I love you, but if you don't start going after what you want in life, you'll forever accept what you're given instead. You've been trying for years to escape the shadow of your father and brothers. Now you have a chance to make your own choices, and you should choose what *you* want for a change." Her mother plated the slices of cake. "Deliver these. The sooner your father eats, the sooner we'll leave."

Before Gia picked up the plates, she hugged her mom.

Macy patted her daughter's back. "Go on."

Outside, Gia maneuvered two plates through the open sliding door. Jayson and her dad sat, their backs to her. There were having a quiet, and she guessed by the low hush of male voices a somewhat intense, conversation. She should interrupt but she was too intrigued by what Jayson was saying.

"Gia deserves it more than I do."

"It's not about *deserve*, Jayson," Jack replied. "It's about want. You want it. The same way you wanted chief technology officer."

Jayson's back stiffened. "That was a mistake."

"I promised you the tech department when you asked for my daughter's hand. You seemed excited about it then."

She blinked in surprise. Had she heard that correctly? She stayed out of sight, content to listen a little longer.

"I never should have accepted it." Jayson sounded as frustrated as he looked. "She graduated MIT with honors,

Jack. She's overqualified for tech and her current marketing position."

"Hell, I know she's smart. I tell everyone that."

"Yes, you do, but you say it as if it's your accomplishment. Then you treat her as if she can't handle the world on her own. When you asked me to take care of her, I thought you were being fatherly. I didn't know you meant for her to settle for a lesser role in your company."

"You didn't take care of her, though, did you? Instead she shows up with that idiot skateboarder at a family wedding. You failed me," Jack snapped, his face going red. "Don't think I haven't forgotten it."

"I failed *her*," Jayson bit out. "Not you. Our marriage had nothing to do with *you*. And since you're retired neither does ThomKnox."

"But you are seeing each other again. That might lead to more. Vice president would be a good position for you, if that were the case."

"Our marriage ended a long time ago," Jayson announced.

Upon hearing that, Gia felt as if someone had plunged a knife into her chest.

"You can't bait me with the promise of VP," Jayson added. "You can't bait me, period."

"I should have fired you the second you divorced my baby girl," Jack growled.

Macy stepped outside, two plates in hand. "*Jack*. What is the meaning of this?"

Jack turned to face his wife, spotted his daughter and promptly pasted on a smile. "There are my girls."

Stunned, Gia was still frozen in place when Jayson turned and met her eyes.

"The ID badge," she muttered. "I thought it was odd how quickly you'd advanced to CTO."

"Because I gave it to him." Jack scowled. "No daughter

of mine was going to be married to a man who couldn't provide."

"Jack!" Macy gasped.

"You underestimate her," Jayson told her father. "And so did I. But at least I had the hindsight to pull my head out of my ass."

Jack opened his mouth to retort but Macy stepped in. "Not another word. Jayson, Gia. We'll be going now. Thank you for the lovely afternoon."

"This isn't over," Jack promised Jayson. Then he turned to Gia, having the decency to look guilty. "I can explain."

"Not now, Daddy." She put up a hand and kept her eyes on her ex-husband. She had issues with both of them right now, but the one with Jayson was paramount.

Her father silently followed Macy into the house. Jayson folded his arms over his chest and waited until they heard the Knox family car leave the driveway.

"I wanted to run tech," she told him.

Jayson's mouth was a grim line. "I know."

"And my father gave to it to you like…some sort of dowry?" Gross. That's what this was. "You never told me. And you had an opportunity to do so the other night."

"I only wanted to protect and care for you. I—"

"I only wanted you to love me!" she shouted, tears rolling down her cheeks. Damn him. He hadn't changed at all.

"I tried! Do you know how hard it is to want to be everything to the woman who needs nothing from you?"

She shook her head, but he kept talking.

"You could make a career out of pushing me away."

"What about the last time we were together?" she asked. "What about you leaving and telling me where we stood? That was you pushing *me* away."

"I know your pattern. The second we get close you back away. I was giving you an out."

"You were protecting yourself!"

"Oh, really?" His expression shifted from disbelief to anger in a snap. "And what about now, when your dad offered me the vice president position on a silver platter? Was I *protecting myself*?"

No.

He wasn't.

"I don't want a pity job, Jayson." She put the cake on the table, the melting ice cream pooling onto the plates in the warm night air.

"It's not pity." Exasperated, he threw up his hands. "I'm damned if I do and damned if I don't. You don't want me to give you anything, but you don't want me to take anything for myself either. And by the way, I *did* love you. So much I was stupid with it. Can you say the same?"

Yes. And she could say that right now, in fact. Judging by everything he'd just said, though, he wouldn't want to hear it. She found herself guilty of doing what she'd accused Jayson of doing—protecting herself.

"You don't have to answer that," he said. "That's the benefit to being divorced. We don't have to answer to each other anymore."

He walked around her to the patio door but before he disappeared inside, he had more parting wisdom. "Being in the role of vice president is your destiny, Gia. You wanted to be involved with tech, marketing? The entire damn company? Here's your chance. Take the VP position and step into your role at ThomKnox. For a change, claim what you deserve."

Then he was gone.

She slumped onto the lounger, her eyes clouded with tears and her mind racing. Her emotions were battling each other. She wanted him, but was afraid to tell him. She wanted to step into a greater position at ThomKnox, but didn't want to risk failing. She'd crowed about wanting a shot at making her own decisions and mistakes. Now she had the opportunity and she was too scared to do either.

And, possibly the most depressing of all… She'd wanted to tell Jayson that she loved him but she couldn't.

He didn't love her. Not anymore.

Chester filled a small shot glass with golden liquid and pushed it under Jayson's nose.

"I fucked up," Jayson said, his speech slurred thanks to the three tequila shots that had preceded this one. He'd come here straight from Gia's. Too pissed off to drive home and stew in his own juices, and maybe a little bit needing the comfort only Chester's empanadas could provide.

As it turned out, Jayson couldn't eat.

Ches, a bartender, had taken one look at him and asked what was wrong and Jay had spilled his guts.

"It happens to the best of us," Ches said. "Now drink."

"I don't want it." But Jay took it anyway. Drinking until he forgot what an idiot he was wasn't a great plan, but it was the only one he had. After downing the liquor that'd done a good job of making his head swim already, he lay back on the uncomfortable outdoor couch. The palm trees overhead canted at an awkward angle and his stomach flopped. He was horribly uncomfortable without a pillow—as if the cushions were built out of the same hard material as the frame. He sat up as quickly as he'd lay down, his head spinning in protest. "I hate this couch."

"So do I," Mason said, stepping outside to deliver a tray of beers in pilsner glasses. "And he paid five grand for it."

Jay sent Chester an appalled look. "Seriously?"

"Shut up. This is not about my couch." Chester moved to sit on the overpriced piece of furniture next to Jayson. "You know I adore you. But, Jay, honey, why didn't you tell her you let her dad give you that position *while* you were married?"

"Secrets like that tend to grow hair." Mason sat across

from them in a chair that matched the couch, but at least he had a pillow that looked squishy.

"Tell me about it. Before I had the chance, we were talking about divorce and then… I dunno." Jay felt his mouth pull into a miserable frown. He knew why he'd procrastinated telling Gia. He didn't want her to hate him and she'd seemed to be heading there at a fast clip already. And if she hated him he couldn't live with himself. Which was where they'd ended up, even though he'd tried his damndest to prevent it. "She hates me."

"She doesn't hate you," Mason argued. "She's pissed off. There's a difference. And by the way, she has a right to be. Probably feels like she was swapped for a flock of sheep or something."

"Thanks, Mas." Jay reached for his beer. Not needing it, but wanting it.

"Don't be mean to your brother," Ches warned his husband as he patted Jayson's back. "He's going through a tough time. Jay, you can stay here tonight."

"Yeah, you can sleep on our five-thousand-dollar patio couch," Mason said with a smile.

Jay surprised himself by laughing. "Pass."

"You were supposed to move on," Mason reminded him unnecessarily. "That's why you took Natasha to the wedding, right? You weren't supposed to sleep with Gia at said wedding. And you weren't supposed to sleep with her over and over again. Especially since she didn't know her own father bribed you."

"Not helping," he grumbled at his brother. Jayson's arms felt like cement. He let them lay heavy on his legs when he leaned back on the couch that might as well have been crafted of that same cement. "I do *not* like this couch, Ches."

Like that, he lost his only ally. "You two hash it out. I'm done helping."

Once his husband was gone, Mas lifted an eyebrow in judgment.

"Like if you lost the love of your life you wouldn't do anything in the world to be close to him again? Even temporarily?" Jay gestured to the house behind him where Chester had disappeared.

Mason blinked. "I didn't realize you were still in love with her."

"It's a moot point, dontcha think?" Jayson lay on the couch anyway, his spine screaming in protest.

"I don't know. Did you tell her that?"

He let out a morose laugh. "Are you kidding?"

"No. I'm not." Mason sounded scarily serious. "If you're in love with her why not tell her?"

"Um, hello? How much have you been drinking? We've said everything we needed to say and most of that was said too many times and the wrong way." Jay took a hearty gulp from his own beer glass. "And she just found out I've been trying to control her for my own gain."

"Have you?"

"Jesus, Mason. No! But that's how she sees it. And if you know Gia—and *I* know Gia—you know that the only thing that matters on this planet is her perspective." He lifted the glass again then set it aside, an idea sparking. "I know. I could quit."

"You're not going to quit. You love ThomKnox."

He did.

"I could step down," Jayson said anyway. "Give her my position. Work in the mail room or something."

"Are you high?"

"No. Drunk." But he didn't feel all that drunk. Sure, the earth was moving under his feet, but he couldn't say he wasn't thinking clearly.

"Tell her how you feel," his brother said. "Man up. Grow some balls."

"Weren't you just banging the don't-date-your-ex drum?"

"That was before I knew you were a goner for her. How long have you been in love with her, anyway? And how much longer are you going to let your bravado stand in the way of what you really want?"

"Jack offered me vice president."

"What?"

"He said ThomKnox is adding a VP position and I was in the running. He said that my being with Gia, and seeing through my promise to take care of her, would stack the deck in my favor."

"What an asshole."

"That's Jack." But that wasn't all Jack was. He was also eccentric and grossly friendly. He loved his family with a fierceness that was hard to understand, especially when Jayson's own father couldn't have given two shits about him. But Jack also had a way of undermining his family when he had his own plans in mind.

"You weren't seriously considering his offer, though."

"No, I wasn't." Jayson shook his head. "Gia deserves it. She deserves the best. That's not me."

"That's not you?" Mason let out a sharp laugh. "Give me a break. You know I know both of you, right?"

A frown pleated Jayson's forehead.

"You'd break your own back trying to prove yourself worthy—trying to prove you're not your asshole dad. Then when Gia doesn't need you to handle her, you sulk."

"Fuck you." Jayson was aware he was sulking now, though, which pissed him off more.

"Listen, man. You chose a strong woman. That's not a bad thing. Give her what she really, truly needs, though. Don't just try and shine in her eyes. Okay?"

What she really, truly needs.

Jayson turned that over long after Mason went inside. Long after the air grew cold and his beer was gone.

Sometime during the night he came to a conclusion about what she needed. It had nothing to do with him or what he wanted.

He was going to have to give up what he wanted more than anything.

And he'd do it. For her.

Twenty-Four

By the next afternoon, Gia couldn't stand her own company any longer. She'd spent the entire morning cleaning the house. She'd thrown out the float shaped like a giant lemon slice because it reminded her of Jayson whenever she saw it. She'd even hauled the big-ass pasta maker out from under the cabinet and put it into a box bound for Goodwill.

She'd stripped the bed and washed the sheets, before going online to order a new bed so she wouldn't have to sleep in the same bed where she'd slept *with* Jayson.

What a mess. What a big, fat, stupid mess.

Her anger had spread beyond the boundaries of her person and her house, which was how she found herself at her parents' home without an invitation.

When her mother opened the front door, Gia stormed in. "Where is he?"

"Enjoying his afternoon iced tea," Macy answered as Gia blew by. "On the balcony."

Shoulders squared, Gia rerouted to the stairs.

"Don't throw him over!" Macy called up to her.

Her father's office led out onto a wide balcony outfitted with chairs, a table and an awning. She stepped into the room, rich with red leather and brass accents. Her father's *lair*.

She'd never before pictured him in here scheming. Until recently.

The French doors were open and she found her father reading the *Wall Street Journal*, a glass of whiskey and the carafe within reach.

"Gia." He smiled. The crinkles around his eyes and his puff of white hair used to be comforting. Not today.

"You owe me an explanation." She stood over him. "And an apology."

"I had my reasons."

"I'm listening."

He gestured to the chair across from his and folded his paper. "Sit. Please?"

She did, because he said *please*. She still vibrated with anger and while she wasn't going to toss him off the balcony she thought emptying his whiskey bottle over the edge might make her feel better.

"You gave Jayson the position of CTO because you didn't think I could handle it. You completely overlooked me." She'd come here for his explanation, but she had a point to make, too.

"I wanted him to feel worthy of you," her father told her. His legs where crossed, and he rested his folded hands on one knee. "I didn't overlook you, Gia. I know exactly what you're capable of. World domination, I imagine."

She didn't smile at his joke.

"You're a powerful woman. I couldn't be prouder of who you've become. But, honey, Jayson isn't from the same world we are."

"This is about image," she said. "You were embarrassed of him."

"No." Her father's voice was firm, unyielding. "It was about him feeling as if he belonged and not like he was limping behind the rest of you. He's a good man. I care about him. I can tell you're in love with him. Still."

She slumped in her chair. "Is it that obvious?"

"I know you're mad at me. I do. And… I'm sorry."

She lifted her eyes to her father's to see if he meant it. He looked like he did.

"I was trying to make up for my mistake. I was trying to offer him vice president so you could finally have the position you want. Then he went on about you taking VP and I started talking out of my hat. You know I don't like to be challenged."

"Pretty sure I inherited that same instinct." She gave him a wan smile.

"Jayson was right. You're the worthiest candidate for vice president. I just didn't want him to leave the company, especially since you two have been…close lately."

"You were bribing him to keep seeing me?" Ugh. That was horrible.

"Incentivizing," Jack corrected. He took her hand in both of his. She tugged it away. "I was wrong to interfere. Then your mother told me you two were, uh, dating."

Gia winced.

"I wanted to make you happy again," he continued. "You've been unhappy. I only ever wanted you to smile."

"Well, giving my job away wasn't the best tactic. I thought he'd earned that position."

"He did. He's fantastic in that capacity. I care too much about my company to hire anyone who didn't make us shine. Honestly, Gia, I thought you'd have given your brothers a run for their money when I announced my retirement. And yet you never wanted CEO."

"No." She shook her head. She had ambitions and aspirations but running ThomKnox wasn't for her.

"And after that, I didn't think you'd want the vice president position."

"I don't know what I want." But she did. She wanted her ex-husband.

"Jayson cares for you."

"He does," she admitted. "But not in the way you were hoping. Not in the way I was hoping."

Her father hummed and released her hand. "I've made my fair share of mistakes in the past—in the recent past. I'll call him and apologize. I owe him that."

"Yes, you do."

"But don't blame him for taking the tech position back then. I practically forced him into it," Jack said. "He took it for you."

"How was taking CTO from me done *for* me?"

"I told him you didn't want it. That you'd…asked me to give it to him."

"Daddy!"

"You were compensated well and I thought you would find your way to a higher rank. I never doubted you. I was trying to make sure Cooper had a place in our family enterprise."

"And he does." Jayson was a big part of the reason ThomKnox was so successful.

"How are things between you two now?" Jack asked carefully.

She shook her head. "They didn't end well. This afternoon there's a party happening at work, so I'm sure that won't be awkward at all."

Her father stood. "This is my fault."

As tempting as it was to let her father shoulder the blame, she couldn't.

"No, you only managed to tip the already leaky boat."

She stood from her chair and touched his arm. "I understand why you did what you did. It was noble, in a way. I wish you would have talked to me, though. I wish Jayson would have talked to me. It would have saved a lot of misunderstanding over the years."

"Would it?" Jack frowned.

She shrugged. "I don't know. I tend to be as stubborn as you are, Daddy."

"Stubbornness is a good quality when you want to graduate with honors." He offered a half smile.

"Not so much in marriage," she said. "Compromising, I hear, is a thing."

"Stop blaming yourself. You did what you knew how to do. You guarded your life and your choices. I'm sorry I didn't honor your union and keep my nose out of it. I'm learning, too." He held out his arms. "Forgive me?"

"Yes." She embraced him, understanding better why he'd done what he'd done. It seemed Jack had believed in her strength after all. Even though he'd gone about showing it in a way she didn't agree with.

"Off you go to claim that VP position, then?" He held her at arm's length.

"I'll talk to the executive team about it," she said. "Taylor. Royce. Brannon." She poked him in the chest. "Not you. You're retired, remember?"

"Trying to," he admitted.

Downstairs, she found her mother in the sitting room on a gray sofa, a blush pink pillow tucked at her back. Macy's charity work often spilled over into this room from her attached office. Gia took in the spread of papers on the coffee table and smiled.

"How'd it go?" Macy asked.

"He was surprisingly open. And he apologized." She sat next to her mother. "I'm assuming you two talked."

"Your father and I might have had a long talk wherein

he agreed he had no right to interfere in your marriage." Macy sipped from her teacup. "Lord knows marriage is hard enough with the two people it involves."

True story.

"Did you and Jayson talk through it?"

"We argued. He left." Gia poured herself a cup of tea.

"I'm sorry."

"I'll see him at work later today. I'm still not sure what I'll say. Daddy's calling to apologize to him."

"Good."

"What are you working on, anyway?" Gia leaned forward and lifted a sheet of paper off the pile.

"A charity for abused women. It's called HeartReach. They help women who are trapped in abusive marriages with children to create an exit plan. You might recognize the chairwoman's name."

Gia's eyes went to a familiar name. Julia Robinson. Aka—"Jayson's mother."

"HeartReach was where she went for support when Jayson was younger—to help her escape Jay's father. I can't imagine."

Neither could Gia. "Daddy said he wanted Jayson to feel worthy. To feel like he fit in."

"Jayson had a father who didn't honor him. Jack wanted to cheer him on."

"The way he always cheered me on." Gia had always been loved. Had always been wanted.

"You championed Jayson, too, dear. When you announced your divorce, you were adamant about us not shunning him from the family. You didn't want him to lose us. Even if you were losing him in the process." Macy patted Gia's leg. "You have a great big misguided heart, like your father."

Gia hummed, finally seeing the big picture. This argument wasn't about roles at ThomKnox or Jayson having a job she'd wanted at one point. Life was about love and what really mattered. Family.

"Remarkable how Jayson turned out nothing like his father, isn't it?" Macy said thoughtfully as she took the flyer out of Gia's hands.

"I used to accuse him of being controlling." Gia shook her head. "He was trying to be accommodating."

"Well, he could have communicated better. Men assume they know what's best. It's our job to correct them. Frequently, it seems."

Gia smiled, then sighed as the gravity of what had happened weighed on her anew. "I don't know what to do. I love him. I don't want to lose him, and I feel like I already have."

"Being brave is hard. Speak your mind. And your heart. Leave nothing on the table."

Gia blew out a breath as she swiped fresh tears from her cheeks. "Easy for you to say."

"Yes. It is." Her mother tipped her head and swiped a stray tear from Gia's face. "Can I do anything to help?"

"You already have. It's my turn to make a few decisions involving what I want. You were right. I need to step out of Daddy's and my brothers' shadows. I've been trying, but I've been going about it the wrong way. That changes right now."

"Good girl."

Gia stood to leave and then turned back to ask, "What if...he doesn't love me back?"

"I don't know how that's possible." Her mother shook her head. "Royce, Brannon, Jack and now Jayson. The men in your life fall all over themselves to protect and care for you."

For the first time in her life, Gia thought about being cared for by the men in her life. Maybe that wasn't so bad after all.

Twenty-Five

When Jayson walked into the ThomKnox building, a cup of strong coffee in hand, he didn't go straight to his desk. Instead, he entered the elevator and pressed a button for the top floor.

The executive floor was humming as per usual. He heard the quiet purr of office landline telephones interspersed with the delicate tapping of high-end keyboards. Like in the tech department, everyone had the sleekest, newest equipment and the flattest screens. Unlike tech, the desks weren't littered with candy bar wrappers or several paper cups that used to hold coffee. It was as if everyone up here knew they were in the presence of greatness. ThomKnox royalty.

Gia belonged up here.

She'd been working closely with Jayson throughout their marriage and after, and now he saw that for what it was. He was holding her back.

As long as he remained closely intertwined with her, she'd continue to vehemently deny herself and give him favor. He knew that was because she loved him—maybe not as a husband any longer, but she couldn't turn off her emotions like a switch.

Neither could he.

He'd fallen in love with his ex-wife, against his better judgment or any iota of common sense. He'd always loved her, even when he'd been trying to bury his feelings for the sake of saving face during their rocky divorce. But since they'd reconnected, he'd felt that love on a deeper level.

No longer was he focused on gaining ground or being right. He wanted to give her what she deserved because she deserved it. Sacrifice, and vulnerability, evidently went hand in hand.

Ultimately, no matter how much money he made, no matter what kind of luxe lifestyle he lived, he didn't belong in the same category with Royce or Bran, and especially not with Gia. He'd been fooling himself. He didn't know if today's sacrifice would make up for years of treading where he didn't belong, but it was a start.

He crossed the room and silence fell. Fingers stopped tapping on keys and interested eyeballs landed on him. He felt Taylor's burning gaze as he stepped past her office and angled straight for Royce's.

They must have heard what happened after they left the house. Gia told them, or maybe Macy. It'd saved Jayson the trouble, he supposed.

He let himself into Royce's office after a brief knock. Gia's oldest brother sat up tall at his desk, his face a mask of anger. He looked as though he had something to say, so Jayson let him.

"Gia always wanted what was best for you," Royce said. "She was brokenhearted and sad after the divorce and still she insisted that nothing change between us. I honored that."

"I know you did." The Knox family had been incredibly accommodating.

"And you repay my family's loyalty by allowing my father to concoct this ridiculous plan? When you'd already accepted the CTO seat because you married Gia. If you think I'll place you in the role of vice president—"

"I don't want to be vice president. I never should have accepted the role I have now. At the time I wanted to please your father and I thought that would help Gia see me as worthy of her."

Some of the fire went out of Royce's expression. He let out a long sigh. "She always saw you as worthy, Coop."

"Sure about that?" Jayson asked. Royce didn't answer. "I was a guy from a broken home who built websites. It was crazy to imagine myself worthy of marrying into the great and powerful Knox family."

"We never made that distinction."

"You never had to. Gia loved me and Jack validated me. You accepted their approval at face value." Jayson took a breath. "I was never going to accept a VP position. Jack was being Jack. He steers his children's lives into the direction he believes is right. He was orchestrating a Jayson-and-Gia reunion."

Jack had called early this morning. He'd apologized for the things he'd said at the party. Jayson told his ex-father-in-law that he wouldn't have to worry any longer. Jayson had a way to fix everything that had happened. To set things right again.

"And now?" Royce asked.

"Now what?"

"You and Gia have been…" Royce closed his eyes as if he couldn't bear saying it aloud. "Spending time together."

"Not anymore." Admitting that aloud hurt worse than he could have imagined.

"Was it only physical for you?" Royce shifted in his chair like he was uncomfortable asking.

"Why else?" Jayson lied. He'd been close. So damn

close. Before Gia had overheard that conversation and learned the secret he'd been keeping—before he'd blown everything, he'd been planning on telling her exactly how he felt about her.

That he loved her. He'd fallen in love with her again, only this time he believed himself incapable of screwing up. He'd committed to honoring her needs—her actual needs—and meeting them.

Then his past had bitten him in the ass and he realized he wasn't incapable of screwing up. He *was* a screw-up. No amount of time could fix that.

"Are you coming to the party this afternoon?" Jayson asked. "It's in celebration of the tablet fix. Gia singlehandedly saving your company and all."

"I'm planning on it."

"Good. I have an important announcement to make."

"I look forward to it," Royce said with a curt nod. Jayson couldn't tell if the other man was lying or not.

Gia arrived at the start of the party, only to bump into the party planner on her way in. "Looks fantastic in here, Joanna."

"Thank you. Everything is in place, Ms. Knox."

Gia didn't correct her by saying that her name was *Knox-Cooper.* She was too tender after everything that had happened to go there. "Wonderful. Thank you."

"You're welcome. My staff and I will be in the background making sure everything runs smoothly." Joanna, her hair pulled back in a smart tight ponytail, turned to straighten the platters of catered sushi.

Music was playing in the background and Gia walked to a bucket of ice to grab a soda for herself. Taylor and Addison were there, smiles bright.

"We're here for you no matter what happens." Taylor offered. "I'm really excited for you."

"Thank you." Gia hugged Taylor and then Addi. "I appreciate your both showing up."

"And miss the action?" Addi asked as she straightened from the hug. "Never."

"Photo booth, ladies!" The photographer interrupted.

"Not me, thanks." Gia waved them off. "You two go ahead."

The photographer shooed Taylor and Addison over to the booth and handed them each masks on sticks. Taylor, halfway to the booth mouthed the words "you owe me."

Gia wiggled her fingers in a wave, relieved at having avoided the embarrassing photo booth.

"If I could have your attention." The low sound of her ex-husband's voice came from the front of the room.

Jayson, dressed in black trousers and a slate-gray shirt, climbed onto a sturdy chair. Not that he needed to. His presence was so commanding he didn't need the chair to establish that he was in charge. His power was as undeniable as her admiration of it. She'd spent years guarding herself from that power, but now she saw the truth. That was simply *Jayson*.

"Not that anyone asked for a speech, but I have one." His eyes flicked to the back of the room and Gia turned to see her brothers enter. Bran gave her a wave, his mouth flinching into a half smile. Royce wore a frown as usual, but when he walked by, he briefly cupped her neck in a supportive gesture.

"I've been a part of ThomKnox for going on seven years," Jayson continued. "I was named chief technology officer almost five years ago, the same year I married one Miss Gia Knox-Cooper."

Smiles around the room were soft, careful. More than a few heads swiveled in her direction.

"Our marriage did not outlast the role, and I've been telling myself for nearly two years that I was okay with that. That relationships work but sometimes they don't, and Gia and I fell into that latter category. It was a lie I've been content with until recently, when I realized that not only was I in love with Gia when we were married, I have been for the entire time we were divorced."

Those soft smiles melted into gasps, Gia's own gasp among them.

"Gia is a gracious, beautiful, incredibly lovable woman," Jay went on. "She's giving. She's tough. She's strong. She's a certified genius mastermind." Nods of support came from several of their coworkers. "She's been in the role of running Marketing, and I know she loves this company with her whole heart, but Marketing isn't where she belongs. She's an MIT grad with a nerdy brain in that gorgeous noggin of hers. She loves code more than any one person has a right to. She found the glitch we're all celebrating." He cleared his throat and added, "Not me. She doesn't need me."

Her chest tightened as those words. That wasn't true. She *did* need him. More than he knew. She thought about her family members who had tried to take care of her over the years. Not because they thought she was incapable or weak, but because they loved her so very much. She'd recently learned that it was okay to lean on others; that it would have been okay to lean on Jayson while they were married.

Needing someone didn't make her unworthy. It made her *human*. Beautifully human, flaws and all.

"And yet I'm the one who's chief technology officer of this company. Or well, I was," Jayson finished. "*Was* CTO."

"No," Gia whispered. She'd made a decision about what she wanted after talking with her mother. She finally knew her goals and dreams and wasn't afraid to claim them. Jayson in the role of CTO was the *right* place for him to be. It had been all along. Her father, while he'd fumbled, wasn't wrong about that promotion.

"I love this department. I love ThomKnox as a whole,"

Jayson was saying. "I love Royce and Taylor, Brannon and Addison, and Jack and Macy like they're my own family." He then locked his gaze on Gia's. "I love my ex-wife enough that I refuse to stand in the way of her living the life she should be living. I should have done this years ago, G," he said, his eyes on her. "I never should have taken the position that was destined to be yours. I should have walked out the door and not looked back when you said you wanted the divorce. I should have left you at ThomKnox with your family to claim what was rightfully yours. No matter how badly I wanted to be in your orbit."

Oh, Jayson.

"I'm leaving ThomKnox, effective immediately," he said as the room erupted in excited chatter. "Gia will take over where I left off, and your upper management is more than capable of filling in the gaps. If there are any."

He stepped off the chair and that chatter grew louder. Panic laced through her stomach until she realized that she could take her power back rather than stand idly by.

"Jayson Cooper!" she shouted. No way would she allow him to make this huge of a mistake.

"My mind is made up, Gia," he said as he walked for the exit.

"And what makes you think you have the final say?" she asked his back.

He turned. Slowly. His face was a beautiful shadow of confusion and hope. She loved his face. She loved *him.*

The room grew eerily quiet. She felt every eyeball snap to her as she closed the gap between her and Jayson, her arms folded at her chest.

"As the newly named vice president of this company," she told him, her voice firm. "I don't accept your resignation."

Twenty-Six

Earlier today

"Thank you all for coming." Gia stood at the head of the conference table and addressed the upper management team of ThomKnox. "I have a proposition for you."

Brannon, tapping a pencil, eraser side down, on the table, shot her an easy wink. Royce, on Gia's left, wore a muted smile. Taylor was grinning like she'd gleaned what was coming next.

"We've been in discussion about adding a vice president position for a while now," Gia began. "And then at the pool party, Daddy decided to offer that position to Jayson."

Brannon frowned. Taylor mimicked his expression. Royce curled his lip.

"Jayson didn't accept it."

"But he had no problem claiming chief technology officer for himself," Royce grumbled.

She blinked. Royce knew plenty.

"Daddy called you."

"He called me, too," Brannon said. "We each received a Jack Knox speech about how he's failed and won't fail us again."

"He does love his grandstanding." Gia shook her head, but smiled to herself. "Jayson would make an excellent vice president. But I'd make a better one."

Taylor elbowed her husband and then bounced in her seat. "I knew it. You owe me twenty bucks."

Royce's smile came out of hiding. "I don't need twenty bucks, but we can negotiate terms later."

"Anyway," Gia said with an eye roll in the direction of her besotted oldest brother, "I want to earn the position of VP on my merits, not based on what Jack or anyone else says. I want this position. I want it to include Marketing and Tech, and then I can oversee both my passions. *And* I want Jayson to stay exactly where he is—in charge of the department he built."

"I had a meeting with the CEO, COO and president of this company this morning," she told Jayson now, aware of many onlookers, said CEO, COO and president included. "I specified that while I'll be overseeing both Marketing and Technology, I would only do it if you were involved. I need you exactly where you are."

"You don't need me, Gia. You never did."

"ThomKnox needs you." She reached down, way down, and found her bravery. Jayson had been brave enough to stand in front of everyone and tell her how he felt. She knew she could do the same. "And *I* need you," she added on a broken voice.

"Gia—"

"I never had the courage to admit that. I never wanted to appear weak in our family of titans." She glanced over at Royce and then Brannon, who each wore compressed smiles of pride. She turned back to Jayson. "Marriage is about admitting you need someone else. It's about being someone's other half."

The lines on Jayson's forehead softened as he tilted her chin gently. "I'm leaving so that you don't feel compelled to take care of me. I'm supposed to be taking care of you."

"I guess we're just going to have to take care of each other." She shrugged, vulnerable and unsure. "I mean, if that's what you want. I don't want you to feel like I'm controlling you."

A slow grin spread his mouth. "How ironic."

She grinned back at him.

"I love you, Gia. I've made so many mistakes. I've been holding on to you without realizing it."

"We both made mistakes." She gently touched his hand, still cradling her face. "And hey, I've been holding on, too. Have you checked my last name lately?"

"You never dropped the Cooper."

"I couldn't let go. Not all the way. Letting go's not the answer and you know it. We screwed up, Jay."

"Yeah. We did."

"I have a better idea of how you can make it up to me and it doesn't involve you leaving ThomKnox. You can't leave me in a lurch and force me to find a good executive to run this department with no notice at all." She affected a stern expression. "Do we understand each other?"

"Yes, boss."

She quirked her lips. "I like that."

He leaned in to whisper into her ear, his voice a low rasp, "Only here. In the bedroom you know who's in charge."

When he pulled away, she felt her cheeks grow bright pink. "Jay," she whispered. "We have an audience."

"Right." He winked. "We'll talk about that later."

Taylor broke the silence. "To our CTO and new vice president!" She held up her plastic cup.

Addison cranked up the music.

The crowd cheered.

By the time the dancing started and everyone had dispersed, Gia and Jayson still hadn't moved from where they stood in front of each other.

"What are you doing tonight?" he asked.

"Oh, the usual." She shrugged. "Making dinner. Having a glass of wine with my laptop. Meeting the installers who are delivering the new bed."

"You ordered a new bed?"

"Yeah. I thought I wanted a different one since that other one was ours."

"And now?"

She tipped her head. "Now I'm thinking we should break in the new one. It'd be a crime to let a brand-new bed go to waste."

"Hell yes it would." He stepped closer and muttered, "Kiss me, Gia."

"No. *You* kiss *me*."

His smirk was one for the books. "Meet me halfway?"

"From here on out."

Epilogue

Laptop aglow in front of her, Gia was curled into the corner of the sofa, her eyes heavy. She just wanted to finish this one last part…

In a flash, the screen vanished, swept up by Jayson, who swapped the laptop for a glass of wine.

"I was busy!" she argued, but took the proffered glass before she ended up wearing it.

"You're always busy. You'd work until your eyeballs rolled out of your head if I let you."

"That's a charming mental picture."

"Can this wait?" He held up the laptop. Then he glanced at the screen. "Candy Blaster?"

"It's strangely addicting."

He sat next to her, his hand wrapped around her waist. "You, Gia Knox-Cooper, are strangely addicting."

She accepted his kiss, her eyes sinking closed. Since she'd taken the vice president position, she'd moved her office from the tech department to the executive floor. Jayson took her former office and she was glad that he finally had his own space.

He was a man in charge, an executive as much as she was, and he deserved more than open office seating.

He'd been sure to remind her that *she* deserved to be at the top of her namesake company. She was a Knox and thereby "royalty" and, he'd also mentioned, again, that vice president was her destiny.

She was beginning to accept he was right. She'd done a lot of sidestepping over the years around taking what she wanted. For all her fighting for her own independence, she'd had a hard time accepting it.

As vice president she could make her mark at the company she loved. Plus, she worked closely with Taylor and her brothers, and Jayson, and that was the best part.

"I was going to ask you about that new—"

He pressed a finger to her lips and shook his head.

"Unless you were going to finish that sentence with the words *sexual position*, I'm not interested."

"Jayson!" She giggled when his fingers tickled her bare skin under her shirt.

"All work and no play, G. Don't you want a break?"

She set the wineglass aside and wrapped her arms around his neck, kissing him rather than answering. He was a lot more fun to kiss than he was to spar with, even though they were both really good at that, too.

He'd moved out of his apartment and back into the house they'd once shared. They had enjoyed plenty of sunbathing in the heated in-ground pool, and they were enjoying their new *and* old beds. Though the new bed had been relegated to a guest room. They preferred their former marriage bed for their room.

"I have a toast." He slipped away from her and grabbed his own glass.

"Now? That was just getting good." She pouted.

"I know but I have something to say. It's your favorite Chardonnay."

The crisp white Chardonnay was hard to turn down. It was her favorite autumn wine. She reached for her glass.

"To our anniversary," he said, clanging his glass with hers.

"Today isn't our anniversary."

"Not our wedding anniversary. The anniversary of the first time I saw you."

"That was New Year's Eve."

"I don't mean then, either. I'm talking about when I first saw you at ThomKnox. I was addressing my staff and stopped midsentence when you walked by. Stevens called me on it, gave me shit for a week about how I couldn't keep my tongue in my mouth."

"No! I've never heard this story before."

He set his glass aside and dropped to his knees in front of her. "Marry me, Gia." He took her free hand—her left hand. "Again."

"Why? I already have your name. You already live in my house."

"Our house."

She barely held back her smile. Her heart lifted, her mind whirred. She wanted to marry him again.

He'd learned he didn't have to prove his worth to her. She'd learned that him taking care of her was how he showed love. Being gracious was her challenge, while his was realizing he could let his guard down.

Nothing would come between them again. She knew it in her soul.

They had already agreed to communicate better, to stop trying to guess what the other one wanted, and ask instead. They understood how to give and take in equal measures. No one had to carve out their own corner. They met in the middle. Always.

"I need a new pasta maker since you threw the old one out. Figured we could register for one." He gave her a half smile.

"I do love your homemade pasta. Can we break tradition and have you make it for Christmas?"

"Gia, I asked you a question."

"I know. I'm thinking!"

"You have to think?"

"Not about the yes I'm going to give you. About which anniversary we'll celebrate in the future. Our old anniversary or our new one? Can we celebrate both?"

Grinning, probably because she'd sneaked her *yes* in those sentences, he said, "We'll celebrate today. The day we decided to make forever official. The day we decided that nothing matters more in this world than each other. The day we went in one hundred-one hundred."

"Because fifty-fifty is for losers," she whispered.

"Exactly." He rested his elbows on the couch cushions and pressed his big body against hers. Heat engulfed her whenever he was near and he was promising never to be far again. "The rings, the license, the ceremony are details. I don't care how it happens, so long as it does. Let's make a real go of it this time, G."

She put her hand into his hair and looked into his earnest, blue eyes. She was grateful, so grateful to have this time with him—to have this chance again. "I love you, Jay."

"I love you, gorgeous. Always and forever."

"Always and forever is a big commitment."

"You think of something bigger than that, you let me know." He kissed her softly and then reached into his pocket to pull out her original engagement ring…only the stone was a hell of a lot bigger than it was the first time around.

She pretended to shield her eyes from the glare.

"I won't do anything with you halfway—not ever again." He slid the band onto her left ring finger.

"How did you—"

"Your jewelry box isn't that vast," he answered. "I stole it and took it to the jeweler for the upgrade."

She admired the chunk of diamond on her finger, glittering in the lamplight. "It's *massive*."

"It's the biggest I could buy without you needing a stroller to push it around in." She laughed and he continued, "Though I'm not opposed to a stroller for you to push something else around in."

"You mean like a toy dog?"

Jayson didn't balk. "Dog. Baby. Your collection of Funko Pop! character dolls. Whatever you want, *wife*."

She put her hand on his cheek and touched his nose with hers. "I like the sound of that, *husband*. I'm willing to give you what you want, too. That's how much I love you."

"Honey," he said in that low, growly sexy way of his, "You've already given me everything I want. Anything else from here on is the cherry on top."

* * * * *

FOUR BRAND NEW BOOKS FROM
MILLS & BOON MODERN

The same great stories you love, a stylish new look!

WED IN A HURRY
KIM LAWRENCE · LORRAINE HALL

Bound & Crowned
LOUISE FULLER · CLARE CONNELLY

Love to HATE HIM
JULIA JAMES · MILLIE ADAMS

RECLAIM ME
CATHY WILLIAMS · DANI COLLINS

OUT NOW

Eight Modern stories published every month, find them all at:
millsandboon.co.uk

afterglow BOOKS

THE CODE FOR LOVE
Her perfect plan has a gorgeous glitch...

NEW YORK TIMES BESTSELLING AUTHOR
ANNE MARSH

✈ International

⛅ Grumpy/sunshine

🍸 Fake dating

OUT NOW

To discover more visit:
Afterglowbooks.co.uk

OUT NOW!

Opposites Attract On Paper

3 BOOKS IN ONE

LYNNE GRAHAM • ROBIN COVINGTON • CHANTELLE SHAW

Available at
millsandboon.co.uk

MILLS & BOON